GREY LADY

When Ben Jacardi is caught stealing coal by boat builder Josiah Armstrong, it is the first stroke of fortune in his short life. With his father dead and his mother vicious and cruel, Ben decides to run away and join Josiah and his wife Kathy. Then Josiah's real son Patrick returns home to rob his father. Unable to pay Ben as his apprentice, Josiah offers him payment in kind: the boat *Grey Lady*. Ben accepts and with his wife, Faith, begins a career on the English canals.

GREY LADY

GREY LADY

by

Jenny Maxwell

Magna Large Print Books
Long Preston, North Yorkshire,
BD23 4ND, England.

British Library Cataloguing in Publication Data.

Maxwell, Jenny
   Grey Lady.

   A catalogue record of this book is
   available from the British Library

   ISBN 0-7505-2031-0

First published in Great Britain by Time Warner Paperbacks in 2002

Copyright © Jenny Maxwell 2002

Cover illustration © Anthony Monaghan

The moral right of the author has been asserted

Published in Large Print 2003 by arrangement with
Time Warner Books UK

Magna Large Print is an imprint of Library Magna Books Ltd.

Printed and bound in Great Britain by
T.J. (International) Ltd., Cornwall, PL28 8RW

To the Coombeswood Canal Trust, where dreams are translated into reality. And to the wildlife that is beginning to return to the waterways.

Acknowledgements

So many of my friends on the canals helped me with this book that I cannot mention them all, but I must particularly thank Tim and Andy Young, who not only taught me the workings of the Bolinder engine, but also allowed me to take their magnificent narrowboat 'Rudd' down a stretch of the Walsall Canal. Bob May and Peter Trijer gave me useful information and introductions, and many good friends at Hawne Basin taught me much, most of which involved rolling up the sleeves. Roy Kenn, Terry Blakesley, Trevor and Carole Roden, Alf Danks, and Ivor and Marion Chambers, thank you all. Peter Roberts and Mike Goodman, thank you too, and Jayne Bradley and her grand boathorse 'Prince', John Else, Jon and Lynne Monk, and last but not least, the bank workers of British Waterways. Thank you all.

Preface

The waters of the canals in the Black Country are still, for the most part. There are no currents, hardly any movement except for the wind flicking at the surface, little eddies around the locks, the wash of the passing boats.

These are not natural waterways. Where they can, they follow the contours of the land. Otherwise there are tunnels and aqueducts and, as a last resort, locks, sometimes dozens of them in a long flight, climbing from a valley like a black and white staircase. The canals lie in the folds of the hills, curving with the hills, across the plains in flat, straight lines, and through the cities. Here, they are often forgotten, sometimes never known, even by those who have lived there all their lives. Under the streets, behind the walls, below the wharves, black water, and sometimes a boat.

Early in the mornings the narrowboats left their moorings, slipping out into the canals while the dark mist lifted. Black cinders crunched on the paths under the horses' hoofs, under the boots of the men. Where grass grew, the hoofbeats were muffled. A mile from the black centre of the city the paths were grassy, the water birds called, and the reed beds grew against the banks. A mile from the city, and fifty years on, the grass was deep and rank on the paths, the reeds had crept into the waterways, and the birds were gone: the waters were choked with filth, poisoned, and there were only the ghosts.

There are ghosts on the canals. A red-haired woman on a flight of locks plagued any boatman with a grey horse. Her lover had had a grey horse. When he abandoned her she drowned herself, but she never forgave him, even after death. Take a grey horse up that flight of locks, and the gates will swing open, the paddle gear will jam, a windlass will fly from your hands and be lost. When at last you lead the grey horse on down the path you will hear laughter behind you.

Don't look back. It's only a ghost.

A headless man walked a tunnel towpath, gone when a light was shone at him, but many swore they had seen him. Part of the wall of that tunnel fell in, and they found a skeleton. There was no skull. They buried the skeleton in the church-yard, and no one has seen him since. It was only a ghost, and never there, when you shone a light.

Travel the canals now, when the waters are cleaner and the boats are quick and light, and you will have to half close your eyes and use your mind and the memories of your ancestors to see the ghosts, but if you can do that they will crowd around you, on these canals. Men, women, children, horses, donkeys and mules; and with them the narrowboats, built for the canals, long and strange, and graceful in this, their own country, their own element.

Look behind the boats, and the men and women, look behind the horses and see those who dug the canals, digging and levelling, clearing and building. Behind them stand the dreamers, those

14

who wondered, and calculated and planned, walked the contours of the hills, and said it could be done.

Yes, it can be done.

A pack-horse could carry two bushels of coal on the muddy tracks they called roads then, a narrowboat, pulled by that horse, thirty tons.

It's never been done. It never will be done. It's crazy.

His Grace the Duke of Bridgewater found a millwright's apprentice, Brindley he was called. James Brindley. His Grace wanted a canal to carry the coal from his collieries into the centre of Manchester, so Brindley walked the route, measured, and calculated, then said he could do it.

Impossible.

Brindley built the canal, His Grace grew rich beyond his dreams, and then they believed. The canals grew out from the industrial heartlands, down into the south, across the land, from the collieries and the mines to the mills and the factories, the rivers and the ports, the great cities.

Can you see them, on the still waters? Can you see the ghosts?

They grew cloudy, dim and scarce, hidden behind the swirls of smoke from the massive black railway engines. The iron rails followed the contours of the hills too: they dived into tunnels, they soared over viaducts, and they could drag hundreds of tons behind them where the horse had pulled thirty. The boats had carried the steel rails and the broken stone on which they lay, the baulks of timber.

But you can still see the ghosts on the water.

You can hear some of them. Not the horses, they are silent, hoof beats muffled by grass and time, but the song of the engines. Listen carefully.

It's a slow song, a heavy rhythm, a little like a beating heart, not quite a chime, not the harsh thud of the roads. Like a muffled bell. Can you hear?

She's coming now, through the mist. You can see her, that long hull tarred black to keep out the water, and the black cloths she carries to cover the cargo. No, she's not a ghost. You can see her, you can hear her. You could reach out and touch her as she passes, and the man at the tiller will smile at you, and nod.

Look, there's her name, painted white on the grey.

Grey Lady.

She's gone now. Round the bend in the canal that follows the contour of the hill, where the big hawthorn dips over the black water.

Grey Lady.

1

Ben Jacardi built *Grey Lady* almost single-handed, as it turned out, and he did as good a job as he could, which meant not far off perfection. It was as if he knew the boat would be his. By then he wasn't being paid, but Josiah Armstrong was a fair man, and hated debt.

Josiah wasn't well. There was nothing you could put your finger on, apart from old age, but he'd told Ben about it one evening. Told him why Sammy and Jed had left, and soon Dave would have to go too, because there wasn't enough money to pay their wages.

Ben had been startled. 'Thought we were doing all right,' he'd said.

'We were. More than all right. Had a bit of bad luck.'

'Josiah Armstrong and Son, Boatbuilders,' proclaimed a red and gold sign over the gateway, and beyond it, behind the half-built boats on the hard standings, there were piles of timber and iron, because nothing was ever thrown away. The name 'Josiah' on the sign was a little different, the red not quite the same colour: it had been painted later, over 'Patrick'. Patrick had died, and left the business to his only son Josiah, who had painted out his father's name and put his own in its place. He'd named his own boy after the old man, but always called him Paddy.

Paddy had been the bit of bad luck.

'Gone off with the money,' said Josiah, and buried his face in his mug of beer.

Ben had been twenty at the time, but Josiah had taken him in when he was ten. He'd caught the boy in the shed, stealing coal, dragged him outside and beaten him with his leather belt.

'You'll earn that coal,' he'd said.

Ben had spat and fought and sworn.

'Hold your tongue,' Josiah had ordered, raising the belt again, and the boy had shrunk away from him, hands raised to protect himself but teeth still bared in defiance.

'What's the matter with you, then?' Josiah had demanded. He'd never heard breathing like that.

He called his wife, who came to the kitchen door and stared at the child, her face twisting in concern.

'Oh, my Lord. Bring him into the warm. Oh, my Lord, that's bad.'

It was bad, and Ben nearly died that night, lying in the corner of the kitchen on the bed they'd made him. It sounded as if every gasp would be his last, deep, slow and rasping, as if the air was being dragged over shingle.

Josiah and Kathy sat beside him all through the night. Some of the time he slept, but when he woke his teeth were bared again. He was frightened, but defiant too.

'Don't be afraid,' said Kathy, and she reached out to touch him, but he jerked away from her, so she drew back her hand and smiled at him, told him to sleep again. She didn't think he would last the night.

18

He lasted that night, and the morning, and she gave him soup. She stayed with him all that day in the kitchen, feeling him watching her except when he slept, and every time he woke she heard him hiss with the pain in his chest.

Every sudden move made him flinch. Each time she approached him he drew away from her, baring his teeth.

'I won't hurt you,' she said.

She wished Josiah hadn't beaten him. What were a few lumps of coal to them? And the boy was half starved. Might not last this next night. He was filthy, too. She wanted to wash him, but thought he was too ill to take the water. And he might fight her and exhaust himself.

'Soup?' she asked, smiling at him. He nodded.

He had fleas and lice, but that didn't worry Kathy. There were ways of dealing with that, after the boy had gone.

He lived through the next night too, and Kathy and Josiah moved back to their own room. They left the door open, so they could hear him if he needed them. Kathy lay awake, listening to him. Sometimes she thought he'd died, that he'd stopped breathing, but then there'd be another breath, long and hard.

'He won't last the winter, though,' she told Josiah, and there was a warning note in her voice, as though it was he who had set his heart on the boy.

Paddy was in the army by then, and Kathy needed someone to mother. Ben was better than a puppy. Dirty little thing, and that language. But he was dying. Must be, a chest like that. Can't

19

turn a dying child out into the cold.

'Where's your mam, then?' she asked one day, and Ben bared his teeth again.

'Not much better than a puppy,' Josiah had agreed.

No one knew where he'd come from, and he wouldn't say. There were too many orphans that winter. It had been cold and wet, with bitter frosts. What was one more thin, dirty boy with ruined lungs?

'What's your *name*, then?'

'Ben Jacardi.'

He hadn't hesitated in giving it, and he could write it, too. That was a surprise: not many boat children could read and write, and there was nowhere else he could have come from. He must have been turned off a boat.

Josiah and Kathy fed him, found him some of Paddy's old clothes, and waited for him to die. Just a few days of kindness before the end, they'd thought.

'Does your chest hurt?' asked Kathy, and Ben shook his head.

'If you're in pain,' she persisted, 'you only have to say. There's medicine.'

They stopped listening in the night for the terrible breathing to end. They grew used to it. In the spring, Josiah took Ben to the doctor.

'My nephew,' he said, because he wasn't a man for long explanations, and didn't mind telling a lie. 'My sister's son. Mam and dad both dead. Going to live with us now.'

Who would argue with that? At least this child had a family to care for him.

20

'What happened?' the doctor asked Ben, but Ben stared him in the eye, and wouldn't answer.

'How long has your chest been like this?'

He wouldn't speak at all to a stranger.

'What can we do for him?' Josiah asked, but the doctor didn't know, although he wouldn't admit it. He told Josiah the boy had bronchitis, as bad a case as he'd ever heard. They were to keep him warm, out of draughts, and Josiah was not to let Kathy get too fond of him.

'Shall we send him to school?'

'If you like.'

Would he last until the spring?

The weather grew warmer, and Ben's breathing was quieter in the night. Kathy fed him well, kept him warm, and was kind to him, but she guarded against growing to love him. How could a boy live with lungs like that?

Josiah wasn't so sure. Ben was growing, and he could run; he wasn't weak. You'd think he'd be thin and pale, but good food and a warm bed had put some flesh on those bones.

'There's nothing catching,' Kathy assured the schoolmistress when she took Ben down to the village. 'Doctor says he can come to school. He can write his name and read a bit.'

For the first few days Ben sat suspiciously at the desk he'd been given, watching through narrowed eyes, speaking, if he had to speak at all, in a sullen whisper. The other children kept away from him, frightened by the noise of his breathing.

Mrs Hart gave him a slate, and told him to write his name. When she next looked he was crouched over it, one arm crooked around it as if

21

to shield it from the eyes of his neighbours. His tongue protruded from the corner of his mouth. His pencil was moving slowly over the surface.

An hour later she looked up to find Ben standing in front of her, holding out his slate. In laborious, careful letters he had printed his name: BENJAMIN SAMUEL JACARDI.

'Very good, Ben. Very good indeed.'

He blinked, and frowned.

'That's very neat writing, Ben. You've done well.'

As if the muscles of his face were stiff, as if he was not sure he could remember how to do it, Ben smiled at her.

At first the schoolmistress thought he was slow, but then she realised he was a perfectionist. If the writing on his slate was not good enough, he would wipe it off and start again, and if necessary again, and again.

'Let me see, Ben.'

'Not ready yet, Mrs Hart.'

At least he had become polite.

The other children lost their fear of his harsh breathing. Two of the girls taunted him in the playground, mimicking the sounds he made, telling each other he was diseased.

'Should be in isolation. We might *all* catch what *he*'s got.'

Sometimes when he came home from school his clothes were torn, and there were bruises and cuts. Kathy mended his clothes, bathed the cuts, and said nothing.

He had chores of his own in the yard. He was to sweep it, and sort out the bits of iron and wood. Anything big enough to re-use was to be put into the bins, wood stacked out of the rain, the smaller pieces chopped for kindling. Scrap metal was to be sorted, iron in this bin, brass in that. Any tools left lying around were to be put in the shed on the bench.

One evening in autumn he came home from school with his shirt torn and his lip split. Kathy watched from the kitchen window as he threw something into the scrap-iron bin. When he came into the kitchen he peeled off the shirt and handed it to her, but this time with a nod and the beginnings of a smile.

'Last time,' he said.

A policeman called. A boy had been stabbed in a fight. Not badly hurt, not even in hospital, but still, a stabbing. Got to ask, because the boy said it had been Ben.

Ben looked him straight in the face and shook his head.

'Not me,' he said.

'Witnesses?' Kathy demanded. 'His word against the other boy, then. Ben's no liar, and the others don't like him. Trying to get him into trouble, that's all there is to that.'

Ben began to help in the boatyard after school. He told Josiah he was going to earn that coal, and Josiah stared at him, trying to remember where he'd heard the words before. Ben looked at Josiah's belt with its big brass buckle, and then it came back.

'I shouldn't have given you such a thrashing,' said Josiah. 'My Lord, boy, it's not even a year. You must have doubled in size.'

Big for his age, whatever that might be, and strong. He said he was ten, and he'd been born in the winter. Kathy decided he was eleven now, and gave him a birthday, the same as her mother's, so she'd remember. 'January the sixth, we'll call it, 1881.' She promised she'd bake him a cake next year.

Josiah took on another workman, Jed, because there was a demand for boats, and he told Ben he'd pay him a wage when he was twelve. Ben could earn two shillings a week, and his keep.

'Don't have to,' said Ben, but he was pleased. Money of his own, earned by right, not just given when Kathy felt like it.

By the time he was twelve he was nearly as tall as Kathy, strong, too, and the sullen defiance was a thing of the past. He was never what you could call sunny-natured, but he could smile at you, and even laugh, although that wasn't a sound you'd want to hear too often. With lungs like that, how could he grow so well? You'd think he'd be sickly.

'Was your dad a big man?' Kathy asked him one day, and Ben said he'd never known him.

Must have died before the boy was born, Kathy reasoned.

Ben was sawing the elm planks by then, and sawing them straight. He took a pride in what he did. No one at the boatyard noticed his breathing any more: they were used to it.

The boatyard was thriving. Josiah took Kathy into town and she bought herself new clothes. At Christmas Josiah gave her a gold bracelet, and told Ben he'd be earning proper wages in the spring, now that he could do the riveting. He was doing a man's work and it was only fair he should earn a man's wage.

Ben could read and write, and his arithmetic was good enough to draw up the bills for the customers, and to check the ones that came in.

'Done with school now,' he said, and neither Josiah nor Kathy argued with him. The boy was big enough to know his own mind, and they were glad to have him around. They were both feeling their age.

'That Alan,' Ben told Josiah. 'Lazy. Get rid of him?'

'Ah. Right, then. Right.'

Josiah was old, and Alan wasn't a patient man, so it was Ben who told him to go, counted out his money, then sat up in the yard for the next two nights in case Alan made good his threats to burn the place down.

'You're a good lad,' said Kathy. 'I reckon Jesus knew what he was about when he sent you here.'

'Good day for me, that was.'

'In spite of the beating?'

Neither of them could forgive themselves for that.

'My mam used a carter's whip,' said Ben. Kathy laid down her work and sat with her hands in her lap.

Ben's father had been wounded in the Zulu wars in South Africa, speared in the chest. It killed him in the end, six months before Ben was born. No, they'd not been married. She was a lock-keeper's daughter, up in Cheshire, and Ben had run away from her. He was sick of being whipped. He

25

wasn't hungry, because the boatwomen used to give him bits to eat. But his mother had whipped him raw, and enjoyed it. He'd been running for three, four months before he got down here. By then the marks had all gone.

'You call that a beating?' said Ben. 'Love taps.'

'But your lungs?' Kathy asked. 'You can't inherit being wounded.'

He didn't know. Only what his mam said, that his father had been speared, and when Ben got the bronchitis, as he seemed to do every winter, he sounded just like his father. His father had come home breathing like that, and died a few months later. Sometimes Ben breathed hard all the time, and sometimes it went away in the spring but came back with the bronchitis in the winter.

'Was your mam's name Jacardi?'

No, she'd named him after his father. His father had been called Samuel Benjamin Jacardi, and she'd named him Benjamin Samuel.

It was the only time he'd talked about it to Kathy, and she suspected he'd never do so again. She told Josiah but he never mentioned it either. They could stop feeling guilty about the beating he'd given a starving child, because it was nothing to what he'd had before, and he hadn't even thought there was anything to forgive.

'A carter's whip,' mused Josiah. 'Maybe they're different, in Cheshire. You'd kill a child, with one of those things.'

At Christmas Kathy would give Ben a hug and a kiss, but only then. Josiah would shake him by the hand. There was never anything more. They were both shy, Ben afraid of presuming, Josiah of

26

being rebuffed. But at work, they relied on each other. Workers came and went, and sometimes it was Ben who told them to go as Josiah became timid and Ben grew in strength and confidence. He had to protect the old man. There should have been a son around to do that, but Paddy had come out of the army, married and moved to London, where his wife had fancy friends. Ben could do any of the work now, most of it as well as craftsmen who had taken half a lifetime to learn. The boats were built to a pattern, to a time, to a routine that he guarded carefully, watching to see that it was done properly, as Josiah had, and as Josiah had learned from his own father.

Then Paddy came for a visit, and Kathy cooked a special meal. Ben stayed out in the yard that evening.

The old people had been looking forward to Paddy coming, and they'd expected his wife too, but she'd stayed behind. No reason given, she simply hadn't come with her husband to meet his parents. She hadn't bothered.

Paddy had talked grandly about his business opportunities in London. London was where everything happened. Everyone went to London. There were canals in London, so there'd be a market for boats there; Josiah should move with the times, and bring the business to London or, failing that, Paddy could be his agent.

'You'll have to buck your ideas up a bit. If I can sell six boats a month you'll have to produce them.'

'Six?' Josiah had sounded bewildered. 'Six a month?'

Ben was planing a rudder, and listening. Six boats a month? Takes three months to build a boat, that means space for eighteen, and there was only room for seven. Eight, perhaps, if you got them in the water early and did more of the fitting out while they were afloat, but that made no sense because it was slower work that way. Who'd make the extra fenders? Mr Hollinshead couldn't make many more, and he wouldn't be rushed. Even if you worked faster, where you would find the extra men?

He wanted to tell Josiah, 'We can't do it.' But Paddy was Josiah's son, his only child, and Ben couldn't interfere.

'Didn't he look grand?' exclaimed Kathy, after Paddy had gone, and Ben agreed, Paddy had indeed looked grand. And yes, he'd spoken like a London gentleman, and no doubt his wife was a lady and soon there'd be a family. Paddy was doing so well in business down in London.

Josiah had looked doubtful. Paddy had said he'd have to buck his ideas up, and he wasn't even sure what it meant, let alone how to do it.

The next day when he went to get the money for the wages, he found the cash box was empty.

Kathy had hardly stopped crying for a week, and even though Josiah was dry-eyed, it had hit him even harder. He'd been so proud of his son, with his grand London-born wife, doing well in business down south, and Paddy was nothing more than a thief.

The day after Josiah told Ben what had happened Ben took Kathy's gold bracelet into Birmingham and sold it, so that they could pay

28

the wages. Then he'd gone to the timber mill and asked for time to pay for the elm, and the manager had looked at him as if he'd never heard the word.

'Time?'

'Mr Armstrong's had a bit of bad luck.'

Bad luck loves company, and the man who'd ordered the boat that was finished had no money either, and asked for time to pay.

Josiah took the train to London to find Paddy, and came back the next day. Paddy and his fancy wife had left the flat in Hurlingham Court Mansions with two months' rent owing. Nobody knew where they'd gone, and no one cared either, except to send on the bills.

Ben told Dave he'd have to leave, and that left only him. Josiah wasn't strong enough for the heavy work, and some of it needed two strong men, better with three.

'I wish we'd been able to keep Sammy and Jed,' said Josiah. 'I know Dave was the better worker, but I liked Sammy and Jed.' They were the ones who had stayed on in the evenings and sat with the old man by the fire, talking about boats over a mug of tea, or beer on pay days.

Ben went to the bank and asked for a loan to tide them over.

'Tide you over what?' asked the manager, but all Ben would say was, 'Bit of bad luck.' He couldn't betray Josiah and Kathy by telling this stranger that Paddy had raided the cash box. The money should have been in the bank, but Josiah hadn't believed in banks. His money was safe in his strongbox under the hearthstone, and no one

29

knew it was there, except family.

Even Ben hadn't known.

'I can't pay your wages, Ben,' said Josiah.

'I know that. You think you're big enough to throw me off the yard, then? Because I don't.'

Josiah had smiled up at him. 'You're a good lad.'

Ben launched the last boat and looked at Kathy in her grey dress and said he thought he'd better take the boat and work it, send money back as soon as he could. He'd call the boat *Kathy,* so he wouldn't forget where to send it.

'You'll need a wife,' said Kathy, ever practical, and Ben nodded. It took more than one to work a boat unless you'd all the time in the world to spare, and no boatman had that, not with a living to earn. He might have hired a man, had he any money, or a boy, who would have been cheaper, but he couldn't afford a man, and he didn't trust boys: they could be careless. Most of the boys working on the canals worked for their fathers, part of a family business, and had been born on the boats. Ben knew some of the families, and he went through them in his mind, looking for a lad who might be suitable, but none he knew well enough to ask would have suited him.

So, a wife it must be, if he could find a woman who'd have him, and he was under no illusions. Few women would put up with a man who breathed as he did, no matter how he might protest that he was healthy. The girls he'd met at school had shown him no more than indifference, and some had professed revulsion.

In the end he asked the daughter of a farm

labourer, a woman nearly fifteen years his senior. She was the oldest of seven children, small and sharp-faced, with a twisted shoulder. She had worked on the farm since she had left school, so was no stranger to a hard life. Her youngest brother had been at school with Ben.

Ben called at the cottage one evening and asked if Faith was at home. Her mother looked surprised, but went indoors and called. Faith came to the door and looked at Ben enquiringly. She hardly knew him. Sometimes they'd seen each other in town, but they'd only exchanged formal greetings. Now he was at the kitchen door of the cottage, his cap in his hand, asking for her. Behind her, the young children gathered, her brothers and sisters. The cottage was crowded, and not very clean.

He asked if she had time to come for a walk with him. She blinked in surprise, then went to fetch her shawl, trying to push the giggling children out of the way. Ben waited, ignoring them, wondering what he could say to her.

They walked through the woods, and he told her he was leaving the yard, taking a boat and working it on the canals. Josiah was not going to do much more in the way of boat-building now.

He did not tell her why.

He did say the boat was his, so he would be what was known on the canals as a Number One, which was the best: a man who owned his own boat. He told her he was strong and healthy, and the noise he made meant nothing. Did it disturb her too much?

'Too much for what?' she asked, cautiously.

31

It was spring, quite warm, but Ben's breathing was just as it had been in the winter. It had come back with the cold frosts, even though he hadn't had bronchitis for three years. It didn't worry him, or those who knew him, but it took a while to get used to a noise like that.

He looked down at Faith, a little sharp-faced woman with one shoulder higher than the other, twisted too, so it tilted forward. She had bright brown eyes and a suspicious look about her. She would have had few, if any, prospects of marriage, and would have been scorned because of that too. He knew how that felt, and could understand the caution with which she responded to his questions.

For her part, looking at him, she saw a young man, tall and strong, very much the sort of young man the girls would have liked, if it hadn't been for the noise he made. That slow, roaring sound. Why had he asked her opinion? Why were they walking through the woods together?

'Could you get used to it?' he asked.

'I expect I could. If I was to hear it often.'

They walked on, and Ben felt shy and uncomfortable. He'd meant to ask her to marry him. He'd thought, There's a woman no man would have, but she's a hard worker. That's what I need on a boat. She'd be glad of any man, so she'll put up with the noise.

But the little woman in the shabby clothes had been quiet, and had listened to him with some interest, courtesy, and something he could only call dignity. Ben felt clumsy beside her. He was too big. He didn't know what to do with his hands. He didn't know what to say.

'Takes more than one to work a boat,' he said. 'Needs two. At least. One leads the horse, works the locks. Other steers the boat. It's usual, on the boats, the man leads the horse and does the locks. And his wife, well, she steers the boat. You see?'

She nodded. She took nearly two paces to his one, keeping up with him, and listening.

'I need a wife,' he said, and she nodded again.

'If you think you could get used to the noise,' he said, and it was only then that she stopped, and stared up into his face. Still she said nothing, but her eyes were wide, and there was a flush of colour in her cheeks. But she was silent, so he drew in his breath and asked her: 'Will you marry me?'

The wide eyes narrowed, and the flush on her cheeks deepened. 'Are you making fun of me?'

'Oh, no,' he protested. 'No, I'm not. No, Miss Carter. Faith. I wouldn't do that. But not many women would look at me, and I thought, I need a hard-working wife, and you're a hard-working woman, and I thought you might be glad to have a man of your own. Get away, maybe. A home of your own. Well, a boat's maybe not much of a home, but I thought. Maybe.'

She wasn't looking at him any more. She was looking down at the ground, and he couldn't see her face. He wondered what she was thinking. He tried to imagine. It was becoming quite important to him to know what she was thinking, and to have her answer, and he wanted it to be yes. Funny twisted little thing that she was. What was she thinking? She was shy, and perhaps still afraid he might be making fun of her, but she was a woman. He knew there were questions she couldn't ask, but she needed the answers.

'This noise,' he said. 'I know it sounds bad, but I'm not ill. I don't think our children would breathe like this.'

She didn't move, she didn't look at him, but he knew he had said the right thing, and after a few moments she spoke. 'I was born with a crooked shoulder. The nurse said it was a birth accident. I don't think...'

What was he supposed to say now? She wasn't going to finish that sentence: She was standing there; looking at the ground, waiting for him. Waiting for a great burst of cruel laughter? It seemed as if she half expected it. He reached out and touched her, on her crooked shoulder, not as if to see what it felt like, but naturally, just a touch on her shoulder, happened to be the one that was a little higher and bent forward, and she looked at his hand, and then looked up into his face, and he asked her again:

'Will you marry me, Faith?'

'Yes, Ben.'

He knew he was supposed to kiss her, but he didn't want to. He wanted to hold her instead, so he put his arms around her shoulders and drew her close to him and stood there, feeling her so little and thin against him, and her heart beating so fast. She was standing still, and quiet, almost as if she was frightened to say anything in case he should change his mind.

'It's hard work on the boats,' he said at last, 'but

you're used to hard work, and I'll try to be good to you.'

He felt her nod. 'I will work hard for you,' she said.

He stood quietly for a few moments, holding her, thinking that it felt right, the two of them close together. The top of her head only came up to his shoulder, and he could rest his chin on it, feeling her hair, soft and smooth. It did feel right. He hoped she thought it was right, too. Her heart wasn't beating so fast now. She just stood still against him, not too tense now, but as if she was waiting, and then he felt her hands, little hands, just touching, just brushing, moving slowly until they slipped gently around his waist, so she was holding him, too. She was hesitant, shy, as if she was not sure she had done the right thing, as if she was wondering if it had been forward of her to hold him like that.

'We'll need a horse,' said Ben, and he felt her relax. It was all right, for her to have her arms around him, then. All right, because he was talking to her. He hadn't said anything about her holding him.

'Can you buy one?' she asked.

He shook his head. 'No.' There wasn't any money. But there were companies needing boats and boatmen and some had their own horses. He hoped they'd hire him a horse until he had enough money to buy his own.

He told Faith about the company horses as they walked back to the cottage, and she listened, nodding. Usually the horses went with the boats. Companies owned the boats and the horses, and they paid the captains, who hired their own crews. But there was plenty of work on the canals, and Ben thought the companies would hire them a horse. Why not? If they had the work to do, and there was a boat, and a crew, why not hire them a horse?

And if they wouldn't he'd find some other way, he thought. He'd found himself a wife; finding a horse had to be easy, compared to that.

Kathy was incredulous when he told her. 'Faith?' she asked, staring at him. 'Faith *Carter*? From the farm cottages?'

'Yes.'

Kathy could think of nothing to say, but questions and objections were flashing through her mind. Must be fifteen years older than you. Hardly know her. And she's not right, she's deformed.

But as Ben talked to Kathy, Faith was thinking the same thing. Faith told her mother, and her mother stared at her, in the way that Kathy had stared at Ben.

'He wants to *marry* you?'

'He needs a wife to work the boat.'

'He did say *marry*, didn't he? You're sure of that?'

Faith was sure of that, but of little else. Faith Carter, eldest daughter of the head ploughman at Fletcher's Farm, was going to marry after all. No more scornful, pitying looks from the other women, the ones she'd grown up with. No more knowing what her mother was thinking and not saying. Eldest daughter never going to be off my hands. What am I going to do with her?

36

All through her childhood she'd heard her mother correcting her sisters, 'You stand up straight now, don't you talk so loud, you brush your hair and keep yourself neat. How do you think you'll get a husband, looking like a hoyden?' Never said it to Faith. Never told Faith to keep herself tidy, or she'd never get a husband. Poor Faith, not much better than a hunchback, it would be unkind to raise her hopes.

'He *did* say *marry?*' her mother insisted. 'I'm not having a daughter of mine living in sin.'

'No, Mother. He asked me to marry him.'

They stood in the kitchen, Faith watching her mother, wondering what she was thinking now.

'Well,' said Mrs Carter slowly, staring across at her. 'Well, then. Well I never.'

The same words echoed through Kathy's mind, but she didn't say them. All she could say was his name. 'Oh, Ben. Ben.'

'She's a hard-working woman,' said Ben, and that was, after all, the main reason he had asked her. That, and the belief that few women would have taken him for a husband.

Kathy managed to smile, at first a tight little twist of her lips that tried to mask her disappointment. Ben was not her son, but she loved him, and she'd had higher hopes for him than Faith Carter.

Ben loved Kathy too, and he'd planned to name his boat after her, but she said that wouldn't do. That wouldn't be fair to Faith, to name the boat after another woman. It would be near enough to an insult. It was Josiah who came up with the name *Grey Lady*. Kathy always wore grey, but

37

Faith, too, had only grey dresses. So Ben painted the name *Grey Lady* on the cabin of the boat, and thought as he did so that it was just as well Josiah had chosen this name because there were hardly any colours but grey and white in the paint store now.

Ben and Faith were married in the church, and two days later they set off, Ben pulling the boat and Faith steering. They planned to go to Birmingham, where there were companies with their own boats and the horses to pull them. It would take them three days, with Ben bow-hauling *Grey Lady*, and Faith standing on the narrow deck, steering a boat for the first time in her life.

2

Faith had never been to Birmingham. She'd never been further from her home than Stourbridge, and that had seemed big. There were blast furnaces there, too, and she'd seen and heard them, the sudden huge noise that sounded as if the air was being sucked away, and the flare of red light searing up into the sky. It had fascinated her, but she hadn't liked it. It had made her nervous.

That first time Birmingham seemed like a scene from hell.

It might have been better if they had arrived during the day, not late in the evening, not in the dark, if it ever could be called dark in that city. As they came through the long cutting, the new line of the canal, she looked wonderingly at the sky, wanting to call out to Ben to stop.

It's on fire, she thought. The town's burning.

Red light glowed on the clouds, and black smoke billowed up from the high chimneys. As she watched she saw the flare, the white light, the red, and the huge noise. WHOMP! WHOMP! She cried out in fright, but Ben didn't hear her. He was too far away, bowed forward under the rope that lay over his shoulders. It seemed he, too, was burning, red light and black shadows all around him.

He was exhausted. The boat, unladen, swam

easily and high in the water, but it had been miles that day, and he thought that the sore place on his shoulder where the rope had chafed was bleeding.

Better not stop. Not much further now. If he stopped he might not be able to start again. They needed to find work within a day or so, work from a company that would lend them a horse. There wasn't much money.

What is that? thought Faith. What is it? Blast furnaces, iron foundries, she knew, but she'd never thought there could be so many. She clung tightly to the long tiller, fingers gripping the wood, felt herself panting with fright.

WHOMP!

'Ah, God, no! No!'

That was so close. And they were drawing nearer all the time.

'Our Father, who art in Heaven, hallowed be Thy name. Thy kingdom come.'

But this was the kingdom of hell, this great city under the burning sky, with all the black smoke and the flames and the sparks, and that terrible noise. Can people live here?

'Deliver us from evil. Deliver us from evil. Deliver us from evil.'

She closed her eyes, and thought of the green fields in spring, thought of skies that were blue, or grey, not that hellish black and red. Thought of the sounds of birds singing.

WHOMP!

'Oh, Ben, please, stop now. Please, no further.'

He stopped. He stood ahead of her on the path, silhouetted black against the red glow, and the rope dropped from his shoulders, on to the path at his feet. The big boat slid on through the black water, and Faith leaned against the tiller to bring her in close to the bank, trying to judge it right this time, so that she was close enough for Ben to take a rope and pull her in tight, but not so near that she scraped against the side.

It was new work, this, and harder than she'd thought it would be. What would it be like, trying to steer *Grey Lady* when she was loaded?

WHOMP! WHOMP!

'I'm not strong enough. Oh, Jesus, what am I going to do? I'm not strong enough. I can't go on.'

But when she saw Ben, he looked so weary she couldn't tell him how she felt. She managed to smile at him. She hoped he hadn't seen the tearstains on her cheeks. Silly, to be frightened of a blast furnace. Heard them before, hadn't she? And don't look at the sky. Get used to it.

There was so much to get used to.

The tiny cabin was no problem to Faith, as it might have been to other women. She was used to being cramped, to making herself small, taking up as little room as possible, and here there were no children running around her, getting in the way. This was her home, and she was proud of it. She liked cleaning it, rubbing the smooth wood with her rags, washing into the corners and wiping dry, polishing the iron range with black lead. Cooking on the little stove, just for her and Ben. At first that had seemed like a game, playing house.

But that night it was filthy. They weren't even in

Birmingham, and a film of sooty dust lay on everything.

'Clean it, then,' she told herself fiercely. 'Make it all clean again. Dirt can come off, can't it?'

But first there was Ben, so weary now he could hardly stand. A big mug of tea, and food for her man, and then her own work, to make her home clean again.

He took off his jacket, and there was blood on his shirt.

'Oh, my Lord.'

There was some pork fat in the cupboard. Goose grease would have been better, but she had none. And then she must make a pad to put on his shoulder. So don't stand there gawping, say something.

'Take a horse back to the stable like that, you'd feel the stableman's fist.'

That's good. Made him smile.

'Sit down, then. You made this cabin, you know there's places to sit.'

It wasn't too deep, the wound on Ben's shoulder, and both of them were used to small injuries. Faith remembered her mother's words, spoken so often throughout her childhood: what you can't poultice you put up with. Ben would have heard them too. A raw patch on a shoulder, well, that wasn't too bad. But it would bleed again the next day.

All through that night she jumped awake as the blast furnaces roared, belching the flames and smoke up into the sky. She knew Ben lay awake beside her, although he was still. By the time they had eaten, and she'd cleaned the cabin and made everything tidy and ready for the morning he'd been asleep, sitting on the bed with his head dropped on to his chest.

It was the first night he hadn't wanted her.

He'd fallen asleep straight away, and she lay beside him, wondering what would happen to them, if it turned out she wasn't strong enough to manage the boat. Wondering, too, if it was only tiredness that had made him turn his back to her as she got into the bed. She knew she was no beauty, and she knew too that some would think she was lucky to have a man at all. He was so much younger than her, and even though his breathing was wrong, as it nearly always was, summer and winter, he was a fine-looking man.

When she was little her mother had made her stay in the dairy out of the way when the cows were taken in to the bull, but no child could grow up on a farm and not know what happened. That night before the wedding her mother had talked to her and said it was all much the same, it was the man's pleasure and his right, and not too bad when you got used to it. Best just to think of something else.

That made sense to Faith. The first time it had been painful, and there'd been blood, as her mother had warned her, so when Ben had fallen asleep she'd crept out of bed to the washstand and cleaned herself, and changed her nightgown, then sat quietly on the chest in the corner of his room with rags pushed up between her legs until the bleeding stopped.

Only four days ago, and now he'd turned his back on her and fallen asleep. And even when he wasn't asleep, and she was sure he wasn't, he was still lying with his back to her, not speaking, not wanting his pleasure and his right.

She had never been so tired before, and still she couldn't sleep. She lay quietly, not moving, fearing to disturb Ben, until grey light was beginning to show in the chinks around the cabin doors. Then she slipped out of bed, and dressed herself, and began her day's work.

On into Birmingham before it was light, and Faith was too tired to be startled by the blast furnaces, too tired to think of her fear as the big warehouses loomed over the canal, and the noise poured over her until she couldn't think, couldn't speak, thought she would be deaf and blind and, dear God, please let me go back to the farm, I can't do this.

Ben trudged on down the path, the rope over his shoulder, feeling the blood running warm again despite the pad Faith had sewn into his jacket the night before. The men and women on the other boats turned to stare: a new boat, new people, who were they, then? What was that boat? What was that name?

'Grey Lady,' said a man standing by the loading bay, and the word ran down the waiting boats, passed on to the men and the women who couldn't read the white-painted letters. *Grey Lady, Grey Lady, Grey Lady.*

'Who are they, then?'

New boat. New people.

'Come from Armstrong's yard. That's the lad from Armstrong's yard, down Stourbridge way.'

'What's he doing here, then? Lost his place at the yard?'

Coal dust, soot and grit, and it was bright morning somewhere up there, but around *Grey Lady* the smoky fumes clouded the air, and Faith clung to the tiller and tried not to notice the men and the women staring as they passed. She looked instead at the horses standing waiting while the boats were loaded. Small, most of them, smaller than the farm horses, and the harness was different.

Ben had stopped walking, he was talking to a man on the path, and *Grey Lady* was drifting on the water. Somebody shouted at her, angrily, loud words telling her to mind her boat.

She looked round, frightened, saw a horse coming up behind pulling a boat, and didn't know what to do. Ben had told her but she'd forgotten, and now she was in the way, causing trouble, and there was another boat coming the other way.

'Mind your boat, woman! Mind your boat!'

What was she to do?

'Help me, God, please. Help me, Jesus.'

She pushed at the tiller, not knowing if that was what she should be doing, and she couldn't remember what Ben had told her, but the man stopped shouting and the horse came past, stepping over the line from *Grey Lady* as it lay on the path, and then the boat with the woman at the tiller, and she nodded at Faith, not unfriendly, just a nod between neighbours, and the boat went on, straight and clear, following the horse.

But that woman had been huge. Faith didn't

45

think she'd seen a bigger woman. Her arms were like tree branches.

Was that how a boatwoman should be?

Ben had stopped talking to the man: he'd watched her, and the boat coming towards them. He smiled at her, and Faith tried to lift her hand to wave at him, but she was gripping the tiller so tightly she couldn't let go in time, and when she did, he was looking away again.

It was better, though. She could remember now what he'd said, about letting the line go slack and leaving room between the bank and the boat so the other boat could get between them, the horse stepping over, as it had, and the boat not getting fouled in their towing line as it rode over, the heavy rope dropping down through the water and lying on the bottom out of the way.

It wasn't so hard to remember, now she'd seen it. If the man hadn't shouted at her, she'd have been all right.

Ben moored *Grey Lady* where she was. There was no point in dragging her through the city while he looked for work. He would go on without her, find a job, then come back. The man on the path had told him where he could ask. The office at the Gas Street Basin would be the best place. They were always busy there.

But it wasn't so easy.

They weren't rude to him, but they wouldn't listen.

'With lungs like that, lad, the canals are no place for you. No, you find yourself work out in the country somewhere.'

At the next place he tried to breathe quietly,

like anybody else, but it was a strain. And there was no work. Next week, maybe, the man said, and Ben nodded, and left, thinking of the few shillings in his pocket.

Next week. Not today. Not without your own horse. Something wrong with your lungs, lad? This is no work for you. There might be work in Stafford, if you can get there. Maybe in a few days.

It was dark by the time he got back to the boat, and Faith met him with a tight, anxious smile. The cabin was warm and clean, but it was bare, too. They had what they needed, or most of it. Other boats, though, had lace plates on the cabin walls, pictures, ornaments; they had white crocheted lace all around the cabin, and the woodwork was painted in bright colours, with the roses and castles that everyone loved.

Faith had made a meal, and there was tea, and the cabin was clean and tidy, ready for an early start in the morning.

'Nothing today,' said Ben, and he tried not to let the worry show in his voice. What if no one would give him work? What would they do? He had married her because he needed a wife to help him on the boat, but that meant two mouths to feed, and if there was no work, that was two people going hungry, and him responsible.

'There'll be something tomorrow,' she said, but there were tears just behind her eyes, and he looked at her, looked a question.

'We shouldn't have moored here,' she said. 'We were in everyone's way. They turn the boats here, and there wasn't room.'

47

They'd sworn at her, she told him, the men, and the women had been rude, and said there was nothing worse than people like her, knowing nothing and coming on the boats. Getting in the way. After it had happened a few times she'd stayed down in the cabin and not come out when the men had banged on the hatches and the angry voices had been shouting. She'd hoped they'd think there was no one in the cabin, but they could see the smoke, they knew she was there. It had made them shout even louder.

'I should have known that,' said Ben. 'I'll move her on a bit first thing tomorrow.'

He did move her, and he asked one of the boatmen where he could moor out of everyone's way. The man pointed on down the canal. Faith couldn't hear what they said, but they talked for a moment or two, and when the man went on he called something back over his shoulder, and he was smiling.

Faith looked at them both, and her spirits lifted a little. One of the boatmen had smiled at Ben and been friendly. Maybe it would be all right. Maybe they'd manage. It might even be that somebody would smile at her that day, too.

There were factories everywhere she looked, and they all belched their black smoke into the sky. Behind them there were always those furnaces, turning the clouds red. Black dirt lay on the top of the cabin. The ropes she'd scrubbed white had grit lying between the strands. How could she keep her boat clean in a place like this?

Well, she could only try.

She began to wash the cabin sides, and when the next boat went past the woman nodded to her. She didn't smile, but she did nod, and there were no shouts, nothing nasty.

Faith nodded back, and watched the boat as it went on, the man leading the horse. It had surprised her the first time she saw it, how far ahead the horse went. She was used to the farm horses, pulling the carts and the ploughs, harnessed between the shafts, but these horses, on the long, long rope, were so far ahead the man couldn't hear even if the woman shouted.

There were children too, living on the boats, and then one went past with a young girl steering. Faith stopped washing the paintwork, and stared.

I'm bigger than her, she thought.

At the bend in the canal the girl leaned against the long tiller, pushing it with her whole body, not just her arms, the way the big woman had done.

Ah, thought Faith. I can do that.

There was a smile on her face as she watched the boat turn under the bridge. A woman on the path on the other side of the canal saw the smile, and called out something Faith couldn't catch, but when she looked across the woman was smiling too and a hand was raised in a greeting.

At about the same time that Faith was watching the young girl steering the loaded boat Ben stood in the doorway of the shipping-company office and asked for a load for his boat. The man at the desk looked at him long and hard, then said there was copper pipe to go to Warwick. He was short of a boat that week, but only for that week, mind. Take the dun horse, and watch out for him. Don't approach him face on, he'll turn.

Ben had learned a bit about boat horses from the boatmen who'd stopped for repairs. A horse that turned away from you and went back down the towpath was dangerous. If the steerer couldn't get the line free in time, the horse might pull the boat round, and there'd be damage.

Ben didn't know a lot about horses, but Faith saw they'd been given a bad one, the horse no one else would take.

It was an easy load, not too heavy, but they only managed by working late into the nights and starting early in the mornings. Ben couldn't leave the horse at all. He had to lead him every step of the way, and couldn't even walk ahead to set the locks. The dun gelding was nervous and stubborn, and shied at shadows. At the locks Ben had to tie him, because he couldn't be trusted to stand. Faith might have handled him better, but that was not the way things were done on the boats. The man took the horse, the woman steered the boat.

They had a bit of luck at Warwick: a load of furniture to take back to Birmingham for a family moving house. Ben had never heard of a boat carrying furniture, but he loaded it without question, glad of the few pounds he'd been offered.

Just before they reached the yard in Birmingham Faith hit the horse on the hock with a mallet.

'Put his foot in a hole,' she told Ben. 'Won't be fit to go out next week, lame like that.'

The horseman had been annoyed and suspicious, but didn't go so far as to call Ben a liar, and the manager had been impressed at the time they'd made, even with a bad horse.

'London,' he said. 'Load of iron.'

London? thought Faith. Only three days ago, I was thinking I'd never been further than Stourbridge, and now I've been through Birmingham, and I've been to Warwick, and I'm going to London. I never dreamed I'd go to London.

It made her nervous, but she was excited, too, and the noise of the blast furnaces didn't frighten her so much now.

Maybe we'll manage, she thought.

Then Ben sent money back to Josiah and Kathy, and Faith protested: she'd had plans for the money, a list of items they needed to buy. Why was Ben sending money back to the boatyard?

'I owe them,' Ben replied, and for the first time Faith was angry enough to raise her voice at him. She understood his words only in terms of money.

'You said you owned the boat. You lied to me, Ben Jacardi. You lied to me.'

Ben made no attempt to explain: his wife would have to accept what her husband did, as women must. It was too late now. They were married.

She did accept it. She was, as he had known she would be, hard-working, and she adapted quickly to her new life, although there were aspects of it she found hard. They were delayed in a village outside Birmingham, waiting for a lock to be repaired, and Faith went out for a walk in the countryside. On her way back, she made the mistake of going into the village shop to buy bread.

As she walked through the door the talk stopped, and the people turned to look at her suspiciously. She waited behind them, puzzled and a little afraid, until it was her turn.

'Are you off the boats?' the man demanded, and when she said she was he pointed at the door. 'Be off with you, then. We don't want your sort here. Go on, take yourself off. This is a shop for respectable people.'

And as she left, the tears starting to her eyes, she heard him again.

'No better than dirty gypsies, the lot of them.'

But if she was excluded from the outside world, gradually she became accepted by the boat people. Almost everywhere the boaters went they were regarded as strangers, suspicious ones at that, so they had formed, over the years, their own sort of community, a tight, protective one. Very few land-based people found their way into it, and not all who worked the boats were welcomed. But Faith liked living on the boat, and she made friends with other boatwomen, who showed her how to manage and treated her kindly. Despised as they so often were, it made a change for them, to find somebody to pity. That poor young man with the bad chest, married to an older woman half-way to being a hunchback, and the pair of them new to the canals, although Ben was a boater by virtue of having built them. But kindness cost nothing, and Faith always offered a cup of tea to a woman on a boat moored beside them at night.

So, this is how you keep the toll tickets in the ticket drawer up by the doors so's they's always handy, and under that's the soap hole for your polishing rags, and when you're settled you'll be making your lace for the cabin. And a few bits of brass, and a lace plate or two on the wall behind the range, and soon you'll be as homely and snug as the rest of us, Mrs Jacardi. And when the babies start coming, there's the side bed for the first, and the cradle goes under here. And these are the shops where they won't turn you away. Stay out of the little village stores, my dear. We only go to the shops by the cut, where they know us, or in the big towns where they don't take notice. Not the village stores, Mrs Jacardi.

Faith learned quickly, and learned first that the best boats were the ones that reached their destinations fastest. Up early in the mornings, and get away to be first in the line at the locks, not held up by other boats waiting in front of you. Learn the ways of the canals, learn that some of those bridge holes silt up, and on which side, so you can steer the boat away, and not drag on the sandbars. Learn how to steer the boat so she runs straight, because that makes less work for the animals.

Get there first, and be first in line for the next orders.

Learn how to load the boat properly and quickly, and get stronger if you're not strong enough. Loading coal, using those heavy wooden barrows with the iron-shod wheels, pushing them along the gangplanks if you can't get the boat in close, and they're heavy, those barrows. Those iron rims on the wheels can slip if you're not careful. Watch where Ben wants that coal put, not in the middle, not at first: you have to load in a way that keeps the bottom of the boat straight and flat. If you load something heavy in the middle first, those bottom planks will flex, and that's bad.

Learn fast, and don't forget.

Learn to keep your balance on those top planks that run the length of the hold, high up over the water it seems when you look down. Keep your balance even in a strong wind. The top planks are only a few inches wide, and they spring under your feet between the stands on which they rest. Sometimes the men run races on those planks, when there's a rally. They run along them, jumping from boat to boat.

If she had to walk on them, Faith was timid on the planks, although Ben found them easy.

Learn how to sheet up your boat, with the side cloths up first, the strings passed over the top planks, the top cloths over that, and a strip of canvas over them all to protect them. Learn the words, so you know. Side cloths and top cloths, all tied down neat and tidy, and the ropes scrubbed white.

That's the work you do when you're waiting to unload, or load: scrub your ropes and wash down the boat. There's water in the cut, and it costs nothing, and there's always rags, so there's no reason for a dirty boat. And the best place to do your washing is at the foundries, because there's always hot water and the men let you use it. We

54

all do our washing when we're at the foundries.

Grey Lady had been well made, and Faith never told anyone there was money owing on her, so Ben was a Number One, and more deserving of respect than many who had been on the canals since they were born.

The boatman's cabin, which was all the home they had, was a piece of craftsmanship, with cupboards and doors of solid oak, fitting snug and close. It was only plain wood, but one day it would be painted, and when Faith saw the other boats, she made her plans for painting her own home, so the cabin would be bright with colour and shining brass. Where the table folded up to make the door of the food cupboard she would have a castle painted, with a bridge and maybe a swan on the water. And on the bed hole too, when the bedding was packed away and the board folded up flat, she'd have that painted, and soon she'd make curtains to draw across for the nights.

In the meantime, everything in its own place, everything spotless and shining, the range gleaming black and the brass near white with polishing, and the clothes and the sheets to be washed in the iron tub that was up in the cockpit, boiled until they were spotless. And the clothes to be made, too; this pattern for a man's shirt, and that for a woman's, with room enough to move.

Faith listened carefully, and asked for advice, and help if she didn't understand, so the women relaxed in her company and came to like her. That nice Faith Jacardi, not too full of herself to ask how things should be done. And her cabin, always clean, and that last shirt she made for her man, nearly as good as I could have done it myself.

Shame about her shoulder, poor soul. And being so much older than her man. But you couldn't wish for a nicer woman.

Faith had always had to be nice, to keep her place in her own home. She'd had to work harder than any of her brothers or sisters, and hadn't dared complain. Her mother said the oldest had to work hardest, that was the way of the world, but there was more to it than that, and they both knew it. The ugly and the infirm have to work harder to keep their places, because that's their apology for being there at all.

When Faith was small it had seemed there was always a new baby in the cradle, and another to come soon. The nearer the time came for the next baby, the harder Faith had to work, because her mother was slow and heavy, and it was as if she had drawn away into herself, saving all her strength for the child that was coming. Most of them died.

When that happened Faith cried, because she loved the babies, even though they meant more work for a child already struggling from daylight to darkness. She would look down into the cradle at the still, quiet face that had been alive such a little while ago, and even as a small child she'd wondered why God let them stay just long enough for people to love them, then took them back. That wasn't fair, was it? And why them and not her, when they were perfect, and she wasn't? She was the one who should have died.

But she didn't die. She just went on working. Up before dawn every morning, up to the farm from the small cottage, out into the fresh air. Faith had always loved that. The cottage smelt bad, smelt of the babies that came every year, smelt of the sweat of working men who were too tired to wash, smelt of too many people in too small a space. Even in the cold winters Faith liked stepping out of the hot, stuffy kitchen into the cold air, and even though it sometimes hurt her lungs she breathed in deep because the air was clean.

Up to the farm before daylight, working in the dairy, listening to the men readying the horses. She wanted to be out with the horses because she loved them, but that was man's work. Cleaning the churns was woman's work, breaking the ice on the water and banging the heavy, stiff brushes to get the frost out of them, scrubbing the cold metal, so cold you daren't touch it, because your hand might stick to it, and when that happened it was like a burn, maybe worse. You could tear the skin off, pulling your hand away.

That was woman's work, while the men harnessed the horses in the warm stable, lifting the heavy collars over their big, gentle heads, buckled everything safe into place, and then out into the fields or, if they were too hard with frost for the plough, into the woods, cutting fence poles. There was always something to be done by the men with the horses. It was hard work for the men, heavy work, out in the open.

Then the cowman would be coming up the lane, and they'd hear the beasts lowing, and everything must be ready, clean and shining. Wash the cows' udders, the water so cold it had made her cry when she was little, and in the winter the chilblains would bleed, and the cracks in her hands looked as if they'd never heal.

Then off to school, after three, maybe four hours' work, and the children from the town still yawning. Faith had loved school, she'd loved her teacher. She'd never wanted to be a teacher, because she knew there was no chance of that, and she had learned early not to want what she would never have. But she did think it must be lovely to be a teacher. It would be so nice always to be wearing clean clothes, and looking neat. It would be grand to live in the schoolhouse, and to have books of your own.

Some of the children could stay on after proper school, and sit at their desks for a while, reading, or doing some more writing. They were the clever ones, who might go on to the big school. Faith could never do that because the cows had to be milked in the evenings as well.

The horses would come in from the fields, and she'd listen to them stamping in the stable while the men fed and groomed them, brushing the dried sweat out of their coats, whistling to them, calling to each other. End of the day, man and beast were ready for rest, and if she'd finished in time Faith would go to the stables to meet her father. She'd stand by the big horse and rub his head, just above the eye, where he liked to be rubbed, and he'd lean his head towards her and blow softly.

'I'd hoped we'd have our own horse by now,'

she said to Ben, at the end of their first year on the boat, but there was no edge to her voice, just a little disappointment. Before they'd married she'd had plans, things she wanted them to have, but nearly half the money went back to the boatyard, and her hopes had been laid aside.

Ben wrote to Josiah, explaining, and he took Faith to a horse fair. She walked a little behind him and stood at his shoulder as he looked at the horses. No one could hear what she whispered. The horses she liked were priced too high, and at last Ben bought a mule, a small, sturdy animal that had lashed out at a man who approached it too quickly. Faith had laughed, smothering the sound in her shawl, then whispered to her husband.

'Too much,' Ben had replied, to the owner's demand. 'The thing's vicious. I saw it kick.'

Faith called the mule Silver, and crocheted him ear covers out of white string, a skill she'd learned from other boatwomen. She told Ben he must always let the mule know where he was, not take him by surprise. 'Speak to him, or whistle, make a noise. Startle a mule and he'll kick, and that'll be your fault,' she said.

Silver never kicked anybody again. He wasn't as strong as a horse but, then, he didn't eat as much.

That Christmas the canals froze over, thick ice that even the icebreaker boats couldn't keep clear. Ben and Faith left Silver in the public stables at the top of the Delph locks in Stourbridge, which was as far as they'd got before the ice locked the boats in, and went home.

Josiah had a bad cough but Kathy was well, and pleased to see them. She told Ben that Josiah still got work sometimes, mending boats, and they were managing. If it was heavy work Josiah sent the baker's boy into town for Jed. The money Ben sent was a help; she didn't know how they'd have managed without it.

Faith's father knew where there was a donkey for sale. He wouldn't cost much, he was old, but he'd be able to help Silver, and he wouldn't eat a lot: donkeys could live on next to nothing.

It was while they were looking at the old donkey, Faith standing as usual just behind him at his shoulder so she could whisper her knowledge into his ear that Ben became aware he loved her. It was not a sudden revelation: it came slowly. As he noted the white hairs on the donkey's muzzle, he realised he listened to her voice for more than information.

He stopped attending to her words. He thought instead of her breath on the back of his neck, not sure if he could feel it from the distance at which she was standing, but enjoying the idea, the warmth, the faint whisper of sensation it would bring. He wanted to tell her he loved her, but her father was there, and John Cobb, who owned the donkey. Then the man named his price. Ben turned to Faith and smiled at her.

'What do you think, Faith?' he asked.

She stared at him, and Ben's smile widened. The situation was ridiculous. Faith's father knew perfectly well that, of the two of them, Faith was the expert. As for the other man, why should Ben care for his opinion? But custom dictated that the man made the decisions and the wife accepted them. It was a natural law. A wife could never know as much as her husband, because she was a woman. Ben was showing contempt for tradition because he wanted to tell Faith he loved her, and he didn't want to wait until they were alone. 'What do you think, Faith?' were the only words he could use to let her know how he felt.

He saw the man look at him sharply, and Faith noticed it too, her eyes nervous in her thin face.

'He's too old,' she said, but it wasn't true. The donkey's teeth bore the marks and shape of age, but his legs were straight and he held himself quite well.

Faith was blushing. She was embarrassed, and probably angry with him for addressing her like that in front of a stranger. The man would think she was forward and managing. It was the husband's job to deal with the animals.

'He's been looked after,' said Cobb, speaking loudly and directly to Ben. He would not discuss his animal with a woman, and avoided looking in her direction. 'There's a difference.'

Now there was a disagreement, and it shouldn't have arisen. The man resented Faith being brought into the deal, and would be stubborn. Ben's oblique declaration might cost them money.

'How old is he, then?' asked Faith's father, and the interest in his voice drew everyone's attention back to the patient little animal standing before them.

The donkey was somewhere between twenty and twenty-four, they calculated. They looked at

61

his teeth again, and at his feet. The hoofs had been kept trimmed, and they were hard and round.

'Good feet,' Faith whispered. 'Good donkey.'

'I like him, Mr Cobb,' said Ben. 'I like him.'

They bought the donkey, and Faith walked beside Ben as they led him back to the boatyard. Her father left them at the barn door to go back to his cottage. He'd been a little too warm in his farewells to Cobb. He'd been embarrassed. He hadn't brought up his daughter to poke her nose into men's business.

'What did you mean by asking me, then?' Faith demanded, as they rounded the corner and were out of sight. 'Showed me up. I didn't know what to say.'

Now that he could tell her he loved her, Ben couldn't find the words. She was in a sour mood, and might even think he was making fun of her. He walked on in silence, listening to the quick patter of the donkey's hoofs on the path behind them. He heard his own breathing, and doubt crept into his mind. Why should she accept his love? She might be a fair bit older than him, but apart from that little twist to her shoulder, which he never even noticed now, she was healthy. She breathed quietly, and he could not. He tried sometimes. He'd tried at school. Mrs Hart had said, 'Practice makes perfect,' one of her favourite phrases, and he had tried. He had practised breathing in only a little bit of air, then breathing it out like a whisper. Again, do it again, and again, but then he had become exhausted by the effort, and he had gasped, dragging air deep down into his starved lungs. With it had come the familiar noise, roaring in his chest, and the long, grateful pauses between those effortful inhalations.

'Why, then?' she demanded again, and there were tears just behind her voice.

'I love you,' he said, and felt as if he was offering her his life.

'Funny way of showing it, then.'

She'd ignored his gift. She hadn't even noticed what he'd done, the danger he'd braved in saying the words.

He felt tears start into his eyes, and his pace quickened so he was striding and she was half running to keep up with him. Behind them, the little donkey broke into a trot.

Better if she'd said, 'I don't love you and I never will.' Better if she'd said, as her brother had once said when they were both at school, 'I don't want your dirty disease.'

'*Shut that horrible noise and die.*' Had that been him? Ben couldn't remember.

He'd never in his life felt so vulnerable. A picture came into his mind of his mother standing over him with the heavy leather whip in her hands, her teeth bared in the half-joyful rage he had come to mimic. He had been small, powerless and frightened, because she was so much bigger than him. But this little woman half running beside him, her head only level with his shoulder, he could pick her up and break her, and she had hurt him.

Her long, heavy skirts were flapping against her legs, and she was beginning to lose her breath as she ran. She wasn't used to this any more. Day after day she'd stood at the tiller of the boat, steering as he led the mule, and now she was running again, and she was out of breath.

'Are you tired?' he asked. 'Do you want to ride the donkey?'

Words, only words, she could pass them by without even looking at them. If she was tired he'd lead her on the little donkey, like the Christmas story.

She gave up, stopped running and stood by the side of the path gasping for breath. Ben turned towards her, and the donkey moved off the path on to the grass, tugged at his rope and dropped his head to graze. There was frost on the grass, which crackled as the donkey moved.

'We forgot to ask his name,' said Ben.

'Blackie.'

Had Cobb told her? Had she known the donkey from the past? Or had she just made up the name? The donkey wasn't black, he was a sooty grey, the colour of a dirty sheep.

Funny way of showing it, she'd said, but to him it had seemed right at the time. It had been like saying, 'Take your place alongside me, not behind me, not in my shadow, but here at my side.' If he had dreamed the scene, imagined it, she would have smiled at him, proud, stepped forward and said her piece about the animal, the equal of any man there.

But this hadn't been his dream, this had been reality, and it had all gone wrong. Faith had said something not because it was true but because she'd had to say something. She'd made herself look a fool, and he was to blame. It was no wonder she was angry.

'I'm sorry,' he said, but once again his offering went unnoticed.

'Blackie's sweating.'

It was an accusation, and it was true: he'd walked too fast. The donkey had had to trot to keep up, and now dark streaks of sweat were appearing on his shoulders and neck. It was a bitter, frosty night, and if the sweat was allowed to cool and chill against the donkey's skin, he might sicken.

Ben took off his jacket and laid it over Blackie's back, shivering in the cold air. It was about a mile back to the boatyard, where Josiah would have laid straw in the sheltered corner by the shed, and now he would have to walk it in the biting cold without his coat, to save the old donkey.

Faith had got her breath back now, so Ben turned away from her and jerked on the rope. Maybe now he would never tell her. Maybe now she'd never know what he'd felt back there in the corner of the barn in the lamplight when his mind had drifted on to the picture of his wife, standing behind him and whispering softly, when the image had been warm and gentle. He'd wanted to take her in his arms, lift her up as if she'd been a child, cradle her, shelter her, take care of her for ever so that nothing would ever hurt or chill her, or come too close to her.

He listened for the sound of her feet on the path behind them, but he could only hear his own breathing, and the tapping of the donkey's hoofs on the frozen earth. He looked over his shoulder, and she was still standing by the path,

65

watching them walk away.

'Are you coming, then?' he called. 'You'll catch your death, standing there.'

She caught them up further down the path, and took her place beside him. He glanced down at her surreptitiously, and her eyes were bright in the starlight, her mouth set and stubborn. She was still angry and upset.

'What's the matter, then?' he asked, and he'd meant his voice to be quiet and reasonable, but the words came out sharp.

'We'd have got that donkey a fair bit cheaper, if you hadn't asked me.'

'Who earns the money?' He was becoming angry now, more with himself than with her, which was worse.

'Ah, and who saves it?' she retorted. 'Putting away little bits, and you sending the best of it back here to pay for a boat you told me you owned. And making me look a fool, and all.'

But he'd had enough, and he turned and struck her in the face with his open hand.

'Hold your tongue.'

Her hand was pressed to her cheek, and there were bright tears running down her face from the shock and the sting of the slap.

He walked on quickly, and she kept pace with him, only a little behind him, her boots scuffing on the path where the grass had grown across it. Ben wanted to stop, he wanted to say something that would explain it all, but he didn't understand it himself. All he had wanted to do was tell her that he loved her, and instead he had hit her, and she was angry with him, and he with her.

He jerked on the rope again, and at the same time tried to turn back to Faith, so the donkey bumped against him and trod on his foot. Enraged, he lashed out at it, and it shied away from him, almost tearing the rope out of his hands, snorting with fright. 'Oh, that's right, beat the animal,' said Faith, and she was crying. 'Not enough to hit your wife, now you have to beat the animal.'

There'd be a bruise on her face in the morning. He could feel the palm of his hand tingling from the blow.

'I'll take a stick to you next time,' he threatened, and she turned her back on him and raised her hands to her face.

He was so frustrated and angry he didn't know what to do. He'd wanted to tell his wife he loved her, and now she was crying, with her hands pressed to the bruise on her face where he'd hit her, and a trusting old donkey was wild-eyed with fright and suspicion. He couldn't understand why it had all turned out so badly, but he knew it had to be his fault. Faith had done nothing wrong, and the donkey had obeyed the jerk on the rope, and been punished for it.

'Stupid clumsy brute, must be half blind.' His breath was roaring in his chest, and his voice was hoarse. He told himself to calm down, but shame was making him mad with rage, and it was all he could do to stand still on the path and not attack either the crying woman or the frightened donkey.

He was shaking with cold, and his jacket was slipping off the donkey's back. He snatched it, and Blackie jumped away from him, jerking his head to avoid a blow.

'May I lead the donkey, please?' Her voice was quite steady, even though her breathing was short, and every now and then he could hear a little gasp. But she seemed to have herself under control.

He handed her the rope, and she took it without looking into his face. She turned to the donkey and spoke quietly, reaching out slowly and scratching his neck under the coarse, tufted mane. After a few moments Blackie's head came down and the white ring to his eye disappeared.

Ben turned on his heel and strode on down the path, too fast for them to catch up. When he reached the bridge he looked back at them, about fifty yards behind him, walking steadily in the moonlight. Faith had taken off her shawl and laid it on the donkey's back to keep him warm in the cold night.

She'll catch her death, he thought, and then, That'll be my fault, too.

At the boatyard he went into the shed and found hessian sacks. He would tie them over Blackie's back to keep him warm. He must find a piece of rope. But when Faith came in a few minutes later she pushed away the sacks and twisted a hank of straw around her hand to dry the sweat off the donkey's back. She wouldn't speak to him as she worked, and he stood helplessly, watching her. Blackie was placid and contented under her hands, dropping his head to nose at the straw, munching quietly, his long ears flopping.

'Shall I get him water?' Ben asked, but Faith shook her head.

He picked up her shawl. She'd dropped it over a pile of timber when she'd taken it off the donkey's back. He shook it out, then held it to his face, sniffing at it. It smelt of the donkey's sweat. Now she'd have to wash it, and that was his fault, too.

He was too tired and depressed to be angry any more. He wasn't even sure that he did love her, after all.

3

After they'd been married for about five years, Faith began to collect little amulets, bits of stone or twigs, which she hung from the brass hooks, or put in vases for a few days, then twisted up in pieces of coloured cloth and hid in corners of the cabin. Ben noticed it, but he said nothing for a while. He knew Faith wanted a child, and he had no objection.

Months and years had passed, and her happy confidence had begun to fade. The little clothes she'd made in anticipation were taken out of the tidy drawers in the cabin and fondled, at first smilingly, later with tears.

'Other women have children,' she said to him one evening, when yet again the cramping pains and the blood had put an end to hopes. 'Why not me?'

It wasn't fair. That Thompson girl, that slut, that 'Rodney boater', as she had learned to call those who allowed their boats to fall into dirt and disrepair, she'd had seven children in five years and didn't care for any of them. One would make Faith happy, just one. Didn't even matter any more if it was a girl, just a child.

A baby in the cradle, so she could lean over it and smile down at it and love it, as she had loved the babies when she was a child, only this would be her own. One baby, one living baby, her very own. It had never occurred to her that she wouldn't have one. She knew they didn't always come quickly: some women had to wait months for the first, but she would have one, soon. Quite soon.

She was healthy. She was even happy, most of the time. *Grey Lady*'s cabin sparkled with white lace and polished brass, and she, like the other women, collected ornaments and hung them on the walls, lace plates with brightly painted scenes in the centre, horse brasses, anything that gave a bit of colour and shine. She was up well before sunrise every day, cleaning and setting the cabin to rights, because she was proud of her home, and she liked it to be shining and clean. But as the months passed it began to seem incomplete. The centre of the home had not arrived. She had made it welcoming and ready for the baby, but the baby wasn't there.

During the day she would stand at the tiller and steer the boat, while Ben led Silver and Blackie and worked the locks. Long though the hours were it wasn't hard, not now she'd learned the ways of the water, certainly not when compared to what had to be done in the mines and the mills, and probably not even as hard as the work she'd done on the farm. They made their living by their work, she and Ben, and she kept her promise to work hard for him.

When he had asked her to marry him, and left her at the cottage, she had already been thinking of her baby. She would marry the young man, and people would stop pitying her and scorning her, and that was good. But it was the dream of

71

her baby that had lifted her head and brought the quiet smile to her eyes as she looked into the years ahead.

'Why not me?' she cried again the next month, and Ben took her to a doctor, who said there was nothing wrong with her. Some women just didn't have children.

His indifference hurt her. There had to be some reason, something they were doing wrong. Maybe they'd committed a sin.

'Give over,' Ben retorted. 'Damned silly, that.'

'Then maybe it's your lungs, maybe that's where there's trouble.'

It had been years since she'd mentioned his lungs. She seemed to have accepted the noise of his breathing, had done so within weeks of their wedding. Now, she noticed it again, because she was looking for something wrong that she might put right. If she put it right, the baby would come. She had to find out what was wrong.

She knew she had trespassed here, but she was defiant.

'It could be,' she insisted, although he had said nothing. 'It could be. You don't know.'

So when they were next in Birmingham Ben went to the doctor and asked. It was not something he did lightly. He supposed the man must be clever, to be a doctor, but if so he seemed to hide it behind a wall of stupidity.

'I'm not here about my chest,' said Ben, but the doctor ignored him. He listened to Ben's lungs, made him breathe in deeply, breathe out. What was the explanation for the noise, when Ben was clearly so healthy?

'I had bronchitis when I was a boy.'

'But you haven't got it now, have you?'

'My mother told me my father breathed like this.'

'You couldn't have inherited this condition,' the doctor said, laying heavy stress on the words and speaking loudly and slowly, as though Ben were deaf. 'It's not medically possible.'

'That's not why I'm here,' said Ben again, but it was no use. In the doctor's eyes there had to be a reason for the way Ben breathed, and the only explanation Ben offered was clearly untrue. If Ben would not tell the truth, then the doctor could not help. Would not, even if he could.

'That was what I was told,' said Ben. 'That's all I know.'

Faith was less angry than resigned when Ben told her what had happened when he saw the doctor. She was sorry she'd even suggested it. Of the two of them, she was the more sensitive about Ben's breathing. She was the one who didn't like meeting new people, she who watched for their first startled reaction, and resented it. Ben had learned to ignore it.

Doctors having failed her, Faith asked the other women. They were kind and sympathetic, and offered what advice they could.

'Don't you worry about it,' said Becky Driver, who had four strong sons and another on the way. 'Worrying makes you ill, and then you'll never fall for a baby.'

'Lie on your back with your legs in the air after you've been with your man,' said Rose Ryder, who had two daughters, and Faith did as she suggested, for the rest of the night, and had such cramp in the backs of her thighs the following morning she could hardly stand at the tiller.

Ben held his peace. He tried to be sympathetic, but he didn't know what to say to her. Awkwardly, she asked if they could try different positions, other ideas that her friends had suggested, but she was embarrassed when she tried to talk to him. She found herself blushing and stammering.

When they moored near one of the missions, Faith would go there and pray. She would attend their services, if she could, when *Grey Lady* was moored nearby. Once she had been to a church, but the other women in the congregation had stared at her and whispered. None of the boatwomen went to church: they were afraid of being insulted. When Faith came back, Susie Brown told her she shouldn't go again: three of the women had tried to go to a church only a few weeks before, and they'd been made to sit in a pew right at the back, away from everyone else, and no one would come near them.

'Like we had some nasty sickness,' said Susie. 'Like they'd catch something.'

So Faith went to the missions instead, but it wasn't the same for her. There was something holy about a church that she couldn't find in the missions. And she didn't like the missionaries, either. They came to the boats sometimes, with their little tracts, brightly coloured bits of paper with writing on them about the evils of drink, about salvation and immorality.

'As if we was savages,' said Susie.

One of the missionaries gave Faith a Bible when he heard she could read, a heavy book bound in dark red leather with a gold cross engraved on the front cover, and he told her to read it to the other boaters, those who were less fortunate than she. Instead, she read it to herself in the evenings. She had a book of her own to read now, a small dream that had come true.

She took to saying her prayers every night, kneeling beside their bed, her hands held in the traditional position, her eyes closed, lips moving. This was how prayer was meant to be done, this was the ritual, and Faith would omit no part of it.

But prayer in church might have been special; it might have worked. So she had tried, and would continue to try in the missions.

'We could maybe confess our sins,' she suggested to Ben tearfully one morning, when she'd woken to find blood on the sheets. 'Go to the mission and confess our sins?'

He'd known anyway that she wasn't pregnant. She'd been short with him for the past two days, and he'd come to recognise the symptoms.

'You've done nothing wrong,' he said, hoping to reassure her.

'We've sinned in our hearts.'

'Oh, give over, that's daft.'

Ben would not go anywhere, let alone to the mission, and confess his sins, even if he could think of any. He'd had no woman but Faith, killed no one, stolen nothing except those little bits of coal, and that didn't count. He would not go to the mission, and he would not bathe in the canal at midnight by the light of the full moon, not only because he did not believe it would help but also because he suspected that it would end in a sudden blaze of torchlight and the noisy cheering of those who had suggested the idea to Faith.

'I do so want a child,' she cried that night, her face pressed against his chest as they lay together on the hard bed. 'I do, Ben. I do.'

'I know.'

He thought she'd fallen asleep after that, but when he woke in the morning his shirt was wet with tears and Faith was lying beside him, so quiet and still he thought she was too silent for sleep, and something like panic clutched at him.

'Faith?'

She turned her head and he felt his heart lurch in his chest, so great was his sense of relief. He thought of telling her, 'For a moment there I thought you'd died,' but he held back. Putting that fear into words might give it strength and substance. Might give her an idea best left alone. Instead, he turned towards her and put his arms around her, holding her head against his chest where his damp shirt clung to his skin. He felt the bones of her face under his fingers, almost sharp-edged. Her skin was soft, not very smooth now, with the hard weather of the winters and the harsh sunshine when the summers were too hot. There were grey hairs among the brown.

She was growing old, he thought, his little wife. Her face was lined, and her hair was going grey, and there was no child.

He wished there was something he could do to comfort her, and all that day as he walked beside the animals, he wondered. On the clear stretches where he could leave them to pull the boat alone he stood at the tiller, watching her working in the cabin, watching the water, watching Silver and Blackie, wondering what he could do.

'Ida Trafford's not well,' he said that evening.

'I know.'

The Traffords worked two boats on the Oxford Canal, and Ida's failing health was a problem to them. They had four children, and the two older boys had to help their father now. The little ones seemed to drain their mother's strength, and she hardly had any left.

'It was Peggy's birth that did for Ida,' said Faith.

'She's not dead yet.' Ben felt the protest rising in his mind, a memory of his fear of the morning.

Faith made no reply. She'd talked to Ida when they'd last moored together. Ida had told her it had been three months before she'd stopped bleeding after Peggy. There'd been other women there too, and Faith had listened to their stories, but even looking at Ida's white face and hunched body, she'd felt nothing but envy. There'd been the baby in the cradle.

She hardly heard Ben's words, but she lifted her head and looked into his face.

'Having a baby wouldn't kill me,' she said. 'And even if it did…'

'And even if it did?' prompted Ben.

'Be worth it.'

There was no point in arguing with her. Almost all Faith's life was turned inward towards having a baby now, and it might indeed seem worth death.

'Shall we take Peggy?' asked Ben.

Ida would probably agree. Boat children were often sent to other families, but usually when they were old enough to work, to be a help. A family overcrowded on a boat would be glad to let a child go to friends or relatives, to keep out of the way of the inspectors now there were new regulations, and to pay its way by helping to work the boats. It was a good arrangement, which was accepted happily by all concerned.

But a baby? Peggy wasn't even a year old.

Ben wasn't sure why he'd suggested it. A baby would slow them down, and it wouldn't even be theirs. But he couldn't get out of his mind the memory of waking with his shirt wet with Faith's tears, when he'd thought she was dead. If she had a child to care for, at least that fear could be laid to rest. Faith would hold responsibility for the baby above everything else.

He'd no reason to believe she'd thought of suicide, except that cold lurch of fear when she'd been so still and quiet. Walking along the towpaths beside the mule, he'd often remember it, and he'd glance back over his shoulder to look at her, standing at the tiller of *Grey Lady*.

That work was too easy for her now. Nothing to fill her mind but her longing for a baby. Nothing to do with her hands but hold the tiller. For a while she'd steered the boat as the other women did, with her back, her hands busy with a crochet hook or a piece of sewing, but that had been when she was making things for the baby. Now she steered the boat, and her once busy hands were quiet and still on the wooden bar. She

78

might be polishing a piece of brass, or perhaps peeling the vegetables in the bowl on the hatch cover, but she didn't make things any more. There was nothing more she wanted to make. She had nothing to watch but the water. She never raised her head to look around any more.

She hadn't answered when he'd asked about little Peggy Trafford. In a way he was relieved. He didn't think he'd want the child on the boat. It would be different if it was their own, at least he supposed it would, but a stranger's baby wouldn't seem right.

He hoped Faith would forget he'd mentioned it. They were on the Trent and Mersey Canal, not likely to be near Oxford for a while.

One night there were pink flower petals on their pillow, and a pink candle burning in the bright holder in the corner. 'What's this, then?' he asked, but she pretended not to hear him.

Old wives' tales, silly bits of magic, he thought. And he was very, very tired. They'd been up the Cheshire flight of locks, not all that hard, not really, but it was called Heartbreak Hill, and he wanted to sleep.

'Ben?'

Not *every* night, he thought. After five years surely most women wouldn't expect a man to do it *every* night. Most women used to complain, say their husbands wouldn't leave them alone, and the men would grumble. Put a wedding ring on a woman's finger and she turns into a lump of wood. Lucky to get a bit more than once a month.

Ben would listen to them, looking down into his pint of beer, wondering what Faith was

79

thinking while the other men complained about their wives always being tired, or having headaches or something else wrong with them. Wondering what she said if the women talked together as the men did. Would the women complain about their husbands always wanting to do it, no matter how tired they were? And what would Faith say, if they asked her?

'Ben?'

'Ah, Faith. I'm tired.'

'Please, Ben. Please?'

What would the other men think? he wondered, as he turned towards her, trying to smile. My wife? I don't have any problems with my wife. She begs me for it. Would they believe him?

But later, when she whispered, 'Thank you,' he winced. That must be some sort of humiliation for a woman, to have to ask, to have to say 'Please' and 'Thank you'. What did that cost a woman like Faith?

So, because he was a kind man, he fought away the desire for sleep and turned to her again, smiling down at her.

'You are more than welcome,' he said, trying to put a little life and fun into his voice. 'You are *more* than welcome.'

And she smiled back at him, not quite believing him, but grateful for the pretence.

The pink flower petals and the candle worked no better than the catkin twigs whose pollen she had collected in white silk, and the queer-shaped stones she'd wrapped in bright pieces of cloth and hidden in the cabin. They worked no better

80

than her prayers, or the contorted positions she'd so shyly asked of him, when he'd tried to hide his anger because he suspected somebody had been mocking her.

They met Jacob and Ida Trafford in Birmingham only two weeks later, and Jacob told Ben he thought Ida might never be well again.

'The little ones drain her strength, and she's not got much left,' he said.

Ben believed him. Ida had said it, and now Jacob, and so he took a mouthful of beer, and asked:

'Will we take Peggy for you?'

Jacob stared at him. 'Peggy's only a baby.'

Ben didn't answer. Jacob would have to think it out for himself. It couldn't be a secret any more, Faith's longing for a child, not now she'd asked so many of the women for advice.

'Is that what Faith wants?' asked Jacob, after a while, and Ben shrugged. He didn't know.

'Be a help to Ida,' Jacob admitted. 'I'll ask.'

When Ben told Faith what he'd said to Jacob she was silent for a long time, staring down at her hands. Then she looked up at him, and there was a tight little smile at the corners of her mouth.

'All right,' she said.

He knew she'd agreed to the terms of a surrender.

She cared for the child beautifully. Nothing was omitted, nothing ever forgotten. Although little Peggy was fretful at first, it only lasted for a few days. Her soft brown hair seemed to glow from gentle brushing, and her eyes grew bright and clear. Faith was always awake at the first muted

81

whimper, cradling the child in her arms as she warmed the milk for her, or poured water for washing into the bowl. By day the cradle in which Peggy slept was tied on to the sliding hatch over the cabin, inches away from Faith's ready hands. In bad weather Peggy stayed inside, warm and safe on the bed, sleeping soundly, or smiling up at her foster-mother who stood on the step, one eye on the boat, the other on the child.

'You spoil her,' said Ben. 'Leave her be. Crying's natural for babies.'

Faith denied it. She could remember crying from the cold when she'd been little, and no one had come. Even if there hadn't been another blanket for her, she said, if somebody had come she would have stopped crying. She'd never been able to bear the sound of a child crying.

There were no more twists of paper in the corners of the cabin, no more flower petals or candles, no more 'Please' and 'Thank you'.

Ben was slightly shocked at himself when he realised he missed it. He felt awkward about approaching Faith now, no longer sure what to say. There was the baby in the cradle, so they weren't alone any more. It seemed wrong, somehow, with somebody else's child in the cabin.

He told himself it was because the child wasn't hers that Faith never laughed with her, as other mothers did. They would pick up their babies, and their wide smiles would turn to laughter as the babies gurgled and kicked. Faith, looking down at Peggy, would smile at her, but never laugh. Ben told himself it would take time.

Faith still said her prayers every night, her hands clasped and her eyes closed, but now they were the words she had learned as a child, and none of her own. She had prayed for a baby, and perhaps Peggy was God's answer to those prayers. How could she dare to show ingratitude to God? Better to say nothing, and look after the child to the best of her ability, as was her duty. Then to slide between the clean white sheets beside her husband, and lie, wondering if he would ever turn to her of his own free will, now that she no longer asked.

Peggy came on to *Grey Lady* in spring, and it turned into a beautiful summer, with clear blue days and warm nights. The early mornings were misty over the canals, but almost as soon as the sun cleared the horizon it had burned away the trailing vapour of the night. By noon the heat was fierce. Ben made a sunshade for the cradle, and draped sacks over the animals' shoulders and backs, soaking them with water from the canal to help them keep cool. Faith's thin face turned gold, then brown, and Ben was the colour of old mahogany. Peggy was sitting up in her cradle and gurgling to herself, fat little fists waving in the air. She had become a happy child.

When they passed Jacob and Ida Trafford they tried to make time to stop for an hour or so, or to moor nearby. Ida seemed stronger, and the bluish tone had gone from her thin lips. She cried the first time she saw Peggy, picked her up and cuddled her, but the baby was frightened by the noise, and wailed in distress. Ida smiled through her tears, gave a little grimace, and handed her back to Faith.

'She looks grand,' she said.

She did look grand. She was growing quickly and strongly, and was crawling around on the cabin floor whenever she was out of her cradle. She seemed so well that the shock was as fierce as a slap in the face when she began to cough, the hard, barking cough of croup.

Ben was more alarmed than Faith, whose youngest brother had suffered from croup and grown out of it, coming to no harm in the process.

'Keep calm,' she ordered Ben. 'She'll be fine if she doesn't get frightened.'

Usually the attacks only lasted a minute or so, but even if Faith could remain placid Ben could not bear to be in the cabin when they occurred. The child's bulging eyes and red face seemed terrible to him, even though she always returned to normal within minutes. Ben would go out on to the deck, or on to the towpath, and if the barking did not stop almost immediately he would stride away until he was out of earshot, then wait until he judged the attack must be over and it was safe to go back.

Autumn came, wet and wild, and by the evenings both Ben and Faith would be exhausted, he with managing the animals on towpaths grown treacherous with mud, she with wrestling the boat off the banks where the wind drove it.

It was hard work, and it was dangerous. They came into a stretch of the Oxford Canal to find another boat blown on to the bank, the man steadying the horse as the woman stood on the

84

planks over the cargo, trying to push the boat away from the bank, a child at the tiller.

It happened so suddenly Faith couldn't believe it. The boat moved away, and then the wind blew again, a fierce gust. The woman's skirts were blown hard against her so she lost her balance and fell down the side of the boat and into the water. Then the wind took the boat too, swinging it back towards the bank. It rocked, once, twice, and it was over.

She hadn't seen what had happened, but she knew. The woman had been between the boat and the bank, and Faith knew how heavy the boats were.

The man with the horse was staring down into the water. He seemed unable to move. It was Ben who took the pole and shafted the boat out into the stream, and Faith steered *Grey Lady* between the bank and the other boat. *Daisy* was the name painted on her, Faith would always remember that. She didn't want to look into the water, so she looked at the name, *Daisy*.

There'd been a big rock in the water, the woman had fallen against it, and *Daisy* had rolled back.

Ben dragged the woman out, on to the path, and still Faith wouldn't look. She held *Grey Lady* steady somehow, the two boats together, their sides rubbing, and she thought, My paintwork will suffer for this.

The boy standing at *Daisy*'s tiller looked stunned, his eyes blank.

'Mam?' he said. 'Mam?'

They stayed to help, and two more boats

85

coming up behind them stopped. One went on to give the news at the next lock, and pass on the message to the family.

All Faith could think to do was make tea, and when Ben came back to the cabin, looking white and sick, she gave him a blanket to lay over the body, because it didn't seem right to leave uncovered the crumpled shape on the path.

After that she was always nervous, walking on the planks, and from then on, whenever they laid the planks on the stands after they'd loaded *Grey Lady*, she remembered *Daisy*, and the woman standing over the water with the long pole in her hand, and the sudden gust of wind.

The wild weather went on into the autumn, and Peggy, confined to the cabin, was whiny and fretful, sleeping only fitfully at night. Faith's face grew drawn under its summer tan, and her eyes looked bruised.

They took Peggy to a doctor in Stoke Bruerne, and he listened to her chest, his face grave. He looked far more serious than Ben had expected. Ben had believed Faith when she said plenty of children got the croup and grew out of it, that it wasn't dangerous. Faith, watching the doctor, began to frown. 'It's just the croup,' she said.

The doctor put away his stethoscope. 'Was it a difficult birth?'

'Not for her.' Ben touched Faith's arm. 'She's not ours,' he said.

'Then she'd better go back to her parents.'

In the shocked silence that followed his words Ben thought only that Faith was startled and alarmed, but there was no grief. There was nothing where there should have been a huge sorrow. He looked across at her, and at the lovely child she held in her arms, and he thought, She never laughed with Peggy. She never laughed, and now she can't cry. Peggy never was her baby. She never did love her.

'Am I doing something wrong?' Faith asked at last.

'No, no, no. Oh, no. This is no fault of yours. The child's lungs are weak.'

Faith looked down at Peggy, at the clear brown skin and the bright eyes, and Ben watched them both, thinking, Her lungs are weak. That's bad, with the croup. And that can't be right. Doctors get things wrong. Listen to me, listen to this noise I make. And my lungs aren't weak. I can work all day, I can run. But they won't believe that.

'Are you sure about her lungs?' he asked the doctor, and the man glanced across at him, one eyebrow slightly raised, a brief quirk of humour instantly suppressed, and Ben interpreted it. Clever lad, the doctor had thought. Fathered your child on another woman and got your wife to nurse it. That's where she got the lung problem. Let's hope your wife isn't bright enough to see the truth.

Slowly and carefully, still frowning, Faith wrapped the baby in the warm woollen shawl and picked her up.

'Thank you, Doctor,' she said.

They would have to tell Jacob and Ida. They asked, and were told that the Traffords were on their way to Chester on the Shropshire Union, on

87

the other side of the country. It might be weeks before they could meet, even if Ben could get a load to take into the West Country.

'I wish we had a regular run,' said Faith, but it was only worry speaking, and Ben recognised it because he felt the same way. With a regular run they could get back to Jacob and Ida. With a regular run they wouldn't have been so far away, with a heavy load of brassware from Birmingham to go down to London, then all that way back again with whatever was waiting for them. It might be two months before they could meet, maybe even longer.

They sent word back with the other boats, nothing to frighten the Traffords but the news that Peggy had the croup.

Sometimes they did have regular runs, mostly carrying coal for the iron trade in the Black Country, but neither of them liked it. They had a good name, Ben and Faith Jacardi. They didn't grumble when they had a long run to do, they didn't mind. It would be different if they had a growing family, maybe, but while it was just the two of them it was all right. While Peggy was little, it was all right.

Ben grew more and more fretful as the days passed and they fought the wind and the rain on their way down the Grand Union into London. He could do nothing for the baby, so he worried about Blackie, who was too old now, he was finding it a struggle. And Silver wasn't getting any younger: they needed a horse. No matter what the families with mules said about how they could live on nothing and still pull all day, a horse was stronger, and faster. And how were Kathy and Josiah managing in this wet weather? Josiah hadn't looked well in the summer. Ben should have made a point of visiting before this last trip. It would only have taken a day or so. Josiah might be ill, and Kathy would need him.

They both wanted to get back quickly, and in their hurry Ben grew careless. A bridge hole was too narrow for both the animals, and Silver, made nervous by the wind, shouldered Blackie off the bank.

It wasn't the first time one of the animals had fallen in, but it was a bad place, steep and muddy, and the wind was fierce. By the time they had dragged the little donkey out he was exhausted and it seemed he'd swallowed too much water. He stood on the path, his head low, mouth gaping, and when Ben tried to make him move he was sluggish.

Faith rubbed him down with dry cloths and tied sacks over his back to warm him, but it was obvious Blackie was in a bad way, and in no fit state to pull the boat.

Ben led the way, himself bow-hauling on the rope with Silver at his shoulder. Faith called to Blackie, 'Come on, come on,' and as the boat passed him the donkey raised his head, and slowly began to follow, his once brisk little footsteps down to a dragging trudge.

They stopped at the next public stables where the horseman looked at the donkey and shook his head. He didn't know, but he thought Blackie had twisted something inside while he struggled to get out of the water, and Blackie was old, not very strong any more.

The tears that should have been in Faith's eyes in the doctor's surgery were running down her face in the dark stable.

The horseman nodded at Faith and smiled. 'I'll make it quick,' he promised, and she went back to the boat and waited for Ben to join her later.

When he came back to *Grey Lady* he had a handful of the hairs from Blackie's tail in his fist. When a good boat horse died the family would often ask for the tail, and it would be hung on the tiller pin, to keep the spirit of the horse with the boat he'd pulled for luck and, although they'd never admit it, for the love of the horse. But you couldn't put a donkey's tail on a tiller. It would look stupid and, anyway, it would stink. Just a fistful of hair was what Ben had, because Blackie had been a good old donkey.

Ben sat in the cabin and watched Faith with the baby, and wondered if he loved her. The night they'd bought the donkey he'd known he did, and then it all went wrong, and he'd hit her. Now Blackie was gone, just a carcass under a tarpaulin in the yard, and that same feeling was in his memory, like an echo.

She'd never been pretty, his Faith. Leaving aside that hunched shoulder, she was sharp-featured and had a quick way of looking at you then looking away, as if something was wrong. But she had those big, sad eyes, and they spoke to him. It was nothing to him that her hair was going grey and that deep lines were etched into her skin. He felt something for her, and it was difficult to understand what it was. He'd look at

90

the pretty girls in the town, and he'd think, as he supposed other men did, that he'd like one of those in his bed for a while, but that wasn't what he felt for Faith. No man would look at Faith and think, I wouldn't mind her in my bed for an hour or so. Little and thin and that shoulder, hair going grey, lines on her face, sharp little face at that, but God help anybody who hurt his wife because he'd kill them. Might throw a fist or two to help a pretty girl, not much more than that, but he'd kill anyone who hurt Faith, and hang for it, and still think it worth the price.

'I wish that hadn't happened to Blackie,' she said, but there was a tone in her voice that told him it was the end of the matter now. 'I wish that hadn't happened' was a way of saying goodbye to the little donkey. That's the end.

'We'll have to get another animal,' said Ben, and she nodded. She'd washed her face and her eyes were dry, although a little red and swollen. He, too, was sad about the donkey, and angry, because it had been his fault. He should have been more careful at that narrow bridge hole, where the arch was so low. He should have made sure they came through with enough space between them, made doubly sure because both the donkey and the mule were nervy with the wind. It had been his fault, and now they would have to buy another animal.

There was enough money. Faith was careful, and they earned quite well. She no longer questioned him about the money he sent back to Josiah and Kathy, although by now she must think *Grey Lady* the most expensive, boat ever to

91

have been built on the canals. But Ben was the man, and would do as he pleased.

'Shall we buy a horse?' he asked.

'If you like.'

He wanted to please her, at least to make her smile. She was sad, he understood that, but it was only a donkey. It was not as if a person had died.

'Will you help me?'

By now he knew enough to make a good choice without her help, but he remembered the horse fair where they'd bought Silver, and he remembered her breath on the back of his neck as she whispered advice, and he wanted that again.

Not too tall, she told him. Look for a horse with short legs. Look for a big chest and a lot of muscle in the shoulders and hindquarters. Nothing flashy.

'Will you *help* me?'

She didn't believe he needed her help, and he grew annoyed, and borrowed a horse, a thin, weedy lemon-chestnut carriage horse with a white ringed eye, and pretended he'd bought it.

'You've lost your wits,' she exploded, and he began to laugh.

'Look what happens when you won't help me,' he said.

'Have you really bought that thing?'

'Ah, give over. Faith, come on, I *do* want your help. You know more about animals than I do. Tell me you'll help me or I'll buy this damned thing.'

Peggy had a bad attack of croup that night, and Ben went out and walked along the path, wondering what he could do for his wife. He couldn't understand her. She'd been truly distressed about Blackie, yet her response to the doctor's words about Peggy had been calm to the point of indifference. It didn't seem natural.

Ben had been to the pub that night to ask about horses. He didn't much care for the dark little canal-side pubs, although he went as often as most men, drank the thin beer and breathed the smoke as he sat on the wooden settle listening to the music, watching the dancing. He danced himself, sometimes. Outsiders who wandered in would watch the big, heavy boatmen dancing and be amazed at how quick and light they were on their feet, and the boaters would hide smiles behind their hands: boatmen needed to be quick and light on their feet. They needed not only their strength but also good balance, standing on the narrow top planks to guide the boats into place when they were being loaded, jumping from the banks on to the narrow gunwales, crossing the slippery lock gates in strong wind. It was no wonder they were neat dancers.

Ben went to the pubs to hear about work, about the state of the canals, all the news he needed to do his job. There's more boats wanted on the Coventry run for coal for the new power station, for the electrics. There's a lock gate broken on the Hatton flight, takes a couple of hours to get through. Peter Hawker's selling up, his boat's for sale.

'I'm looking for a horse,' said Ben, and the men scratched their heads. Peter Hawker used a pair of mules and they thought he'd sold them. A horse. There's that one from Banbury that the

Littlemores borrowed a few weeks back? No good, that one, lame as often as not. The gypsies down by the railway sidings might have a horse? No, only ponies, and half starved at that, waste of time going there. A horse. Well. There's a couple of dealers in the town. If you know what you're looking for. If you're careful.

Faith went with Ben the next day to look for a horse. Silver was old now, and couldn't manage *Grey Lady* alone, not day after day with a full load, and if they were to make good time back to Birmingham, where they could pick up news of the Traffords and find a way to meet them, they would need another animal. Strong though Ben was, progress would be slow if they had to rely on him to bow-haul *Grey Lady* alongside the mule.

But horses were expensive, and Faith shook her head stubbornly over all that were available. Not worth the money, she insisted, and besides, it was time they got a young animal with some work left in him, not other people's leftovers.

'A mule, then?' asked Ben, who was becoming impatient and exasperated, but Faith wouldn't have it. Ben had said they could have a horse, and Faith intended to find the right one.

They gave up in the middle of the afternoon. Peggy, wrapped in a shawl in Faith's arms, was becoming fretful, which might bring on an attack of croup. If they worked into the night they could at least make it to the next town, where there'd be a stable for Silver and perhaps news of a good horse.

But they were back in Birmingham before they

94

found an animal that met with Faith's approval, two days later than they'd been expected. Because the load was so heavy Ben had had to bow-haul the boat to help the mule almost all the way; it had been too much for one small animal to manage alone. His shoulders had been rubbed raw by the rope. Faith had smeared grease on to the sores and sewn padding into his shirt, but it hardly helped: The first hour of the morning was the worst, but then the scabs would break, and although the wounds bled, they were less painful.

Faith was determined about the horse. This time they were to get a good animal, even if it meant waiting.

'I can stand the pain,' she said, as she opened the pot of grease, and Ben grinned. It was his own fault for saying they would have a horse.

Peggy remained a sunny-natured child, and when the weather was fine and she could be outside to watch the passing landscape, she slept better at night. Despite his sore shoulders, Ben felt more confident. Perhaps the doctor had been wrong. God knows, that had happened often enough in the past. He liked little Peggy, her smiles, the way she waved her hands towards him, her efforts to speak.

'Ba. Ba. Da ba. Ba.'

'What do you suppose she means?' he asked Faith, but she only smiled.

Back in Birmingham, the manager knew what had happened to Blackie because word had gone back by the faster boats, the fly boats that changed horses every few hours and took precedence over all the other canal traffic.

95

'Bad luck,' he said, but he wasn't pleased. They were two days late, and customers wouldn't care about a donkey that had fallen into the canal.

'We're looking for a horse,' said Ben, and the girl who worked in the office checking the toll tickets looked up and said she might know of one that would do.

'You get on with your work, Miss.' Selby had had enough: the Jacardis were late, and he had no patience with young women who put themselves forward when they should be earning their pay.

But that evening she came down to the canal to where *Grey Lady* was moored, and called out to them:

'Mr Jacardi? Are you there, Mr Jacardi?'

Her brother worked in the market, and a man had been killed the day before when a cart had rolled over him. He'd had a horse, and the widow would need the money for it. Yes, she thought it was a young horse.

It was a piebald cob, with ugly black patches smearing into the white coat, and a pink-rimmed eye, but it was the horse Faith had described, short in the leg with a powerful body. He was called Billy, he was ten years old and he was used to hard work, so Ben didn't bother to ask Faith. He gave the woman the money she asked and said something awkwardly sympathetic about the death of her husband.

'You can take his bridle,' she said, 'but I can sell the harness, and it's not boat harness, is it?'

Ben gave her a luck penny for Billy, and a shilling each for the two children.

'God bless you,' she said, patted the horse then

96

began to cry, so Ben led him off and didn't look back.

Selby listened with a little more sympathy to Ben's account of Peggy's croup, and what the doctor had said. Someone else could take the steel he'd marked down for them and they could wait a day or so to see if there was a load that would take them on to the Shropshire Union where they could meet the Traffords.

'It's an ill wind,' said Faith, as she looked at Billy. 'Poor woman. But that's a good little horse, my Ben. That's the one we wanted.'

Almost as soon as they were on the Shropshire Union, Ben saw three magpies, and muttered to himself as he led Billy, '"One for sorrow, two for mirth, three for a funeral, four for a birth."'

That night Peggy died, and as he looked down into the cradle at her waxen face, so still and so quiet, Ben could think of nothing but the three black and white birds he'd seen in the willow tree.

They stopped in Brewood, a pretty village, and the word went round the canals that little Peggy Trafford had died of the croup while in the care of Faith and Ben Jacardi. Two days later Ida and Jacob came and there was a funeral.

She had been a lovely baby, but no one cried for her. Faith was resigned, and Ida sad, but although Faith had taken such care of her, she had never loved Peggy. Ben stood outside the churchyard after the funeral, and felt it was all wrong. Somebody should have been crying for Peggy, but everyone had been sad, no more.

He tried to explain to Jacob what the doctor

had said about Peggy having weak lungs, and Jacob patted his shoulder.

'Nobody's saying it's your fault.'

It wasn't anybody's fault, but little Peggy Trafford had died of the croup, and she'd been a beautiful, happy child, and nobody had cried for her.

4

'God didn't mean me to have a baby,' said Faith. 'We were wrong to take Peggy.'

Ben didn't know how to answer her. It had been his idea, and with his sorrow over the child he had the even greater burden of guilt. If he hadn't suggested it, Peggy would have stayed with Ida and Jacob, and though she would still have had weak lungs, and probably croup, her death would not have touched Faith.

'It would have happened anyway,' the women said, and Faith would nod, and Ben would know it was true, but ask himself why it had to be put into words.

The women were sympathetic, and they spoke kindly to Faith and of her, and said how well she had cared for the baby, but the unspoken words hovered around their heads on black wings.

The baby had died.

A week later when they reached the depot, Ben asked if they could be sent north rather than down to London again. Faith was not grieving for the baby, but Ben was beginning to suspect, behind the kind words and the sympathetic smiles of her friends, a sort of triumph. Faith had cared for Peggy Trafford better than they had cared for their own children, but thin, untidy Harriet still lived, and Rose might have scabs around her mouth but she was running along the path, and Moses grizzled with the discomfort of a filthy nappy sagging around his knees, but he was alive.

Faith accepted the kindness and the sympathy, but Ben found himself resenting it, and growing angrier every time. So they waited a couple of days in Chester, and then went up to Ellesmere Port and on to Manchester, and Faith, freed of the work with the baby, helped him with Silver and Billy, and admired the little piebald horse, and complimented him on the bargain he had struck.

Faith only said it once, but Ben knew she believed she had gone against the will of God in taking Peggy. She was not meant to have a child. She had accepted surrender, but now surrender meant defeat, and Faith had been defeated by God. She accepted it, but she didn't go to the mission any more. Her prayers at night had become a routine, and were therefore perfunctory. Her eyes were closed, her hands held at her breast, her lips moved, but there was no thought any more, no feeling, nothing of the desire and despair that had given them such urgency only a little while before. There was no longer any fear of offending God with ingratitude, but there was nothing now for which Faith wanted to pray.

Faith knew what lay behind the sympathetic, pitying eyes, because she had seen it so often before, all through her childhood. She had seen it in the eyes of women who looked at her own mother, and said what a good child she was, and she had known even then what lay behind it. Your child's a hunchback, Mrs Carter, but I'm a good,

100

kind woman, and I'll find something good and kind to say to you, poor Mrs Carter with your deformed child.

Ben encouraged Faith to help him with the animals, which none of the other boaters did. The cabin was the woman's place, almost her realm, and the animals and the rest of the boat were for the man. The women could handle the horses, often led them or held them at the locks, but it was not their job to do so, and they would have felt uncomfortable taking any part in their management.

'Something wrong with Billy's feet, I think,' Ben said.

Faith went with him into the stable, lifted Billy's feet one by one, frowned down at them and felt them, probing and rubbing. Then she shook her head.

'Nothing wrong.'

She never questioned him when he asked for her help. She simply went with him, and looked, ran her hands over whatever he had said worried him, then shook her head and told him there was nothing wrong.

He would have done anything to shake her out of her placid resignation. He would have preferred the sharpness of her voice when they had first married, the way she snapped about him sending money to the boatyard, her accusations that he had lied to her. He would have preferred the amulets in the cabin, the flower petals, the way she wouldn't meet his eyes when she asked him if they could try something Janet Crowe had suggested because Janet said she only ever fell for a baby when they did it this way.

'Shall we get a dog?' he asked one day, when they'd unloaded grain in Wolverhampton, and a rat had run out almost at her feet, but there was no enthusiasm in her reply. If Ben thought they needed a dog, then yes.

'Do you want one?' he insisted, but he knew it was no use. Slowly, but with great determination, Faith was killing what there had been in her of motherhood, and with it she was destroying herself.

She was not doing it consciously. She did not see what Ben saw, a woman wanting to die, but she wanted to shield herself from the pain of what seemed to her like a loss. There was no baby, and no hope of a baby. It hurt too much to be borne. Somehow she would build a wall of indifference between herself and the world. If that meant there would never be any joy, at least it also meant there would be no more anguish.

Ben remembered the morning when he had woken and thought she was dead. He wondered if it would be worse to live with a dead woman or without her. Living without her would somehow be tidier, although the shell that had been Faith still functioned. Faith could still clean and polish the cabin, still steer the boat, very well now, neatly moving it into the locks up against the wall, with room enough for another should there be one waiting with them. She was quick and neat, stronger than he would have thought possible, with such a thin little body. She wheeled the barrows of coal, she clamped the dogs on to the sacks of corn, she handled heavy baulks of timber. The food she cooked was good, and she counted the money carefully and kept it in the brass tin behind her rags in the soap hole. She was the perfect boatman's wife.

When they saw a child in a cradle, Faith would look down at it and smile, and say it was a pretty baby, and Ben, listening to her, thought the words sounded like stones, thudding into her flesh.

'What sort of a god do you worship?' he asked one night, as she climbed into bed after saying her prayers. She told him it was God and Jesus, the ones they'd learned about in school. She didn't seem surprised by his question, and if she noticed the tone in which he'd asked it, which was intended to goad some sort of anger out of her, she did not respond to it. She had to worship her God, but He had defeated her, and she did not feel called upon to defend Him.

They went back to the boatyard for Christmas. Kathy hugged Faith and looked sharply into her face, then turned to Ben and kissed his cheek, the once-a-year kiss he had come to expect. Josiah shook him by the hand and clapped him on the shoulder.

That night when Faith was asleep Ben told Kathy about Peggy, how Faith hadn't really loved her, but now she seemed to want to be dead. Having had a baby to look after, even one she didn't love, she was lost without it. She had nothing to do, and she'd given up the idea of having one of her own.

Kathy sat in silence, listening to him, then said she would try to think of something, but it must

103

be hard to want a child and not have one.

She and Josiah had not heard from Paddy since the Christmas when he'd come, and left with all their money. She didn't mention him to Josiah, she didn't talk about him to anybody. At first, when people had asked, 'How's Paddy?' they'd said, 'Down in London, seems to be doing well.' Now people had stopped asking. Her only son had gone out of her life, and the last memory she had of him was the Judas kiss he had given her as he left, with all their money in the smart suitcase he'd brought with him.

'Did you ever tell Faith?' she asked Ben, and he shook his head. Faith had assumed at first that he sent money because he was paying for the boat. After the first bitterness, she'd never asked again, but as he thought about it a question arose in Ben's mind.

'Is *Grey Lady* mine?'

Kathy laughed. 'Of course she is, Ben. She was yours before you took her. That was your wages for building her, and two or three others. Of course she's yours.'

Ben nodded. Of course she was his. He knew every plank, every stud, almost every knot of wood. He'd built her. If there was anything that needed repairing, he could do it quickly. He'd helped the other boaters too, when he could, when he'd had time. His skills had made him a few friends, and probably saved them plenty of money.

'You're a proper Number One,' said Kathy, and he smiled at her.

It mattered to him, the extra respect accorded

to the man who owned his boat, and there were few on the canals with a boat as good as *Grey Lady*.

He changed the subject and told her about Billy, their good little piebald cob, or mostly cob, and how he'd come to buy him. Kathy tut-tutted about Blackie, 'What a shame, that nice old donkey,' and exclaimed over the woman who'd sold them Billy. The death of a market man was too common for more than a passing expression of regret, but Kathy was concerned for the plight of a young widow with two small children.

Ben fell silent, and Josiah came in from the yard, clapping hands stiff from the cold and standing in front of the fire, smiling at them. He wanted to tell Ben about the yard, how business was picking up, with Number Ones bringing boats for repairs. Soon he might be able to hire Jed again, and they might even think about building a boat, if there was a safe customer.

Kathy looked between the two of them, but when Josiah turned away she shook her head at Ben. He understood her: of the two of them, Kathy had always been the realist. Passing trade in repairs was a help, but Josiah was old now, and if boats were ever to be built at Armstrong's again, it wouldn't be under his direction.

Ben didn't show his disappointment, but he felt it. By now, if he had not been supporting Josiah and Kathy, he would have saved quite a lot of money, but as it was there was just enough put by for docking, should *Grey Lady* need repairs, and a little to tide them over the freeze. Being a Number One meant he earned more than the hired men, but it also meant he earned nothing when *Grey Lady* was empty, when they were waiting to be unloaded, or when there was nothing to be carried.

He had hoped the yard would be able to start work again some time, because he would have liked to save his money, but each time he and Faith visited the yard that hope dwindled. Kathy and Josiah would never be able to manage without him.

Ben, too, was a realist, but even he sometimes thought of how things might have been. If Faith had had a son within a year of their marriage, as he had somehow assumed she would, and if he had not had to support the old people, they could have had two boats by now. Quite small children could lead the horses, and they might have hired a man to steer another boat.

But, then, if Faith had had a son within a year of their marriage, she might have had a daughter every year since, and the cabin would have been crowded out, and there would have been no money at all after they'd fed the family.

Faith's God didn't offer choices, and Ben felt another surge of resentment, and with it the beginnings of loneliness. Soon his only friends would be the old mule and the strong young horse. And Silver would have to go soon. He and Faith didn't need him, now they had Billy. If Ben was honest with himself, it was nothing more than sentiment that kept Silver in harness.

He didn't want to lose Silver. Still less did he want to lose Faith, but she was steadily drawing away from him, into herself, or something like oblivion, and he could neither bring her back nor follow her.

Kathy was a wise woman, and she lay awake that night thinking about Faith, and wondering where the problem lay. She fell asleep just before dawn, having told herself she would find the answer before morning. When she had difficulties, she would turn all her ideas over in her mind until she could no longer stay awake. Then she would tell herself to find the answer, and give herself a time limit.

'Faith cannot see a use for herself in this life,' she told Ben in the morning. 'She believes women are for bearing children, and nothing else, so if she can't have children she's of no use.'

Ben pondered on her words, and saw little sense in them. 'She's of use to me,' he objected.

'Any fool can steer a boat,' Kathy retorted, and Ben said a lot of them did, which made Kathy laugh. But then she laid a hand on his arm and looked earnestly into his face.

'All women need to be needed,' she said. 'She needs to feel needed for something only she can give, like a mother to a child. Something special to Faith.'

He found himself talking about it to Billy, muttering to him, 'Something special to Faith, what is there that's special to Faith, then, Billy?' And the horse turned one ear towards him, listening to his voice.

'Talking to yourself, then, Ben?' a boater demanded, grinning at him as they passed, and Ben grinned back, said he was talking to his horse, never had a stupid answer from him yet.

'What's special to Faith?' and Billy blew softly into his brightly painted nose bowl, reminding Ben that it was empty and he was hungry.

Kathy had been wrong in her belief about Faith. Faith knew that she was of use to Ben, and she had never believed that a woman was only for bearing children. What Faith did not have, and had never had, was love. A baby would have loved her, and she would have loved her baby. She had never allowed herself to dream of love, until Ben had asked her to marry him, and she had seized it, and dreamed it, waited, and longed for it, and then it had been taken away. There was, after all, to be no love.

She had never looked to Ben for love, although he had sometimes said the words. He had wanted a worker, and had promised to be good to her. They had made their bargain. Faith had not expected love from Ben.

Silver went to the knacker's yard. For a few days Faith wiped her eyes with her apron, and Ben strode in grim silence alongside his good young horse, telling himself that after all it was only an old mule, couldn't pull worth a note. Damned stupid, getting upset over a mule. But he'd been a good old mule, and Faith took the hairs from his tail and plaited herself a little bracelet. Then she found Blackie's hairs and made herself another, slipping them both on to her wrist and stroking them. She, a woman, had no need to pretend she wasn't sad about the animals. Women were allowed to be soft like that.

'Needs to be needed,' he muttered to Billy. 'That's what Kathy said.'

'Do a bit of painting on the boat?' he asked Faith, and she said she didn't know how. He thought she did. She'd seen it done, watched the craftsmen with their brushes, the deft strokes that made a rose petal with one quick turn of the brush, the traditional designs of the yellow castles over the blue water. No one really knew for sure where the designs had come from. Some said from gypsies, but when Ben had looked at a Romany covered wagon he'd seen only bright gold swirls and curlicues.

'Try anyway?' he insisted. 'This boat needs painting.'

So she agreed, and he bought paints and brushes, and in the summer evenings they worked. After a little while Faith seemed to be taking an interest, and when there was a bout of wet weather, which kept them off their project, she painted the water jug, carefully setting the lines with damp string so her designs would be straight all around the difficult slanted surface. She liked blue, and she painted blue daisies in defiance of reality and custom. She painted the handle of the mop blue and grey and white because she wanted *Grey Lady* to be what she claimed, grey, and never mind that the mop handle looked drab: it fitted with the boat's colour scheme. She painted castles on the inside panels of the stern doors, a task that took weeks because she was like Ben in her search for perfection and would wipe away days of work if it didn't come up to her standards.

But at last the boat was painted, bright and clean and gay with brilliant colours, and there was nothing more to be done. Ben could not keep Faith interested in checking every night for scratches and touching in their work. Once more she became the meticulous boatwoman, cleaning and polishing, cooking and washing, steering *Grey Lady* and leading the horse over the hills when Ben had to pole the boat through a tunnel or steer her behind the tug, saying her prayers at night to her God, and steadily killing her spirit.

'Don't you think the canals are beautiful?' a boatwoman called to them one afternoon, when the beech trees were blazing gold on the embankment and the sky was so blue and clear it almost hurt to look at it. Ben nodded at her: they were beautiful, these waterways, and sometimes, when he went up the locks, or through a tunnel, he marvelled at the work, all done by hand by hundreds of men cutting through the land to make the arteries for the lifeblood of trade in the industrial revolution.

He tried to picture those men with their picks and shovels, working so hard and in all weathers, earning good money, and he wondered whether they had looked ahead in their minds as they dug and shovelled, carried and built, to days like this when the water was clear and still under the blazing trees, and the brightly painted boats moved along the canals, carrying coal, iron, brass, grain, everything that needed to be moved from one part of the country to another.

He wished he knew more about them. He'd heard that many had come from Ireland, because there was near starvation there and money here. 'Black Irish', they'd called them, because so many had been dark men with black hair, and there was a flight of locks near Stourbridge called the Delft, or the Black Delft, and it had come from the words Black Delve. The locks had been delved by the Black Irish.

That's what he'd heard. Maybe it was true.

There was this about water, even if it was in channels dug by men: it was always a natural thing so it always brought its own beauty.

He tried to express some of this to Faith, and she listened dutifully. That was the word he'd been looking for, and it came to him that night. She'd become dutiful. The work she did was her duty so she did it as best she could, but there was no joy in it, no sense of achievement, no pride, although she did it so well.

'Don't you wonder about those men?' he insisted, and she smiled, shook her head and went on with her cooking.

'Well, I do.' He was stubborn now. He would get her to talk to him. He would make her take an interest. 'I wonder about them, I do. I want to know about them. They don't deserve to be forgotten.'

'It's just history,' she answered.

'Well, what have we got if we haven't got history?' He wasn't even sure what he meant by that, which made him even more stubborn. 'History's us, isn't it? What happened before. It's like where we've come from. Coventry this time, that's history, a little bit. Or your great-great-something-grandfather, what did he do, then?'

111

She shrugged, and he pressed on.

'Was he a farm worker? Was he?'

'I expect so.'

'So there's generations behind you, working the land. Dozens, maybe. It's your roots, that. You're part of the land, you are, like the trees back there. Those beech trees. You're like them.'

'That's daft.'

It was, he thought. It was daft. He hadn't been able to tell her what he'd meant, and maybe it was nothing but rubbish, but there was something true in what he'd felt about history back there among the beech trees. It was a new thing for him, this curiosity, and the sudden feeling of respect for the men who'd dug the canals, the feeling that they deserved better than oblivion.

'I want to know,' he muttered. 'I want to know about them.'

It didn't stir any response in Faith. She handed him his plate, and he took it, and began to eat.

There had to be something that would bring her back to life.

Two days later there was a message. Kathy had had a fall, and wasn't feeling well. Nothing to worry about, but if they could manage a load down that way they should call in when they had time.

Perhaps the lock-keeper who gave them the message had been a little too reassuring, because it was nearly five weeks before they moored *Grey Lady* at the towpath and Ben walked through the kitchen door to see a man he didn't recognise sitting in Josiah's chair.

112

The man stood up and looked at Ben sharply. 'Who are you?' he demanded.

'Ben Jacardi. Where's Kathy?'

'Oh, yes. The boy who worked in the boatyard. Do you usually walk into a house without knocking?'

'Where's Kathy?'

'That'll be Mrs Armstrong to you.'

Faith was at his shoulder, staring at the stranger, and Ben, feeling the beginnings of anger along with recognition, thought briefly of introducing them. Faith, this is Patrick, Josiah and Kathy's son.

'Where's Mrs Armstrong, then?'

A woman came down the stairs and stood with her hand on the newel post staring at them with one eyebrow raised. She was tall and slim, dressed in a tweed suit. Her hair was cropped close to her head. She looked very smart, and very out of place, a town woman wearing what she thought was appropriate for the country.

'Who's this?' she asked.

'One of the workmen. Ah. Jacardi. Asking about my mother.'

Faith touched Ben's elbow, but Ben was watching Paddy. 'Still waiting for an answer,' he said.

The woman turned her head towards him, eyes widening, an expression designed to show her amazement at his impertinence.

'Don't take that tone with me.' Paddy stared hard at Ben, who knew he was supposed to drop his eyes and mumble an apology. Did this man think Ben knew nothing of what had happened?

113

Ben stared back, straight into Paddy's face. Nothing to say to you, thief. Where is your mother? It's her I want to see, not you.

Nothing to say, but there couldn't be silence in a room where Ben Jacardi stood, and the woman had never before heard the slow roaring of his breathing.

'If you are *ill*,' she said in tones of incredulity, 'would you *please* leave this house?'

Ben felt Faith draw in her breath, and knew she wanted to explain. Ben's not ill, madam. He always breathes like that.

'Don't speak,' he said, too quietly for the man to hear, and he knew Faith would be silent, but he felt her distress. He knew, too, the answer to his question, and so did she, but she knew nothing of these people, except that they were rude and scornful but also what she thought of as gentry, so entitled to their rudeness and their scorn.

'Mrs Armstrong?' said Ben again.

The man looked them up and down once more, and spoke in a tone of indifference.

'I'm afraid you're too late. Mrs Armstrong died on Monday. The funeral took place yesterday.'

Again, Faith drew in her breath, but a small movement of Ben's head kept her silent.

'Mr Armstrong?' he asked, but the man had turned away and was picking up a sheaf of papers from the table.

'You have no need to concern yourself with my father,' he said. 'Adequate arrangements have been made. You may leave now.'

Ben stood motionless, watching him, but. Faith

114

plucked at his sleeve and breathed, 'Please, Ben. Please.'

He took her arm as they went through the door. He was trying to think. Kathy was dead, and Josiah had had arrangements made for him. By the thief. By the man who'd ruined him and caused Kathy so much anguish.

'Just a moment, Jacardi.'

That bloody arrogant voice stopping him on the path because he couldn't help it. A voice like that would always stop a man like Ben, because it was a voice of command, it had to be obeyed. Never mind the anger, never mind that it came from the mouth of a thief, it was a voice that must be obeyed.

'That boat, I believe it comes from this yard?'

'It's my boat.'

Don't come any closer, Patrick Armstrong. Stand there on the path a good few paces from me and say your piece in your bloody arrogant voice, in a voice I have to obey. But you've been in the army, Patrick Armstrong, *Paddy* Armstrong, you know the meaning of the word mutiny, don't you?

'In that case you'll have a receipt.'

No. No, Paddy Armstrong, there's no receipt, because there was no sale. Your father gave me that boat in place of the wages he couldn't pay me because you'd stolen his money. All the money he'd earned over the years, and because you stole his money I've been supporting him and your mother for more than ten years, with *my* boat, and *my* work, and the blisters on my hands and the soaking cold rain in the winter and my back aching from working frozen lock gates.

Now come and take that boat away from me.

There was no conscious change from thought to action, only the sound as he moved forward of Faith screaming, only the feel of Patrick's fist in his face because the thief could fight, and his bloody arrogant voice didn't mean he wasn't a hard man.

He hadn't been taken by surprise, either. By the time Ben reached him Paddy had been ready, and as soon as Ben had been within reach a fist had smashed into his mouth, rocking him on to his heels, and Paddy was backing away, quick, watchful and wary.

Blood was running down Ben's chin, the taste of it in his mouth, and for a moment he felt as if he was swimming, as if he was looking at Paddy through water, but there was no pain. There was anger of a sort he'd never known before, and the sound of Faith screaming was another goad, a woman screaming behind him and an enemy in front of him, like an old memory of fires in the night and the wild noises of an attack.

I want him dead, he thought. I want him dead.

The other woman had come out of the door and she, too, was screaming, but there were words: 'Stop it, for God's sake, stop.' Another voice of command, another voice he should obey, but the command in his own mind was stronger.

There was terror in Faith's screams. She'd seen fights before, drunken brawlers, boys mostly, swinging fists or even weapons at each other, but nothing like this, two grown men in combat, and she'd never seen Ben like this, when rage had driven out even the memory of reason, turning

116

this into a fight in which either man might die.

The other man had something in his fist, and he was quick and strong. He had a weapon and Ben had nothing but his anger, but that might be weapon enough.

He knew something was thudding into his body and his face, knew it was hurting him, and he could see the man's smile through the mist of blood: the man was smiling because he was enjoying the fight, taking pleasure in it. He was winning, and he liked that. He was breathing fast, and smiling, and that fist kept jabbing out, something glinting under the blood, something in his hand, get it. Get it.

Something in his hand, and he was a hard man, Paddy Armstrong, but now Ben's hand was there too, gripping that fist, and Paddy Armstrong's quick fist was no match for an arm hardened by ten years of working the heavy locks, and the smile had turned to a grimace, because something hard in a fist was a good thing in a fight, until another hand caught it and crushed it against the fingers, crushed metal against bone. Smile now, Paddy Armstrong, smile at me now. I can see you through the blood. Smile now.

The smile had gone, and the face had gone, because Paddy had turned his back, quick and lithe, and Ben's arm was twisting and there was an elbow coming back at him, fast towards his groin as Paddy dropped low, almost to his knees. The thief knew too many tricks.

But Ben had released the fist and stepped back so the elbow only grazed his thigh. You missed, thief. And Paddy was off balance for a moment, just long enough for a kick in his ribs. Smile again, Paddy Armstrong, smile after that if you can.

He was rolling away, it had hurt him, but it hadn't stopped him, and this was a boatyard with plenty of weapons to hand if you could reach them. Now he had something long and heavy, a piece of elm, in his hands, and he knew enough not to aim it at Ben's head. Instead he swung it low, swung it fast, and Ben felt something give in his knee, a feeling he remembered as pain. There was no pain now but he couldn't use the knee, and he was down on the ground with Paddy standing over him, still with the heavy length of elm in his hand, and Paddy thought he'd won and this time the weapon came for Ben's head.

He managed a kick at Paddy's ankle before he threw up his arms to defend himself, and it was enough to cost the man his balance and take the weight out of a killing blow. But what landed was bad, across his forearm, with the same sound there'd been in the knee, and now he couldn't stand, and one arm was useless, and Paddy was hardly hurt at all and he still had the elm.

All Ben had was the sound of Faith's screams and his own rage. It would have to be enough. There was blood in his eyes and memory from years ago of fire, and a woman screaming, and an enemy who would have to die if anything was ever to matter again. In the flickering light of his anger he saw the wood swing towards him again, and this time he rolled towards it, and kept moving, feeling it smash down across his shoulders, but it didn't matter. What mattered now was that Paddy

118

was within reach of his right arm, the arm he could still use, and his right leg which could still kick.

He heard Paddy grunt as the foot thudded into his shin, and Ben's teeth bared in triumph. It hurt him, I hurt him, he knew about that one, I hurt him.

Now Paddy was coming back with the elm, but he was holding it differently: he was using it like a spear, not a club any more, jabbing it at Ben's face, at his throat, at his chest, and Ben was kicking out at him to try to keep him at a distance. The rage was as strong as ever but he was trying to think too, beginning to use his mind just as Paddy was growing careless, believing he'd won, trying only for the finishing blow that would cripple the man who had dared to attack him.

So Ben fended off the elm, and twisted away, then dropped his hands and allowed his face to show fear, and made as if to speak, knowing what the response would be, and then as Paddy, that hateful smile of triumph back on his face, lunged forward with both hands driving the weapon towards Ben's head, Ben raised his strong right leg, caught the wood, dragged it towards his own face, and Paddy, off balance again, fell forward on to Ben's foot and was lifted off the ground as Ben gripped his throat, and heaved him clear over his head to smash face first into the hard cobbled ground.

Then he was with him again, alongside him, on top of him, punching at his face and Paddy was grunting and gasping. Now there was real fear in his eyes, fear, anger and disbelief, and the fear

119

was growing stronger and stronger, and the screams were louder and Ben's fingers were digging into the soft flesh of the man's throat, but only one hand would grip. Ben heard himself curse in fury and frustration, because he wanted to kill, and one hand wasn't enough to kill the thief.

Something was behind him, dragging at his shoulders and his arms, screaming his name.

'Ben, no! Ben, no! No, don't, Ben, don't kill him! Ben, don't kill him!'

One hand wasn't enough, not for that, so he punched down into the hateful face again and again, hearing screaming in his ears, feeling hands on his arms trying to stop him. He twisted his fingers into Paddy's hair, and slammed his head down on the ground, but the screams were louder, and his hand was pulled away.

He couldn't kill him because his damned hand wouldn't grip, and because something on his back was holding his arm.

'Don't, Ben! Please, Ben, don't kill him.'

The other woman was screaming at him too, and Paddy was staring up through bruised eyes, blood on his mouth, not believing what he was seeing. Then the bruised eyes were closing and the hands had slipped from Ben's arms, and Ben knew it was over, that the screaming weight on his back was his wife, and that he couldn't kill Paddy, not because his hand was injured but because he wasn't a killer, and it was too late.

The murderous rage had gone, and there was nothing to do but roll away from the other man and leave the women to drag Paddy out of reach in case Ben attacked him again. But Ben knew he would never touch Paddy now, never look him in the face, never speak to him, not only for hatred but for shame: he'd wanted to kill him, and hadn't been able to do it.

Faith was sobbing, and that other woman was saying Ben would be in prison for this, or transported and flogged, she would see to it.

Ben raised his head and called to her, 'I'll tell the judge about Josiah's strongbox. You ask your man first. You see what he says about that.'

And Faith, hearing reason in Ben's voice, came back to him, speaking over her shoulder to the woman.

'Take your dirty man and get him out of here. I saw what he had in his hand, the filthy thing. Take him away.'

And to Ben, 'Don't you worry. She's never fought a working woman, no, and she won't want to start now. You'll be all right, my Ben.'

Ben whispered to her as she stooped over him, and Faith turned back and shouted.

'Where's Josiah Armstrong, then? Where is he?'

The woman looked up, at first defiant, but then uncertain as Faith moved towards her.

'He's with some people called Cartwright in the village.'

'Jed,' said Ben, and moved his hand to touch his swelling lips. 'That's good. Leave her now, Faith.'

She was beside him again, helping him, kneeling and pulling his arm around her shoulders, climbing slowly to her feet, taking him with her, gentle as she could be with her arm around his waist, but every touch hurt now, and he knew his teeth were bared at the pain.

She was whispering to him, but he couldn't make out the words. It didn't matter. There was encouragement and concern in her voice, and that was enough for him.

Every part of his body hurt. Every punch had left a bruise, and every bruise was a centre of pain, throbbing and aching, but Faith was beside him and he could lean on her as they made their way back to *Grey Lady*. He wondered at Faith: thin and small and as good as finished, he'd thought, but here she was, stronger than she looked, supporting him, almost all his weight on those narrow shoulders where she'd pulled his good arm across them. She'd shouted down that woman, Paddy's fancy London wife. If she'd had to she would have fought, and that would have taken more courage than he had shown, because she didn't know what had happened. She only knew that Paddy had tried to lay claim to *Grey Lady.*

'Ben. Oh, my Ben. Come on, my Ben.'

At the steps she tightened her grip around his waist and almost lifted his feet off the deck so he wouldn't have to put any weight on his injured leg as she helped him down into the cabin. She pulled down the bed, the heavy slab of solid oak that folded so neatly into the cabin wall by day, laid out the blankets, and helped him on to it. He was filthy with blood and with dirt from the yard, and he tried to protest, *her good clean blankets*, but she hushed him, smiling, then brushed tears from her eyes.

Ben lay back on the bed and let her take off his clothes and wash him, her hands gentle. The water was warm and soothing even though she hurt him. Knowing she was caring for him soothed him, and he listened to her voice, not to the words but to the soft sound of a woman speaking to a man who'd been hurt, a man who needed her care.

When he fell asleep she must have gone out, because he woke to see another woman in the cabin, and Josiah standing behind them both, his old cap in his hands as if he was in church. He looked anxious, and much older, and his hands were trembling. He was wearing black. That was his good Sunday suit he was wearing, and somebody had dyed it black for him.

Ben tried to speak to them, but the pain in his mouth was suddenly fierce, and he felt a scab break, and blood, and the other woman said he shouldn't talk.

'She's a nurse,' whispered Faith, bending over him and dabbing at the blood with a clean cloth.

Ben closed his eyes and waited for the questions about his breathing, but there were none. Faith must have told her. A woman would listen to another woman, might not believe her, but she would listen. Not like that doctor in Birmingham, or even the one near Stoke Bruerne who'd looked at him and thought he was little Peggy's father, and that Peggy had inherited his lungs.

He listened to his own breathing now, and it hurt. Every breath hurt, so he was trying not to breathe too deep. That made it quieter, his

123

breathing. A couple of ribs must have gone, then. Funny that, he thought. Get hurt, and the breathing goes quieter. Get better, sounds like I'm dying.

His arm was broken, the nurse said, and Faith nodded. She'd known that. She'd seen the blow for one thing, and that was why she'd taken his good right arm when she'd helped him into the boat. The nurse wanted to straighten his arm and splint it, bandage it up nice and strong so it would set straight, and it was going to hurt, no help for it.

Josiah was telling him there'd been whisky in the house, and he would have given Ben whisky for the pain, but it was all gone.

Paddy, thought Ben, and maybe he'd said the name, because there was blood on his lips again, and Faith said it wasn't only the whisky that had gone. That fine pair had gone too, and God alone knew what they'd taken with them.

Ben wanted to say, 'Don't talk like that in front of the nurse. This is a family matter, not for outsiders.'

Old Josiah looked so confused now, and his eyes were watering. How was he going to manage without his Kathy?

Ben did manage not to cry out when the nurse set his arm, but there was sweat on his face and tears in his eyes, and he thought, What about my knee? Hurts like hell, that knee. Doesn't feel like it's lying straight, either. Damn Paddy Armstrong, for drinking all the whisky.

He must have passed out when they set his knee, because his next memory was of Faith straightening the blankets over him, and there was a hard, set look to her mouth that meant she was trying not to cry. He touched her arm, but couldn't smile at her. He wanted to say, 'It's all right. It's not too bad.' Would have been a lie, because nothing had ever hurt like that before, but he should tell her it wasn't too bad.

Josiah was mumbling something, sitting on the little painted stool by the stove in the corner of the cabin, and the nurse was putting on her coat.

At least she's finished, he thought.

When the nurse had gone Josiah and Faith sat together, and she held the old man's hand. Ben lay watching them. They didn't speak much.

He watched them, and he listened when they spoke, but he was thinking of Kathy, and remembering that he'd named the boat *Grey Lady* because of Kathy's grey dress, and not after Faith. Kathy's grey dress was one of his earliest memories of his life with her and Josiah, standing at the stove in the kitchen, the woollen fabric, the softness he could imagine he would feel if he were to touch it. Soft and warm, he thought, and now, whenever he thought of warmth, whenever he was cold, and in winter he was often cold, it was the memory of Kathy's dark grey dress as she stood in the kitchen that came into his mind, a picture as clear as if he had only seen it yesterday.

As he lay watching his wife and the man who was as close as anybody could be to a father, Ben did not wish that they had come earlier and seen Kathy before she died. He'd seen people who were dying. He didn't want to have seen Kathy like that. The last time they'd spoken she'd told

125

him Faith needed to be special. She'd said Faith had to be needed for something only Faith could give.

Now Faith was sitting on the step, and Josiah was on the little stool, and she was holding his hand. Had Josiah's hair been so white when they were last here? And if his hands had trembled before, Ben hadn't noticed. Kathy had always been the stronger of the two, but Ben had thought that Kathy was realistic, while Josiah was hopeful. Josiah had always thought something better lay ahead, and that had given him whatever strength he had. Without Kathy, would he be able to look into the future with hope? And without hope, would he survive?

Ben drifted in and out of sleep, thinking of Faith, of Kathy and Josiah, of Jed Cartwright and his wife. How had Paddy arranged that?

At the thought of Paddy bile rose into his mouth, and he gagged. Immediately, Faith was on her feet, and as he shook his head to let her know he didn't need her, he remembered once again that Kathy had said Faith must feel she was needed.

He fell asleep again, and when he woke it was morning. The night had passed, and Faith was sitting on the step, watching him. Josiah had gone.

He tried to ask, 'Where's Josiah?' There was pain in his mouth, and Faith stood up and came to him. She was tired, he could tell, but she hadn't slept: she'd watched over him all night.

'Josiah?'

Had she understood that mumbled name?

126

Josiah had gone back to Jed and Violet Cartwright, because he hadn't wanted to be on his own in the house here. Paddy had said they were going to sell it, and the yard. There'd be enough money to look after Josiah in his old age.

Thief. Thief. Should have killed you.

'Don't you worry. He's all right now.'

By that evening Josiah was back in the cottage; Jed and Violet Cartwright and their three children were with him. Faith sat beside Ben and told him what she'd arranged. They would all live there together because the house in the village was too small, and another baby was on the way. The rent was more than Jed could manage now that he had only the job at the corn merchant, which didn't pay as well as building boats. They'd all live at the cottage, and they'd look after Josiah and take care of the place, and the yard, and if Paddy came back Jed would warn him off, and let Ben know.

Ben lay quiet, marvelling at the way she had handled it, so calmly, and getting it so right. Josiah had always liked and trusted Jed. He took Faith's hand and squeezed it gently. If he spoke, the scabs on his mouth would break open again, so he could only tell her by touch: 'You've done well. You've done the right thing. Thank you, my Faith.'

'What was that about a strongbox?' she asked him later in the evening, and he thought, I should tell her now. All these years I've kept their secret, but Faith had proved her place with them, and she should know.

When he opened his mouth to speak she laid

127

her fingers across his lips, hushing him, but her face was grave.

'Will you tell me tomorrow?' she asked, and he nodded.

She brought another woman the next day, a tall old woman in a dark dress, who said little but who listened to Faith. When she touched him Ben felt her fingers dry and cold, barely brushing his skin, but those fingers hovered over the places on his chest that hurt the most, as though they were asking their own questions.

Faith told her about his breathing, about his father having taken a Zulu spear in the chest, and somehow surviving for nearly a year, and Ben having had bronchitis nearly every winter as a child, how he'd breathed like that when he was ill, and now he breathed the same way all the time. How Ben's mother had said he sounded like his father when he had the bronchitis.

The tall woman listened, interested, curious.

She took a little pot of oil out of a bag, and gave it to Faith, who put it on Ben's lips and on the other cuts on his face. It smelt like new-mown hay.

'Who was that?' Ben asked, after the woman had gone. Faith told him she was someone she knew. She was good with injured animals.

Ben wanted to laugh, and Faith understood, and smiled down at him.

The scabs on his lips hadn't broken when he'd asked.

She gave him something to drink, something with a bitter, pungent taste under the sweetness of honey, which made him drowsy. As he fell asleep he remembered he had to tell her about Josiah's strongbox.

When he woke later that night, he told her the story of that Christmas visit ten years ago, and she said nothing, didn't seem surprised, only nodded, and went on polishing her bright brass ornaments.

'Well?' he asked in the end, unable to understand her quiet acceptance.

'It had to be something like that,' she answered. 'You're no fighting man.' Some men would have resented those words, but from Faith they were not belittling. If anything, there was respect in her voice. 'You're better than that,' was what she'd said.

But I beat him, Ben thought, and the pride was fierce and satisfying.

The nurse came, looked at his hand and his knee, asked him if he could feel it when she pricked him with a needle, looked at the scabs and the bruises and made him turn over, because his back was hurt, a heavy weal across the shoulders where Paddy had got in his last full blow with the elm, and when she'd finished Ben was exhausted. He supposed she had to see if everything was healing as it should, but what she did hurt him, and tired him, and, in a way, angered him too. She didn't ask, she just did what she thought she should, treated his body like a piece of meat on a butcher's slab.

The tall old woman didn't ask either, but she listened to Faith, her head lowered so they were almost at the same level. When she looked at him or touched him or asked him questions, he didn't feel even the edge of the resentment that arose

129

when the nurse was there. The old woman had authority about her, and she didn't pretend she knew everything. That was why she listened, and why she thought about the answers to her questions, because she knew there was always something to learn, and because learning was her business, more than anything else.

'Where was the wound in your father's chest?' she asked him one day, when he was well enough to sit up. He couldn't be sure he remembered exactly what his mother had told him. High up, he thought, and near the middle.

'When your mother told you about it, what was she wearing?'

'Her red dress.'

Bright red it had been, but faded from washing and drying in the sun. She used to wear a white leather belt with it, a belt with a metal buckle that had been painted white, but the paint had flaked off, and the metal showed through. The dress had once been the colour of blood, his mother had said. And she'd told him the Zulu had been crouching on the ground and had come up behind his spear, and the point had hit the bone in the middle of his father's chest, and cracked it, then turned off to the side, to the right side, not the side where the heart was or Jacardi would have died there on the stony ground of South Africa. It had gone into the lung high up, almost into the throat, and ripped it. Should have killed him.

Did, in the end.

He'd been telling the old woman things he'd never wanted to remember, certainly never

130

wanted to repeat, but she had a right to know, because she wanted to learn. Something else to think about, that was, while he was waiting for sleep. That, along with the men who'd dug the canals.

Her hand was on his chest, high up on the right-hand side, away from the heart, with the fingers pointing to his throat, and she was frowning down at those fingers, as though it was there that the answer lay, if she could only understand it.

'What's in that drink?' he asked her when at last she took her hand away.

'Poison,' she answered, and they both laughed.

'Ah, but it is poison,' said Faith, after the woman had gone. 'Too much of that, do you no good, my Ben.'

It took the edge off the pain, and it sent him to sleep.

Ben began to worry about getting back to work. How long would it be before he could walk on the injured leg? It hadn't been broken, had it? Why couldn't he walk on it now?

The nurse said he had to be patient. 'It'll take as long as it takes,' she told him. The old woman explained that the ligaments that held the knee straight had been stretched and torn, which was sometimes worse than a broken bone. She traced the lines of the ligaments on his own knee, from here down to here, and across here. When she'd finished, he understood why he should keep it still and straight, then use it only a little at a time, not go stamping around. If he wanted to he could be back at work quite soon now, but then the

131

knee might never be completely right.

It was Faith who said that he could steer the boat and she'd lead the horse. Ben hadn't thought of that. He looked up at her, little and thin but with a spark in her face at last, and thought of her with his big iron windlass on those heavy double locks on the Grand Union, and some of the stiff deep ones on the Trent and Mersey.

'You'll never do it,' he said, but there was a bit of a laugh and a challenge in his voice.

She might, then. Ask him a month ago, and he wouldn't have believed she could have carried him down into the boat.

Josiah came in every day, sat on the painted stool by the steps, and asked him how he was doing, 'Mending all right, boy?' If Faith left them alone for a while, to go into the village or spend some time in the cottage with Violet, Josiah would cry for Kathy. He wore his black suit every day, but it was his old cap he'd crumple in his hands, not the smart black hat someone had bought for him, which didn't fit and didn't suit.

'Mrs Webster came every day,' said Josiah, and Ben thought, That's her name, then, that tall old woman.

'Never missed a day, never a day since Kathy fell.'

She'd known from the start what the doctor and the nurse had only later come to realise. Josiah talked about Kathy, how her back had hurt, and then it had gone to her stomach, so she'd been bent over with the pain, and had to take to her bed. Mrs Webster had come in, not done much, not what you'd call doctoring, just come in and sat with her. Kathy knew it was bad. She knew she was dying. So did Josiah, in the end. Not that Mrs Webster had said anything. But she'd come in every day, and been with them. When Kathy had died and the doctor had been and gone it had been Mrs Webster who'd seen to her, made her right and decent. Put a posy of rosemary in her hands, for remembrance, and because it smelt like a clean summer day.

Paddy had been there by then, with his Hermione, and they hadn't liked Mrs Webster much, but she'd hardly spoken to them, only enough to be polite. Hermione had said it was impertinent of a stranger to interfere, but Mrs Webster hadn't interfered. She'd only come to visit each day, and then gone, and when Kathy had died, Josiah had asked her to see to Kathy, to make everything right. And she'd done that, and gone home, and he hadn't seen her again until Faith fetched her for Ben. She hadn't interfered at all.

'I can't quite take to Hermione,' said Josiah quietly, and Ben thought, Me neither. No, nor her rotten thief of a man.

'I always think of Kathy in the summer, in her garden,' said Josiah, and Ben nodded, and thought, I always think of her in winter, in her kitchen. The warmth of the grey woollen dress, the woman who'd been kind when he first knew her, and kind at the last. But he could picture Josiah's memory too, Kathy in her blue summer frock tending her vegetables, and now and then taking a moment or two to look around at the

133

grass and the trees, all green, and growing under the summer sky.

'Everything all right with Jed and Violet?' asked Ben, and Josiah said it was grand having children in the place again. He liked children. Liked the noise and the mess and never knowing what or who was going to come crashing round the corner pretending to be a horse or a dragon or Lord alone knew what next.

Ben was fond of Josiah, but it was Jed's visits he enjoyed most, because Jed was friendly, and cheerful, and not too bothered by the fact that Ben had been hurt. He'd been in a few fights himself, and was not impressed by cuts and bruises, although he did admit the knee was bad. For reasons that were inclined to be ribald.

'Faith make a good jockey?' he asked, and Ben, remembering some of the positions she'd asked him to adopt in the past, laughed in a way that Jed did not quite understand or quite like.

Faith had sent word to Birmingham that Ben had fallen off a lock, an accident that could easily be believed when there was frost around and the gates were slippery with ice. Word had come back wishing him well, asking when he'd be back at work, and this time Mrs Webster considered his question carefully, and she listened to Faith.

'Can you do it?' she asked directly, when Faith said she'd work the locks and lead the horse, once Ben was well enough to steer the boat.

'Two weeks, then. Keep it bandaged. Take your weight off it, and keep it still and cold. Make sure it's always held straight.'

The next day she brought with her the slippery

134

white inner bark of a willow tree, and showed Faith how to bind it round Ben's knee to keep it cool. She told her not to take too much from one tree, and only to take it from one side of a healthy branch, or she'd hurt the tree.

Ben laughed when she said that, and she looked at him sharply. Straight away there came into his mind the memory of the glorious beech trees on the early autumn morning, and he thought, She's right, it's bad to hurt trees. Then he thought, How did she do that?

From then on he was never quite at ease with Mrs Webster, although he would always be grateful for what she had done for him, and for Kathy and Josiah.

So he got off the bed every day, and tried to walk around without bending the knee, holding it straight and stiff, thinking it would be easy, and finding it was almost impossible, as well as exhausting. He couldn't keep his balance properly, and fell against the cabin wall, hurt his broken arm and swore at himself.

The nurse took the splints and the bandage off his arm, then made him turn it, and clench his fist, which he could only do hissing with pain. He was to exercise it now, she said, a little at a time, a few times a day. He overdid it on the second day, and it became swollen and inflamed. Faith laid wet cloths over it, and told him he had no sense at all, he was more trouble than the children.

They were all over the boat now, clambering around on the roof of the cabin, saying it was a pirate ship, and trying to slide down the cloths until Faith grew angry because they might damage them, and new cloths cost a lot of money.

'Those cloths are for keeping the rain off the cargo,' she yelled at them. 'You rip holes in those and I'll take a stick to your backsides.'

They ignored her, so Jed took the threatened stick to their backsides, and after that there was no more trouble with the cloths, although the top of *Grey Lady*'s cabin was still the bridge of a pirate ship.

When the weather was fine, and Jed wasn't working at the corn merchant's, he'd started to clear up the yard. There was iron that had rusted beyond use, elm that hadn't been stacked properly and had rotted to wet dust. There was copper and brass to be put aside for cleaning later. There were tools, some still good, some rusted paper-thin.

Ben watched him for a while, then made his way to one of the workbenches, found a wire brush and began to scrub rust off iron tools. That was better exercise for his arm than what the nurse had told him to do, and more useful too.

'Nearly enough stuff here to build another boat,' said Jed later that afternoon, half joking.

Ben looked around, and wondered. 'You could make a start, if you've got time.'

Not all the wood had been badly stored, as his own body could testify. That length of elm had been as hard as iron.

It would cost money, and there was no reason why Jed should work for nothing. Rent free in exchange for feeding Josiah and looking after him was one thing; slave labour was different.

They agreed that Jed would make a start on a boat, work on it whenever he had time, and when Ben could afford it he'd send some money. When the boat was finished they'd sell it: Jed would have half the profits, Ben and Josiah a quarter each. Or maybe, if it had all gone well, they'd think about building another boat. Maybe.

When they put the idea to him, old Josiah broke down and cried. The next morning he went out into the yard, took down the red and gold sign and painted out the words 'and Son' in scarlet, as close to the original colour as he could find.

Josiah Armstrong, Boatbuilder.

Maybe.

5

Exactly two weeks after Mrs Webster had pronounced on Ben's injuries they set off with *Grey Lady*, Faith leading the little piebald horse, and Ben balancing as best he could at the tiller. For the first five miles he watched anxiously, wondering if Faith would be able to manage, but after that he kept his anxieties for himself. He'd never realised how heavy the boat was, how much effort it took, in a wind, to keep her off the banks. He couldn't brace himself properly, with his injured leg; all the strength had to come from his arms.

There were only a few places where Faith could leave Billy to pull the boat and come back to take the tiller from Ben. Billy was a good young horse, but he was new to the canals, and needed leading in places where a more experienced horse could have picked his way alone.

By the time they stopped to rest the horse, Ben was almost exhausted.

They didn't make very good time that day. In the middle of the afternoon, when there should still have been three hours' work left before dark, Faith came back to the boat and said she could go no further. She was too tired.

She was lying, and Ben knew it, but he was in no fit state to argue. He stumbled down into the cabin and sat on the steps by the stove, leaving her to lead Billy on to the next public stables for the night. By the time she came back, Ben was asleep.

He jerked into wakefulness as her weight on the boat rocked it and thought that if he'd taken Billy to the stables, Faith would have had the cabin clean and a meal cooking on the little black range when he got back.

Fifteen miles and ten locks, and he'd wondered if she'd be able to manage.

She said nothing when she came into the cabin, only took off her shawl, shook it out and hung it on the peg. In answer to his question she told him Billy was tired: it would take him a few days to get back into work ways after his holiday. But he'd eaten his feed and she'd left him comfortable.

Faith wanted to look at his knee and his arm before she did anything else, but Ben was ashamed of having fallen asleep, and grumpy with her attentions. She waited for a few moments to see if he would be reasonable, then gave up, and began to prepare the meal.

Ben went back to the steps, sat down and watched her.

Watching Faith became his main preoccupation over the following days. Watching her leading the horse, one hand on the bridle, the other holding her long skirt out of the mud. Watching her working the locks, leaning on the windlass because the paddle gear was stiff and heavy, so she had to brace herself to pull the windlass up, and then lean again, until the shutters lifted and the cogs turned quickly as the pressure eased. He listened to the water rushing as the lock chamber filled, or emptied, and he watched her standing, waiting, for the few moments when she could rest. Then pushing on the heavy balance beams, and at that point Ben would feel himself pushing with her, knowing how heavy they were, those gates, knowing every lock, and that one's a bitch, take care, Faith. Take care, that's slippery, where the bricks have worn smooth. Then almost a sense of relief as the gates moved, slowly at first, and swung open.

Well done, Faith.

If the path up to the lock was straight and easy Faith could leave Billy and go on ahead. By the time the boat reached her, she'd have the lock ready and the gate open, and she'd be standing waiting for them, ready to draw a paddle so the rush of water would check *Grey Lady,* stop her slamming into the gates or on to the sill. Ben should have been able to close the gates behind him, levering them away from the chamber walls with the pole, then hearing them slam as the rushing water caught them, but he wasn't quick enough now. He was out of practice, and he couldn't move fast enough with his injured knee. Faith would have to come back, and close the gates. It made them slow.

Sometimes Ben would imagine Billy looking down at him, as if the little horse was wondering why Faith was doing all the work.

And she couldn't always leave the horse. If boats were moored, or the path was tricky, she'd have to lead him all the way, then work the lock. That meant hauling *Grey Lady* into the chamber. Faith had her own way of hauling the boat. Not for her the rope around her arm and shoulder; she simply wasn't strong enough for that. Faith would pull backwards, the rope behind her waist then pulled forward over her shoulder, and she'd lean back against it. It was a good way to move the boat.

Billy trusted her. It was bad practice to walk towards the face of a loose towing horse because he might turn and go back down the path, which was dangerous. The wise boater stood at the lock and called the horse to him, 'Come on, then. Come on, my beauty.' And the horse, hearing praise and reassurance, would walk on, bringing the boat with him. A trusted horse could be left to pull the boat alone, and the man could go on ahead to set the lock.

'Come on, then, my beauty. Come on, Billy.'

At first the short black ears had flicked with uncertainty, and the horse had stopped, and looked. It was the wrong voice.

'Come on, then, Billy. Come on.'

Go on, Ben had thought. Walk on, Billy. It's all right.

And, as if he'd heard Ben's thoughts, Billy had dropped his head and walked on until he reached Faith at the lock. Then he'd stopped, as he'd learned to do for Ben.

'Come on, then, Billy.'

Not that Billy wasn't used to Faith or happy with her. When they came to tunnels it was Faith who led him over the hill while Ben waited with the other boats for the tunnel tug to tow them through, or, on the shorter tunnels, poled her, or legged her if he could find somebody to help

141

him, lying on the broad wooden board and walking the tunnel walls, sideways, an awkward, cramping movement that nevertheless took the boat through the dark man-made caverns at a good speed. Faith would take Billy's bridle and they'd set off, briskly, up the hill and down the other side, and as often as not she'd be waiting for Ben by the time he got through, walking the horse up and down the path to keep him warm and supple.

Poling the boat alone was as hard as work could get, because there was no room to walk on the gunwales, with the tunnel so low. It had to be done crouched on the stern deck, pushing with arms and shoulders, braced against the door. It was slow and laborious, not a task he enjoyed.

So, when they came to the first tunnel where *Grey Lady* had to be poled, Ben said he'd do it. When Faith tried to argue he shouted at her, because he was sick of being helpless and only half useful, sick of standing on the damned deck and steering the boat while his woman strained on those heavy locks. This might not be a long tunnel, but he wasn't having her leaning on that pole and trying to force a heavy boat through the water and mud. Anyway, he doubted that she could do it. She was a brave woman, but she was nothing more than a little slip of a thing, and this was work for a man.

Silently, she boarded the boat and pulled the pole free from the ropes that held it against the side cloths. She handed it to him, then she jumped back on to the path, stood at the horse's head, and watched.

'You go on,' he ordered, but she shook her head.

He couldn't do it. He couldn't brace himself to get the leverage on the pole, not with only one leg. He couldn't balance like that. He'd fall, maybe fall into the water, lose the pole.

Faith said nothing, but she left Billy standing on the path, took the stern rope and pulled the boat in.

'You'll have to ride him over the hill,' she said.

Billy had never been ridden. Boat horses weren't ridden, except sometimes by small children. They had enough to do, pulling a heavy boat, without carrying anything on their shoulders. But Ben couldn't walk that far, not up the hill and down the other side, not if he didn't want to damage his injured knee.

They couldn't stay where they were. It was nearly dark, and Billy needed a dry stable for the night. They should have stopped at the last town, but it was too late to regret that now. No one else would be coming through the tunnel until morning, so there was no hope of help, and no one to lead Billy over the hill for them.

And Ben couldn't ride, had never had any reason to learn.

Faith made a stirrup out of her hands and told him to put his foot in it and get up on the horse that way, please, Ben, don't argue, it's cold and I'm tired, I want to get through that tunnel. Please.

So he did it, and when Billy threw up his head and began to sidle around, upset by the strangeness of a weight on his back, she took the horse's

143

bridle and spoke to him, reassuring, but there was also the note of command in her voice. Behave yourself, Billy, and all will be well. Trust me. Get awkward, and I'll belt you, I mean it.

'Just hold on,' she said to Ben. 'He knows the way.'

But Ben kept the horse standing on the path as Faith untied the mooring line, jumped back on to the boat and took up the pole. He was so angry at his helplessness he could have cried. He watched her drop the end of the heavy wood into the water and brace her shoulder, push her feet against the back of the cabin, and slowly, so slowly, *Grey Lady* moved, inching out into the channel as Faith pushed as hard as she could. She looked up and smiled at Ben.

'I can do it,' she called, but he couldn't answer her. He watched his boat and his wife until they had disappeared into the forbidding black hole that was the mouth of the damned tunnel, and then he pulled at one of Billy's reins and told him to walk on. Billy turned to the path, tossed his head and flattened his ears, his back hunching. Ben grabbed a handful of his mane and tried to keep his balance.

'Walk on, Billy,' he said. 'Walk on, my beauty.'

If he fell and landed on his bad knee, he wouldn't be able to climb on to the horse's back again. He might not even be able to walk. Faith would get the boat through the tunnel, and he wouldn't be there. She'd wait for a while in the cold rain, but then she would have to climb the hill to look for him and Billy. By then it would be dark.

'Walk on, Billy. Go on, my beauty.'

144

He nearly slipped off as Billy took to the path, scrambling on to the flints, trying to get away from the weight that had never been on his back before, only half reassured by the familiar voice.

'Go on, Billy. Steady, my beauty. Steady, Billy.'

Ben dropped the reins and clung to the collar, sliding sideways as Billy shied at a bush and pulling himself back, so the collar twisted under his hands and the little horse snorted and tossed his head, his ears flattening. Ben, upright again, straightened the collar and spoke to the horse as soothingly as he could. Billy broke into a trot, and once more Ben was nearly thrown.

'Whoa, Billy. Walk, you little bastard.'

How was Faith managing? It was black as pitch in that tunnel. He should have lit a lamp for her. A woman on her own, she might be frightened. There were rats in there. Suppose one got on to the boat in the dark and frightened her? She didn't like rats. He should have lit a lamp. Damn, he should have done that for her. A lamp on the cabin would have been a comfort for her.

'Whoa, there, Billy. Walk on, my beauty.'

Her arms would be aching by now. It was hard work. And there was that bit half-way through where the roof got lower. He should have warned her. She didn't know about that. She wouldn't be able to see it in the dark, and she'd be facing the other way, it could catch her on the back of the head. Could knock her cold, knock her into the water. She might drown.

Should have warned her about that place, should have lit a lamp. He'd been so stupid, never thought. So bloody stupid, and angry because he

145

couldn't pole the old bitch of a boat, never even stopped to think about a lamp, and the rats, and that bad place in the tunnel, she might be about there now.

'Oh, keep your head low, my Faith. I'm sorry I didn't tell you. Didn't light a lamp for you. Just keep your head down, my darling. Keep your head down and you'll be all right. And the rats won't hurt you. Don't you worry about the rats, they won't touch you.'

Her shoulder would be getting sore, where the pole digs in, her poor little twisted shoulder. Sometimes he'd had to stop and rub that place on his shoulder, and he was twice the size of that little woman. Such narrow shoulders, she had, and that hard pole. He could have made a pad out of something, tied it to the pole to make it easier. He hadn't thought.

'Walk on, Billy. Good lad. Come on, my beauty.'

He wanted to hurry now. He wanted to be on the path by the canal, waiting for her. He could call out to her, call out that he was there, was she all right? She might hear him and answer.

'Come on, Billy. Come on, boy.'

They were almost at the top of the hill. Ben's legs were aching with the effort of gripping the horse's shoulders, and there were cuts on his fingers from the coarse hairs of the mane. But that didn't matter. He had to get down the other side, be there and call out, and if there was no answer he'd tie up the horse and he'd swim through the damned tunnel until he reached her.

'Come on, Billy.'

146

Going down the other side of the hill was even worse. Billy's head was low, and Ben slid forward, almost went over the horse's ears, and was only saved when Billy threw up his head in alarm, hitting Ben's nose and making it bleed.

'Come on, Billy.'

There was a muddy patch and Billy slipped, one forefoot sliding forwards, and then Ben did fall off, over the horse's shoulder. He managed to catch the reins and Billy pulled away from him, frightened and upset.

'All right, boy. All right, my beauty.'

Ben scrambled to his feet. He couldn't get on to the horse's back again, but he could hold on to the collar, and that way they'd get down the path and back to the canal.

'Walk on, Billy. Walk on.'

It was nearly dark. It was cold and wet. The horse needed his stable, needed a good rub-down and a feed, and he'd be damned, if he'd leave that to Faith tonight. If he could ride the animal over the hill he could set him to rights for the night. And he'd buy something at the pub for them to eat. He'd not let her cook tonight, not if she'd poled that great heavy boat through the tunnel.

A full-sized boat, *Grey Lady*, because that was what earned the money, but there were times it took a strong man to handle her. He'd never thought, when he built her, that one day there'd be a little slip of a woman struggling with her through a dark tunnel.

He was slipping on the mud, and his knee was hurting. It had started with an ache, and now it was burning, like there was hot iron in it. Maybe it would never be right again, and he'd have to live with a crooked knee. So be it. There were worse things than a crooked knee. Getting knocked out in a tunnel and going face down into the black water was worse than a crooked knee.

'Go on, Billy. Go on.'

But they were on the towpath. They'd slid down the last few yards on to the towpath, and the black water was at his feet, and the black mouth of the tunnel was only yards away. He stopped and shouted as loudly as he could, 'Faith? Faith, are you there? Are you all right, Faith?'

And he heard her voice calling back to him: 'All right, Ben. All right.'

He'd never known relief like that. He'd never known it could hit you like that, like a blow, so sudden, so hard. There were tears in his eyes and running down his cheeks with the rain, and he sat down where he was, on the muddy path, and that was how Faith saw him when at last the boat came out of that black tunnel, sitting on the towpath and crying, with the tired little horse standing at his shoulder, and the rain soaking the pair of them.

6

Ben took Billy to the stable that night, and he bought them something to eat at the pub, because Faith admitted, with a very weary smile, that it would be good not to have to cook that night. But when he came back to the boat the cabin was shining clean, the white lace had been washed and pinned back into place, and the brass glowed from its polishing.

He watched her eating the beef and oyster pie he'd brought home, and he wished he could tell her how much he loved her, but knew he'd feel foolish. He didn't have much of a way with words.

All he had, then, was his body, so he used that, and with every move and every touch and every kiss he thought, I love you. I love you. And he watched her tired smile turn to a look of wonder, then joy, and for the first time he, too, felt joy, because of his love for her, and because of the happiness he saw in her eyes.

I love you. I love you.

She was brave and very dear to him. There was nothing more precious in his life than his little sharp-faced wife, who looked as if a touch of wind could blow her off her feet, and who had poled a heavy boat through a black tunnel because her man couldn't do it.

I love you.

He wanted to protect her from everything that might hurt her. Protect her from the wind, the sun and the rain, from the storms and the cold in winter, from the harsh midday heat of summer, he wanted to keep her safe and by his side, because he loved her.

Could she love him? If he tried very hard, with everything of himself, could he make her love him?

'I love you,' he whispered, and when he looked again she was crying. He laid his face against hers and kissed her cheek, tasting the salt of her tears, feeling her mouth move in a smile.

I love you.

'When you were in that tunnel,' he said later, 'if you didn't answer me, I was going to swim back for you.'

'Not ride the horse through the water?' she asked, and put her fingers on his lips to feel him grin in the darkness.

'Damn that for an idea,' he said. 'I'm no horseman. Billy could tell you that.'

She was lying close against him, skin against skin, warm and gentle. She moved her arm so it lay across his chest, and he stroked it.

'Did you hit your head on that low place?'

She hadn't. She was smaller than him, so she'd only got a few cobwebs in her hair. And she hadn't seen any rats, but the lamp would have been nice.

'Light it for me next time,' she said, and he didn't reply, but put his arms around her and pulled her close to him, then stroked her hair where the cobwebs would have brushed it, and

150

thought he'd die before he let her do that again. He'd plan better in future, so they didn't get to a tunnel at a time when there'd be no one to help.

When they met them, the other boaters did help. When they reached the locks, Faith didn't have to open the gates if there was another boat: the men did it for her. Someone would have helped them at the tunnel.

'I love you,' he said, and it wasn't so difficult to say the words after the first few times. 'I love you.'

'I love you, too.'

Did she mean it? How could he know?

It hadn't been much of a life for her, with him. It had been hard work, and there'd been bitterness when she'd thought he was paying Josiah and Kathy for the boat, when she accused him of lying to her. He hadn't really cared then what she'd thought. It was his money, and he'd do whatever he wanted with it. It wasn't her place to argue.

Was she asleep? She hadn't said anything for a few minutes now, his little wife, all quiet and warm and close up against him, naked; they'd never slept like that before. It hadn't seemed right, not quite decent, not like married people. He had his nightshirt and she wore that thick cotton nightdress, and now here they both were without a stitch between them, and she'd gone to sleep with her head on his arm and neither of them had thought about putting on their nightclothes.

He thought his nightshirt would make good polishing rags, just the sort of stuff she liked for

151

her brass, and the idea made him want to laugh. He was trying to keep still, but he must have moved a bit, because she lifted her head.

'What are you laughing about?' she asked, so he told her, and she said he was daft, and then she started to laugh, too. They might tear up her nightdress and plait it into ropes, save buying new ones. It was good strong stuff, wasn't it? Shame to waste it.

Then they were both laughing at the silly jokes, and the more they laughed the more helpless they grew with laughter, until he thought he would fall off the bed and pull her down on top of him. Then she was hugging him again, and she was saying, even while she was laughing, that she loved him.

'Oh, Ben, Ben, I do love you. I do.'

It was true, then. She did love him, because she was saying it laughing. That made it truer and stronger and much more real than if it had been solemn. It was better than those words she'd repeated in church at their wedding. It was better than anything, laughing in the dark, and saying she loved him.

He woke before her in the morning, seeing the first gleam of light at the porthole, feeling the strangeness of the cotton sheet against his skin, and Faith's hair soft on his arm.

'What's this, then?' he whispered to her. 'You're a wicked, sinful woman, you are. Lying here in bed with a man, without your clothes on.'

'I'd better get up and put some on, then, hadn't I? And I'll go to the mission and say I'm sorry.'

She was always awake in flash, was Faith. One

moment fast asleep, the next wide awake and all her senses working.

He pulled her close, held her tight against him so she couldn't get out of the bed.

'And are you sorry?' he demanded, and felt her little hand creeping across his chest, the fingers tickling the hairs.

'I won't go to the mission and say I'm sorry,' she announced, in the voice of a little girl, 'because it would be a sin to tell a black, bitter lie.'

They lay together for a little while, warm and close, then he patted her shoulder and said she was a hussy, and should get up and get dressed.

'And dress warm,' he added. 'It'll be a cold day.'

He must buy her some warm boots as soon as he could. Those towpaths could be cruel in the ice, and it would be winter soon. Faith must have warm boots, and even when he was well enough to lead the horse himself, she'd be glad of them when she was off the boat.

All that day as they worked the boat he watched her, and sometimes she would look back, and he'd raise his hand, and she'd wave, and he'd be glad, but then anxious, in case she should lose her footing while she wasn't watching the path.

Like daft children, he told himself. They'd been married for years, and now they were like a pair of silly teenagers.

If he could ride the horse over the hill he could open those gates, and when they came to the next flight of locks he called her back down the towpath and made her take his place at the tiller. When he braced himself against the balance

153

beam the pain in his knee didn't matter, because Faith wasn't having to do the heavy work any more. She could lead Billy on the towpath, but he'd work the locks, even if changing places made them slower. It was only a few minutes.

Word had gone round that Ben had injured himself falling off a lock gate. Boaters called out to ask how he was, and when they met on the locks the men helped him, too, just as they'd helped Faith. It made him feel a little foolish at first, but he was grateful for their friendship, knowing that one day he would be doing the same for an injured man, who might in his turn be feeling a little foolish.

'Didn't happen at midnight by a full moon, did it?' he heard Rose Ryder call out to Faith, and Faith laughed. For a while he was puzzled by the question, but then he remembered that had been one of the tricks she'd been told to try when she wanted a child. He looked into her face as he and Sam Ryder pulled *Grey Lady* into the lock, looking for a sign that the joke might have hurt her, but she smiled at him.

There were only two more locks in the flight, and the Ryders had helped enough, so he told Sam he could manage, and thanked him. Almost as soon as the man's back was turned he stepped down on to the deck and gave Faith a kiss, only to hear Rose laughing at them from the other boat.

'Leaving Billy standing,' said Faith, pink in the face with embarrassment. 'What are you thinking about?' She was annoyed with him for showing her up in front of the Ryders. She did laugh

154

eventually, but Ben thought it was probably only to stop him pestering her with his half-humorous apologies so that they could move on to the next lock, which Sam had left open for them.

'Be here all day,' she scolded, but the Ryders were out of sight, so he kissed her again, and although she pushed him off it was not before she'd given him a quick hug.

That night she fussed over his arm and his knee, worrying that he might have strained them, and he let her look and probe, touch and question, and he smiled over her frown of concentration, and moved his leg as she asked, and bent his arm so she could see it in the light of the oil lamp.

'Do you know what you're looking for?' he asked at last, and she said she thought his knee was swollen, and she must put some willow bark on it.

'Leave it,' he said. 'If you think I'll let you go out in the dark looking for a damned old willow tree you're very much mistaken. And it's raining.'

But the next day when they passed a willow tree she stopped, took out her knife, and peeled some bark from one side of a healthy branch, as Mrs Webster had told her. When they stopped at the locks she refused to take the tiller until he'd let her bind his knee with the cold white strips.

He watched her tying them into place, and thought it strange that he'd never liked anyone fussing over him, touching him, yet now he could watch her deft fingers and feel her gentle hands, and take such pleasure in it. This was a delay, the boat tied up by the lock, the horse standing idle with a thick sack across his back, and canal work was judged on the speed at which a boat could reach its destination. Even though he and Faith had the excuse of his injuries, standing idle here should have worried him, but it only made him smile.

'All right now?' he asked, as she tied the strip of clean cotton into place, and she agreed that it was. But he was to be careful not to twist the knee, he should use his other leg as much as he could, rest this one, try to keep it straight, and so on, until he laid his fingers across her lips, and made her laugh.

The trip took them two days longer than usual, but the manager didn't complain. He'd expected it, allowed for it, and as he said, wrought iron wouldn't rot. Ben stood with the money in his hand and tried to calculate. Warm boots for Faith, yes. And Jed had said he'd need nails and rivets, as soon as Ben could send some money, but what about Josiah? Jed and Violet would feed him, and he had no doubt they'd take good care of the old man. At least a little money should be put by.

Faith knew what was worrying him, and she said, quietly, that a man must have some money in his pocket.

He should have told her before. He should have trusted her with Josiah and Kathy's shameful secret. It would have been easy for her to accept that he had to send money back if she'd known it was all they had to rely on, that and the little bits Josiah could earn from the passing repair trade.

There'd be none of that now. The more he

thought about Josiah the more Ben wondered at the change in him. He'd always been vigorous and energetic, except when he'd been ill, or after Paddy had stolen his money. Now he was just another old man, with shaking hands and a bewildered look in his eyes. Josiah Armstrong would never work again.

But before anything else, Ben took Faith into the town to the cobbler in the main square and bought her a pair of warm sheepskin boots. She laced them up, and stood in front of him, and he knew she was wriggling her toes in the thick fleece and loving the feel of it. When she looked up at him he was smiling at her.

'Want them?' he asked, and she nodded, her eyes shining with pleasure at his gift. As he handed over the money he knew he'd never bought anything that had made him happier than those warm new boots for his wife.

She told him time and again how glad she was to have them, and he believed her because the winter began with wicked weather, driving sleet and wet snow that froze in the nights so the towpath was rutted with ice, and the snow lay wet on top of it. Ben did most of the walking himself, a little more every day, but it was hard, keeping his feet on that surface, harder still opening the lock gates with green ice on the standings. Even when he slipped and fell and Faith cried out in alarm for fear that he'd damaged his knee, he was fiercely glad he could do that work again, and not leave it to her or to the other boaters. He'd hated being less than strong and able.

Freezing sleet, slush or ice under his feet, often in pain from his knee, almost always weary from the hard work, soaking and cold, Ben had never in his life been so happy. Faith had her warm boots and a good shawl, and there was enough coal to keep the range well stoked, so the warmth drifted up on to the deck and kept her from the worst of the cold. Billy was young, strong and willing, and happy enough with sacks over his back to keep off the worst of the winter weather, and there was the friendship of the other boaters, which seemed stronger now. Perhaps they had caught some of Ben and Faith's happiness, and reflected it back to them. The Jacardis were nearly always greeted with smiles and a few neighbourly words. Some evenings they'd spend on other boats, with other families, all crammed into the tiny cabins, sitting wherever there seemed to be no more than a square inch of space, but all drawn together by the adversity of the hard winter.

It was the wind that was the worst, sometimes strong enough to blow a man off his feet, and then, if he went into the water, he'd need to be quick to get out, and strip off his sodden, freezing clothes. Nearly everyone had chilblains, and there were even cases of frostbite.

Word came down the Grand Union that Ida Trafford had died of pneumonia, and been buried in Nantwich. Jacob was still working the boat, with the two boys helping him. The youngest child, the girl, had gone to live with her grandmother.

Christmas came, and the ice closed in. Ben and

Faith forced their way through to Birmingham, and from there they went by public coach down to the boatyard, leaving Billy at the stables at Gas Street. The roads were hardly better than the towpath, tracked in rutted and frozen mud. They had to walk the last few miles, and Faith was so worried about Ben's knee that she was almost oblivious of her own weariness.

Jed and Violet made them welcome, gave them warm drinks and sat them close to the kitchen fire. The children were asleep upstairs, but Josiah was wandering around, pleased to see them but a little vague. He seemed to be looking for something.

'He's all right,' said Violet, when the old man wandered out of the kitchen. 'It's just his age.'

But Josiah couldn't be that old, could he?

The boat Jed was building in the yard was coming on, but the bad weather had been a problem. You couldn't work with soaking wood, not if you wanted to make a good job of it. But Jed was clearly proud of what he'd achieved, so Ben went out with him, with a storm lantern, to look at what he'd done, and when they came back there was snow in their dark hair.

'White Christmas,' said Violet. 'Snowball fights tomorrow.'

She was very pregnant, the baby due in only a month, and although she seemed happy and comfortable, Ben told Faith that Jed was worried. The doctor had left, and the nearest was ten miles away now. There was only that nurse, and Jed didn't think a lot of her.

'There's Mrs Webster,' said Faith.

159

They stayed at the cottage for nearly a week, because there was no chance of moving *Grey Lady* off her moorings in Birmingham until the ice melted. Sometimes Josiah seemed to forget who Faith was. Ben would see him looking at her, puzzled. He couldn't remember the children's names either.

'It's just his age.'

Violet was kind to him. Josiah's talk had become a little rambling, but she'd listen to him as she did her work, and she'd answer his repetitive questions patiently.

Jed told Ben that Josiah had taken to hiding the money Ben sent, stuffing it into the toes of his slippers or into the tea caddy. Jed never knew when he was going to find a sixpence somewhere.

'Proper old squirrel.'

Ben decided to send Jed the money for Josiah: Jed would keep enough to buy Josiah's tobacco and Josiah could have the rest to hide and lose and do with as he wished. No matter what he did with it, Faith had been right: a man had to have some money in his pocket.

The bitter frosts gave way to rain, and Faith and Ben went back to Birmingham, to work.

Faith was glad to be home. *Grey Lady* was cold and dusty, with a chill that had soaked into the cabin walls. Ben lit the range, and soon water was running down to the floor, steam rising. Faith busied herself with mopping and cleaning the cabin while Ben went to the office, and to fetch Billy.

There was plenty of work. It had piled up during the freeze, and the manager asked if they could help with another boat. He'd only the one man to work it, and he was desperate to get the pottery from Stoke to London. Three people working two boats was possible, if not easy, so Ben agreed.

Anthony Kender was a man Faith couldn't like. He had a way of eyeing her, and smiling to himself, as if he knew something discreditable about her and was laughing at it. The boat he worked was a dirty old thing, the name *Valiant* almost illegible through the mud. But Kender was a hard worker, even Faith had to concede that, and he handled the two horses so well that Ben said he might have been born in a stable. So Faith held her peace, and tried to ignore the man, who never spoke to her disrespectfully, or tried to become familiar with her.

On the third night Kender brought a woman back to *Valiant,* and all night there was singing and laughing, songs that Faith had never heard and Ben didn't want her to hear. In the morning he confronted Kender. 'Next time you bring a slut back to your boat, you moor well away from mine.'

After that, they only spoke when they had to, and when they returned to Birmingham Ben asked the manager to pair them with a different boater, if he had to send two boats together.

It happened quite often, but never again with Anthony Kender. None of the married men wanted him near their families.

'Something about him I could never like,' said Sam Ryder one evening in the cabin of *Benevolence* when the two families met in London. 'I

161

wouldn't have him near Rose or the girls.'

But the Ryders' twin girls are only ten, aren't they? Ben thought. Then he saw Rose looking at him, her usually lively face still and grave, and felt sick.

They took the two boats together back to Birmingham, and it was one of the happiest journeys Ben and Faith had ever made. The Ryders were good friends, and cheerful company in the evenings, and two boats working together could make their way up the canals faster than one alone. Rose was a quick, clever boatwoman, skilled in all the crafts she needed, but she told Faith she could write little more than her own name, and only read a few words; she'd wanted better than that for the girls.

'But what can you do?' She seemed resigned to her daughters' lack of education.

Faith thought about this for a long time. She and Ben were unusual on the boats for having had an education, and Faith had found that most boat people did not want their children to go to school. They thought it would make them discontented, and when they voiced that objection, Faith thought she could hear other echoes. The children might come to despise their parents and the way of life on the boats.

Better to keep them uneducated than to lose them. Better that they couldn't read than that they couldn't handle the boats. The boat families needed willing workers with strong arms, not scholars.

And yet there were some, like Rose, who wanted more for their children, who seemed prepared to risk losing them, if it meant a better life for them.

A few nights later Faith asked Ben if she thought the Ryders would take it amiss if she taught the girls a bit of reading and writing. She could buy slates, and when the families met, they could do a bit. What did he think?

He thought he wanted to sleep, and get on in the morning, not stop to go shopping for school slates, but Faith sounded serious.

'We've been lucky,' she said. 'We went to school. We were never boat children.'

Lucky hadn't been how they'd been described at first by some of the boat families. Although it wasn't too difficult to learn how to handle a narrowboat on the still waters of the canals, a few treated new boaters as if they were interlopers with no chance of mastering the skills, a hindrance and a nuisance to the real boat people. But Rose and Sam hadn't been like them. Rose had shown Faith how to crochet the ear stalls for the mule, and had been friendly and encouraging. Never mind that Rose had also been the one to tell Faith to hold her legs up in the air all night after being with her man if she wanted to fall pregnant, Rose had meant no harm by her joke, and for all Faith knew, perhaps she hadn't been joking.

'Ask her, then,' said Ben at last. 'You ask Rose tomorrow.'

Rose's happy response to Faith's offer led Faith to suspect that Rose had hoped for help but hadn't liked to ask. Rose wouldn't hear of Faith buying the slates and pencils: the girls would have their own so that they could put in a bit of practice between the times *Grey Lady* and *Benevolence* moored close to each other.

Sally and Jane Ryder were good children, quiet and obedient, and they worked hard, although not with great enthusiasm. By the time the Ryders and the Jacardis parted company, they could write their names and had learned most of the alphabet.

'I'm no teacher,' Faith told Ben. 'They should have done more.'

Rose and Sam were pleased with their girls' progress, and thanked Faith for her help. They must have spoken of it to others, because only two nights later Susie Bedwell was knocking on the cabin door with her son Moses at her back and a new slate in her hand.

'I wondered...' she asked shyly. 'Mrs Ryder said ... because Moses ... well...'

From then on nearly every night saw at least one child in *Grey Lady*'s cabin, and occasionally as many as five. Sometimes Ben wanted to protest: after a hard day, the last thing he wanted was his boat full of other people's children and his wife doing teacher's work, but although Faith seemed a little bewildered by their sudden popularity it made her happy. When the children went home, instead of being tired she was at times almost wild with enthusiasm. Had he seen how well Tom Waterford had written out his lines? And Daisy Farraday, wasn't she a bright little thing?

Ben folded her into his arms and agreed, and kissed her grey hair. If teaching the children made her happy, he could hold his peace. If it all

164

became too noisy he could go to the pub, and if the fathers of the children were there, he was always sure of a pint. And of a loving welcome when he returned to his boat to find it deserted apart from Faith, and clean and tidy, and Faith happy with the progress of at least one of the children.

She had never dared to dream of becoming a teacher. She remembered her days at school, sitting on the bench at the long desk, looking up at Mrs Mannering, and later at Mrs Hart, and thinking of what it must be like. The children in the cabin were like a gift. There, now, Faith, that's for you. Teach them.

When she next made herself a skirt she chose a black fabric, and it was long, almost to the ground. She had remembered Mrs Hart's white blouse with the lace at the collar and a cameo brooch, but she did not try to make a blouse like that, or dare to wish for a brooch. Somehow, it would have seemed presumptuous.

There was some trouble: one of the women told Faith she was trying to turn the children against the canals, and others agreed with her. Faith was setting herself up as better than anyone else, and Faith was a nobody, just a farm labourer's daughter. There was nearly a fight over it, but the woman's husband backed away from Ben and said it was up to the women to sort it out, but he'd be damned if his children would waste their time on Faith's stupid schooling.

Faith was upset and angry, but she wouldn't turn the children away when they came to the boat.

'I'm no teacher,' she'd insist again and again, and Ben would ask her, 'What's a teacher, then? Moses Bedwell can write his name. Who taught him?'

'I love you,' she said, snuggling her cheek up against his chest. 'I do love you, Ben.'

Every night they'd curl up tight against each other, close and warm, and even if there was no more than that loving embrace, and a goodnight kiss, Ben could spend hours of the day dreaming of the night to come, when he and Faith would be alone, and close, when his harsh, rattling breathing would stir her soft hair, and she would be so quiet and still as she slept, with her arm across his chest and her little fingers half curled, just touching his shoulder. Every time he moved in the night she'd stir a little to adapt to his new position, and it would still be much the same, still close, and quiet, with the love she held for him there even in sleep.

Faith could hardly believe in her own happiness.

Out of that dreadful night when Ben had fought Paddy, and she had thought Paddy would kill him, had come love, from Ben to her, and with it the realisation she had never dared acknowledge until then, that she loved him and had done so for years. She might even have been a little in love with him when he asked her to marry him. She still thought of that evening sometimes, and remembered standing there in the woods by the edge of the field, his arms around her, his chin resting on the top of her head, when she had wondered if it would be all right for her to hold him, too. And then she had dared to try, and he had talked about horses, so she knew he didn't mind. His shirt had been clean, a little rough, and it had smelt faintly of lavender, not enough for him to notice but Faith had known that somebody had spread it over a lavender bush to finish drying in the sun.

They had married, and he had taken her to his bed, and what had followed had been what she had expected, in the darkness with no words spoken, a man and a woman coupling, as the beasts did. She had tried to think of something else, as her mother had suggested, and she had thought of the woods by the fields and the scent of lavender.

She had worked for Ben, and she had overcome her fear of the great industrial cities, although she still disliked them. She could not feel it was right, that red glow on the clouds, the noise, the grit and the dirt, and when Ben said to her, 'Only another ten miles,' she would smile, but every step grew heavier with her reluctance to go into that noise and dirt, and that unnatural red light in the sky.

Dark times, those had been, with no baby, and little Peggy dying because God was punishing her for her presumption in taking on a child when He had forbidden it. Dark days, grey nights, with no hope, and the love she held for Ben hidden deep within herself, so deep she hadn't even known it was there.

She had worked for him, had kept her bargain. Grow stronger, Faith. Do not complain about the weight of those wooden barrows. Don't tell him

167

you still have nightmares about *Daisy*, the woman falling between the boat and the rock. Don't say, 'I can't lift this sack, it's too heavy.' Never say, 'I'm tired.' Never tell him that he can go to the pub at the end of his day's work, but you still have two hours ahead of you, cleaning, cooking, washing, polishing. You made your bargain, now keep it until you die, and perhaps that won't be too long, since you don't want to live. Not too much longer maybe, with no hope and no love.

Until he'd been hurt in the fight with Paddy she'd never allowed herself to consider her feelings for him. He was her husband, and she'd promised to love, honour and obey him. She did obey him, and she wasn't very sure what was meant by 'honour', so she did her best by not joining in the conversations of the other women when they turned to complaints about their husbands.

But love, to Faith, was a frightening thing. All her love had been turned inward, to the child she'd never doubted would come her way, and it had been rejected because the child had not come. That pain had been dreadful, and Faith would not, if she could help it, leave herself vulnerable to anything like that again.

But then Ben had been hurt.

During that fight Faith had been truly frightened. She'd never seen Ben so angry, never seen him move so swiftly and with such purpose as when he went for Paddy Armstrong, and she'd thought he'd kill the man. Paddy had still been on his feet with that smile on his face, with Ben

168

pulled up short by just those two punches, his face white. She hadn't understood that: Ben was big and strong so how could two punches do so much damage? And then she'd seen the dull gleam of unpolished brass in Paddy's fist, and the fear had gone the other way. She knew what that thing was, because her brother had had one, God knew where he'd got it, and he'd shown it to her, laughing about it.

That thing could kill a man. There'd been pure terror then, for her man, and there was only one reason for that. Love. She loved him, and he was in mortal danger.

If Ben had died, she would have tried to kill Paddy herself.

Caring for Ben afterwards, listening to the nurse who had said the doctor was too busy, and going to find Mrs Webster, all the things she'd done for Ben had been because she loved him. He needed her, and she loved him, but she hadn't thought further than that. She was doing what she had to do, as best she could, because she was his wife. She loved him, but she'd never expected him to love her in return.

Then she'd got *Grey Lady* through the tunnel, and although she had tried to make light of it, it had been hard. After only a few minutes she'd begun to doubt that she could do it. The pole had seemed so very heavy, pulling it out of the water, pushing it down again, leaning her shoulder against it, and it was dark in there. For a long time it seemed that the light behind the boat, where they'd gone in, was always going to be bigger and brighter than the one in front, where she would, eventually, come out again. It was dark and cold, water had dripped from the brickwork, and her shoulder was sore from the pole. And the boat seemed hardly to move at all, no matter how hard she pushed.

A little more than halfway through, she'd heard Ben shout, and she'd answered. She was all right, she'd called, but she wasn't really. She didn't think she was ever going to get out of that tunnel. All her muscles were sore and aching, and the pole seemed twice as heavy as when she'd started, and the boat was going so slowly she'd have sworn they were aground and she was trying to push her over a sand bar.

But she had got through, and there he'd been, sitting on the muddy path in the rain, crying. For pain in his leg, she'd thought at first. He must have fallen and hurt his knee, but he'd never cried after the fight. There'd been sweat on his face, and some terrible language when he'd thought she wasn't near enough to hear, but he'd never cried. Men didn't cry, and she'd been embarrassed to see the tears on his face, and hear him making that noise, pretended she hadn't noticed.

Then that night he'd held out his arms to her, and she'd thought, Oh, no. No, I'm so tired. Surely he can't expect that, after I've poled the boat through the tunnel? But it had been her duty, so she'd smiled at him, and it had been different. All the time he'd been looking down at her face, watching her, and he'd kissed her, and he'd stroked her, and he was trying to please her.

'Do you like that?' he'd asked. 'Tell me what

170

you like. What would you like me to do?'

She hadn't known how to answer him. He'd never asked before, but he'd been smiling down at her.

'Tell me,' he'd said. 'Tell me what you like.'

She'd felt shy, and she'd turned away her face, but his hand had been under her cheek turning it back again, so she was looking up at him and he was smiling.

'You used to be able to tell me,' he'd said. 'You could have written a book, the things you told me to do.'

She'd laughed, and he'd laughed too, and kissed her again, and she held him close and remembered the scent of lavender, the way she'd felt holding a man close to her for the first time in her life, how she'd been excited, and a little fearful, and curious.

That night it had been like starting all over again.

He had whispered love words in her ears, and he had never done that before. It hadn't been easy for him to call her the loving names. He was clumsy with the words, trying to think what to say, and that was when she began to think, He loves me.

She'd started to cry, and he'd understood, and kissed her again, and he'd said the words: 'I love you.'

Everything had been different since then. He needed her, and he loved her, too. The desperation she'd felt since little Peggy's death had gone. She didn't want to die any more, not unless Ben died. Then she'd want to go with him.

171

There was still that dark, cold place inside her that should have been filled and warmed by a baby, that would never heal, but it wouldn't kill her. She could live with it, now.

And she could look into the future, too. She could see a life ahead that had happy times in it, summer evenings spent with her man. Fine evenings when they didn't have to plan to get to a stable for Billy, because he'd be happy tethered on the path, not needing the shelter. Summer nights out in the country, with the soft sounds of the horse grazing, and the night birds calling, and Ben's harsh breathing that she'd come to accept, and now to love.

Even the winters were good with Ben, even when the whole bitter day was spent longing for the night, when they could be out of the cold wind, safe and snug in the cabin, with the little black stove warm in the corner.

And the wild nights, like that time last March when *Grey Lady* had been empty, and the wind had been so strong she'd dragged her mooring stakes and been rocking so hard Faith had thought she might go right over. They'd pulled her half a mile to the next lock, and the bottom gate had been open. Perhaps they should have thanked God for that because Faith would never have held the boat on her own in that wind, nor kept her feet on those slippery bricks had Ben held the boat and left her to open the gate. They'd gone into the lock, and Ben had closed the gate, and suddenly it was all calm and still, *Grey Lady* steady in the water. Ben had jumped down on to the cabin and he'd been laughing.

They'd ridden out the storm in the bottom of the lock, lay there listening to the sound of the wind roaring in the trees above them, pictured those trees bending and lashing, and she'd hugged herself, and rolled around on the bed for sheer glee, because it couldn't get them down there.

So there would be good times ahead, and even though winter was coming Faith was content, and felt safe. She had her good warm boots, plenty of wear left in them yet, even though the fleece had worn away in the place where her toes went, her own fault because she'd liked wriggling them in the warm softness. And they had coal enough, because there was always some to be kept when they carried it. Filthy job, cleaning out the boat after a load of coal, but worth it, because no one said a word about the little bit the boaters burned on their own stoves, or complained about some put away for the trips when they carried iron, or glass, all the things that wouldn't burn or keep them warm.

She'd knitted gloves to keep her hands busy as they moved along the waterways, thick oiled wool to keep out the wet and warm the hands. She could knit even when she was teaching children in the evenings, a ball of wool in her pocket, fingers quick with the needles, looking over the shoulders of the little ones as they wrote on their slates, wrote their names carefully, each time a little neater than the one before. Each lesson a few more rows of Faith's knitting, the gloves and the thick warm socks.

And the glow she felt when they came to a

173

mooring in the evenings and a woman would look out and see them, and smile. There'd be a wave and a shouted greeting, and the children called, 'Come quick, it's Mrs Jacardi, find your slates and wash your faces, it's Mrs Jacardi. Meg, change that pinny, you're not going out in that. Peter, let me wash your face for you, you're not fit to be seen. Now, hurry. And take this with you.'

They'd often bring little presents, a packet of tea or some home-made biscuits, sometimes a pretty lace plate with bright ribbon threaded through the holes in the border to hang on the cabin wall, and once a Measham teapot, a lovely thing in Faith's eyes, a grand present in the tradition of the boaters. There were four children in the Baker family, and now, thanks to Faith, every one could write its name, and make out most of the words in a children's book. Thanks to Mrs Jacardi, and thanks took the form of a Measham teapot.

'There won't be room to put the windlass in the cabin soon,' Ben commented, after Mrs Baker had handed over the teapot, and Faith put it proudly on the little shelf over the stove, but he was pleased that she'd been given such a fine gift.

Spring came at last, wet and wild at first but welcome all the same after the winter. It was marked in Ben's memory by the day on the Staffordshire and Worcestershire Canal when he'd stopped at her shout.

'Oh, Ben. Look!'

The steep cutting he and Billy had walked past with their heads low as he watched his footing was a dark cloud of bluebells, tens of thousands of them under the trees. He'd told the little horse to stand, and he'd run back, climbed the cutting and pulled an armful for his wife. Half an hour they'd lost as he gathered the flowers, and then she had to put them in water and find safe places in the cabin. She'd scolded him for the delay, but she'd been pleased he'd done it.

Word went round that Mrs Jacardi liked wild flowers, and when the children came in the evenings the girls often brought little posies for her, whatever they had seen growing on their way.

Summer came, and Faith would teach the children out of doors, sitting on the grass, or the benches, but in the clean fresh air, until the nights began to draw in again, and the cold carried the hint of the coming winter.

Jed finished the boat, and Ben found a buyer for it near Middlewich, not too far to travel to collect her.

Jed's oldest son William was helping in the yard now, after school, just tidying up and sorting the scrap metal, the work Ben had done when he'd first started. Violet had had a little girl early in the new year, no problems with the birth, but Jed told Ben that Violet was looking after two babies now, little Emily and old Josiah.

'He's no trouble,' Jed told him. 'He doesn't know much about what's happening. He's fond of Violet.'

'Can she manage?' asked Ben.

She told him herself when they were next passing that she liked Josiah. He was a bit like an old dog in front of the fire, just dozing the days and nights away, but did no harm to anyone. He was inclined to confuse her with Kathy. He couldn't remember her name now, so she answered to whatever he called her. It didn't matter.

They'd made a good enough price on the boat for it to be worth building another, and Jed was keen to start. Maybe, if the winter wasn't too bad, he could finish one by early summer, even working alone most of the time, hiring an extra man when he had to have one, and with young William to help. If that sold quickly he might give up his job at the corn merchant and come back to building boats full-time. What did Ben think of that idea? Wouldn't it be grand, to get Armstrong's building boats again?

It was the women who were cautious. Violet reminded Jed that he had four children to support now, and she had no mind to lie awake at night worrying about where the money was coming from. That same night, Faith reminded Ben of Paddy.

'He's Josiah's son,' she said. 'When Josiah dies, the cottage and the yard will be his. Who are you working for, Ben? Do you want to build up a business for Paddy to inherit?'

Why hadn't he thought of that? And how could he explain it to Jed?

'I'm in no mind to work for Paddy Armstrong,' he said, 'or to put money into anything that'll make him rich.'

But it was a dilemma he couldn't resolve. Jed was a good friend, and he wanted to build boats

176

and pass on his skills to his sons. Josiah's lucid moments were now so few that he could not be asked to reach an agreement about the use of the boatyard. When he died, Paddy would inherit.

'Keep all the receipts,' said Faith. 'Keep records, Jed. Write everything down with the dates and the money, pounds, shillings and pence, and don't forget a farthing. What was Josiah's share we'll call rent for the yard. And Violet taking care of him, that's the rent for the cottage. There's four of us to say it was agreed before Josiah lost his mind, and it's a fair agreement, isn't it? We're not cheating anyone.'

'There was Mrs Webster, too,' said Violet. 'She was here. She'll be a witness.'

Back on the towpath, leading Billy through the mud of a wet autumn, Ben knew it was the best they could manage, but he wasn't happy. He couldn't see ahead to what would happen, or when, and it made him uneasy. Faith was less worried, more inclined to be fatalistic. They had done all they could to protect themselves, and even Josiah, and now they could only trust to their luck, or perhaps to God.

Ben mused over those few words as he walked beside his horse. Faith's religious beliefs had never interested him, while his own were as vague as it was possible to be and still exist. Faith's beliefs in the Christian God and the teachings of the Church were absolute, but she did not love God. Fear was what she could understand, and submission to the will of something omnipotent, but fear didn't make possible love as she understood it.

177

She still said her prayers every night, and every night Ben waited for her eyes to open and her hands to drop. It was only then that a smile would touch her face, and love show in her eyes. But not for God.

Faith, repeating the words of the Lord's Prayer and the Creed, trying to keep her mind on them, found her own will returning, beneath her apparent submission, begging for a child of her own. There was no hope in her mind but the unspoken plea had become as much a habit as the set words of the familiar prayers. Other people's children, learning a little reading and just enough writing to get by, were no substitute.

Jed finished another boat, sold it himself, and started a third, this time with a customer waiting for it. William had left school and was spending all his time in the boatyard, and even Violet was coming round to the idea that Jed should leave the corn merchant and work only on the boats.

But Josiah was weak now, she said. Still like an old dog in front of the fire, dozing, not doing much, not able to see or hear too well. And a bit smelly. They'd have to burn that chair, one day.

The day Josiah died, that would be. And what were they to do when that happened?

Faith and Ben had little money. They sent most of what they saved to Jed for materials for the boats, and for Josiah, and Ben began to wonder if they were walking into a trap. Josiah might die at any time, and then there'd be Paddy, who might have lawyers. With all their money tied up in the boats being built on the yard, what would happen if Paddy turned them off before those boats could be launched? They might never get their money back.

But Jed had to make a living, and Ben didn't want to hinder him. All it needed was a little time, and then they'd have their money again, wouldn't they?

But he was growing more and more uneasy.

There was still plenty of work for boats, even though the railways were taking most of the trade. The canal companies still needed men, were always looking for more. Ben and Faith worked long, long hours, worked on until Billy was tired.

Ben fretted about money. When they had to wait at the wharves to be loaded or unloaded, when a broken lock held them up, when the canals froze, whenever there was a delay and they were earning nothing, his thoughts turned to the boatyard, to what might be happening there.

Violet was pregnant again.

All the time Ben fretted about Paddy, wondering what they would do when he came back. He could turn them all off the place in little more than an instant, and where would Jed take his big family then?

'Without Jed there's no business,' said Faith. 'Paddy's a vile man, and a thief, but I doubt he's a fool.'

Violet was writing down every penny spent in the yard, and she was paying William wages, as well as Jed. Ben stifled his resentment: he'd been older than William before he earned that sort of money, and William's wages would cut into the profits. David would be leaving school next year,

179

would Violet pay him the same? Violet was a kind woman, and a good mother, but she was greedy. Most of William's wages came straight back to her for his keep, and when the coal merchant made an offer to buy the ends of wood to split up for kindling, Violet agreed, but the money the coal merchant gave her didn't find its way back into the business.

'It's only pennies,' said Faith, but she too was uneasy. She didn't begrudge the pennies, but she didn't like the fact that they'd been taken. Sometimes she'd think about the boatyard and remember that it had been Ben who ran it until he'd taken her and *Grey Lady* on to the canals, and now it was Jed, but more and more it was Violet. If they went back, who would be in charge? Who would make the decisions? Jed and Violet might not be willing to stand aside for Ben, and there were the two boys to be considered as well.

She'd brought Jed and Violet back to the cottage because they were friends, but the real friendship had been between Josiah and Jed.

She put the worries aside. There was nothing she could do, and it was too early to think seriously about going back to building boats. Even though the railways were doing well, there was still plenty of room on the canals for a hardworking boatman, provided he kept his wits about him and his boat and horse in good order.

Then Ben was made an offer of a regular run, taking pottery from Stoke-on-Trent to London, and hardwood back. It was good money, and more security, but it meant they would seldom be near the boatyard. They wouldn't even touch Birmingham, let alone the Staffordshire and Worcestershire Canal.

Ben wrote to Jed and told him they would have to keep in touch by letter from now on, unless there was an emergency, and Jed's reply, which only caught them a month later when they got back to Stoke, told them he was content enough with the arrangement: there was an order for another boat once these two were finished, and Violet thought that one more order within the next two months would make it worth hiring another man.

After their third trip to London they were asked to make a special journey, up the Trent and Mersey and the Shropshire Union to Chester. There'd be another load in Chester, but not for a few days, so they wouldn't have to hurry, and the customer would pay them for the wait.

It was a bit of a treat, that offer, and the manager smiled at Ben when he asked, because the Jacardis were good workers, and deserved a bit of a treat.

On the second night, when they moored at Middlewich, Faith remarked to Ben that they must be near the place where he was born.

He hadn't noticed. They'd been along this canal before, he and Faith, but it was only now and then that he'd raise his head and look around as he walked along the towpaths beside Billy. You watch your footing, on those towpaths. They could be slippery, or narrow, and if you weren't careful you or the horse could be in the cut. It happened now and then. The boaters called it

181

'taking a look'.

Billy took a look on that slippery bit just before Nantwich. Old Silver took a look there once, do you remember?

Yes, now he gazed around at the high buildings and the white heaps of salt for which the town was famous, he did remember. He'd taken a look himself on this stretch, when he was about eight. Had he been running away from his mother?

Just up there, beyond the lock cottages, that row of houses behind the lock, that was where he'd been born. His grandfather had been the lock-keeper there for a while, and his mother had stayed on in the town when her father had left. He'd never known why.

'Ben?'

He hated this town. He'd never thought of it before, but he did hate it. The only people who'd ever helped him had been the boaters, and that was why, when he ran away, it had been down the canal. He'd spent his days hanging around the locks, hoping for a chance to help, hold the horse or take a line from the boat, shivering in the winter cold or sweating in the sun.

He'd hold the horse or take a line, and that was nearly always followed by the present of a slice of bread with a scrape of dripping, or a mug of milk. Something for a thin, hungry child with bruised legs.

He came to know some of them, not by name, not *their* names, anyway. He never asked.

'How are you today? What's your name, then? Ben, that's a nice name. Can you hold that rope, my dear? Don't let her run on to the gates, now.

That's a good boy. Here, have a slice of this. Take care, now, Ben. 'Bye, Ben. Take care, now.'

'Ben?'

That had been more than twenty years ago, and here he was, looking back along the broad canal to that little row of red houses behind the lock. He pointed to them, and glanced across at Faith.

'There. That's where I was born. Third house from the end.'

It was a nasty little house; it had been cold and damp. Sometimes, when his mother had been worse than usual, he'd hidden himself in the coalhouse beside the privy in the garden. Stayed there all night sometimes. Made it worse when he had to come out in the end. His first memory was of crouching there behind the heap of coal, the smell from the privy mingling with the scent of the honeysuckle someone had planted against the fence.

'I wonder if your mother's still alive,' said Faith. Ben shuddered. 'God forbid!'

She stared at him in surprise, a look of alarm on her face. He reached across and touched her hand. He hadn't meant to startle her.

The white belt with the painted metal buckle. The paint had flaked off it so the metal showed through, he could remember that. He could remember her undoing that buckle, and sliding the belt through the loops of her faded red dress, and folding the leather. He'd watch every slow, deliberate move until she was standing there, holding the belt, waiting. Then he'd raise his eyes to her face.

She'd always be smiling, when he looked into

183

her face, while she held the belt, and waited.

'I love you, Faith,' he said, and her answer was like a talisman. He took it into his mind: 'I love you too, my Ben.' He held it there, tight, hearing the words over and over again as he remembered his mother. 'I love you too, my Ben.'

You've been a bad boy again.

I love you too, my Ben.

What happens to bad boys, Ben? I've told you before, Ben. This is for your own good. Don't you dare say a word to anybody. Do you know what happens to little boys who tell tales, Ben? They get their tongues cut out. I've a good sharp knife in the kitchen, Ben. It's there specially for little boys who tell tales.

'Ben?'

When the boatwomen had asked him about the bruises on his legs he'd said he'd fallen down the stairs, and they'd believed him. Why not? They didn't know about the specially sharp knife in the kitchen drawer to cut out the tongues of little boys who told tales.

One day he'd come in and there'd been a whip in the kitchen, a thing like a big black snake. She'd only used it once, because she'd knocked him out with it. Two blows across his back, he hadn't been able to breathe, couldn't draw in his breath to scream, just felt his knees give way, then nothing. When he'd woken up there'd been a sharp knife on the table, to remind him of what happened to boys who told tales.

Third house along in that row behind the lock, where the damp made the paper peel off the walls and water ran down the windows until the frames were rotten. A sash cord had broken, and

184

the glass was cracked. It made a shape like a star. In the moonlight it would twinkle at him, that crack in the glass. It was beautiful. He'd heard somewhere that you could wish on a star, so he did, on the star in the window. I wish I was somewhere else.

Bright morning, down by the locks, the day after he'd wished on the star, something seemed to tell him, Go on, Ben. Go somewhere else. You can make your wish come true.

So he'd walked across the lock gates on to the towpath. He'd looked one way, he'd looked the other, and then he'd started walking, and the star in the window had made his wish come true.

7

Faith held him very close that night, lying almost on top of him, as if to shield him from nightmares. She only ever slept lightly, half a breath away from full wakefulness, and when he opened his eyes in the morning she was looking down into his face, searching for the signs of misery she'd seen the night before, when he'd told her about the little house behind the lock.

'I'm going to find out where she is, that evil thing. What happened to her,' she told him that morning. 'Nothing worse than not knowing, my Ben.'

He'd wanted to argue, to order her to leave it, to make ready while he fetched Billy, but now he'd told her about his mother it was her story, too. She needed to know. If there were terrors to be confronted, they were hers as well as his, but he could not bring himself to tell her any more. He would not go with her. If his mother was there, Faith would have to confront her alone, and if not, the search was hers alone, too.

No one knew of a woman who'd lived in the house with a little boy. One of the neighbours had only been there ten years, the other fifteen, and it was more than twenty years now since Ben had wished on his star and walked away from Middlewich.

The house where he'd lived was empty.

But Faith would not be put off by a small setback. She stood at the gate and thought. Then she set off for the church. Ben's father would have been buried somewhere, and the churchyard was the most likely place.

There was a man cutting the grass in front of the church, and he stopped when Faith spoke to him. Jacardi? About thirty years ago? About that time, maybe?

He pointed down the slope and said she could try down there. He only cut the grass, but he seemed to remember a name like that. He warned her she was to be quiet. There was a funeral taking place.

She found it quite quickly, a plain slab of sandstone with the name Samuel Benjamin Jacardi cut into it, and the dates, 1849-1880. There was nothing else, no epitaph. But at least there was a headstone, she told herself. Somebody had paid for a funeral and a headstone. Ben's father hadn't been buried in a paupers' grave, anonymously, with all the poor souls who'd had no one to bury them, and no money to mark their passing.

Further away she heard voices chanting, one louder than the rest, and looked across briefly at the group gathered around a new grave before turning back to the one at her feet. It was a weedy patch of grass, with no flowers, and nowhere to leave any. Faith knelt down beside it, and thought, Hello, Samuel Jacardi. I'm your daughter-in-law. You didn't even know you had a son, but you have, and he's a good man, and he married me. You didn't pick much of a mother for him.

187

There was a clump of groundsel under her hand, and she pulled at it, but the ground was hard, the roots held firm by baked earth.

She had a little pair of scissors in her bag, so she took them out and dug at the weed. Come out of there, you.

She beat him, Samuel Jacardi, and she frightened him, so he ran away. He ran down the canals until he got to the other side of Birmingham, right down the Stourbridge Canal, and he found a place where he could steal coal. Cost him a beating and saved his life, shouldn't wonder.

She looked up as a shadow fell across her. An old man in a cassock and surplice with a prayer book in his hand stood staring down at her, his eyebrows raised interrogatively.

'Did you know Samuel Jacardi?' he demanded.

Faith rose to her feet and bobbed a curtsey.

'I'm married to his son, sir.'

The man stared at her in surprise, then with a look of astonished relief on his face.

'The boy lived, then? We all thought he was dead. Everyone thought she'd killed him.'

'Not quite, sir.'

'Oh, may the Lord be praised! She was telling the truth. Well, we thought she was lying. May we be forgiven, she told the truth.'

'Where is she, sir?'

But he held up his hand to stop her. 'Wait there,' he commanded. 'I must finish my duties. We must speak further.'

Faith knelt by the grave again as he strode away, faintly resenting his air of authority. It was as if he had interrupted her conversation, and she couldn't remember what she'd been thinking before he'd come. She picked at the grass, dug out another groundsel, and waited.

He came back a while later, striding through the graves towards her.

'Where is he?' he demanded. 'Where's the boy? Why isn't he with you?'

But Faith was in no mind to be interrogated. This man at least should have protected Ben from his mother, and he had failed. She rose to her feet and looked coldly into his face until he saw the accusation in her eyes, and became less certain of himself.

'Where is his mother, sir?' she asked.

He found himself stammering, as if he had to explain himself to her. His voice was hesitant, the words hurried.

'I don't know. The men came to see me. They told me she'd killed the child. We all thought that was what had happened. Where could he be? Then she disappeared, too. I suppose she ran away rather than face a charge of murder. They wanted to see her hang. They'd already been to the magistrate. There wasn't anything I could do.'

Faith looked steadily into the vicar's face, and watched the eyes drop, and colour come into his cheeks.

'We were all guilty,' he went on. 'It was too late by then to do anything about the boy. We should have helped him years before.'

'Yes, Vicar. You should.'

They stood in silence for a while, Faith looking around the graveyard, thinking that it wasn't a bad place for a soldier to lie, but wondering, now she had found the father and lost the mother, what had brought Samuel Jacardi here.

'It's thirty years ago that Jacardi died,' said the vicar at last. 'You say you're married to his son?'

Ben, thirty years old, and she? Faith knew what he was thinking, and kept her resentment firm in her mind. This old man should have befriended the child, and had failed him. He had no right to know about Ben now.

'Did he come from these parts?' she asked, but the vicar said no. Not from Middlewich.

After the silence had gone on for several moments Faith looked up at him again, and saw him gazing over her head, his chin raised, an expression of conscious nobility on his face.

'He swore me to secrecy,' he said. 'I cannot break my vow.'

He seemed to be waiting. For what? Faith wondered. Martyrdom?

If he would not even answer her simple question there was nothing more she wanted with him. She turned away and sank to her knees beside the grave, ignoring the man who stood over her. She wanted him gone, so she could continue her reverie, her conversation with the man who lay under the dry grass.

It took a few minutes. The vicar waited for the protest that never came, and at last, perhaps catching an edge of Faith's contempt, he turned and walked away, the black cassock brushing the grass and the weeds that grew between the graves.

'Samuel Benjamin Jacardi, I think your line

190

ends with me,' she said. 'I'm sorry for that. It wasn't for want of prayer. When we come back through Middlewich I'll bring flowers for your grave.'

On their way back, a little less than a week later, she brought the flowers, and Ben, too. He'd been there once or twice as a child, with his mother, and he stood beside the grass that covered the grave and looked at the stone as Faith put her offering in a jar, and set it in place.

'She's gone,' Faith told him. 'She's gone, Ben. That woman, your mother. You can forget about her, she's finished. She'd never dare come back here.'

'Yes,' said Ben, and he knew she was speaking the truth. His mother was nothing in his life now, only a dreadful memory, and Faith would shield him from that, if it ever threatened him.

For the first time, he wondered about his father.

'I would have liked to bring a grandson,' said Faith, rocking back on her heels and looking critically at the flowers in their plain jar. 'It does seem sad, him lying there alone, and no grandson.'

Ben looked down at her, seeing, as the vicar had, the grey hair and the sharp face where hard weather had etched lines deep into the skin. She was beginning to look as if it was her own grandson she should have brought to the soldier's grave.

'I did bring a fine son, though,' she said, smiling up at him.

Ben thought, There's only Faith in my life.

191

Kathy's dead, and Josiah's feeble-minded and it won't be long for him. There's only Faith. If she dies before me, there'll be no one in the world for me. Only a horse, and a boat.

'What are you thinking?' asked Faith.

'I'm wondering what I'd ever do without you,' he answered.

It was close enough to the truth. Had he told her his thoughts word for word it would have brought the tears to her eyes, although she would have known he could never blame her.

She was getting old, and he supposed he must be, too. Funny idea, that. One day they might not be able to work the boat any more. One day one of them would die, and leave the other alone. Faith had brothers and sisters, but there was no one for him. The only one in the world he might acknowledge as a blood relative lay at his feet, no more than bones now.

Samuel Benjamin Jacardi, he thought, you died before you knew about me, or so she said. I never doubted her. What brought you to this town? You had a terrible wound in your chest, and you died of it. Why did you come here, to a woman like that? Not even pretty, and certainly not kind, my God, never that. Whatever brought you to Middlewich, and the arms of Gillian Nicholson?

What did you look like? People used to say I had her eyes and they were her best feature. What did you give me? I'm bigger than most, were you a big man? I suppose I've got your dark hair. Hers was ginger. Auburn, she used to say. Who were you? I've never met anybody with my name. Never heard it spoken.

Samuel Jacardi, have I got an uncle or an aunt somewhere? Maybe even grandparents? I've got a little space to wonder about that now, now that she's stepped aside, that woman you bedded. You never loved her, though, did you? No one could have loved her.

'I wonder what he was like,' said Ben.

Faith came to stand beside him and look at the name carved in the sandstone.

'Have you never wondered before?' she asked.

He shook his head. It was strange, thinking of that now, but Gillian Nicholson had been his childhood, standing in front of him and between anything else that might have entered a child's mind, tall and thin and smiling, in a faded red dress with a white leather belt folded in her hand.

'I never looked beyond her,' he said.

'She's gone now. She's out of it.'

'So what brought him here? Who was he? A son ought to know that, oughtn't he? I should try to find out. A son ought to know about his father.'

He didn't know if he was making any sense with his words. He wanted her to understand, maybe so she could explain it back to him, because he knew nothing but confusion at that moment.

'"Honour thy father and mother," or something like that. That's the Bible, isn't it? I can only do half that. I ought to try.'

'You never cared about the Bible.'

'I know.'

The words were wrong, then. He hadn't said what he meant, didn't even know what he meant, only that there was something he should do about the dead man under the weedy dry grass.

'Help me, Faith. I don't know what I'm supposed to do.'

She took his hands in hers, looking up at him, puzzled by the expression on his face. He tried to smile at her. How could he explain to her that not having a child of his own only left him the option of looking backwards if he was to find a family? And he didn't know why finding a family had suddenly become important. It was something to do with Gillian Nicholson having run away. By doing that, she'd stepped out of the light, and let him see beyond her.

He didn't care about her family. Her father had left Middlewich, left her with a child to rear, must have known what sort of a woman she was, and still left a young child at her mercy. No, the Nicholsons were not for him, whoever they might be. If he had a family at all, anywhere, their name was Jacardi.

'We ought to be getting on,' said Faith at last, and she was right. Mooning around in a graveyard wasn't getting them back to Stoke-on-Trent. What would people think of them leaving the horse tethered and the boat moored with seven hours of good daylight still ahead?

'What did he look like, then?' Ben asked Billy, as the horse approached him at the next lock and stood waiting quietly as Ben pushed on the balance beam. 'What did my father look like? I know more about your father than I do about my own. Yours was a farm horse. Mine was a soldier. What sort of a soldier? What regiment? What rank? I ought to know. I ought to find out.'

'I ought to find out,' he repeated to Faith that evening. 'I ought to find out. How do I do it, my love? How do I find out?'

'I don't know. How would I know?'

'Think about it. You're the one with the brains.'

Faith looked at him doubtfully, wondering if he was teasing her, but there was only a worried frown on his face, and a restless look about him. There was something he should be doing, and he didn't know what it was, or how to do it. But he wouldn't stop fretting until he did know.

'The vicar wouldn't tell me where he came from,' she said.

Ben only looked more helpless, more confused. 'What, then?'

'I suppose we could write to the army,' she said. There can't have been that many soldiers called Jacardi wounded by a Zulu. Maybe they've got a list. Maybe they'd write back and tell us.'

So Faith did write, once they'd got back to Stoke and talked to Mr Wright in the office whose son was in the army. He said they should write to the War Office, and he found the address for them. Faith and Ben worked on their letter that evening, sent it off, and wondered if they would get a reply.

It arrived about four weeks later, an impersonal, formal response, telling them that Captain Samuel Benjamin Jacardi of the 1st Battalion 24th, 2nd Warwickshire Regiment, had died at the Battle of Isandhlwana on 22 January 1879, and had been buried there. The War Office had no knowledge of a grave in Middlewich.

195

'He was an officer,' Faith exclaimed, but that wasn't what they had wanted to know. They read the letter until they knew it by heart, but it answered none of their questions. The man in the office said he'd ask his son about Isandhlwana; he seemed to think it had been a disaster, and that no one had survived. Wasn't Isandhlwana a hill somewhere in South Africa? He thought a small troop of British soldiers had been attacked by Zulus.

'Who's that buried in Middlewich, then?' Ben wondered.

Faith replied it was his father, Samuel Benjamin Jacardi, as it said on the headstone.

'What about the wound in his chest?' she asked. 'Are you doubting that? What about the way you breathe?'

'Could have been just a story,' said Ben. 'Maybe he just had something wrong with him. That's why I breathe like him. All the doctors say you can't inherit something like that.'

He was even more unhappy and disturbed than he'd been before they sent off their letter.

'I want to know,' he said. 'Even if it's bad, I want to know.'

Faith felt helpless in the face of his bewilderment. She'd never known him like this, so uncertain, so worried. He couldn't seem to rest, couldn't leave the subject alone.

'Who buried him, then?' he demanded, a few nights later. 'Who paid for that headstone?'

'Your mother?'

He didn't seem to hear her.

'That costs money. Funerals and headstones,

they cost money. Who paid?'

'Not your mother?' Faith repeated.

Ben smiled at her.

'No, not my mother. She wouldn't have paid money to bury him.'

Faith still saw Ben's mother as some creature out of a nightmare, not something to believe in once morning had come. She did not doubt what Ben had told her, but trying to understand a creature like that, who had beaten a child and laughed with pleasure as she did it, was impossible. Her own son, and she'd taken joy in his pain. Not human, his mother. But dead bodies have to be buried, and someone has to pay or the bodies go into a big pit all together, when there are enough of them, and earth is shovelled over them at the expense of the parish, or so Faith had heard. And Captain Jacardi had been buried properly, with a place in a churchyard and a headstone.

Captain Jacardi, her father-in-law. An officer in the 1st Battalion 24th, 2nd Warwickshire Regiment. She wasn't sure what all the numbers meant, but she knew a captain meant that he had been an officer, and that meant he was a gentleman, somebody important and special.

'It wasn't him,' Ben insisted. 'That man in Middlewich is my father, but he isn't any Captain Jacardi, is he? Tom Nobody, that's who he is. Captain Jacardi's buried somewhere near a hill in South Africa.'

He still wanted to know, and how was he ever to find out who his father was now? A dead man with a stolen name. Somebody had paid to bury him. When they were next in Middlewich he might ask that vicar who had paid for the funeral. There'd be records somewhere: that couldn't be a secret, protected by some vow.

But there wasn't much chance of getting back to Middlewich because there was trouble in the air, in Europe, in North Africa, and it was even touching the canals of Britain now. Back to the Black Country for *Grey Lady*, to carry coal to London for the big factories, where they were making more and more guns, then back with whatever had come in, from anywhere in the world. Anything that had to be carried up the canals *Grey Lady* would carry. Young men were leaving the waterways and going into the navy.

There was going to be a war.

Faith found herself frightened in a way she couldn't understand. All this fuss, and all this excitement, and she couldn't feel touched by the excitement. She saw boys with sparkling eyes talking about going off to be soldiers, and all the time she and Ben were going up and down the Grand Union, coal one way because guns had to be made, timber or corn or stone, whatever there was in the docks, back the other, and it was having to be done faster and faster, because there was going to be a war.

Faith didn't tell Ben she was frightened. She didn't know anything about war, only that it meant fighting, and lots of men being killed, and then Ben came back to the boat one day very quiet, and she left him alone until late that night, when he said he'd tried to enlist but they wouldn't even let him go for a medical because of

198

his chest.

Ben, her Ben, had tried to enlist without even telling her. If they'd taken him he might have been killed. The man hadn't been nasty, he said. Just told him, 'No chance, old chap. You go back to the canals, that's valuable war work. Don't feel bad about it.' But there had been boys there, lining up to sign their names on a paper that promised them their share of glory, and Ben had been told to go back to the canals.

He was still fretting about the man in the grave in Middlewich. He wanted to know if his father had been a soldier. He couldn't seem to see his way past it, and it was driving him half frantic. He couldn't forget it, so Faith wrote again to the address Mr Wright had given them, and this time she didn't word her letter as a careful, formal request for information: she wrote in the words of a troubled woman worried about her man, and she told the story, and asked for help.

Somebody in that huge building in London read her letter, and took time he didn't have to search through old boxes of records, and he found a photograph, the name of a next-of-kin, Mrs Charlotte Jacardi, widow, and an address in Coventry. There was no letter this time; perhaps rules were being broken. The name and address were copied on to a plain sheet of paper, and that and the photograph were sent to the canal-company office in Birmingham, with an instruction that the envelope was to await collection by Mrs Benjamin Jacardi. Ben found it late one night when he and Faith had dragged their way back from London.

'It's you to the life,' said Faith, as they looked at the stiff portrait of the man in the uniform of an infantry officer. 'Don't you tell me that's not your father. I don't know how he got back to England or why he went to Middlewich, but don't you tell me that man isn't your father.'

8

Ben and Faith had never worked so hard before. Coal had to be carried to London, as fast as a horse could pull a boat down the canals, as fast as the railways could carry it, as fast as the roads would bear it. There was no time now for teaching children in the evenings: the evenings were spent on the move, pushing the animals as far as they could go, and then, if there was still light, leaving them at a stable and taking another, because no one had time to wait for a horse to rest. The men had to manage without rest.

In August, war was declared.

Faith could not remember having been so tired. She still tried to keep the boat clean, her precious brass polished, the range black, when she could find a shop that sold the blacking, but the only time she had was when they were waiting for *Grey Lady* to be unloaded or to take on a new load. At those times Ben would see to Billy, or whatever horse they had borrowed, feed him and find whatever shelter there was for him, and then he'd fall asleep, lying on the bed in his clothes, one arm thrown across his eyes to keep out the light.

Faith worked quietly, so as not to disturb him.

When they had time to talk, their conversation was of ordinary things, things they had hardly thought of before: evenings when they could moor because the horse was tired, or they'd done enough for one day, when they could heat some water on the range and have a good wash. Some days Faith thought of hot water and soap as a token of paradise.

'It'll all be over by Christmas,' they heard, and Faith thought of counting the days to Christmas, but she didn't know what day it was now. Sometimes she'd hear church bells and think, Sunday. Later it would be, Was it yesterday I heard them? Or the day before?

It wasn't the work that made her tired. She'd worked hard all her life. She didn't know what it was about war, but it brought with it a feeling like a dark grey cloud. She wasn't really old, was she? Why was she so tired, then? At the end of every day, why was she so tired?

And this boat had been made to carry heavy loads, but not on canals that were silting up because there was no one to dredge them. Water up to the gunwales, she'd often been like that, but now they found it hard to drag her through the bridge holes where the mud and silt piled up. How can Ben pole her through this tunnel? She's running aground in places we never had trouble with before.

The railways were doing well. They heard of the big wages that could be earned on the railways, pay rises nearly every week, it seemed, and the men on the railways didn't have to go to the war.

Christmas came, and brought horror with it: young men had come home from the war, not as conquering heroes but as cripples, young men who should have been starting their lives, looking at the future with courage and hope. What was there for a young man who'd been blinded or lost his legs?

When Faith cried herself to sleep at nights it was not only her own exhaustion that brought the tears, it was the dreadful pity of it all, the waste of all that hope, strength and courage. Gone, with the guns and the barbed wire and the bombs. All gone.

There was no hope in the spring. The longer days, the bluebells brought nothing. There was no end in sight.

'I hate this war,' she said to Ben. 'I hate it. I hate that Germany.'

Ben had gone beyond hate. Young men had gone to France, and come back old, with lungs ruined by gas, breathing as he did, but with pain in their faces. There was nothing to be done for them.

Faith began to dread going into London. It had been bombed. When they had to wait for *Grey Lady* to be unloaded she became more and more nervous. And often they were hungry. There wasn't much food, and the shops refused to sell to anyone who wasn't a regular customer. There never seemed to be any bread, except when a lock-keeper or his wife came out and offered them a loaf. They understood the problems of the boaters and did what they could to help, most of them.

Ben took to poaching. As they went along the canals, Faith would watch him, and see his head turn as he looked into woodlands, and into farms where there might be poultry. Then, after it was dark, he'd go out, and he'd come home with a pocketful of eggs, once or twice a chicken.

This was more than carrying a catapult in his pocket for the occasional rabbit, setting snares in the evenings or taking a few potatoes from a field beside the canal, which all the men did when they could, and which the farmers almost expected. This was more than taking a little food from the cargo, if they were carrying food, or exchanging it for coal when that was what was on *Grey Lady.* Faith tried not to give it the name, tried not to think about it, but it was stealing.

The war went on, and the factories made more guns, and more tanks, and there were always more boys growing up to be almost men and going to the war. And there wasn't enough food, and there wasn't enough sleep, and there weren't enough boats on the canals to carry what needed to be carried, and when there were, there weren't enough men to work them. The canals weren't being maintained; they were more and more difficult, not only silting up in the bridges and the tunnels but the towpaths were becoming weedy and overgrown. There were places where the horses couldn't get through and the boats had to be poled while the animals took to the road. No one seemed to be listening.

They were earning good money. The work they were doing was essential, carrying the coal and the iron to the foundries, the food back from the ports. They were keeping the factories supplied with raw materials and the people from starvation. But they felt as if they'd been forgotten. Who cared for the canals, and the people who worked on them? All the talk was of the railways, and *they* were always being repaired. The boats carried roadstone for the railways, the boats were dragged over the silt to take the stone to repair the railways, which was always urgent, always a priority. Long lines of boats made their way down the overgrown canals, struggled through the weeds and the rubbish, the sand bars and the broken paths, to take the stone and the steel to the railways. The men who worked the boats earned good money, but they couldn't buy food with it. That was saved for the regular customers.

The boat people used the canteens that had been set up when they were near enough to them, and the lockkeepers tried to help, but they'd been forgotten. All the news was of the war, and the war effort made by the soldiers who were fighting in the mud, and the people at home working in the factories and the foundries, and the men on the railways. No one remembered the canal people.

They tried to live as they always had, keeping close to their own kind, meeting at the smoky little pubs when they moored together in the evenings, singing their songs and dancing to the music of a fiddle or a squeezebox, but the lightness had gone from the dances, and the music could not lift the spirits of the exhausted men.

Neither Faith nor Ben felt anything when they had a letter from Violet telling them that Josiah had died and been buried.

'Why didn't she tell us before?' Ben wondered, as he read her letter. 'We might have got to his funeral. Why didn't she tell us?'

They asked if they could take a load down to Worcester, so they could visit Josiah's grave, and the manager agreed. It was long past the time when the Jacardis should have had a couple of days to themselves. They could take coal down to Stourbridge, then glass to Worcester, and there might be a load of grain to bring back. These were heavy loads, but they could have a day on the way to visit Josiah Armstrong's grave.

When they reached the boatyard they found the answer to their question.

Paddy Armstrong had come back after Josiah had died, and Jed and Violet had bought the cottage and the yard from him. The scarlet and gold board had been painted again, and there was no mention of Armstrong on it, nor of Jacardi. The words made it all very clear:

'J. Cartwright and Sons, Boatbuilders.'

9

Jed found it difficult to meet their eyes, but Violet seemed coldly defiant. They had done nothing wrong, she said, although no accusation had been made. Mr Armstrong had come to his father's funeral, as was only natural, and Jed and she had asked him about the cottage and the yard. He'd said he had other interests, and couldn't run the business himself, so if they made him a fair offer, he'd sell to them. Nothing illegal about that, was there?

'Thirty pieces of silver?' Faith asked, and Violet retorted that she wouldn't be spoken to like that in her own kitchen.

Her own kitchen, thought Ben. She could call this her own kitchen, and say the words as if they were completely natural. She was standing at the stove where Kathy had stood, her dark blue dress nearly sweeping the flagstones. The picture of Kathy in her dark grey one still stood in his memory as a symbol of warmth and safety. But where Kathy's head had been bent towards him with a smile and kindness, Violet's was raised high with triumph and defiance.

'What about the money we sent you for materials?' asked Ben.

Violet looked at Jed, and said she'd been under the impression that it had been for Josiah, for his tobacco, and such things as that. Of course, what had been sent since Josiah had died would be given back, wouldn't it?

Ben stared coldly at Jed, who sat with his hands between his knees, looking at the floor. Jed was a good ten years older than Ben, but he looked younger. He was successful. He owned his own business, which he'd bought legally from the man who'd inherited it. He had a shrewd wife, and five children, and he was doing well out of the war.

'Well,' said Violet, 'now we all know where we stand, shall I make a pot of tea? There's no reason not to be friendly, is there?'

'Jed?' asked Ben quietly. 'You're very quiet, Jed.'

Jed looked up, shrugged, tried to smile.

'You taught me how to use an adze,' said Ben. 'I was barely big enough to hold it. Do you remember?'

Jed nodded.

'You helped me build *Grey Lady*,' said Ben.

Violet broke in. '*Grey Lady*'s yours,' she said quickly. 'No question about that. That was instead of your wages, wasn't it? We're not making any claim about *Grey Lady*, are we, Jed?'

'No,' said Jed. 'No, *Grey Lady*'s yours, Ben.'

'What about that pot of tea, then?' asked Violet, comfortably.

Faith touched Ben's arm, and tried to smile at him as he turned to her.

'I want to go back to the boat.'

'Not just yet.'

'Please, Ben.' And then she added words that frightened him, because she'd never used them before. 'I don't feel very well.'

208

Her face was white, and there was sweat on her upper lip.

Ben stood up abruptly, taking her arm as she rose to her feet, looking down at her.

'Come on, then,' he said, and he turned his back on the people he'd thought were his friends, and he helped his wife out of the kitchen that had once been the centre of his home.

'What's the matter?' Violet called after them. Jed followed them into the yard and echoed her question, but Ben ignored them both. Faith was clinging to his arm, holding on to him as if her own legs couldn't carry her.

'What is it?' he asked, as they made their way across the yard to *Grey Lady*. 'Are you in pain? What is it?'

'I don't know.'

She felt sick, she said. Maybe she'd eaten something bad. Maybe that bit of fish had been off. She wanted to get back to the boat, and she didn't want to stay here. Her voice broke as she said that.

Ben helped her into the cabin and made her lie down. He spoke to her reassuringly. They'd move on when she felt a bit better, because he didn't want to stay here either. He'd fetch Billy out of the shed, and they'd go on another couple of miles.

He was talking because he didn't know what to do. She was ill and she'd never been ill before. Small and thin, but never ill. What was to be done? What did she want him to do?

What would she have done, if it had been him?

'Shall I go for the doctor?'

She said she didn't want a doctor. She'd be all right soon. Just that bit of fish, probably. It hadn't tasted quite right. And Violet.

She began to cry, helplessly.

'That makes me feel sick, too,' he said, and wondered as he spoke if it was shock that had affected Faith.

It had been a shock.

He, too, felt cold and a bit sick. He'd never thought the Cartwrights would treat them like that. His fear had been of Paddy Armstrong coming back and turning them all off the place, but that Jed and Violet would do a thing like that had never crossed his mind.

'We should have thought,' whispered Faith.

Jed had been Josiah's friend. Josiah had never really known Violet until she moved into the cottage after Kathy died, and by then it was too late; anyway, she'd been kind to him. She'd looked after him, and done it well. Josiah would have had nothing of which he could complain, and he was losing his mind. Ben had never known her either, although he had thought she was a greedy woman, taking every penny she could get. But he had never thought that she could be so treacherous. Nor that Jed would let it happen.

Neither of them doubted that it had been Violet.

'What should we have thought?' Ben asked gently. 'That our friends would betray us? Why should we have thought that?'

Faith had no answer. She closed her eyes, and tears brimmed out from under her lids. Her face was still white, and there were dark smudges

210

under her eyes. Shock, Ben thought again, and exhaustion.

'I don't want to stay here.' She was close to sobbing. Ben fetched her washcloth, and wiped her face with it.

'As soon as you're feeling better I'll fetch Billy,' he said. 'We'll go another couple of miles. He can stay out tonight. It's not too cold.'

When he went to fetch the horse Jed was out in the yard, waiting for him.

'There's always a place for you here, Ben,' he said.

Ben shook his head, and looked the man straight in the face.

'I don't think so. I don't think I could ever feel easy here with you, now.'

When he got back to the boat Faith was crying, but she insisted she wanted to move off. They'd planned to stay for the night, and visit Josiah's grave in the morning, but now she wanted nothing more to do with the place. Ben hitched the towing line to the mast, and led Billy on down the path. He didn't look back at the cottage, but Faith, clinging to the tiller, saw Violet standing at the kitchen window, and Jed at the door of one of the sheds. How could they do that? she asked herself. How could they do that, and live there as if they'd done nothing wrong? Nausea made her choke, and she leaned across the tiller, retching, as her eyes filled again and bile rose in her throat. She couldn't remember ever having felt so ill.

'It's only money,' Ben said later that night. 'We never thought about buying the place, did we?

We'd never have saved enough, even if we hadn't sent anything for Josiah.'

They hadn't even got the money they'd sent since Josiah had died. About fifteen pounds, Ben calculated, and they'd left without it. He didn't care about that. He couldn't see himself standing in that kitchen holding out his hand for that fraction of the money he'd entrusted to the Cartwrights. What was fifteen pounds compared to what had been stolen?

No, they would not have saved enough to buy the yard if they'd sent nothing back, but they certainly would have done if they'd stayed at the yard and Ben had built boats instead of working them, taking the place of one of Jed and Violet's boys. If they had stayed at the yard they would have seen what was happening, kept an eye on the money, not given Violet the opportunity to put so much into her own pocket. If they had been at the yard, they would have been there when Paddy came back. They might have been able to do something.

Why hadn't they done that? he asked himself, but he knew the answer. He couldn't have turned his friends out of the cottage, and he and Faith couldn't have lived there with them. He was a better boatbuilder than Jed could ever be, for all that Jed had taught him, but there was only room for one family at the boatyard, and the Cartwrights had five children; the Jacardis none.

Faith could not stop crying, and could not understand herself. It wasn't as if they'd ever

212

thought the cottage and the yard would be theirs. But she was so dreadfully tired, and it had been a shock, and it had made her angry. It wasn't so much that Violet had cheated them: it had been that Violet seemed to see nothing wrong. 'Done nothing illegal,' she'd said, and then she'd offered to make a pot of tea. She hadn't only cheated them, she'd wanted them to accept it and remain friends.

Faith tried to stop the tears and the sobbing, tried to smile at Ben, worried at the look of concern on his face, but she couldn't. Her stomach was churning, and the tears flowed no matter what she did. She could hardly bring herself to lift her head from the pillow Ben had placed under it.

'I'm just tired, I expect,' she said, and he stroked her forehead, and mopped her face again.

'Go to sleep, then. Go to sleep, Faith.'

The morning brought no improvement. They went on down the canal, with Faith clinging weakly to the tiller, at times leaning over the side to vomit. Her stomach was sore, and her eyes were swimming. Now and then there was double vision, two black and white horses on the towpath ahead of the boat, two men leading them. It became difficult to steer, and when the wind rose just before they reached Kidderminster, Faith told Ben she couldn't manage any more.

She had never said that before.

Ben moored the boat, took Billy to the stables then went into the town to find a doctor.

'She's only a little thing,' he told the man. 'She can't take much of this, being sick all the time.

213

She'll wear herself out.'

The doctor agreed with Faith that it was probably a piece of bad fish. She was to drink as much as she could, and try to rest.

'Got to get on down to Worcester,' whispered Faith, and the easy tears rose to her eyes again. She was never ill, she told herself. Never like this. Bit of a cold maybe. Never been so bad she couldn't work.

She tried to get up in the afternoon, dress herself and clean the cabin, and Ben came in to find her sitting on the bed, the tears running down her face, too weak to stand. Gently, he took her polishing rag out of her hands and put it back in the soap hole.

Another boat pulled up alongside them, and Ben went out to see. It was the Cooper family, George Cooper curious to know why the Jacardis had stopped outside the town in the middle of the afternoon. When he learned Faith was ill he said their second boy, Edward, could steer *Grey Lady* for them, if that would be a help, until Faith was herself again. They could manage without him on this trip. There'd be plenty of men to help unload when they got to Gloucester, and they could pick him up from his granny's house on the way back. She lived in Worcester.

'You take our Edward,' urged Mary. 'Do him good to do a bit of work for a change,' and the boy grinned at her, and said he'd be happy to help.

Another year or so and that nice lad will be off to the war, Faith thought, and fought to keep the tears out of her eyes.

Whatever is the matter with me? Whatever can be the matter with me? A bit of bad fish, a bit of a shock, and I'm all to pieces. It's stupid, this.

By evening she felt a little better. She came out on to the deck, saying the fresh air would do her good. There was some colour in her cheeks, and she managed to smile at young Edward, and compliment him on the way he handled the boat.

The following evening when they reached Worcester Edward went off to see his grand-mother, and Faith and Ben waited at the dockside for the glass to be unloaded. Faith was still pale and weak, but she told Ben she was on the mend, she'd be fine again by morning.

By the time the iron was loaded it was too late to set off, so Ben and two of the loaders pulled *Grey Lady* out of the dock on to the canals, and moored her there. Boats weren't supposed to be moored at the dockside overnight any more. Sometimes there were explosives.

Faith woke before daylight, and crept out of the cabin. She felt sick again, and weak. She didn't want to worry Ben. She was stiff and sore from vomiting, and she wasn't sure she'd be able to steer the boat. So low in the water, with all that iron, so heavy. Hard to steer her now.

Three years, this war had lasted, three years, and they'd said it would all be over by Christmas. Last time they'd been in London the place where the nice man had let her have half a loaf of bread had been bombed. It was black, just a burned hole in the ground. Nothing. But what was worse for Faith was that she'd only thought, No bread today, then. On her way back to the boat she'd

215

been so ashamed of herself. The nice man might have been killed, and she'd only thought of the bread.

That's war for you, she thought. Turns everyone into monsters.

Both her brothers were away fighting. At first farm work had been too important, they hadn't wanted to take the men off the fields. Then there hadn't been enough soldiers. They didn't say it, but everyone knew why. It was because so many had been killed. Take the men and boys off the fields, out of the mines, away from the foundries and turn them into soldiers, because the army needs soldiers for the Germans to kill.

How much longer? she wondered, as she watched the light growing in the morning sky. If we could only know how much longer, it would be easier.

But it was good to be away from that London run. It wasn't so frightening here. Even if there were bombs, this was more like home, here in the west and up to Birmingham. She wished they could stay here.

I wish we knew how much longer.

When Ben came out Faith was still standing on the deck, but she was no longer clinging to the tiller. She was upright, and watching the beginnings of the sunrise. She smiled at him, and reached out to touch his face.

'Better?' he asked, and she said, yes, she was better. Better than yesterday, but not completely recovered. She still felt giddy and weak.

Ben lit the fire for her, and made tea. There were some biscuits, stale and soft now, but she

216

ate one, slowly, and thought that, after all, she might manage today.

It was a fine June morning, a beautiful day to be on the water, with a light wind and clear sky, and once they were out of the town Faith began to feel happier. Here, for a little while, it was possible to forget the war, and maybe they'd be able to buy some food. At Lincombe Ben told the lock-keeper that Faith had been ill, and he fetched his wife, who was kind and concerned, and gave her soup. It was good soup, with beef, and it made her feel better. But there was only half a loaf of bread to spare, and that not very fresh.

Hunger was becoming a serious problem for the boat people. No one seemed to think it unreasonable that shopkeepers should keep their goods for their regular customers, but the boaters couldn't be anybody's regular customers. Stealing and poaching was now part of their way of life, and those who lived alongside the waterways grew suspicious and hostile.

There were still a few shops that would sell to them, one or two opened specially by the government alongside the canals, and there were the canteens, too. But there weren't many, and they were often short of supplies. Working long hours, heavy work on the locks or loading and unloading coal, iron, sacks of grain, day after day, the boat people needed good food and enough of it. Some of the men complained that they could no longer lift weights that had been no trouble before.

Some were luckier than others. Those who had

217

land-based families could rely on them for help. Those who carried foodstuffs could take some for themselves and, provided the depredations weren't too obvious, nothing would be said. Coal could be exchanged for food, but who wanted blocks of the salt destined for the chemical factories? Who wanted tar, or pig iron?

Sometimes a shopkeeper would sell them leftover bits that weren't good enough for the regular customers. Not quite fresh enough, perhaps. A bit of bad fish for a halfpenny.

Later in the afternoon Faith began to feel dizzy again, but she managed to cling to the tiller, and to steer the boat, although it took more strength than she thought she had, laden as *Grey Lady* was, water lapping almost to the gunwales. When they stopped for the night she went down into the cabin, her knees buckled and she sank to the floor, which was how Ben found her, with the tears running down her face again.

'Fetch Mrs Webster?' she asked, and Ben said, yes, he'd go. It was only a few miles. Faith was to rest on the bed. He'd be as quick as he could.

He followed her directions and found the house, the last in the row, and knocked on the door. It was late, and getting dark, and he wondered if she'd open to him, or look through the window, see a man and leave the door barred against him. He wondered what he would do, if that happened.

He was now seriously frightened about Faith.

But Mrs Webster opened the door and stood looking at him, questioningly, a tall old woman in a dark dress. There was something fierce about

218

that hooked nose; she wasn't the sort of woman to worry about opening her door. It would take a brave man to attack Mrs Webster.

Ben didn't know why he thought that, looking at her. She was, after all, an old woman living alone. But he knew he was right: this was a woman who was afraid of nothing mortal, nobody's easy victim.

'Mr Jacardi?'

Somehow he'd thought she would read his mind. She'd written in it after all, put that picture of the beech trees there. She should know why he was there.

'My wife.'

He couldn't say any more. His chest was burning with some sort of pain, and his throat was dry. He'd never been so frightened.

'My wife.'

'I'll come,' she said, and she left the door open as she went to fetch her coat, and a bag, which he took from her to carry the four or five miles. Would she expect him to have a horse for her? A trap, maybe, for her to ride in?

This was no frail old lady needing his assistance to walk four or five miles. She kept pace with him easily, and she didn't ask him any questions, hardly said a word, only a warning about the path now and then, because she knew her way down to the canal. Probably knew all the paths and roads around here, all the trees where you could take the bark.

If anybody could help Faith it was Mrs Webster. Faith hadn't asked for a doctor, or the nurse, she'd named Mrs Webster. The doctor had already seen her, and told her she was tired and had eaten bad fish. They already knew that. Waste of time, he'd been, yes, and Ben had had to dip into his pocket for him to tell them something they already knew.

Ben wasn't limping now. For a while he'd thought he'd be lame for life, with his knee not quite straight, but Faith had done what Mrs Webster said with the willow bark, and he'd obeyed her too, keeping it as straight and still as he could. He'd done that because she'd explained it.

'They're like straps,' she'd said, 'the ligaments. They hold the joint together, like a bit of harness. That one's stretched, and that one's torn. That stretched one, that'll shrink back, but the torn one, we'll need a bit of luck. And you keep it straight to give the luck a chance.'

A bit of luck was horseshoes and a rabbit's foot, a black cat crossing your path. A bit of magic, more like. Not all that stuff like conjuring a white rabbit out of a hat, and not like some warty old hag putting spells on a neighbour's cow, but magic for all that. Maybe Mrs Webster didn't understand it all herself, but she was trying to learn. She'd had her hand on Ben's chest as she'd listened to what he'd said about his father's wound, her fingers pointing up the way the spear had gone in, and she'd been thinking about that, and putting it all together with what she knew about what was inside a man's chest. Would have cut through that, but not this, because that would have killed him right away. That's what she'd been thinking. And how that big blood vessel must have been set a bit further back than in most men so the spear missed it. But how the boy had inherited it, if that was what had happened, she could not fathom.

And that was what she was thinking as they walked along the path, and Ben suddenly realised it, and knew he was reading her thoughts. It startled him so much that he nearly tripped on a root. It was she who caught his arm when he'd thought he'd been guiding her.

She'd known Kathy was dying before Kathy knew it herself.

Oh, God, don't let my Faith be dying.

'Is bad fish really bad?' he asked.

She answered him right away, no dressing it up in kindly words, no reassurance. 'It can be the worst.'

In some ways it was a relief to hear those words spoken so clearly and calmly. She'd told him the truth, and he didn't have to wonder about it. She was to be trusted like that. He was still as frightened as before, but this woman would do what she could, and if she couldn't help Faith, then Faith was beyond help.

Faith was lying quietly on the bed when they reached *Grey Lady,* and Mrs Webster came down the steps, took off her coat, handed it to Ben, and told him to leave them alone but stay within call. He went out on to the towpath, and he walked a little way down it to the wide bit of tussocky grass that led up to the road where he'd tethered Billy. The horse was grazing quietly, and Ben sat on the stump of a tree and watched him. Strong, stocky little horse, ugly little thing if you minded

221

about colours, and that pink nose and pink-rimmed eyes, but he'd done well for them, had Billy. He wasn't young any more. Still as good as ever, never sick, never lame, but not a young horse. Another five or six years, and Ben and Faith would be thinking of replacing him. Ben wished there was something else for an old horse, something better than a knacker's yard. He'd heard stories of places where old horses could go, live in a nice paddock, but he'd paid no attention. It had seemed a daft idea at the time, like keeping an old pair of boots with the soles worn through. What use was an old horse?

Because it was easier than thinking about Faith, Ben watched Billy, and thought about him, thought about the years they'd had together since he'd bought him, and begun to teach him to pull a boat instead of a cart. Billy hadn't needed much teaching. He'd always been a willing little horse, never lazy, never stubborn. It hadn't been long before Ben had been able to leave him to walk the path alone. 'Baccering', they called it, and there were tricks some of the boatmen used. Tie an old boot to the line just behind the horse so it sounded like somebody walking. Never needed to do that with Billy.

Get to the top of a flight of locks, and give him a drink, and Ben would rest the bucket on his knee, so the horse could drink easily. Every few moments Billy would lift his head and look around, taking an interest, enjoying his break, just as a man might. Ben would wait with the bucket on his knee, knowing the horse wanted to drink again. He knew that, because when Billy had had enough he'd nudge Ben's arm with his nose. Silly, to think of a horse thanking him for a drink, but he always did it when he was ready to go on.

If Faith died, the best friend Ben had was that little piebald horse. No family, not without Faith. And bad fish could be the worst. In five or six years, it could be Ben on his own looking for a new horse, wondering what to do with the old one, because he'd be damned if Billy went to a knacker's yard, not if Faith died.

There were boats with engines now. It had started with steamers on the rivers, towing strings of trows, narrowboats and barges, but now there were diesel engines, too. Getting quite common. You could hear them coming, thudding along the cut, and at first the horses had hated them. There'd been a few mishaps. Even Billy, who could stand most things, had stopped dead in his tracks and his head had gone up when he'd heard that noise and seen the smoke. Smelt it, probably.

So maybe, when it was time to think about Billy getting too old, he wouldn't look for a horse at all. He'd look for an engine. What would Faith think of that?

He didn't want another horse, or a mule or a donkey. Faith had cried when Blackie and Silver had died, and he'd wished he could, too. But men don't cry, and certainly not over something like dead animals, it would be soft. So he'd get an engine. And Billy, no, he would not send Billy to the knackers. No. Next time he was near a boat with an engine, he wouldn't only ask those polite

223

questions, he'd ask the others. How much did that cost? Where did you get it? Could I put one in my boat? How much does that diesel stuff cost and where do you buy it? All those things he'd never asked. He'd ask now.

'Mr Jacardi?'

She had a voice, that Mrs Webster. Not what you'd call loud, but you could hear her from quite a distance.

Please, God. Whatever it takes, you tell me what you want to make Faith be all right. I'll do anything.

Faith was still lying on the bed, looking towards the steps, her face white, her dark eyes sunk, with what looked like bruises all round them. Dark brown shining, shining eyes.

Mrs Webster out on the path, doing up her coat.

'Faith?'

She held out her hand to him, and he took it. It was damp and hot, and it was trembling.

God, whatever it takes. I'll do anything.

'Ben,' she whispered. 'Ben, I'm going to have a baby.'

10

But it wasn't pregnancy that had made Faith ill:
it was food poisoning. The bad fish was still
dangerous, and Mrs Webster, although smiling in
response to Ben's bewildered reaction and
Faith's incredulous delight, was cautious. Faith
could lose the baby. She was not a young woman,
and she was weak.

Rest, and as much to drink as she could hold,
said Mrs Webster. Fresh air. Sunshine, if it was
there. And good food.

That was what stopped Ben. Faith needed good
food, and there was none to be had unless he
could steal it. So he would have to steal.

He took Mrs Webster back to her house, and all
the way he was asking questions, few of which
she could answer. She didn't believe the baby
would inherit his breathing, but she hadn't
known he could inherit it from his father, so she
wasn't sure about that. But if Faith's twisted
shoulder was a birth accident, the baby wouldn't
have it.

Good food, fresh air, nothing strenuous that
she wasn't used to, but don't turn her into an
invalid.

Her voice was friendly, normal, answering his
questions, but he was always aware of the
distance between them, of his own unease in her
presence. He could never forget his memory of

225

the beech trees, and the way she had conjured it into his mind when he had laughed at her concern for the health of the willows. There was something about this tall old woman that was like a warning, always present, never spoken, never quite forgotten. And yet he would allow her closer to him than anybody except Faith, because of her search for knowledge. She would ask him questions, and touch his body, and he would answer and watch her hands. The doctors, those men of supposed learning, Ben would tell the doctors nothing more. They always believed they knew more than he did, that they had nothing to learn from him, so they never would learn, not from Ben Jacardi. But Mrs Webster, no matter that she made him so nervous, he trusted her. She didn't know everything, maybe not as much as the doctors, but where they had stopped their studies when they left their universities, she went on, and would do so until she died.

'If happiness can heal, she's as good as cured,' said Mrs Webster at her door. 'Good night, Mr Jacardi. Let her rest here for a little while, and be here for the birth, if you can.' Then she reached out and touched his forehead, and her eyes seemed to go cloudy and dark.

'When you have power over your enemies, be merciful,' she said. 'Your child and theirs will need each other.'

Ben stared at her, and then she was looking at him, everything quite normal again, but she touched her own forehead, and seemed to wince.

'Good night, Mr Jacardi,' she said again.

There was starlight, bright starlight, and Ben

226

ran nearly all the way back to *Grey Lady*. He arrived out of breath, and stumbled down the steps, laughing. Faith was awake, watching for him, smiling at him.

'Oh, Faith, darling Faith.'

'We're going to have a baby,' she said, and Ben dropped to his knees beside her, taking her hands in his. Yes, they were going to have a baby. Mrs Webster had said something about the baby, he couldn't quite remember what, but he knew she'd seen the child.

She'd said nothing about Faith, his darling wife who lay on their bed, white-faced and weak, but smiling up at him. What about her? He was looking down at her, trying to answer her smile, but there was dark anxiety clouding his mind, and he didn't know what to do.

'We'll stay here for a few days,' he said, and Faith tried to protest. They were needed, with this load, back in Birmingham. No time to wait here.

He listened to her as she fretted about losing time, and he smiled down at her because, compared to what he feared, her worries were so small, such little problems. A few strong words from whoever was in the office, a couple of dirty loads because they'd been late, but Faith had nearly died. She was alive, with a light in her eyes he'd never seen before, but she had nearly died, and she wasn't well yet. What were a few strong words and a bit of extra work cleaning the boat compared to that?

The next morning Ben went to the cottage where Faith's parents lived, the same farm

227

cottage from which he had fetched her that summer evening to take her out into the woods and ask her to marry him. A child told him where to find Mrs Carter, and he went to the farm, and found her trying to lift a churn on to a stand. He took it from her, and she thanked him, and asked him what had brought him off the canals.

'Faith's going to have a baby.'

Mrs Carter leaned back against the wall and pressed her hands to her face. 'A bit late for starting that sort of thing, I'd have said,' but when she lowered her hands he saw she was smiling at him.

'How is Faith?'

'Not too good.'

He told her about the bad fish, how ill Faith had been, what Mrs Webster had said, and when he left he was carrying a boiling fowl to make soup, and a basket of vegetables. He was to call as often as he could. Mrs Carter could always get something good to eat from the farm.

And what he could not come by honestly, he would steal. He'd made that resolution as soon as Mrs Webster had spoken. They'd tried to buy food, and they'd been turned away. They'd made do with what hadn't been good enough for regular customers, and Faith had nearly died.

Faith said she was well enough to go on that afternoon, but Ben refused to move, and when she tried to argue he said he'd lame Billy if she wouldn't rest, and then they'd have to stay. He'd been joking, trying to make her laugh, but when she tried to get up and dress herself he repeated the threat, and he meant it.

'I will,' he said. 'I'll do it.'

Mrs Webster came back that evening, and she brought a basket of apples. She nodded approvingly at Ben's chicken soup, and told him tea would help. First thing in the morning, before Faith lifted her head from the pillow, he was to make her a cup of tea and give her a dry biscuit. Even if she vomited it up again, that was better than nothing, less of a strain.

Where do you steal biscuits? he wondered.

It was a question that kept returning to his mind over the next two days, when they stayed moored in the quiet cutting while Faith recovered. Ben looked into the near future, and saw himself as a thief.

It was not his conscience that troubled him: it was his lack of skill. He thought briefly and resentfully of the times Faith had, returned from a shop empty-handed, her money refused, and remembered that even then the idea of stealing from those shops had crossed his mind, not because of need but for petty revenge.

Mrs Webster came, and brought gifts of beef to be boiled into strong soup, wrinkled apples that still tasted sweet and firm and, most important of all, calm encouragement for Faith.

The vomiting and retching subsided, but weakness remained, and fear that her weakness could cost her the baby. When she opened her eyes in the mornings Ben saw the immediate question on her face: is the baby all right? Am I still carrying my baby? A few seconds as her mind searched her body, tension until the answer came, yes, all's well. Not until then would she

229

look at Ben and smile.

Mr Carter came on the second day, leaning on a walking stick, a little out of breath. There was a slab of cheese in one of his pockets and a loaf tucked into his jacket. How was his daughter today? And the babby that was to be?

Of them all, only Ben had no fear for the child, and he could not quite remember why. He knew the baby would be born, but he did not know whether Faith would come through the birth well, or even alive, nor if the child would be whole and healthy. That, it seemed, depended on him.

On what skills he could develop as a thief.

A few eggs from a hen-house, a cabbage from a garden, that had been easy. That meant nothing more than walking quietly, and listening out for a dog. It had troubled him no more than taking a shovel to the coal they carried. He'd never done it before the war, when they'd been able to buy their food, but he might well go on afterwards. He could do it, and save a few pennies. Since the Cartwrights had stolen their money, and they had so little put by, he would need to save pennies. He'd had to cut into the money they'd saved for docking to pay the doctor at Kidderminster.

The trains ran fast and smooth on well-maintained tracks while the boats carried heavy loads on waterways that were silting up, pulled by horses that stumbled on broken paths. When he heard the boat grinding on the bottom as Billy dragged her over another bar of stones and mud Ben thought of the elm, of which *Grey Lady* was built, being worn thinner every time: she'd have to come out of the water quite soon. It would cost a lot of money to replace the bottom of his boat, and he had no money now, or very little.

Bastards, spending all that money on the railways and none on the canals. Canal companies saying they couldn't pay higher wages because they weren't earning enough, boats standing idle because boatmen were in the navy now, out on the seas, and boats getting damaged on neglected canals. How could he save the money to put a new bottom in his boat?

Biscuits, and beef for good strong soup. That meant stealing from shops, and shopkeepers were wary of strangers.

Faith claimed to be strong enough to steer the boat, so they set off again, and Ben watched as he led the horse, or left him to pull the boat on his own, watched for gardens and hen-houses, and it was no longer the casual glance to see if a door looked rotted around the hinges or hasp; it was a calculating, careful look. A window might be forced or broken.

He looked at cottages, too. Regular customers lived in cottages. They could buy good food, and bring it back to those cottages, where a latch might be left unfastened.

Now that good food had become overwhelmingly important, it seemed to Ben that even his chances to steal had been reduced. *Grey Lady* was in the Black Country, in Birmingham and Wolverhampton, carrying coal again, and where he had previously looked from the towpath into fields and woods, where there might at least be the possibility of snaring a rabbit, now he looked

231

into blast furnaces and wharves.

It was a strange, eerie landscape, especially at night. High buildings loomed over the water, dark and menacing against a sky lit red, seeming as if they leaned down over the boats, threatening them. There were iron skeletons of the cranes and gantries, red fire in caverns where men shovelled the coal the boats had carried. There were black brick arches, like great mouths, and boats would sometimes slip into those arches, and although Ben knew it was only to be unloaded and that they would slip out again a few hours later, it always seemed to him as if they had been swallowed and would never return.

Evenings were not spent trudging on paths made slippery by rain, thinking ahead to places where stakes could be driven into firm moorings, but on dirty gravel and cinders, looking to moor only in a place that would be quiet enough to allow some sleep. It wasn't sweat and dust he brushed out of Billy's coat, but black grit. Hours were spent waiting to load and unload coal, in an atmosphere blackened by floating soot, and Ben, leaning against a wall and listening to the other men talking, wondered whether Faith needed clean air as well as good food.

There was nothing he could do about that, so he listened instead to men as resentful as he was of shopkeepers who would not sell to their wives, of the stretches of the canals that were almost impassable, of the lies they had been told about the war. Some had not waited as long as he had before turning to theft.

The first time, he was lucky. They were in

Tipton, between Wolverhampton and Birmingham, and Ben went into the town. A young lad was trying to push a barrow through a narrow gateway, struggling with it. Ben took a handle from him, helped him, grinned in response to his thanks, and walked on his way with a slab of bacon under his jacket. It had been easy.

Faith knew exactly how much money they had, and she knew the price of bacon, too.

'Be careful,' she said. 'Ben, my love, do be careful.'

They had friends, women whose children could read a little and write their names because of Faith and now tried to repay her with gifts of baby clothes to lay by, with advice, with a kind ear, when they had time to talk. Some of them Faith trusted enough to tell of her fears about Ben, now he had taken to stealing, and that was how he came to find himself in a gang.

They had been unsure at first, and so had he. He hardly knew some of these men, and as for them – Ben Jacardi? Him that breathes so loud and slow? Draw attention, he would.

'Can you breathe quiet?' demanded Saul Preston bluntly, and Ben said he could, for a little while, not for long, not without going giddy and his face red, but a minute or two, if he had to.

Their methods were simple. There would be a diversion, a fight, shouts proclaiming a fire, anything to draw the attention of a shopkeeper and other customers, to take them crowding to a door, and behind them a pair of quick hands could reach over a counter and snatch whatever was within reach and small enough to be thrust into a capacious pocket before the thief joined the others, to look and exclaim. Moments later interest died and the spectators would turn away as the fight broke up or the fire was discovered to be a false alarm, the men walking off in opposite directions.

One fight, one puff of black smoke with shouts of alarm, was enough for four thieves to take what they had already noted as they waited in four different shops. Butchers were the favourites, slabs of meat laid out on white marble, or grocers where the paper packets of sugar stood neatly on shelves within arm's reach. Dried fruit, tea, butter.

Biscuits.

It was not always the same men. The boats were on the move, so the members of the gang could never know who would be there, to steal, or to set the fires. It would be Ben's first thought as they pulled in for the night. Who's here? Are there enough of us to go into town tomorrow? Nods of greeting would be exchanged with all the boaters, but after some of those nods there would be a questioning tilt of the head, which might be answered with a smile, or a wink, and he would know, there are enough of us.

A handful of rags soaked in oil carried in a tin would make black smoke, the job for one man, and for the others, there were the shops to raid.

Sugar, flour, salt, biscuits, bacon and beef.

A gold watch.

They were on their way back from Manchester when that happened, *Grey Lady* loaded with zinc. They moored up with four other boats late one night, and when Ben went to the pub he saw men he knew, who nodded to him and made room for him, and asked him if he would join them the next morning.

Yes, he said, if he could have the grocer, and they agreed. Ben Jacardi was like that, always wanted the grocer, always took a packet of biscuits and some tea. Terry can take the butcher, and there's a fishmonger here: Jack can have that. Tony will do the smoke.

Tea and biscuits, dried fruit and butter. Beef, and some sausages. A couple of fish and some eggs, but who had spoken of the jeweller?

Ben waited to hear what the other men said about that, but none seemed to want to catch his eye, and after a few minutes his dropped, too. Sam was a good thief, quick and bold, and had always brought back more than the rest of them. He'd never claimed more, though, when it came to sharing what they had taken. He'd taken his share and no more, content with the grin of approval they gave him.

No one can eat a gold watch, but no one cared to challenge Sam, who knew a pawnbroker in Worcester who would give him a fair price.

Sam never took his watch to Worcester, because the police came for him that night. He'd been a little too clever, a little too greedy. A jeweller isn't a grocer, and the jeweller had had only one other customer in his shop when the shouts went up as the black smoke billowed out into the street. There'd been Mrs Jefferson, and a small man in corduroy, with a red kerchief tucked into his collar, who'd said he was looking for a birthday present for his wife.

Corduroy, and a red kerchief. A boater.

A small man, yes, with a gold wedding ring on his finger. A jeweller would notice that. Quite a broad ring, it had been, and worn thin. But the man's knuckles had been swollen, so the ring wouldn't have come off.

No grocer would have noticed a thing like that.

Oh, yes, the jeweller was pretty sure he'd know the man again. And, come to that, Mrs Jefferson would too. Probably.

So, Sam Dobson, quick Sam Dobson, thief Sam Dobson, who set the fire, then? Who'd been in the fishmonger's, where a pair of mackerel had gone missing? Swam off, did they? And the biscuits and butter from the grocer?

Questions are asked when a valuable watch goes missing, and other shopkeepers had answered some. They'd started with much the same words: 'Now, there's a funny thing, then.'

One man stealing a bit of bacon for his pregnant wife, because he couldn't buy food when he tried, now that could be understood, and dealt with leniently, but a gang, and boaters at that, little better than vagrants, that was a different matter. A gang planning their crimes and stealing from honest, decent tradesmen, respectable people, nobody could say that should be dealt with leniently. That was a serious matter, and an example must be made.

Quick Sam Dobson, not so quick with his fingers broken, and not so quiet either. None of them blamed Sam when, in the end, he gave the names.

236

There was no sympathy either for Sam Dobson, named as the ringleader, when he told such dreadful lies about the police, when he said they'd broken his hand to make him give the names. All decent people knew that thieves would say anything to get themselves out of trouble. Sam Dobson had named his gang to try to gain favour and, given the choice between the word of a thief and that of a sergeant of the police, who would they believe? The thief had broken his hand trying to escape from his cell, when it had become trapped between the bars over the window and he'd slipped and fallen.

Faith knelt beside her bed, and prayed. Everything she had, she offered to God if God would save Ben. Everything except her baby.

She and two of the other women went to the church, because prayers in a church might be holier than prayers on a boat. They crept in, and they went to a pew at the back where no one would notice them, and they prayed for their men. Sam Dobson's hand had been broken. God, save Terry and Ben and Tony. Please, God, don't let them break our men's bones.

Sarah Dobson was ill, first time ever that that big, tough woman had known a day's sickness, but now she was in her bed and the nurse said it was bronchitis and might turn to pneumonia. She lay there, coughing, and nothing anyone did seemed to help her. Her two children sat beside her, quiet and frightened, watching their mother coughing herself into exhaustion, thinking of their father locked away in the prison, wondering what was to become of them.

'Is she going to die?' Nellie asked Faith, and Faith kissed the top of the child's head, and said no, and hoped she wasn't lying.

There was money in the soap hole, saved for docking *Grey Lady*, and getting a little less every day. Faith had never touched that money before, and every time she took a few more pennies she thought of the money Violet Cartwright had stolen from them, and her hatred grew fiercer.

There was nothing any of them could do, and one by one the women moved the boats on, working alone, or with their children. Faith stayed longer than the others, watching them as they went, wishing them well, praying for them as the horses pulled the long, heavy boats away, led by children, or walking alone. She watched little Nellie Dobson, only eleven years old, standing on tiptoe at the tiller of the boat as Joey, three years younger, led the horse away, and she prayed for Sarah and Sam, and wondered what had gone wrong with a world that could see two little children working a big boat alone, and nobody lifting a finger to help them.

The next day she collected Billy from the stable, counting out the money she owed for him.

Time to go home.

She'd tried to write a letter to her parents to tell them what had happened and ask for their help, but she was too ashamed. She didn't know how to explain that they'd had no choice.

Thou shalt not steal.

If she could have done, she would have stayed away, but there was the baby, and she needed to be at home.

Faith could lie very convincingly, when it was a matter of the welfare of her baby. She told the shopkeepers she'd just arrived from London, moved into a little house on the outskirts of the town, and was hoping her husband would be back from the war before the baby was born. He'd been wounded, and sent home, you see. But the wound had healed, and he'd gone back to his regiment to fight.

Yes, he was a very brave man, and she missed him dreadfully. But the war must be over soon.

The nurse had said she should have beef tea. Did the butcher have a little beef to spare? And did the grocer perhaps have some tea and some biscuits for the wife of a brave man who'd gone back to the trenches once his wound had healed?

Then move on a few miles, because sooner or later someone would mention that they'd seen that little woman with the twisted shoulder getting on to a boat. She'd lied, then. She was nothing more than a dirty boatwoman, no better than a thieving gypsy.

Carefully, Faith moved the big boat on, just a few miles every day, the piebald horse towing it, as he had done so often, alone, obedient to her voice. Carefully, so as not to strain herself, she worked the lock gates alone. Another town, a safe mooring, a stable for Billy, a new butcher, who might perhaps have a piece of beef for the pregnant wife of a brave soldier? A grocer, with a little tea and a packet of biscuits?

Every night Faith knelt beside her bed, and prayed for Ben, for her baby, and for money. Please, God, money, because there isn't much left now, and it's still a hundred miles until we're home.

Sometimes it seemed as if she was praying to Ben. I love you, my Ben. I do love you. I do miss you. Take care of yourself, my love.

Oh, God, please take care of Ben.

No more money, but a Measham teapot to sell, and a couple of lace plates. A nice pair of crocheted curtains to screen off a bed at night? Hand-made, and good work? A few brass ornaments, just for a few shillings?

Only forty miles now, but that's too far. No more money. A painted stool for sale? A good warm blanket, plenty of wear in that, a few shillings? A little brass lamp? A pretty little brass lamp?

A little piebald horse?

11

When she said goodbye to Billy, Faith felt as if she had lost everything. She was standing alone in front of the little horse, who was lipping at her hand with his soft, pink mouth, and there was no one else. One hand at Billy's head, one on her belly, where the child lay quiet. Everything was quiet. It was almost silent that evening, grey clouds overhead, black trees outlined against them, everything so very quiet, and so very lonely.

They hadn't wanted a horse. It was a boatyard, not a livery stable, but yes, you can moor here for the night, my dear. Go into the kitchen and see my wife, there'll be a cup of tea. I'll take care of your horse, he can spend the night in the shed, he'll be safe.

They'd been so kind to her, and Faith had been too weary to lie any more. She'd told them what had happened, that Ben was in prison and she had no money and had to get home for the baby.

'I don't need a horse,' he'd said, 'but I'll buy that good boat. I'll give you enough for her to see you home and safe with plenty for you and the baby.'

No, not *Grey Lady*. No. All she had left that she could sell was Billy.

So kind, they were. They'd given her money for him, and said she could leave the boat there, and they'd watch it until she came back for it. Just a few shillings a week, and pay when you come back for her, she'll be safe here.

Somebody would buy Billy from them, and she was to go home by train, and then by taxi if there was one to be found, or a pony-trap if not. There was enough money paid for Billy for that, and a bit left over.

'God bless you,' she'd said, and then she'd slipped out into the yard to stroke Billy's nose and wasn't sure if it was right, after what God had done for her, to ask one more thing, that He take care of a horse, too. How much could you ask of God before He grew tired of your prayers?

She'd be home that night, back in the cottage, and tomorrow she'd answer the questions, and hope they'd understand. Two strangers had understood, and given her a fair price for Billy and a safe mooring for *Grey Lady*. What about her God-fearing mother and father, could she hope for as much from them?

Thou shalt not steal.

Honour thy father and thy mother.

Ben had stolen for her and the baby. If ever a father deserved honour, it must be Ben, for breaking a commandment for his child.

'Time to go, my dear.'

Kind man, giving her money for a horse he didn't need or want, enough to take her home.

Goodbye, Billy. Good luck.

So Faith went home alone, and late that night slept in the bed she'd slept in as a child, and she'd been too tired to cry, too tired to do more than hug her mother and say she'd tell them every-

242

thing in the morning, but for now, please, only sleep.

She dreamed of two little children on a heavy boat, and the boat was going through a long dark tunnel, and the children were frightened.

'They saved their food for respectable people,' she said to her father the next day. 'There wasn't enough for us. We're not respectable people.'

How could she ever have doubted them? They were old, and they were God-fearing, but they knew people had to eat.

'The Bible's not only about thou shalt not steal,' said her mother, and she was wiping angry tears from her eyes. 'There's a bit about the stranger at the gate, too. Damn them.'

Faith had never heard her mother swear before.

She was home. Where were Nellie and Joey Dobson? What had happened to Sarah?

There were only two months now before the baby was due, but she was home, and there'd be food from the farm, and Mrs Webster not too far away when her time came. The Carters were poor people, and their clothes were shabby and worn. The cottage was in a poor state too, the roof patched with bits of tin, the window-frames warped for lack of paint, rotted by rain, letting in the draughts. But there was enough food from the farm, and it was good and fresh, and there was warmth. Wood could be cut. Warmth, and shelter, and good food was all Faith needed, to keep her baby safe.

Ben should be with her about the time the baby was born, if it didn't come early. Two months to rest, to wait, to feel her baby growing and

243

moving, two months to become calm and patient.

At first she seemed able to do nothing but sleep. Ten hours every night, and then only two or three hours later she felt her eyelids drooping, and went back to the narrow bed in the room under the sloping eaves, and slept again, and woke, and drowsed, and lay quietly feeling her baby moving and stirring in her belly.

Ben, my love, take care of yourself. God, please, help Ben. Look after Ben.

There were three children in the cottage, two little boys and an older girl. Her brothers were in France and their wives worked every day in the town, leaving the children at the cottage early in the mornings and collecting them at night. As if the old people didn't have enough to do, working on the farm.

When Faith thought of that she began to make some effort to help. They were old, her mother and father, and they were having to work as hard as young people because there were no young people left to do the work. So Faith looked after the children in the cottage during the day when her mother went to the farm, and Mrs Carter admitted it was much easier in the dairy without having to watch the children.

Easier to come home to a clean kitchen, too, with a meal halfway to being cooked, and the children washed and tidy, ready to go home to bed.

Faith made the children rest in the afternoons, and she rested with them. They lay on the floor of her room on folded blankets, and she lay on her bed, and the whisperings and scufflings died away as the children fell asleep. Faith lay quiet, and dreamed, and thought of Ben, and counted the days to the time he would be free.

They'd flogged him and put him in prison, and left her on her own. No one had asked about his pregnant wife, a hundred miles from home, with no money except what had been saved to dock the boat. *Grey Lady* needed docking now, because she'd been worn thin over stones and silt that should have been dredged. No one asked how children could manage with their father in prison and their mother ill. The nurse had said bronchitis, could turn to pneumonia if they weren't careful, and she'd left. Who was to be careful? The children? Nellie and Joey, taking their parents' place to work that big boat all the way back to Braunston?

Big Sarah Dobson, strong as a man and twice the size of Sam, who was little and quick and clever, and who could twist a bit of old rope into a fender as soon as tell you about it. Would he be able to do that again, with his hand broken? Would there have been a doctor in the prison to treat a broken hand?

Faith mused over all these things as she lay on her bed in the afternoons, the three children sleeping near her on their blankets, but she pushed away the anger and bitterness. She had become placid. She had made herself calm and placid, in the same way that she had nearly killed her own spirit after Peggy Trafford died, because she had a very strong will and a very strong spirit, and she could make herself be what she wanted to be.

Quiet and calm, waiting for her baby, waiting for her man. The fury that she turned away from herself might have harmed her baby.

The days passed, and the children came in the mornings and went at night, and the old people sat with her by the fire in the evenings, only the three of them in the cottage now. All her brothers and sisters had gone, married and left home, leaving her mother and father alone, and Faith wondered how they would manage when they grew too old. Who would look after them?

For now, they looked after her. If they thought she seemed sad, they fussed over her, and tried to make her smile, but Faith wasn't sad. She was doing what was right for her baby, eating good food and resting, and keeping herself calm. She'd brought the baby clothes with her, those little dresses and shawls she'd made years before, then packed away in a corner of a cupboard. Now they were lying neatly folded and carefully aired in the chest at the foot of her bed. All white, they were, because she didn't know if it would be a boy or a girl. No blue, no pink, everything quite plain, but good and well made. Tiny neat stitches in soft cotton, nothing to chafe a baby's delicate skin, she'd made them all with love, years before, and put them away with love, too, even though she'd been in despair, for the baby she loved that had never come.

Monotonous days, they might have been, one passing like the one before, and the next the same. Early mornings, her mother lighting the lamp and bringing her a cup of tea and a dry biscuit, then up to light the fire and make the breakfast, have everything ready for when the children came, and pack sandwiches for her father to take out into the fields, and her mother off long before daylight.

It was winter, cold and dark until late in the mornings, and dark in the afternoons, but still and quiet. Black shadows on grey land, dark skies, the sun veiled behind thin cloud. Cold mist rising from the frosted, brittle grass. The log pile stacked high beside the kitchen door, only a few steps to bring in the warmth, to keep the children warm, to keep her baby warm.

Please, God, keep my Ben safe. Please keep him warm.

A Christmas baby, Faith had thought, back in the spring when Mrs Webster had come in the night to see her. She'd lost track of the days by then, and it had been hard to count. When was the last time? What day, what week, what's the day today? Was it yesterday I heard the church bells, or the day before? I was ill I couldn't stand. My legs weren't strong enough to hold me, and that vomiting, my stomach hurt, and my head, it was like drums. I can't remember.

My dear, you're going to have a baby.

Try to be here when the baby's due. I'll come and help you.

So, try to be home for Christmas, because it might be a Christmas baby, but I don't know. I can't remember what dates.

The war ended, and Faith, who had cried for the young men and for the waste and shame and pity of it, only smiled when she heard, and waited with her old parents for news of Moses and

Daniel, waited to hear that her brothers were safe, that they had not died in those last few days.

They would be home in the spring.

Keep warm, keep calm, and when the pain is coming too often, too regularly now for it to mean anything else, tell Pamela to go up to the farm and fetch Granny, say Auntie Faith said she should come now. And Grandpa, to go and get Mrs Webster. Saul, you go up to the top field, and tell Grandpa he must fetch Mrs Webster. Put on your coats, it's cold. Take care now, and then come straight home. David, you stay here with me. No, there's nothing wrong. Just fetch Granny and Grandpa.

Too old to have a baby, and a first one at that, but keep calm. The baby's coming.

'Mother, it's time.'

'I know, my dear. We've got everything ready, nothing to fret about. Mrs Webster won't be long, I don't believe, because Mr Fletcher said your father was to take the trap, and that cob's a trotting demon. Now, you just come up the stairs carefully. David, you stay down here. And Pamela, you look after the boys for me. Grandpa won't be long.'

Too old for a first baby, and now these pains are something fierce. But keep calm, and don't cry out or you'll frighten the children. Just keep calm.

'Hold my hands, my dear, and bite on this bit of wood if you need to. It helps a bit. It won't be long before Mrs Webster's here. That cob can go like you wouldn't believe, and it's only a few miles. Hold my hands.'

248

She'd thought the baby would be born in the cabin, but *Grey Lady* was forty miles away, moored up in a boatyard. That cabin would be cold and damp now, would take a bit of cleaning when they fetched their boat. Fetch her back here, borrow a horse because Billy had gone. No more money. Sorry, Billy. Sorry, Ben, but you'll understand, I know that. I know. Won't be the first time you've pulled that boat. Remember the grease I rubbed into your shoulders? I wouldn't let you buy a mule. You'd said we could have a horse, and we were going to have a horse, because you said so. I won't let you be a liar. You never did lie to me, though I thought you had. Wish you'd told me about Paddy Armstrong. Could have trusted me.

There were strong hands helping her, lifting her, a calm voice telling her what to do.

'Turn towards me now. That's right. Now, put your foot on my shoulder, and you push as hard as you can. Go on, now, Faith. You can do it. Now, stop. Breathe, Faith, breathe deep. Not long now.'

Not a Christmas baby. Too soon, and I want my Ben. I wish my Ben was here.

Bright fire crackling in the grate, night had fallen, and there were towels warming on the fender. Her mother was watching, anxious old face, it's a hard birth because she's too old for a first baby.

Keep quiet, bite on the piece of wood, because the children are downstairs and they mustn't be frightened. Going through a dark tunnel on a big boat, I dreamed that, didn't I? There'd have been a tug to take them through the tunnel, if they had any money to pay. Someone would have helped them. Those men on the tunnel tugs, they would have helped two little children, money or none, but the children would have been frightened. It's a long, dark tunnel, a long way before you can see the light.

Light from the fire, cracking warm and bright. Bright gold, and red, and there's blood, too much blood.

Something to drink, something warm and strong.

It was daylight again. The window was grey with the morning.

Drink, Faith. Breathe deep. Not long now. Foot against my shoulder, bite on the wood and push as hard as you can.

So tired. Pushing. Pushing a boat through a tunnel, but Ben was waiting. It was hard, and tiring, but Ben had been there.

Push, Faith. Not long now. Don't you give up now. Push.

'She can't.'

'She must.'

'She's exhausted.'

Yes, she was exhausted. They were all exhausted, Faith and the two women who were with her. Her mother was crying softly, and Mrs Webster's eyes were sunken with weariness, but when she leaned over the bed and spoke her voice was hard and steady.

'Faith, you listen to me, Faith Jacardi. You will give birth to this child. Your man went to prison for this child. Don't you dare give up now.'

Hour after hour this had lasted, these pains, and struggling and straining. Not long now, not long now, but she was too weak. Can't push any more. The light isn't getting any stronger. It's getting dark now. I can't do any more.

'Drink this. Drink it now. Faith, do you hear me? Drink.'

'Our Father, Who art in Heaven, hallowed be–'

A hand, hard and strong, *slap* across her face and her name shouted at her, and she was starting up with the shock and looking into the blazing eyes of an angry old woman.

'Faith Jacardi, don't you *dare* give up! Don't you *dare!*'

'...kingdom come, Thy will be done, on Earth...'

'Now, push. Wake up, or you'll feel the weight of my hand again. Push.'

'They flogged him. They flogged my Ben.'

'I know. Now you save his child, Faith.'

'...forgive them that trespass against us. And lead us not...'

Slap!

'Oh, Mrs Webster, no! Don't hit her.'

'Wake up, Faith Jacardi. Wake up and save this child for Ben.'

For Ben. Just for Ben. Wake up, and bite on this bit of wood, and do what she says. Old, she is, but she's strong and clever.

'Can't do it.'

'Yes, you can. Wake up.'

Stay awake, and push, and drink, because I've lost so much blood now. Drink. What is this? Tastes horrible. But she's strong and clever, do as

251

she says. Drink, and push, and stay awake.

'Push, Faith. Yes, my dear, now it really is nearly here. Push again. Yes, my dear, the baby's coming now. Good girl, Faith. Good, brave girl. Well done, Faith. Well done, my dear. It's all right now. Well done, Faith. He's here now, your baby. He's here, and he's alive.'

Take the baby, then. Hold him close and safe, and everything was worth this, a tiny boy, his face red, his fists clenched and his eyes tight shut. Smeared with blood, this little baby. Mouth opening and closing, eyes screwed shut, and then he gasped, and he was breathing. A little cough, and he was breathing. He didn't have to cry. No one smacked him, no one hurt him, and he was breathing, quietly, quietly, and the screwed-up eyes opened. Blue grey, blurred, his opening eyes. Could he see her? Could he see the face of his mother? Perfect little boy, with his fingers curled into fists, and his blurred blue eyes, and his quiet breathing.

'He's perfect, Faith.'

No one forced him into the world. No one dragged on his arms to pull him out of his mother, twisting him and breaking his fragile body. Perfect, this tiny baby, his arms moving and his face screwing up again, so Faith held him close to her, held his arms to his side, gentle and loving. Keep him close and safe, because it's strange for him, this freedom, able to move his arms and his legs, to kick and wave, but there's his mother's heart beating, and this is a familiar and comforting sound.

'He's perfect, Faith.'

Ben, we've had a perfect baby. He breathes quietly, and his shoulders are straight, not twisted but level. He's only little, and he's very red, but it's normal, that. Ben, we have a son.

The children were there, staring wide-eyed at the tiny child and his exhausted mother, and Faith, dazed with disbelief and bliss, looked at them, and at her father who was standing behind them, tears on his lined cheeks, and at her mother beside him, still praying.

'Sleep now, Faith.'

Tall woman behind them all, smiling at her, triumph on her face. A bad one, that, a hard birth, but they came through, mother and child, safe and whole, and the baby perfect.

You can sleep now, Faith. Hold your baby, your perfect tiny son, hold him against your heart, because that's a familiar, comforting sound to a tiny child new in a strange world, and sleep. Rest now. Gather your strength to nurse your baby.

It was dark in the room, only the glow from the firelight, when Faith woke, and the baby woke with her, opening those blurred blue eyes, little fists waving gently and mouth working, so Faith put him to her breast, and he began to suck. Tiny boy with little wisps of dark hair, little hands relaxed now, on her breast, hungry and sucking, eyes closed again.

'What's his name?'

Her father sitting on the chest at the foot of her bed, keeping watch over the sleeping mother. A weary woman can sleep hard, and a baby can be overlain, so her father had been watching. Her dear old father, who had taken her in, and

253

understood, and now watched to see she didn't overlie her baby.

'What's his name?'

How could she ever repay him, except by naming her baby after him?

'James,' she said, and she saw him smile.

'He's not cried yet,' said her father, but she had no answer. Why should he cry, her little James? He was with his mother, his hunger nearly satisfied now, hearing her heart beating, feeling the warmth of her arms around him. Why would he cry?

'Your mother's asleep,' said her father. 'You had us quite frightened for a little while there, my girl. Do you want your mother?'

'Let her sleep.'

'Do you want his shawl now?'

No. Leave him as he is, naked and perfect in her arms, leave him warmed by the glowing fire and by his mother's body.

'He's perfect,' she said, wonderingly, and the baby sighed, and slept.

'Are you thirsty, my girl?'

She was. Her mouth was dry, and she hadn't realised, until he asked.

'A little.'

Mrs Webster had made beef tea before she left. She'd be back in the morning, and Mr Fletcher had said they could use the trap and the cob as long as was needed. So Faith should drink strong beef tea, and red wine. Where did this come from? Red wine?

'You lost a lot of blood. You nearly died, Faith. Your mother thought we'd lost you.'

254

There was a tremble in his voice. He was old, and he was tired, and he'd been frightened, because he loved her and she'd nearly died. She held out her hand to him, and he took it. He must be tired, but he'd sat at the foot of her bed while she slept, watching to make sure she didn't overlie that precious baby.

Even if I had died, she thought, it would have been worth it.

There were no thoughts of death, apart from that. She was weak and tired, but she was alive, and so was the baby. He slept, or opened his eyes and nuzzled for her breast, and sucked, and slept again. Sometimes he sighed, or murmured, but he didn't cry. Faith's mother fretted about it, thinking it wasn't natural, but Faith was content. Why should he cry? He was warm, he was fed, he was with her, sleeping close against her body, where he could hear her heartbeat.

It was a dreaming time for Faith. It would be a while before she would recover from the birth, quite a long time before she would be strong again, having lost so much blood. Mrs Webster never spoke of her weakness and exhaustion as if it was an ordeal, but her mother worried.

Sleep. Feed the baby, wash him, keep him warm and clean, and sleep again. Hold him close and safe, and dream contentedly, because she was out of the tunnel now, and there were no more visions of darkness and fear. The three children came into the room and looked at the baby, touched his head with tentative fingers, whispered to each other, and left them to sleep again. There were other visitors, too, who came into the room, and spoke kindly, left gifts for her and James, and Faith would look at them, and smile, but she hardly ever spoke other than to thank them, and it was never more than a moment before her eyes returned to her baby. The visitors looked at the baby, and looked at Faith, and saw a woman and a child so absorbed in contentment and love that they were oblivious to anything outside themselves.

Ten days after the baby was born Ben came back, and he went into the room where his wife and child lay sleeping, and he knelt by their bed and laid his head on the pillow beside them, and he slept too. It was his first sleep for three days, because he had walked the hundred miles that had separated them, and had not stopped to rest until he had reached them.

When Faith woke a little later, opening her eyes to find him beside her she touched his thin face, and kissed it, and then for the first time since she had reached home she cried, because Ben's crisp dark hair that she had loved to stroke had turned grey, and there were lines on his face, and he was old.

12

It was not only his hair that had turned grey. Ben's view of life seemed to be seen through a grey haze of sullen resentment. He had become taciturn, almost monosyllabic. He was reluctant to meet anyone's eyes, looking away over their shoulders, or down at the ground.

When he and Faith were alone together she caught glimpses of the man she loved, but as if from a distance. They spoke together, they touched, they lay in their bed together, and the walls of the prison lay between them.

He knew Faith had nearly died bearing the baby, and he knew who had saved her. He thanked Mrs Webster, and as he did so his voice broke, and he raised his hands to his face. She took him out of the room, and talked to him, but he would never tell Faith what she had said. When he came back to her he was calm again, and he looked at the baby with a thoughtful frown on his face.

'He's perfect, Ben,' said Faith.

He nodded and kissed her. 'Yes.'

'Don't you want to hold him?'

'He's so small.'

He was growing quickly, and his eyes were beginning to focus. He would smile at his mother, and although Mrs Carter insisted it was only wind, Faith knew it was not.

'James,' said Ben, looking into his son's face. 'James.'

He seemed to be tasting the name.

James seized his father's finger and grasped it strongly. Ben was surprised at the strength of the grip, even impressed. He took to offering the baby his finger, and each time James gripped it and held on to it he smiled.

There were thin white scars on Ben's back.

He had got into the habit of sleeping on his stomach, his face turned to the wall, of sleeping as close to the wall as he could. Faith tried to bring him back to their old way, but even if he did fall asleep holding her, it would only be a little while before, in his sleep, he would turn away from her, and from then on sleep restlessly, but always returning to the same position, close to the wall, his face turned towards it.

Faith stared at the scars, and pushed away the rage that might have disturbed the placidity she needed for the baby. She touched them as Ben slept, and he sighed in his sleep, but didn't move.

She slept more lightly than ever now, alert to the needs of the baby, who spent the nights in a cradle at the side of the bed. Faith responded every time he woke, rejecting her mother's advice to let him cry, that it was natural for babies to cry. She would pick him up and nurse him until he fell asleep again. Sometimes when she fed him in the night Ben would wake, and watch them both. One night she reached out for him, and drew his head close, on to her other breast, and all three of them lay together. James opened his eyes at the change of position, and father and son gazed into each other's faces, grave and curious.

Ben found a job on the railway. No one mentioned his breathing. They all assumed he'd been gassed, and were amazed that he could do a normal man's work. The pay was good, and there were opportunities for theft.

He was a thief.

He had learned how to be a thief in prison. He would never again work in a gang, leaving himself at the mercy of another thief, and he would never again be an honest man, if his wife was in need.

'You don't need to steal,' said Faith. 'We have enough.'

He wanted to fit an engine in *Grey Lady*. She needed a new bottom, too, and that would not be cheap. He would not buy another horse, and he would not go back to the canals until he had enough money, either earned or stolen, to set up his boat as he wanted her.

He listened to Faith, and he talked to her. He explained, as best he could, how he felt, but there was a gulf between them on this. All he would concede to her was that he would only steal from the companies, from the wagons on the railways; since she felt so strongly about it, he would not break into people's houses, nor pick pockets, although that skill, too, he had learned.

When she asked him about prison he tried to tell her what it had been like, but she stopped him. He was searching for unfamiliar words to tell her of a grey hell of helplessness and misery, and he grew more and more tense as he stumbled over his explanations, so she laid a hand on his mouth, told him to stop. He wanted to forget, if he could, and she would not remind him by asking him to speak of it.

That was not the way to break down the wall.

Ben went to the boatyard where Faith had left *Grey Lady*, taking money with him to pay for her moorings. When he came back he said that they could fit an engine for him, a Bolinder, and put in a new bottom, but he wanted to do most of the work himself. He wanted to learn about the engine. He knew nothing. He could work at the boatyard to help pay for the engine, but it would be quicker to keep his job on the railways and save his money.

Billy had been sold to a local dairy, and had pulled a milk cart for a while, but then he'd been sold again, and no one knew where he was. Six months earlier, Ben would have been distressed. Now, he didn't seem able to feel anything for the horse. Faith and the baby were his world, or the part of it that mattered. *Grey Lady* was their home, and he would take them back to her, when he and the boat were ready. Perhaps there it would all be right again.

In order to get the boat ready he would work, and he would steal. Some of what he stole he could show to Faith before he took it to the shops and the yards he had been told about in prison; some he could not. Faith did not like him stealing, and particularly did not like him stealing from the passengers, or from houses, and thought he had promised not to do it. But Ben was a thief, and he would steal. He was good at it.

He didn't need the diversions, the shouts or the

black smoke. He needed only for someone to look away for a moment, for a foreman to turn his back when no one else was around. And he knew what to steal. There was no point in taking anything, no matter how valuable, no matter how easy, if it could not be sold quickly. Keeping what he had stolen was dangerous, and therefore foolish. Steal and sell, as quickly as possible. And the money? Where did you get the money? Saved it. Worked for it. Wasn't always a railwayman. Was a Number One, and we were careful. Had a lucky win on a horse, a bet between friends.

The men he worked with said he was a surly bastard. He'd hardly ever speak. Wouldn't even say where he'd been gassed. Never stop for a word or two, never even give you a fag, lucky if you got a light. And don't trust him either.

Not because they knew he was a thief; far from it. Because he would not join in their own small schemes. A few bits of copper or brass, there's a scrap-dealer who gives a good price. Not that bastard Jacardi, wanted nothing to do with it. More fool him, leave him out of it.

So Ben stopped taking what he had stolen to that particular scrap-dealer, and went a little further afield when the work finished in the evenings. He carried rabbit snares and a catapult. He was going out to get a rabbit for the pot. Nothing wrong with that.

Worked hard, mind. Always worked hard. Wouldn't think he could do it, with lungs like that. Probably the Somme, that was probably it. Funny, though. Most of them that got the gas can hardly lift a hand. Jacardi, he can go all day.

261

Funny, that. Something strange about Jacardi. Leave him out of it. Leave him alone. Surly bastard.

Moses and Daniel came home from France, and didn't want to talk about the war. They'd been lucky, leave it at that.

Old James had told them the boys would be bound to ask. Their uncles had come home in uniform, been soldiers, so the boys would be bound to ask. Make up a story or two.

'Would they like a story about my best mate drowning in the mud at my feet, and me not strong enough to pull him out? Or the rats that ate the bodies, that be a good story? Sorry, Dad. Sorry. You're right. We'll try to tell a story.'

'Dad, how long is Ben going to be here? Can't stand the way he breathes. Reminds me... How long?'

Not much longer. A wallet here, a lady's pearl brooch there, silver candlestick from a house on the other side of the village, a couple of pounds from the collecting box in the church. Money earned on the railways. Money saved and counted, three hundred pounds would do it. Forty miles to the boatyard, walk that in a day now, no trouble. Work on *Grey Lady*, no wages but your keep and all the materials, the elm and the engine. And the boat out of the water, work on her here. Line out the cabin, make it warm and dry, and then bring Faith and Baby James home. Home to *Grey Lady*.

A bit of information, what's on those trains with the guards? Where do they stop? A silver-gilt carriage clock from a crate in a van. Fragile, handle with care, blue and white china, Meissen. Worth a bit, that. Anything else going to that address? No more china, no. Too difficult to place, too easy to break.

They've got a big dog at that house, but they're not there in the week, and there's a new housekeeper. She's nervous of the dog, gets the gardener to shut it in the stable at night. The stable's on the other side of the house.

Twenty pounds for telling them that.

Save the money and count it, put it in the tin under the floorboard. Tap that floorboard back down, quietly, rest the leg of the bed on it. No sign that it's ever been moved.

'Ben Jacardi, how much longer are you going to be living in this house?'

'Oh, Moses!'

'No, Mother, we've a right to ask. We're crowded here now, and he frightens the children. Faith and Baby James, that's different, but we've a right to know. How much longer, then?'

'I go tomorrow.'

'No need, Ben! Moses, you've no right to speak like that. Ben. Ben?'

He'd wanted to leave some money for Faith and Baby James, but there wasn't enough. There wasn't even the three hundred pounds yet, but he'd go. He'd find the rest somewhere. Get *Grey Lady* out of the water, put a new bottom on her and an engine, a big thing of brass and green-painted iron, a thing he didn't yet understand but had to have. No more horses for Ben Jacardi. No need to look for a stable every night: an engine doesn't need shelter in the cold.

Faith was silent, but when she thought he was asleep he heard her crying, and there was nothing he could say to her. He wanted to explain, he wanted her to understand, but he could not understand himself, and had no words with which to explain.

He wanted to tell her, I am the same man. Grey-haired and scarred and a bit thin, but I am Ben, and I love you. I love you just as much as I did that night you poled *Grey Lady* through the tunnel. I love that boy, too, that little baby. I love you both.

He tried to find the words. He tried to rehearse them in his mind, and thought of turning to her and telling her, but the words shifted before he could move, and instead he was thinking, No, I am not the same. I am grey-haired and scarred and a bit thin, and my thoughts are grey too, and the scars go down to the soul, and what can I tell you? I only know I love you, if that's still worth anything.

Better to pretend to be asleep, and not to know you're crying.

Faith lay beside him, as quietly as she could, and wondered if her love would be enough to heal the wounds. She wanted to tell him that she loved him and understood, but she did not understand, and doubted if she ever would. It must have been terrible, to have done that to him, but it was over, and they were together, weren't they? Now he was going away again. Why couldn't the three of them go together? They would have managed, somehow. He hadn't even spoken of it. He hadn't even said he wished she was coming with him.

But it was better he didn't know how much that hurt, so she would be as quiet as she could and let him sleep. He had a long way to go tomorrow. He needed his sleep.

Ben didn't bother to tell them, at the railway, that he was leaving. He kissed Faith, touched the baby's head, and couldn't even bring himself to look into her eyes. He didn't think he could have borne that, looking into her eyes. Hardly any time at all, and he was going away again. So he walked off, and didn't look back, and felt the lump in his throat would choke him, and he was nearly blinded with unshed tears.

Faith could hardly see him as she walked away. Her mother came up behind her and laid a hand on her shoulder, but she, too, could think of no words.

'It won't be for long,' she said at last, and Faith thought, No, it won't take him long. Whatever it is he has to do to the boat, it won't take Ben Jacardi long, he's good with boats. But there are other things that may take for ever, and still not be right.

Through his choking misery, Ben knew it would be good to be back on a boatyard. As he walked along the paths, he wondered whether he would be able to remember the skills Josiah and Jed had taught him, or whether he would be clumsy with the tools, or slow.

It turned out to be much as he had thought.

At first it had been difficult, and he had paused with the adze in his hand, hefted it, willed himself to remember, for his hands to work as they had worked before, quickly and surely.

Freddie Johnson told him to take his time. He knew Ben was a good boatbuilder. The more he had looked at *Grey Lady*, the more he had admired the skills that had gone into her. She was a lovely boat, and the man who had built her knew what he was doing. He had hoped Ben might stay on and work at the yard. The competition in the boatbuildmg trade was getting fierce, and only the good ones would survive.

'Take your time,' he said. 'Put in a bit of practice. Smooth off those planks, the short ones. See how you get on.'

But Elizabeth Johnson had been nervous of him. She tried to avoid him, and after a few days asked Freddie if they couldn't get rid of him.

'I don't like him. Doesn't look you in the eye, hardly a word out of him, the man's barely civil. And that noise he makes, it's horrible.'

'Gas, Lizzie. He can't help that.'

'I suppose so. I don't understand that. Mrs Jacardi never said anything about gas, did she? You'd think she'd have said. Please, Freddie. Tell him to go.'

But Freddie had reached an agreement with Ben, and was reluctant to break it. It shouldn't be long before the work on *Grey Lady* was done. There'd been enough money to buy the engine, and while they were waiting for it to be delivered Ben could finish the two butties on the hard standing. That would pay for the elm for *Grey Lady*'s new bottom, and for most of the materials he'd need to convert her.

'I don't want him in the house. Freddie, he

266

does make me nervous, he really does. He frightens me.'

Freddie tried to laugh her out of her fears, but although he would never admit it to Elizabeth, Ben made him nervous, too. There was a bitterness about the man as sharp as an east wind. Little Faith Jacardi, pregnant, exhausted and desperate, had touched him. He'd wanted to help her. He'd wished, when he waved her goodbye from the platform as the train steamed out of the station, that there had been more he could do for her. He'd bought the horse, kept the boat, and taken her to the station, a packet of sandwiches in her pocket, and still wished he could have done more. Nothing about her had prepared him for Ben.

He didn't know what to do about Ben.

Ben slept and ate in *Grey Lady*'s cabin. As soon as it was light enough to work, and for as long as it was light enough to work, he worked. He finished the two butties and painted them, and he helped Freddie and two men from the town to launch them. He poled them out to their moorings, and then the four of them winched *Grey Lady* out of the water and up on to the big iron trestles.

As soon as she was settled into place Ben was under her, eyes and hands moving quickly over the grooves and hollows in the hard elm, the places where it had worn thin, worse than he'd thought, and those where she was still sound, better than he'd feared. This to be cut out and replaced, and this, from here to here, but the middle was still good.

Measure, and think, and remember.

I made her, he thought. She's mine. More than just buying her, I made her. Even fought for her, once. Oh, but she's a good, tight boat, *Grey Lady*. Dry as they come. But this here, take this out now and put in new, as tight as I did before.

The skills had come back. The tools had become as familiar to him as his own hands, and he hardly had to think now as he worked with them. Years ago he had used tools like these to build this boat. He'd been a boy. Josiah had watched him, Jed had come in and helped when it was work for more than one man, but he had built this boat.

Freddie Johnson was on the other side of the trestle, crouching and peering up at the bottom of the boat. Ben glanced across at him and looked away. My boat. I made her, not you. Mine.

'I thought she was good when I offered to buy her,' said Freddie. 'She's even better than I'd thought.'

Ben never did smile, but for a moment Freddie thought he could imagine how that tense, hard face would look with a smile on it.

Ben had always tried to load *Grey Lady* heaviest in the fore-end and the back-end, leaving the two centre areas lighter, to keep the bottom planks tight up against each other. When Billy had pulled *Grey Lady* over the bars of stones and silt by the bridge holes Ben had heard her rolling and scraping, hard and loud as the bows hit, quieter as she rode over them, and then again the grinding until she was free, and into the deeper water. It had made him wince, that noise, as if it

268

was his own skin being dragged across the gravel, grazed and cut.

Not as bad as he had feared, though. The fore-end and the back-end, he'd replace all of that so she'd be as good as new, and a few of the planks under the cabin, where he'd thought that the whole bottom would have to come out. Could have been so much worse. Should have earned enough money to buy those planks by now. Could be in the clear now. Could be floating free. Only a few more days.

Freddie was calculating, muttering to himself as he peered up at the boat's bottom.

'Seems I owe you,' he said. 'Just the five on the fore-end and a couple on the back-end, what's the damage under the cabin?'

'The whole of the fore-end, the whole of the back-end, four under the cabin.'

'But there's no need,' protested Freddie. 'There's years of wear.'

Ben felt anger flash into his mind. My boat. I know her, every rivet, every knot of wood. I felt her go over those stones. Mine. And I'll make her right.

'The whole of the fore-end, the whole of the back-end, four under the cabin.'

No sign of a smile now, nothing on that face to suggest it had ever known how to smile. Freddie backed out from under the boat and straightened up.

'Your boat,' he said. 'We'll have to change the stern anyway, to take the propeller,' he added as he walked away.

The evenings were growing longer and lighter,

and Ben worked until he could no longer see to do so. She'd been a tight boat, hardly needed to lie in the water more than a day or so before the wood swelled up enough to make her dry. She'd be like that again, his boat. And build the engine room, because that brass and iron thing he had to learn about would be here next week. Could you come to know an engine the way you knew a horse? Know how it felt on a cold morning, stiff and a bit reluctant to start work? Know when it would stop? How strong was this engine? And that bronze propeller, those blades, turning the water the way Freddie had said, sucking it back behind the boat, so it made a hole in the water and the boat fell into the hole. He couldn't picture that.

Got to learn all this. Got to learn from Freddie. Freddie was good to Faith. Got to try to remember how to be friendly. Got to learn. Freddie's going to teach, so try to be friendly. He's a good man.

Shut up in the prison, it hadn't only been walls and bars, it had been a cage around his mind. Whatever you do to my body, I can keep you out of here. This is me, and you cannot touch me here. Thieves there'd been, real thieves, and men who had robbed others with knives and clubs, men who had raped. Ben could understand the thieves. Stupid men, most of them: some could hardly speak, let alone read or write. What they stole, they spent, never thought anything about it. Never thought of what would happen. Life meant stealing, and spending, and getting caught, and prison, wait to get out again, steal and spend.

270

Some hardly seemed human. One, a big man about Ben's age, so far as he could tell, was like a huge, bewildered child, always trying to please. If you could make him understand what you wanted him to do, he would do it, and look hopefully for approval.

Stand there. If anyone comes, hit them on the head with this.

Yes, Andy.

Ten years in prison.

Shut out the anger and the pity along with everything else. But learn. Learn how a window catch, even a stiff one, can be moved quietly. Learn how coins from a pocket can be slid up a sleeve without clinking, what can always be sold quickly, and what takes time. Learn who will buy, and what to say to them, when you first go into the shop or the scrapyard or the pub with something to sell. Learn the names to give. Learn the places to avoid.

Learn to watch, and listen, and say nothing. Learn not to look anyone in the eye. Learn to answer with as few words as possible, and then stay silent. Be quiet, be still, be invisible.

Survive.

There'd been noises in the night. It had never been silent. Murmuring noises, men snoring, whimpering, sometimes crying. Turn to the wall, keep close to the wall, so if you whimper in your sleep no one will hear.

Keep your distance. Some of the men look at you, look you up and down. Don't look back. Keep away for as long as you can, but think and plan, and when it happens, be ready, know what

271

you will do, and do it as violently as you can. Make a name for yourself, a man best left alone.

It was time to unlearn some of that, if he could. Freddie Johnson was a good man, and he'd been kind to Faith. Time to unlearn, if you can.

'Good morning, Mrs Johnson.'

Look at her, he told himself, but his eyes dropped, he couldn't help it. She was too surprised to answer, and she backed away from him. Why had she done that? He'd wished her a good morning.

Should have looked at her. Should have smiled. Try again tomorrow.

The engine came, in a big crate on the back of the carter's wagon, and Freddie and Ben lifted it clear with the pulleys on the iron frame. *Grey Lady* was ready for her engine, eight feet of cargo space lost to make room for it. But the boat can earn more with an engine than with a horse, go further, and faster, if the water's deep enough. Don't have to stop in the towns for a stable.

Big and heavy, the iron painted red and green, the copper pipes and the brass dull. There'll be a shine on them before long.

Freddie knew what he was doing, how to swing the main part, that heavy bit, on the chains and through those side doors. Freddie could do it by himself, probably. He'd watched Ben working on the boat, told him how to lay the new oak keelsons alongside the main one, long as you like, he'd said.

'Spread that load as far as you like. Five feet out into the cargo space because that engine could shake herself loose if you give her a chance. Do

272

that first, build your engine room over that, and give yourself room.'

'Yes,' said Ben, and then, remembering, 'Thank you.'

Freddie checked, uncertain, looking across at Ben. Their eyes met, and Ben seemed to flinch away, but glanced back again, and held the look, steady.

'Right,' said Freddie at last. 'Raise the cabin roof too, because there's a shaft to go under the floor.'

'Yes,' said Ben again. 'Yes.'

Working on the boat he didn't have to think about Faith, didn't have to worry. When it was too dark he'd stop, eat something, then try to sleep, but often he'd lie staring up into the dark, thinking about Faith and the baby. James. His son. It had been bad for her, too. How desperate had she been before she'd sold the horse? Pregnant, and working the boat on her own. He'd known she would try to get home before the baby was due, and thinking about it had driven him nearly crazy. Some of those locks were so heavy. Would there be anyone there to help her? No money, either. Just a few pounds in the tin at the back of the soap hole that wouldn't last. Little Faith, on her own, not a young woman any more.

Those were the nights when he'd buried his face in his arms and pressed himself against the wall, because he, too, would be whimpering.

She was safe at home now, and the baby was perfect. As time had passed he'd dreamed of coming home to her, and he'd walked for three days, and found her asleep, and slept beside her, but the grey walls hadn't come down. He'd tried to reach her. He'd wanted so much for it all to be as it had been before.

He'd been freed from the prison, but he couldn't escape.

Now all his hopes were here, on his boat. This was their home, *Grey Lady*. Perhaps here it could all be as it had been before. Perhaps, if he made her as good as she could be, this boat, Faith would understand that he did truly love her, even though the words when he said them didn't sound the same any more. He had to force himself to say them: I love you. 'I love you, too,' she'd said, and she'd smiled, but the smile was like his words. She'd made herself smile. Inside his mind he'd been crying out to her, 'But I do love you, Faith. I do.' The smile she'd put on her face as she answered had hurt more than he could have believed.

He'd rebuild that whole cabin now, and while he was doing it he'd put an extra layer of wood inside, to keep her warmer, because there was a baby, and Faith loved that baby. Keep her baby warm for her.

Freddie told him what to do, but not how to do it, and sometimes he came over and watched. He told Elizabeth she might have to get used to Ben Jacardi and his strange ways, because if he could, he'd keep him.

'He's not so bad,' said Freddie.

Elizabeth sighed. 'Perhaps not.'

Ben had been trying to unlearn those strange ways. He sometimes managed to smile now, and he could look Freddie or Elizabeth in the face

274

when he wished them good morning. He couldn't look at strangers, but the Johnsons were people he felt he could speak to, although it still made him feel tense. When he knew people were near him he was uneasy, although it was not so bad if it was only Freddie. But he couldn't stand anyone behind him.

He was only relaxed when he worked on his boat. Then, he was confident and comfortable. Freddie told him about the keelsons, and about the engine bearings that had to be fixed to them, with bolts or spikes, better to use spikes, as he had on the main keelson, driving them up through the elm, right through the hard English oak, hammer the roves down on to the spikes to hold them tight against the wood, split them and turn them, clenches hammered down flat. Nothing this side of Judgement Day would move a keelson that Ben Jacardi had fixed.

More oak laid on the new keelsons to carry the weight of the engine, and cross members to hold everything steady. Ben, frowning over his work, felt as if he was making a cage for a dangerous wild animal. What sort of a thing was this that could shake his boat to splinters if the bearings weren't long enough? Need to be careful, with something that strong and that savage.

Have to change the stern of the boat, too. *Grey Lady* had been shaped like a fish, to swim through the water so it flowed past her and behind her, washing against the hull and sweeping away. But leave her like that now and the propeller would suck in air down the sides, and that's no good. Air in the propeller, cavitation, Freddie called it, the

275

boat would hardly move. Sit there on the water with a load of froth at the back-end. Got to build a counter, said Freddie. The counter is a rounded shape, and it goes down just under the water, and that covers the propeller, so there's only water gets into it, no air.

Freddie had said Ben should make plates, set them out from the hull, that would do. Have to change the rudder, too. Ben had listened, and thought about it. When Freddie built a motor boat, he made the stern rounded, not like the horse boats. Ben looked at the drawings of Freddie's boats, and he looked at *Grey Lady*. He didn't like the plates.

He wanted to rebuild the whole stern instead, so she looked as if she was a motor, not something messed about to make do. That seemed to Ben to be second best, and that wasn't as good as *Grey Lady* could be. She had to be as good as he could make her. Second best wouldn't tell Faith what he needed to tell her, when he didn't have the words.

'Take you two weeks to rebuild the hull. More,' said Freddie.

Ben nodded, then checked himself. 'I owe you?' he asked.

Freddie shrugged, and said it wouldn't be too much. If Ben would work a week or so on the new motor, that would cover it.

So Freddie made the drawings for *Grey Lady*, and showed Ben where she would have to be changed, and where she could stay the same.

Take off all the planks from two feet up from the bottom, leave that fish shape. Freddie called

276

that a swim. Cut more planks, and make the iron framing for the new counter, set all that in place, and then he had to work on Freddie's new boat to pay what he owed for the timber and the iron.

He missed Faith. He missed James, found himself thinking of his face, solemn, blunt, no edges to the bones yet. When the baby was asleep it was as if he had thrown himself into oblivion, almost as if he had made a decision, fallen asleep, and gone there. Gone to sleep, another place. Fallen asleep, down until you land there, in that other place.

James awake, sucking on Faith's nipple, looking into Ben's face. Thinking about me, aren't you? Ben had thought. What form do a baby's thoughts take? No words, but you're thinking for all that.

Had he followed Freddie's advice Faith and James might have been with him by now. Only replace the bottom where it had worn thin, never mind the scars and those grooves, leave them. Put in plates instead of building out the counter. That's the way most of the horse boats are converted.

The huge rudder had to be reshaped too, a big angle cut out of it so it swung under the counter.

'She'll be lighter to steer,' said Freddie, and Ben had thought, That's good. Faith's stronger than she looks, but bearing that baby took a lot of the strength out of her.

They put *Grey Lady* back into the canal, slid her down the turf bank. There was a loud slamming noise as she hit the water, a sheet of spray right across to the towpath, a wave washing along the bank, and then *Grey Lady* was rocking and settling. Ben jumped aboard, scrambled down into the hold, and watched for the signs of water seeping through the caulking between the planks. In a few days the elm would have absorbed enough water to swell and make the hull tight and dry, but Ben had always been anxious, just after a boat was launched.

She was low at the stern now, with the huge weight of the engine. The prow rose high out of the water, black, almost menacing. But she was all right. The water seeping in, just little trickles, that would soon stop. She was fine, his boat. She'd be dry and tight, like before.

Freddie stood on the gunwales, looking down into the hold, watching the planks, and when Ben came out of the cabin he smiled at him. For the first time Ben smiled back spontaneously, without any thought.

'Good boat,' said Freddie. 'I'm still offering you that job, Ben. You think about it. A boat's no place to bring up a child.'

Ben shook his head, but remembered to look into Freddie's face and smile again as he did it.

'Think about it,' repeated Freddie. 'I'll give you a good price for this boat. Or you could sell her yourself, if you think you could get a better one.'

But *Grey Lady* was nearly ready, floating stern low, the big bronze propeller in place, the rudder, curiously light now, rehung to take advantage of the water that would rush past it. It would be different, the way she handled.

Ben wrote to Faith, and said she could come home now, then found himself wondering if she

278

would still think of *Grey Lady* as home. He had tried to put the cabin as she had left it, but it seemed dull without her brass ornaments, without the lace plates behind the range, without her precious Measham teapot. He hadn't even noticed that her curtains had gone. He polished the brass, what there was of it, rubbed it until it shone, but he never could bring it to the nearly white gleam that Faith managed.

They'd be together again the next day.

They arrived at the yard exactly as Freddie fired up the engine for the first time. Ben had watched, listened, and done as he was told, with oil and paraffin, lighting the blow lamp, pumping the levers in the oil box, watching Freddie. Ten minutes to heat her up, Freddie had said, and there were levers and rods, this sprays oil, and that makes the engine go faster. Ben had put his hand to his head, and thought, I was mad to do this. Mad. I'll never learn all this.

But Freddie was confident and sure, and he showed Ben how to set the iron peg into the slot in the big flywheel, and roll it back, then kick it forward, hard and quick, and be quick yourself, because she can kick back, like a bad-tempered mare, but this mare's nine horsepower and can throw you clear out through those side doors, to say nothing of breaking your leg.

There'd been a bang louder than anything Ben had ever heard, startled him, and startled the baby awake as Faith stepped down from the pony-trap. Ben shook his head, and Freddie grinned at him, rolled the flywheel back again, kicked again, and the engine fired. That was the noise Ben had heard before, those new boats on the canals, not quite a thud, not quite a chime, somewhere in the middle, and Freddie was moving levers and talking to him, but he couldn't hear.

James was looking towards the boat, where there'd been that loud noise, and now a different noise, and Elizabeth Johnson had come to the door to welcome them, so Faith turned away from *Grey Lady*, and walked towards her.

James began to cry. At first it was only a little noise, a whimper of protest, and Faith's hand rose to his head to stroke his hair. It's all right.

He cried out again, loudly, then howled, louder than he had ever cried before.

'He's frightened of the noise,' said Elizabeth. 'Bring him in.'

But Ben had heard, and was swinging himself out of the boat, calling her name, so Faith turned towards him. James was crying louder and louder, tears welling up into his eyes, and he was beginning to struggle.

'Here, let me take him,' said Elizabeth. 'You go to your man, I'll take the baby inside. It's the noise.'

'No,' said Ben, and never did understand how he knew what his son wanted. 'Bring him to the boat.'

'He's frightened of the noise!'

'No.'

It wasn't so loud. Not too loud, once you got used to it. It was a good noise. That was how this engine was supposed to sound. James's tear-filled eyes were wide, and he was still hiccuping from crying, but he was staring towards the boat, towards the sound he could hear, a sound like a heartbeat, not quite regular, but going on, and on, never stopping. He wanted that sound. He wanted to listen. He wanted to be close to it.

'Bring him to the boat. Please, Faith. Bring him to the boat.'

And please let her still think of it as home.

She stepped on to the deck, carefully, because for the first time she was holding her baby as she did so, but it felt good and familiar under her feet, even though he'd changed it. It was wider now, but it was still the same feel. *Grey Lady* moved as she had before, when Faith stepped on to the deck.

Down the steps, and the cabin was different. It was bigger too, wider, and higher, but only the one step down. Different but familiar, and the sound of the engine was clear and loud and strong, and James was wide-eyed, staring towards that sound.

Different, but familiar, a heartbeat for a baby, a home for a woman.

Faith turned, looked around her. Ben was standing on the steps, watching her with so much anxiety in his face she felt as if her heart would break.

'Oh, my Ben,' she said, and she laid the baby on the bed and held out her arms to him. 'My Ben. It's all right, my Ben. We're home now. We're all home now, Ben.'

13

Freddie Johnson liked engines. There was a kind of logic to them that appealed to his sense of order, as horses never had. If you knew about engines you knew what to do when something was wrong. Horsemen made the same claim for the animals, but Freddie could never understand that. He'd been kicked by horses, and been told what he'd done that made the horse kick, and he never could see the logic. This horse doesn't like that, and that horse can't stand this, and even though it had been an engine that had broken his leg, while horses had never given him worse than bruises, Freddie would never build another horse boat.

For Freddie, a boat without an engine was nothing, a dead thing in the water waiting for a heart to beat.

Grey Lady had always been a good boat, and Freddie had known it from the first time he saw her. Now, though, with the Bolinder thudding in the engine room, with the smoke lifting from the chimney in neat white rings, with the smell of oil and the shine of steel, *Grey Lady* had become a thing of real beauty, a living, breathing thing.

Freddie watched and listened, tightened a bolt here, adjusted a spray there, touched a lever, paused, listened, touched it again, and all the time he was humming to himself, a happy man.

Well, Ben Jacardi should be pleased with this. He'd done a good job, making ready for the engine. And that cabin.

Had that been a baby crying, a few minutes back? Had Mrs Jacardi come then, and brought the baby? So busy with the engine he'd hardly noticed, but now he came to think of it, Ben had gone. First time they'd fired up the engine, what sort of a man would be off out of it, then?

He went to the door between the cabin and the engine room, and there was Ben Jacardi, his arms around his little wife, his cheek resting on her head, and on his face a look of such relief, of such exhausted joy, that Freddie turned away, because he could not understand, and looked instead at the baby lying on the side bed, listening to the engine. The baby's eyes were round and wide, and he was staring at the doorway, and at the man who stood between him and the engine.

That was where the noise came from.

Thump. Thump-thump. Thump. Thump.

That was the heartbeat of the boat, and the baby wanted to see. Freddie smiled down and thought, I'll take you to see, then. That's what you want, isn't it?

But Faith spoke first.

'Mr Johnson. Good afternoon.'

Freddie snatched his cap from his head and nodded to her.

'Mrs Jacardi. I didn't mean to intrude. I was working on the engine.'

She and Ben were standing alongside each other, but Ben still had his arm around her shoulders, holding her close to him. Freddie wasn't sure what to say. It seemed a bit indecent somehow, the man holding his wife like that with a stranger present. It was a bit embarrassing.

He gestured towards the baby.

'Likes the noise of the engine, doesn't he?' he said, and she smiled.

It was Ben who picked up the baby, and Freddie stood aside to let him carry James into the engine room, to look at the heart of the boat.

There it was. Big. Green and red, with brass and copper polished, shining under oil, the flywheel spinning, the whole engine not quite moving but not quite still, alive and warm, and beating.

'Aah,' sighed James.

Thump. Thump. Thump-thump. Thump.

'Aah.'

'He only wanted to see,' said Ben, and James smiled, sighed again, and his eyes began to close.

'He looks like a born engineer to me,' said Freddie.

He was the first to say it. James opened his eyes and looked at this new man, and then one small hand reached towards the engine, fingers out-stretched.

'Aah.'

Ben took him back into the cabin and laid him down gently. James slept quietly on the bed, fists curled up beside his head, face turned towards the heartbeat of the boat.

When at last Freddie was satisfied with all the adjustments, when he could no longer stay in the engine room whistling softly through his teeth, hefting spanners and screwdrivers as he looked

284

for something more to do, when he turned off the engine and the thump, thump, thump slowed and stopped, James sighed in his sleep, frowned, then relaxed again.

'It's going to take a while before I know all this,' said Ben to Faith, when Freddie had gone.

Faith nodded, but she hadn't heard what he said. She was looking around the cabin.

'You've put it back just like before. Only the steps look different.'

He'd tried. He had worked so hard, wanting *Grey Lady* to be her home again, but he couldn't remember exactly how it had been. The brass rods that ran from the engine room to the hatch, the brass wheel, the handles, all those pieces that Freddie called the controls, he hadn't been able to hide them, but at least he'd polished them, and Faith always had liked a bit of brass. Between the engine room and the cabin, he'd painted the door with the castle scene like the one on the bed hole, yellow castle, blue water, and swans. It wasn't quite as good as Faith would have done it, but he hadn't had much time. He'd missed her. He'd wanted her to come home to him and to the boat.

Her hair was all grey now, none of the brown left. It was white at her temples. There were deep lines on her face, too. Out in all weathers, that was what had carved those lines, wind and sun, snow and rain. A boatwoman's face now. Faith had been a farmgirl, but she'd become a boatwoman, not only in her skills but in her wariness of outsiders.

She must have been truly desperate to ask the

285

Johnsons for help. But there'd been boats in the water, narrowboats like *Grey Lady*, and the people had been kind. Rough words would have sent her on her way without protest, but their kindness had broken through, so she'd told them her secret, because she didn't know what to do next. My man's in prison, and I'm pregnant, with forty miles to travel before I'm home, and I've no more money, and nothing left to sell except the horse.

'We'll get some new lace plates soon,' said Ben. 'And I'll make you another stool.'

'We'd better get back to work, then.' Faith was smiling at him.

'I don't understand that engine yet,' Ben said.

She laughed. 'It took a year or two before you understood the animals. It never stopped us.'

James stirred in his sleep, one hand opening and reaching out. His mouth worked, and then he was still again. Ben and Faith watched him.

'Born engineer,' said Faith, smiling again. 'Better ask James about the engine. He loves it.'

'Better ask Freddie to teach him, maybe,' said Ben, and although he was smiling too, Faith could see the doubt behind it.

But it didn't take him as long as he had thought it would. The following morning he looked at it again, a big lump, with bits running off here and there, pipes and things, and gadgets. That flywheel with the peg you kicked to start it. A blowlamp to heat it all up before you could do anything else. A box down there, Freddie had said it had to be full of oil. The oil box, that was it. And diesel, that comes from a tank up on the bulkhead, and down through those pipes.

Brass rods running through the cabin to the side of the hatch, the controls. Controls, yes, like reins on the horse maybe. Push, and pull, and turn.

Never learn all this.

Then Freddie had come over to the boat, walking very quietly, because he thought Faith and the baby might still be sleeping. He didn't know Faith. She'd been up with the range lit and a polishing rag in her hand while Freddie had still been dreaming in his warm bed. Baby James would sleep through a brass band playing six feet away.

'Good morning, Mr Johnson.'

'Mrs Jacardi? You're an early riser.'

Freddie and Elizabeth Johnson were easy and pleasant with Faith, Ben thought. No problem to smile at her, say how bonny the baby looked, how nice it was to see her again. They were still nervous of him, though, despite him always trying to smile when he spoke. He usually looked at them now, didn't he?

He had thought about the offer of a job. He would have liked to build boats again, but not here. Not with Mrs Johnson trying so hard to hide her dislike of him, and not feeling that Freddie was comfortable with him, either. As for Baby James, Faith had taught other people's children. James wouldn't suffer for lack of schooling, no matter where they lived.

'Have you thought about my offer?' Freddie had asked, and Ben had said he had. Then he'd remembered to smile, and look him in the eye before answering.

Learn to start up this engine. That's the most difficult. Pump up that blowlamp, and get it lit, and then there's the diesel and the oil, this bit of pipe, that thing, that with the oil. The oil box, why can't I remember that? And there's the spray, with those injectors, whatever that means, have to adjust that. Pump on these levers in the oil box, four of them, until they're stiff, until they resist, that's what Freddie said. Then push them down until they click. Each one of them, and never forget that. Keep an eye on that blowlamp. Ten minutes in cold weather, maybe as little as six or seven when it's hot. Swing that flywheel up to top dead centre, see that mark? There, on the steel? Right. Slot in the peg, swing it back, and then kick.

And don't you kick me back, you evil old mare.

Thump. Thump. Thump.

Do it again. Kick down a bit harder.

Thump. Thump. Thump-thump. Thump. Thump.

That's it. Let her run a moment. Shut down on that spray, now she's running right.

James will be awake now, only for a few minutes maybe, lying in his cradle with his eyes wide open, listening. It's more than a smile on his face, it's like a look of wonder, or would be, if he wasn't just a baby. Wide eyes closing again, a little smile, turns his head, says something in that quiet voice of his, nothing we can understand, not yet, but it's something to him.

The engine's running now, and you can feel it, all the way through the boat. Freddie was right about those keelsons, and the bearers on them. Make them long and make them strong, because an engine like that can shake a boat into splinters, given a chance. She can kick like an evil old mare, but she's running sweetly now, and a baby, born engineer, he's falling asleep to the song she sings. Strong as nine horses, and more dangerous than the worst of them if you don't handle her right, shining under the oil, and she'll carry this boat for thousands of miles.

There's explosions going on inside that cylinder head. You squash down that diesel so hard, compression's what Freddie calls it, then it explodes, because that pressure makes it hot. Explosions, like a bomb, blow you to pieces, lull a baby to sleep.

Faith was standing at the door between the cabin and the engine room, watching, in a faint blue haze of smoke. She had one hand on the doorframe, and the cuff on her sleeve was trembling from that little movement of the engine that runs right through the boat now.

Will she get used to that? A horse boat, that's quiet and still, going through the water. There's only the sound of water against the hull, slapping at it, a gentle noise, a good noise. Wherever we go now there'll be the sound of the engine, and that shaking, nothing to upset you, nothing to do any damage, but it's there. Will she get used to it?

'It's a grand-looking thing, isn't it?' she said.

Ben thought, Thank you, my love. You said the right words.

'She'll be lighter to steer.'

Faith was looking at the brass and the copper,

289

a smile on her face.

'Whose job is it to clean all that, then?'

'You keep out of my engine room, woman,' he threatened, and her smile turned into a laugh.

Out in the garden, hanging the washing on the line, Lizzie Johnson heard Ben laugh in reply, and when she had finished she went to the workshop and asked Freddie whether Ben had accepted his offer.

'No.'

'Try again,' she suggested, and he looked at her in surprise. 'He's different now Faith's here,' she said.

Ben, holding his wife in his arms, resting his face on her hair, thought that it wasn't only being with Faith that made everything all right, even though he was worried about the engine because he still wasn't sure of it, and there wasn't any money, and he might still owe some to Freddie. It was being with Faith on *Grey Lady* that mattered. Anywhere else, he liked to have her with him, but it was only here, with her, that he was complete.

The baby, little James, might change that, might disturb it. Somehow Ben would have to accept that, and learn how to include him, because although Faith loved Ben, James was the centre of her life. Even now, her face pressed against his chest, her arms around his waist, she was listening for the baby, loving Ben, but listening for James.

James, sleeping in his cradle, dreamed of his mother, warm and close, dreamed her grey hair and her eyes set deep in her lined face, dreamed her voice and her heartbeat, thump, thump, thump, thump-thump, thump.

14

James's first memory was of the engine. His mother laughed when he told her of it, and said it wasn't possible he could remember so far back, but he knew he did. He hadn't been able to walk at the time, although he could pull himself around, standing and holding on to anything within reach. He remembered sitting on the engine-room floor and watching the flywheel.

'I'd never have let you anywhere near the thing, not with the engine running,' Faith protested, and although she laughed as she said it, he knew he'd hurt her feelings. An engine room was a wickedly dangerous place for a child. She would never have been so neglectful.

He did remember, though. And he remembered knowing perfectly well that he shouldn't touch the flywheel. He could watch and listen, and join in the song if he liked. He could hum the song of the engine, and watch the flywheel turning, but not touch until the song stopped.

When he could stand up properly, he was allowed to help keep the engine clean. He was given a piece of rag, and told to wipe the surfaces, but he didn't need to be told. He didn't like there to be dirty smuts on the engine. He wanted it all to be clean and shining, and so, whatever he could see and reach, he wiped away. If he couldn't reach, he would tell his father.

'There. There. Look.'

James measured his growth in terms of the parts of the engine he could reach with his rag.

He knew his family, and he knew his friends, but he couldn't understand why the engine wasn't part of the family. His mother said it wasn't alive, it wasn't part of any family, it was a machine. That made it different.

'Why?'

She tried to explain. It was metal, for one thing. It wasn't alive. Nothing that wasn't alive had a family.

That wasn't good enough for James. He didn't believe it wasn't alive. So, he counted his family and his friends. First, his mother and father. Next, the engine, but when he said his prayers he decided to say that one, 'God bless the engine,' in his mind, not aloud. There were Grandpa Carter and Grandma Carter, and Uncle Moses and Uncle Daniel and Aunt Judith and Aunt Rebecca. And some cousins, Pamela and Saul and David.

When his mother was showing him how to write his name, James asked about the other family names, and she wrote them, too, and explained who they were. Grandpa and Grandma Carter were her mother and father. Grandpa Carter was called James, too.

James liked writing his name, and the names of his family. He liked writing the word 'engine', too, but he didn't tell his mother about the engine being part of the family, because he knew she didn't understand that. It was a shame, because she understood nearly everything else.

293

Not quite as much as his father, but nearly.

When it came to questions about his family, his first was, why had he no brothers or sisters? It seemed a strange thing, when the other children on the boats had brothers and sisters, but he had none.

'I'm too old to have any more children now,' his mother said. 'Women can only have babies until they're a bit younger than me. I don't know why I didn't have you earlier.'

It didn't seem to James that his question had been answered, and that was not good, but before he could protest his mother asked him if he minded not having brothers and sisters.

'No.'

He much preferred being on his own. He would play with other children, when the boats moored near each other in the evenings, but on the whole he thought they were rather silly, and he couldn't see why they liked playing those games. There never seemed to be any room in their cabins either. If he wanted to sit at the table and write or draw, he couldn't. The other children crowded around him and jogged his arm or squashed him. It didn't matter, because he could always go home, and his mother would make sure he had room to write and draw, with no one disturbing him. If he had had brothers and sisters, they, too, would have crowded around him.

He accepted that the reasons for not having brothers and sisters would not be explained to him. His questions were turned aside, so he stopped asking.

He was nearly eight years old before he

294

realised his father was a man like other children's fathers. Until then, James saw Ben as something completely different. Most importantly, only Ben worked with the engine, and Ben and the engine made the boat move through the water, taking them all somewhere else. Most of the other boats were still pulled by horses, and to James there was a difference. In those boats, it was the horses that made the boats move, not the men. Ben and the engine were partners, and between them they governed almost every aspect of James's life.

James saw a cow giving birth to a calf in a field by the canal. Ben stopped the boat, and they watched. The calf slid, black and wet, from its mother, and she, bloody matter hanging down between her hind legs, licked it until it staggered to its feet. A new and separate being stood alongside its mother. Only minutes earlier, they had been the same creature.

'Everything's born like that,' said Ben to James, as he pushed the boat back out into the canal.

James nodded. 'Except you,' he said.

Ben, jumping back on to the deck, looked down at him in surprise. 'Why not me?'

James didn't have the words to explain, and now he was bewildered. No one had mentioned a Grandpa and Grandma Jacardi, and he knew his family, didn't he? He knew everyone he had to mention in his prayers? Sometimes the list seemed to grow longer and longer, as his mother remembered the names of his cousins. But that was all her family, all Carters, except the aunts, and they had been until they'd married.

'Why not me, James?' asked Ben again, and he was smiling, so James smiled back, and spread out his hands, the gesture he made when he thought that what he was explaining should have been obvious.

'No Grandpa and Grandma Jacardi.'

Had Faith been there, Ben would have left it to her, but she had gone ahead to set a lock, and by now would be wondering what had happened to them.

'They're dead,' said Ben. 'Come on, your mother might be worried.'

He didn't mention it to Faith, and that night she was startled when James ended his prayers with 'God bless Grandpa and Grandma Jacardi,' and then, before she had time to recover, as he scrambled into bed, he wanted to know what dead meant, and where they were.

Ben watched them both, and Faith looked at him, her eyebrows raised.

James became impatient.

'Where are they?' he insisted.

'They're dead,' said Ben again. 'My father was a soldier. He was killed before I was born. My mother was a lock-keeper's daughter.'

Faith leaned down and kissed James's forehead.

'She was a bad woman,' she said. 'We don't like talking about her. Now go to sleep, and I'll tell you what being dead means tomorrow.'

She did tell him the next day, but James became impatient with her. He wanted to know more. He wanted to know whether Grandpa Jacardi had had any brothers and sisters. He wanted to know about being a soldier.

Death he accepted and seemed to understand without any difficulty. His father sometimes brought back rabbits he had killed with his catapult, and they were dead. They had been like the rabbits he had seen nibbling the grass beside the locks early in the mornings, and scampering away into the bushes when *Grey Lady* approached, but life had gone out of them, and now they were dead.

Faith had half expected him to be upset at the idea that everything died eventually, including them, but he was impatient to return to the subject of Grandpa Jacardi.

'We don't know very much about him,' Faith said, and James wanted to know why not. The fact that he had died before Ben was born was not good enough for James. He had to say the names of all his cousins in his prayers, even the ones he had never seen. It wasn't fair.

He became defiant and argumentative. He was going to pray for Grandpa and Grandma Jacardi, and he was going to pray for the engine too. And he wanted some more Jacardis, or he wouldn't pray for all the Carters.

Faith left him alone in the cabin and went up on to the deck to stand beside Ben. She had little hope that James would forget his questions: he never did.

Even when she thought she had turned them aside successfully, it was only a matter of time before he asked again, if it was something that interested him, and his family interested him very much indeed.

Ben, steering the boat, listening to the engine,

remembered the evening nine years earlier when he had stood beside a little piebald horse and waited for Mrs Webster, and known that, if Faith died, as he had thought she might, he would be truly alone.

Faith was old now, and not quite as strong as she had been. She complained that the locks weren't being maintained properly. Some of them were almost too stiff to work. The hinges hadn't been greased. Ben agreed with her, but knew the truth. The locks were no heavier than before, but Faith was old. James would be alone in the world sooner than most men.

'We'll try for orders to Middlewich, and see what we can find out, shall we?' he asked, and she nodded.

Ben remembered that they'd intended to do that, once. But James had been born, so it hadn't seemed to matter. They had a family now, in their son. They could look into the future, not the past. It hadn't occurred to either of them that James might want to know about the past.

Salt, then, from Middlewich to Wolverhampton, with a day or so to be spent in the Cheshire town, looking for someone to answer questions.

It was a new vicar, a young man, and he told them he'd only been in Middlewich for two years. He wasn't sure he knew all his living parishioners yet, let alone the dead ones. But he took them into the vestry and found the right book, and laid it open so they could all read what had been written at that time.

There was the record of the funeral, and a note that the expenses had been paid in advance.

Another book then, a heavy ledger bound in brown leather, and there it was, back in the autumn of 1879, money given to the vicar by Samuel Benjamin Jacardi in advance to pay for his own funeral, and for a stone to be set up when the grave had settled, with only the name and the dates. There were two signatures.

Ben looked at them, and thought, My father's hand travelled across that paper. He reached out and touched the page, touched the signature. Perhaps there was something of his father still there, on the heavy cream paper, some tiny fleck from the skin of his hand that had rested there ever since, waiting for his son, and now transferred.

Black ink that had faded a little, turning brown. It was a bold, square sort of handwriting. Perhaps there was something to be learned from that, from the style of the writing. What sort of man would write in such a style? Would anyone ever know? Would anyone ever look at a piece of writing, and say. 'That was written by a brave, clever man, that by a fool, that by a dreamer and that by a man who worked with his hands'? What would they make of Captain Jacardi's signature?

'Dr Ramsey died before I came here,' said the young man in the dusty cassock. 'I never met him.'

That answered Faith's question and left it unspoken. The old man had not passed on the secret that had been entrusted to him.

What now? she wondered, and glanced across at Ben to see on his face the same expression she had noticed years before, when he had not known what to do, how to find out about his father, and he had wanted to know. James, standing beside him, was looking up at her, and waiting, and there was a question in his eyes too, but with it the certainty that she would know what to do now. She was his mother.

'What now?' This time it was said aloud, to the vicar, who looked back at her enquiringly.

'We must find out about Captain Jacardi,' she said. 'He has a grandson now, who wants to know.'

There was nothing else in the leatherbound books in the vestry. Ben's christening was recorded, and there his mother had written in the name of the father and his rank, Captain Samuel Benjamin Jacardi, but nothing more.

'We must go to Coventry, then,' said Faith. 'That was where he came from. There can't be that many named Jacardi.'

So simple, thought Ben. Like the way she wakes up in the mornings. Of course, we go to the place he came from. They'll know there.

But the vicar, as he lifted the heavy books back on to the shelves, asked if they would like to visit Dr Ramsey's widow first, in case she knew anything about Captain Jacardi. After all, she'd been in the town at the time, and a husband would talk to his wife, wouldn't he?

This was said with a smile to them both.

She still lived in the vicarage. He, a young bachelor, had no need of such a big house. He lodged with a family, he said. He took them out on to the road, and pointed to red-brick gables and a white gate. She would be there. She never

300

went out.

'She doesn't receive many visitors,' he said, and there was a note of warning in his voice. 'Don't be too disappointed if she won't see you.'

At first she did refuse. The maid who came to the door said the mistress was not at home, but they could leave cards, if they wished.

Those words made Faith stubborn. She would not be sent on her way with her questions un-answered.

'Please tell your mistress that Captain Jacardi's son begs the favour of a word,' she said, and the maid, who had been closing the door in their faces, hesitated.

'Captain Jacardi's son,' repeated Faith, and added, 'she will know the name.'

She did know the name, but it was still a suspicious little face that peered out at them from under a white lace cap, and the black eyes were narrowed. They grew narrower still as Ben approached her down the length of the long darkened room, and then a hand was cupped to her ear, and the look of suspicion turned to amazement, and something like fear.

'His son?' she demanded. 'His *son?* No, stay there. No closer, if you please. Stay there.'

She held a lace handkerchief to her lips, and the narrowed black eyes were widening. She was shrinking back into her chair.

'Only his son, madam,' said Faith from behind him. 'No ghosts.'

There were frightened tears on the old face, and Faith went to her in concern and sympathy.

'Only his son,' she said again.

301

She looked across at Ben, and saw him through the old woman's eyes in the half-light that crept through the drawn curtains, a tall man with a face gaunt from suffering, his breathing sounding like the sea on shingle, slow and rasping.

Mrs Ramsey reached out her hand. Faith took it, and felt it thin and trembling in her grasp.

'Yes,' said Mrs Ramsey. 'Yes, you are his son. You must be. I never thought to hear that again. What do you want, Mr Jacardi? What do you want with me?'

She kept Faith's hand in her own, but her eyes were fixed on Ben, and she was still fearful, still fascinated. Now and then she looked at the boy who stood beside him, a quick glance, and back to Ben's face.

'What do you want with me?' she asked again, and Ben turned helplessly to Faith.

'We want to know Captain Jacardi's story,' said Faith. 'He has a grandson now, who wants to know about his family.'

Faith felt the thin hand in hers tremble, then stiffen, and the old woman lifted her chin.

'It's no story for a child.'

'It was no life for a child, but he was left to face it,' said Faith, and the thin hand left hers and was raised to the wrinkled face.

'Oh, I know. I know. We should have stopped it. I can't be bound by my husband's promises any more. But you must decide how much to tell the child. I won't speak of this in front of him.'

'I want to know,' said James stubbornly.

'Then I'll tell you later,' said Faith, and she went to him to take him out of the room.

'Promise?' he demanded.

'I promise.'

When she came back Ben was sitting on the sofa facing Mrs Ramsey, but still at a distance from her. Every time she looked at him she seemed to want to shrink into the corner of the big wing chair in which she crouched, as if to be as far away from him as she could. As if she still believed he was his father's ghost.

'Captain Jacardi was wounded at the battle of Isandhlwana,' she said. 'He was left for dead. There was a burial party, I believe. Yes, that's right, I remember he said ... but he was still breathing, so they left him. They said they'd bury him later. Nobody believed he could live, with such a wound. He was unconscious most of the time, but he heard that.

'It was very sandy, and it was windy. The sand soaked into the blood. It covered the wound. I understand it stopped the bleeding, before he died. The burial party left, and they left him. I don't know why. Perhaps the Zulus came back. Captain Jacardi said that he regained consciousness once, and there was a black man there, who gave him water.'

She stopped speaking, and her eyes turned away into the distance, a dreamy look crossing her face.

'Perhaps they weren't all savages,' she said. 'My husband... He said your father was very struck by that kindness, from the black man. He said he wished he had learned the language, so he could have thanked him, but then he said he couldn't speak anyway, so it didn't matter. I do remember

303

that very clearly, my husband telling me about the black savage and the water.'

She clasped her hands in her lap, still looking away from them.

'My husband said he wanted to be a missionary, and I would have liked that, but nothing came of it. He was a dreamer, you see. Not a man of action. He would always rather dream than face the realities. I didn't know that at the time, when I married him. I listened to his dreams, and I made the mistake of thinking they were plans for our future. I would have liked to go to Africa.'

Ben and Faith waited in silence, and after a little while Mrs Ramsey looked back at them. She frowned as if she could not quite remember who they were, and then she seemed to flinch, but she went on.

'He was found by a deserter. George Nicholson. Your uncle, Mr Jacardi. Nicholson was looking for things to steal. He thought your father was dead, and he tried to steal his boots. When he realised he was alive, he made his plans. He was a dreadful man, Nicholson, but very clever, very quick-witted. He was a sort of adventurer. He'd gone to South Africa because he wanted to be rich, and he'd heard there was gold. He didn't find any gold. Then he enlisted, because he thought that would be a cheap way of getting back to England, but there was fighting, and that wasn't to his taste, either. So he deserted. By the time he found your father he was down to his last few pennies, and living off the land.

'But he took his opportunity. He would bring your father back to England. A wounded officer would be sent home, you see, with a soldier to care for him, and Nicholson decided to be that soldier. The only difficulty he could see was keeping your father alive, at least until he was on a ship and on the way home. He took the revolver and he shot a deer. He made Captain Jacardi drink the blood. The Captain said it tasted disgusting, but Nicholson forced him to drink it. Nicholson said there was a tribe that lived on blood. I don't suppose it's true. I would have liked to learn about the black people, but my husband didn't know anything. He only pretended he knew. He didn't. Captain Jacardi knew a little, but he said he hadn't met many black people. He was sorry about that. He said he would have liked to meet the black people.'

Faith felt Ben stir restlessly beside him, but she touched his arm, and thought, She's old. She's bound to ramble a bit, while she's remembering. Be patient, she'll come back to the story.

'The man who speared him, he told me about him. He said there was a lot of white on his shield, and that meant he was a warrior with some experience. They'd been told the Zulus were blood-crazed savages, but that was wrong. The Captain said when he saw the man, he was crouching down, and he'd reached them without them even noticing him. He said the man looked very calm, and he held his spear, and he looked into the Captain's face. Captain Jacardi had a revolver, a Webley he said it was, and that was the gun Nicholson took to shoot the deer. The

Captain had shot the Zulu with it, but he was too late. He said the man came up behind his spear from his crouching position by the rock, and he wasn't a blood-crazed savage at all, he was a disciplined soldier using a weapon with which he was entirely familiar. That was what the Captain said, and I believe he knew.

'The Captain couldn't talk very much, because of his wound. It tired him, talking. But he knew I was interested in the black people, so he tried. He was very kind to me. I think he understood I'd thought I was marrying a man who was to be a missionary. He, too, had been mistaken in his marriage. He didn't tell me about that. He told my husband. The Captain only talked to me about Africa, and the black people.

'Nobody survived the battle of Isandhlwana, did you know that? Nobody at all. Well, they were wrong. The Captain survived, for a little while. But no one knew, except Nicholson, and the Captain, and he only told my husband. Oh, and his friend, of course. Yes, he told his friend, he must have done. But the secret would have been quite safe there, because of the scandal. His friend wouldn't have told anyone. No.'

Ben moved again, and again Faith touched his arm, and they waited in silence. The old woman's eyes were closed, but her head was still erect, and her thin hands clasped and unclasped in her lap.

'Nicholson kept him alive, and he found a farm, a Boer farm, and they helped. The Captain said they didn't want to help, but they were devout people, very religious, so they had to help

306

him. They took them both in. The man thought he was dying. He even dug a grave. But the Captain didn't die. Nicholson took the Captain's money and bought a bullock cart, and that was how they got back to the coast. The Captain said he thought the bullock cart was more likely to kill him than the Zulu's spear, but he was still alive when they reached the coast, and there were ships, Royal Navy ships, so Nicholson's plan worked.

'Captain Jacardi still couldn't speak, you see, only a word or two. And he told me once that he didn't really care by then. Nicholson was a thief, a deserter and a rogue, and the army was better off without him. Captain Jacardi should have denounced him, but he told me he couldn't be bothered. He was dying, he always knew that, and Nicholson wasn't important enough to be worth the effort.'

Mrs Ramsey looked across at them, and her voice sharpened as she remembered, as her interest quickened.

'But strangely enough Nicholson seemed to like Captain Jacardi. The Captain had always thought Nicholson would kill him as soon as they were on the ship and it was out at sea. It would have been the logical thing to do. The ship wouldn't have turned back or put into port just for a common soldier. He fully expected Nicholson to suffocate him with his pillow, and he couldn't have stopped him. It was very strange, don't you agree?'

'Yes, madam,' said Faith, and felt Ben nod beside her.

'But perhaps it was because the Captain was someone to talk to,' said Mrs Ramsey. 'After such a long time on his own, if it was a long time. I don't know. I don't know very much about Nicholson, I'm afraid. I never met him, or his sister. No. I only know what the Captain told my husband. Nicholson talked about Middlewich, about his family. His father was the lock-keeper. Yes, well, I expect you knew that, but the old man left. I think his daughter...'

She turned away again, and there was an expression of distress and distaste, perhaps embarrassment on her face.

'I'm sorry,' she said after a little while. 'I find it difficult to speak of her. Of ... of Miss Nicholson. Your ... your mother, Mr Jacardi. I'm sorry.'

Ben didn't know what to say. He tried to smile, turned it into a shrug instead, then felt that had been rude, so he looked at Faith.

'We understand,' she said.

There was a long silence, and again Ben began to feel restless. Again Faith touched his arm, and he waited until the old woman began to speak.

'Captain Jacardi told me nothing about the events that followed his return,' she said. 'I remember I asked him what brought him to Middlewich, and he turned the question aside, most courteously, most adroitly I might say, and I never asked again. I believe I assumed he simply visited the town now and then, and called on my husband when he did. But then he died, and he was buried here, and I went to his funeral. I couldn't understand why he was being buried here, in Middlewich. I asked my husband, and he said the Captain had sworn him to secrecy, and he wouldn't break a sacred vow.'

Faith remembered the old man in the churchyard, the expression of conscious and martyred nobility on his face as he had used those words to her. She understood very well the ironic note that had crept into Mrs Ramsey's voice.

'Of course he did tell me in the end, because I wouldn't ask again. So he told me, and he swore me to secrecy too, and now I'm breaking my promise to him. As he broke so many of his to me.'

A quick frown, displeasure at herself, and then she went on, quickly, before they could speak, if they had wanted to do so.

'The ship docked at Portsmouth, and Captain Jacardi wrote to his best friend in Coventry, where he lived. He had thought, you see, to spare his wife the shock of his sudden reappearance. He asked his friend to meet him, in Coventry, having prepared the way for him.

'His friend did meet him, at the station. His friend told him that his wife had remarried. Very shortly after the news of his death had reached her. His friend had called at the house to offer his condolences, you see. And had done so. Captain Jacardi's ... widow ... was carrying his best friend's child, and so there had been a wedding. A bigamous wedding, following a disgraceful adulterous liaison, on the very day that the woman received the news of her husband's death.

'Well, that was how my husband told me the story.

309

'Captain Jacardi and his ... wife had a son. His name was Charles, and he was three years old. The scandal, if Captain Jacardi had resurfaced, would have harmed the child most dreadfully. It was already bad enough, the marriage so soon after the husband's death, the child no doubt spoken of as being born prematurely, or perhaps they planned to travel abroad for the confinement, and change the dates. I don't know. But the Captain loved his son very much, although there was, I believe, not much feeling for his wife. She was very beautiful, and very extravagant, and very spoilt, and he, if my husband is to be believed, was resentful to the point of hating her most bitterly for what she had done, most of all for depriving him of the comfort of his son for the last few months of his life.

'You see, he decided to disappear. To allow his death at Isandhlwana to stand. To keep the scandal to a minimum so it would not harm his son. He would not even go home to his parents, in case the truth should emerge through them.

'He told his friend to bring him money, and he told him, too, to take his new wife and his stepson for a walk in the park on the following morning. Captain Jacardi sat at a table in a coffee-house that morning, and looked at his son for the last time. Then he came to Middlewich to find George Nicholson, and he offered him money to care for him for the remainder of his life. It could not be more than a few weeks, a month or two at the most. His heart was beginning to fail, you see.

'But he met Nicholson's sister.'

She would not look at them. For the last part of the story she had been staring towards the window, her eyes only occasionally moving back to them, but now her head was turned away, and there was the lace handkerchief in her hand, held to her lips as if to wipe something unclean from them.

'He hated his wife, but could do her no harm without harming his son,' she said softly, her voice muffled in the white lace. 'But in Gillian Nicholson he found another woman he could hate without harming the boy. And so he lived with her. And she ... she was a strange ... a bad woman, yes, a *bad* and *evil* thing. I don't understand it myself, I ask you not to press me on this. I am told doctors know of it, there is a term. She ... she took joy in his pain. For her, pain was something that pleased her. And he was ... in great pain.'

Ben and Faith sat in silence, and Ben thought, I knew this. I don't need to ask any questions. The man would have been better than the boy, to satisfy that lust, but she smiled at me, too.

And Faith took his hand, and thought of the woman who had taken joy in her child's misery, and watched the old woman, and thought, So now we know who he was, and why he was here, yet we cannot take this any further, because if we do we destroy what he tried to protect. We cannot go to Coventry and ask about the family. We have to leave it here.

She looked at Ben, and rose to her feet, and he followed her. Then he turned back to where the

311

old woman crouched in the big chair, her face turned away, the handkerchief held to her lips. 'Thank you,' he said.

15

James always remembered the day they had gone to Middlewich to see the old woman. He had waited quietly in the hall, sitting on a high-backed chair, looking at the door that had closed behind his mother, or down at the black and white tiles on the floor. She had told him she wouldn't be long, and she had promised again to tell him the story of his grandfather.

The maid had walked past once or twice, and then she had stopped and talked to him, asked him his name. He had answered her politely, and when she came back the next time she had held out her hand.

'Come to the kitchen,' she said. 'Cook's made some jam tarts... It's warm, in the kitchen,' she added, as he hesitated.

He remembered the warm kitchen, and the cook, who looked as if she'd been covered in flour, and the big table with jam tarts on wire trays, cooling from the oven. He remembered the smell of baking. He wanted a jam tart, but he didn't ask, he only looked at them. The cook laughed, took a blue plate off a kitchen dresser, and put two jam tarts on it, one with apricot jam, the other with strawberry.

The cook and the maid had jam tarts too, sitting at the big table, and they'd all talked, but the maid had been listening for the drawing-room door, and when she heard it open she'd been in the hall to tell his mother and father where he was, so when they left the house his father was carrying a brown paper bag, and in it there were more of the jam tarts.

He thought he'd been good, while they'd been in the big, dark room with the old woman. He'd remembered to say thank you to the maid, and to the cook, and they'd both smiled at him.

He'd wanted to go to the churchyard to see Grandfather Jacardi's grave, so they'd taken him. He'd stood for a minute or two, staring at it, reading the name and the dates.

'Is he down there?' he'd demanded, pointing.

'His body is. What's left of it,' his father had answered, and his mother had looked across, sharply.

James had looked down at the ground, frowning. Then he'd crouched, knelt, pressed his ear to the grass, his eyes screwed tight shut. Ben and Faith waited, watching him.

'Can't hear anything,' he'd said.

He remembered walking back to the boat, how quiet everyone had been. His father still carried the paper bag with the jam tarts in it.

He remembered hearing that Grandpa Jacardi had been a hero, not only because of fighting in South Africa, which he could understand, but because of choosing to die in a strange place, with only a bad woman to look after him when he was ill because he'd loved his son so much.

It took him a long time to understand that.

Faith talked to him quietly about Grandpa Jacardi. She still hadn't said anything about the bad woman, but she said the bad woman wasn't a real grandmother, and shouldn't be called Grandma. If James wanted to give her a name, it was Miss Nicholson.

Faith usually talked quietly, when she was explaining something. He didn't think he had ever heard her talk loudly, although she could shout if she had to, sometimes to other boats, or people on the towpath. But only three days after she told him about Grandpa Jacardi she was shouting, and at his father. She had never done that before.

There had been a letter waiting for them at Wolverhampton from a company of lawyers in Stourbridge, and it had been forwarded from the office in Birmingham. Mr Young in the Wolverhampton office said it was like a post office in there these days, letters going everywhere, but Mr Young was usually only joking when he said things like that. He was a nice man. He had a packet of biscuits under the table, and he used to give them to the children.

This was much more interesting to James than the letter from the lawyers.

There were no orders for *Grey Lady* in Wolverhampton that day. They could wait until Friday, if they liked, said Mr Young, or they could go empty to Liverpool. There might be something they could pick up on the way.

'We'll wait, then,' said Ben, and he handed the letter to Faith.

'Hunter, Parkinson and Rudd. Something to your advantage?' she wondered, looking up at him. 'What could that be?'

315

'I don't know.'

'You'd better go, then.'

Ben went the next day, alone, on the train, and he came back late that night. James was asleep, but he heard the footsteps, and woke. Still sleepy, he listened to his father and mother talking, not to the words, but to the sounds of their voices. He liked the sounds of their voices.

Ben still seemed dazed, as though he had seen something he could not quite believe, but he told Faith immediately what he had learned.

'Josiah left me the cottage and the boatyard,' he said. 'Not Paddy. Me.'

Faith sank down on the seat, staring at him.

'After Paddy stole the money,' he said, 'he and Kathy changed their wills. The lawyer, he was an old man, he died before Josiah. There was this will in his desk. His son was in the army, only came out a few weeks ago. He found it. It's been there all this time.'

'No one knew?' asked Faith.

'That damned thief Paddy, he knew. When Kathy died he was sniffing around, went to the lawyer to see what she'd left him. There's a note the old man wrote about him coming. The will says he's already had his inheritance. He knew it wasn't his to sell. Faith, it's ours. The boatyard's ours.'

Faith's voice was very, very quiet.

'Jed and Violet?'

'No, it's not theirs, even though they paid. It's ours. All they can do is try to get their money back from Paddy, if they could ever find him. I don't think there's much chance of that. Faith,

316

it's ours. I can't believe it. Only a week ago we had the docking money and a few pounds in a tin. Now we've a cottage and a boatyard. I can't believe this. I can't believe it.'

It was then that Faith began to cry, then to scream and to shout, and James was so frightened he couldn't move. He had never heard her like this, screaming.

'Damn them! Damn them! May they burn in hell! You were flogged and sent to prison because of them! I nearly starved while they lived in our house. Damn them!'

'Now, Faith, don't say that. They didn't know. Don't shout, you'll wake James.'

'Damn them! I want them dead and rotting. I want them dead. Years it's been, years, damn them.'

'Faith, darling. My love, no. They didn't know.'

'Ben, it says in the Bible, "They have digged a pit for my feet and are fallen into it themselves." It says in the Bible, and it's true. It's their turn to starve. Give them a boat and send them on their way.'

'They're too old for that.'

'I'm too old! I can't do it any more, I can't work those heavy locks any more. I've worried and wondered, and... Damn them! May they burn. Turn them out. It's their turn to worry and wonder now. Turn them out.'

James began to cry. He couldn't help himself. He tried to cry quietly, he tried not to let them know he was awake and had heard, but he was too frightened, and the first muffled sobbings rose to a high wail of distress and fright.

Immediately, Faith was on her knees beside the bed, reaching for him. Her face was streaked with tears, and he had never seen her like that before. He didn't want her. He cried again, and held out his arms to his father.

Ben lifted him off the bed and held him close, talking to him, telling him all was well, nothing to worry about.

'Stop crying, James. It's all right now.'

But James looked back at Faith, at her wide and angry eyes, at the white hair streaked across her face, and he thought she looked like a witch. She'd turned into a witch, and she'd been making bad spells for someone.

'Don't,' he said. 'Don't. Please.'

'Don't what, James?' asked Ben gently, but James was still staring at his mother. 'Don't what, old lad?'

'Don't make bad things come.'

Ben and Faith looked at each other, and Faith pushed her hair away from her face and wiped her eyes.

'No,' said Ben.

She tried to smile at James, then nodded to him.

'No. No, we won't,' she said. 'We won't.'

But although Faith was prepared to promise to do nothing bad to Jed and Violet, she did not intend to forgive them. She tried to smile at James, tried to be herself again, but she could not drive away the memories of everything that had happened since the Cartwrights had bought the business from Paddy Armstrong. Ben had had to steal because she needed good food. He had

318

been caught, and flogged, and imprisoned, and she had sold everything they had to stay alive, and work the boat home.

But Ben, holding James in his arms, feeling the boy's fear, suddenly had a memory of Mrs Webster standing in front of him, her hand against her forehead as if she was in pain, and he knew that it was important to promise not to hurt Jed and Violet.

'We'll do nothing bad,' he said again.

The lawyer had agreed to write to the Cartwrights, telling them about the will.

Ben lay awake that night, trying to think of the future. He would make boats again, as he had always wanted to do. James would go to school. Faith would no longer have to struggle with heavy lock gates, or steer a boat against strong winds in the winter rain. But against all that, he could only remember Jed as he had first known him, when Jed had been a young man and he a sullen boy. Jed had worked with Josiah, and later with Ben himself, showing him how to use the tools, how to hold them, how to keep them sharp. Jed had been kind to Ben, and in only a few days, Jed's world would come to an end.

'Leave it for a week,' the lawyer had said. 'I'll tell them you'll be coming, shall I?'

He was a young man, the lawyer. 'Peter Hunter,' he'd said, holding out his hand. 'We should have met before now.'

Young, but he seemed to know what he was doing. There was no disputing the will, it was clear and direct, nothing to argue about. The house, the yard, and the business belonged to

Benjamin Samuel Jacardi.

Ben had nodded, said, 'Yes, please write to them,' but he really wanted to go home to *Grey Lady*, to talk to Faith, so he hadn't been listening to Hunter. I'm a man of property, he'd thought, as he walked out into Market Street. He'd dreamed of making boats again, and sometimes wondered if he might do it, if he could find a boatyard that would employ him. Then, when he'd had the chance, when Freddie Johnson had offered him a job, he'd refused.

Maybe it wasn't making boats he'd wanted at all. Maybe it was his youth again. He smiled to himself in the darkness, remembering summer evenings with Josiah and Jed, when the work was finished, sitting in the yard on the gunwales of a half-built boat, listening. Listening to the talk of the next boat, of the last customer, listening to birdsong, listening to hoof beats on the towpath, looking a little sideways, not at the thin grey horse but at the pretty girl who led it. Thinking perhaps she was looking a little sideways at him, too, and from this distance she couldn't hear him. Could she?

Over the water, sounds carry. He'd learned that early, made a remark to Jed about a different girl, and her father, must have been fifty feet away on the boat, he heard, and he'd threatened to come ashore and sort it out, that dirty tongue.

Summer evenings by the side of the canal, with the work finished, and Kathy making a meal, and maybe if it was warm and fine the meal would be a picnic to eat in the garden.

Remember instead the rain and the sleet, that

320

time he'd cut his hand on a chisel, sudden dull pain at the base of his thumb, a deep, deep hole that he'd looked at, and dark blood welling up out of it. He'd thought, Jed told me not to hold the wood in front of the chisel, and that's why. I'll not forget again.

Remember lifting the planks out of the steamer, so hot it could blister your hands. Get it set up right, and quickly before it cools, get that clamp fixed in place. Blisters on your hands? You'll have to get used to that, boy.

Hate that job.

Caulking a boat in the winter rain, hands so cold you can't feel them, can only look at that strip of black muck, push it against the crack, hold the caulking tool against it and hit it with the hammer, force it between the planks. So cold you can't feel your hands, so why is it, when that hand slips, and the hammer hits the fingers, there's nothing hurts worse?

Those hot steamed planks in the hot dry sun, so thirsty your throat seems to be swelling, but can't stop there, boy. Get that damned thing in place, while it can still bend.

Remember coming home from school in the evenings. And think of James coming home down the track. There's nothing wrong with the way he breathes, no one's going to pretend they could catch something dirty from James. He's clever. Faith's taught him as much as she can, now. Time to hand over to someone else. Think of James coming home from school, those dark, eager eyes looking ahead, looking for his father to tell him what he'd learned that day.

Remember Kathy in the kitchen door, smiling at them all, hot drink ready, maybe a few fresh biscuits. Leave the mouldy old boats, come on in and get warm. Faith, standing in the doorway, smiling out at them. Leave it. Come in and warm yourselves, I've made tea and there's a cake cooling on the wire rack under the window. Never got a chance to get cold, did it? Tastes better hot anyway.

Faith, his darling wife, looks like an old woman now. Screaming at him that night, she'd never done that before. All those memories, it had been too much. She'd looked like a witch, her eyes all wild and filled with tears, her hair streaked across her face.

Bit of bad luck, that had been, old Mr Hunter dying, the young one in the army, and not really wanting to leave it, either. Strange, that. You'd think, after that war, everyone would want to be out, never put on a uniform again, get as far away as they could. But not him. Only came out when the other partner wanted to retire. Kept putting it off. Slowly, and reluctantly, the man had weaned himself away from what had been his life, away from the noise and the action and the shine of the military machine, back into the quiet, dusty, thoughtful life of a country lawyer. Looking at leather books, at crisp, white letters, at dusty old papers in the back of his father's desk drawers.

Oh, my God. Josiah and Kathleen Armstrong's will. Dated January 1898. Left in the back of a drawer, or more likely pushed there by accident, when other things were dropped in front of it.

Pencils, pens, dear Lord, an old quill, where had that come from? Sealing wax, a box of it, and a little brass lamp for heating it, and the two heavy bronze stamps with the oak handles, and a thick roll of yellowing paper, right at the back, behind all the rubbish.

Oh, my God. Josiah and Kathleen Armstrong's will. How the devil do I set about finding Benjamin Samuel Jacardi now?

Remember that thief Paddy Armstrong, remember him. When Kathy died he knew full well that he was out of the will, but did he slink off back to his den, as he should have done? Moved poor, bewildered Josiah in with the Cartwrights and tried to sell the place behind his back. Money to keep the old man in his retirement, he'd have said. And then, when Josiah died, come back quick and see what there is to steal, and Violet offering him money. What would she have known about a will? The Cartwrights never knew Paddy had stolen everything that Christmas.

Buy the place from you, Mr Armstrong?

Not a bad woman, Violet Cartwright, not really. Nothing dishonest, not in Violet's eyes, never dishonest, not that. Those bits of wood, they'd only be burned, only a few shillings, hardly worth writing in the books.

That money you sent, I thought that was for Josiah. Nothing to do with the business. Of course, what you've sent since he died, we'll give you back. Of course.

Bought the place fair and square from Mr Armstrong. Mr Patrick Armstrong, that is.

That little bit of greed has grown into a mighty tree, Violet, and now it's coming down, crashing down, and look what it's bringing with it. You and Jed, years of work. Your home. The work of your sons. All dragged down, because you turned into a greedy woman.

There was grey light at the porthole, and Ben turned his head to look at the coming dawn. Faith stirred as he moved, her hair drifting over his shoulder, gleaming in the darkness. Her eyes opened, a little sigh, and closed again. The same sigh from James, the same sound, in, a jerky little noise, as though they'd been surprised, a pause for a second or two, and that soft, long breath. Faith and James, so alike. Tough and loving, bright and gentle. His darling wife and his perfect boy, who was growing strong now. Lifted the boat pole yesterday, and slid it under the strings against the side cloths, grunted with the effort, but he did it.

Growing tall and straight and strong, and it's time he went to school.

Ben looked at the grey light in the porthole, closed his eyes, and at last he slept just as James opened his eyes, and remembered the promise that nothing bad would be done.

Faith was quiet all the next day, and the following one, when Mr Young came out and said there was a load of empty oil drums to go back to Nantwich, then back down to Worcester with timber. Ben had thought she might refuse, and say they should go to the boatyard, but she nodded to Mr Young, took the paper from him, and made ready to cast off. Half-way through the morning, when they were at the top of the locks, Ben asked if she was all right, and she nodded, then shook her head.

'What are we going to do about the Cartwrights, then?' she asked. There was a quick, angry gleam in her eye as she said their name, but then it was gone. She still wanted to throw them off the place, make them suffer as she had done, but she was no fool, his Faith. They'd been running that business for years. If there was to be a business worth running, they would have to stay, at least for a while.

When at last they reached the yard, nearly two weeks later, they were both subdued, even a little apprehensive. There was no doubt about their right to the place, but Ben had made no decisions. He'd told Faith they would just have to do what seemed right at the time, and she'd listened to him, and nodded.

Jed came to the kitchen door of the cottage as they pulled into the bank, watched as Ben jumped ashore, then went in to fetch Violet. She had grown fat since they had last seen her, and she stood at the door, staring at them, her arms folded as Jed walked slowly down the path to meet them.

'I suppose you've come home,' said Jed.

Ben nodded. 'I suppose we have.'

Jed took the bowline and tied it to a mooring ring as Faith stepped off *Grey Lady* and walked up to the cottage.

'You'll have to pay us what we gave Paddy Armstrong,' said Violet defiantly, as Faith approached her. 'That's only fair. We bought this

325

place from him.'

But then she began to cry, lifted her apron to her face, and wailed into it. Disjointed words, muffled by the fabric, sounded through the high, keening voice. 'Only fair. Have to pay.'

Faith walked past her, and Violet stood aside to let her through. Ben watched. Violet was huge beside Faith, a great wide woman in a crimson dress with her flowered apron crushed up against her face, sobbing. Faith said something to her as she walked past, but Violet only wailed again.

'Only fair,' she called after her. 'Just what we paid, that's only fair, isn't it?'

'James needs to go to school,' said Ben, not knowing what else to say to Jed, and Jed nodded, not looking at him. He was taking a long time with the rope, tugging at it, looping it into a hitch, coiling it.

'There's a job here for you,' said Ben. 'For you and William, if there's enough money in the business to pay your wages.'

'And Violet?' asked Jed.

'No. No, not Violet. I think Faith can do what Violet's been doing. But you and the lad, I'd like you to stay. Not in the cottage, I don't mean that. Just work here. Fair wage. We'll stay on the boat while you find somewhere else to live. A week or so. What do you say? Can you work for me? Because that's what it will be. Work for me, in my business. Could you do that?'

Jed was nodding before Ben had finished speaking, but still not looking at him. Still looking down at the rope in his hands. Then he did look into Ben's face, quickly, and away again,

326

out over the water.

'We could do that,' he said. 'We were going to ask. We'll need the work, now.'

16

After that first evening Faith did not go into the cottage again until Violet and Jed left, just over a week later. For most of the time she stayed on *Grey Lady*, cleaning and polishing while the men were on the yard, and in the evenings looking at the account books and the files of letters, trying to work out how much money there was in the business, in the materials and the tools, and, more importantly, in cash.

Nothing would ever bring her to trust Violet again.

'Four hundred and thirty-five pounds seventeen shillings and fivepence,' she told Jed, two nights before the Cartwrights left. 'And if I'm wrong, you'll have to prove it.'

'As much as that,' Ben marvelled.

Faith shook her head at him.

'There are bills to pay,' she said, 'but they haven't been paid, so the money has to be there. Don't you let Violet tell you any different.'

Jed sat on the cabin steps looking down at his hands.

Ben hardly spoke to Violet at all, except to wish her good morning when he saw her. She seemed to have collapsed. She had been a big strong woman, and then she had grown fat, and now it was as if she couldn't carry herself around. She held on to things, to doorframes, to the backs of chairs, to the edges of tables. Her eyes were vacant and usually unfocused, and her mouth hung open. Sometimes she would try to pack her belongings into boxes and cases, but she hardly ever finished a task, and it was Jed who would fill the half-empty containers, and fix the lids.

'You want to check what we're taking?' he asked Ben on the morning they left, and Ben shook his head, feeling faintly sick. He wanted Violet out and away, and, although he couldn't express it even to Faith, he wanted the cottage scoured, every inch, ceilings and walls, doors, windows, floors, scrubbed, washed and rinsed of every trace of Violet Cartwright. She had never been a dirty woman, but Ben felt as if she had tainted the cottage.

It seemed that Faith felt the same way. She watched the cart move away up the track, and then she seemed to brace herself. She took buckets and brooms into the cottage, and she threw open all the windows, even though it was raining. Smoke began to rise from the chimney, and Ben knew she had put the big copper on to boil. She would need plenty of hot water.

James wanted to help in the yard. He had no great interest in the cottage, and hadn't reacted at all when Faith had told him he was to have a room of his own. He wanted to be with his father, and the new boats.

Most of all, he wanted to be with the engines. There were two in the shed, in big wooden crates, and James peered at them between the slats. He reached through to touch them, to stroke them. He murmured the song of the

329

engine, humming to them. This is the song you will sing.

Ben pulled the slats off the side of one of the crates and gave James a strip of cotton rag and a bottle of oil. He told him, 'Once it's clean I'll give you the polish for the copper and the brass. Non-ferrous metals, James. Remember? Copper, brass, anything that isn't iron or steel. Gold and silver too. Won't find them on a Bolinder, though.'

'Non-ferrous metals,' said James. 'Copper, brass, silver, gold.' And he nodded to himself in satisfaction, and rubbed his oily rag over the block. 'Non-ferrous metals.'

It was two days before Faith moved their own possessions into the cottage, and when Ben followed her into the kitchen he found she had done exactly what he had wished, although he had never expressed it. The place was still damp from the scrubbing it had received. White paint on the ceilings showed the grey plaster under-neath, and Faith frowned at it, said it would all have to be whitewashed again, and the walls too, when the weather was dry. In the meantime, there were fires burning in every room, and the windows, the glass sparkling, remained open. Wisps of steam escaped through them into the damp air.

Faith watched Ben a little anxiously when he came into the big bedroom that first night. The brass bedstead gleamed from polishing, and the sheets were white and crisp, boiled, starched, ironed, but it was still Josiah and Kathy's bed. Ben smiled at her.

'I never thought I'd be sleeping in that,' he said.

'Do you think they'd mind?'

'No. No, not them. Never.'

She must be tired, he thought. Dawn until dark she'd laboured in the cottage for the last two days, but it was clean. It smelt of soap and wax polish, and the crisp smell of clean linen. The polish was dull on the damp floorboards, but once they'd dried there'd be a shine, and the smell was good.

'I love you, my Faith.'

'Ben. Love you too, Ben.'

'We're home,' he said, and he held out his arms to her.

Silky white hair, no colour at all now, but soft and shining and beautiful. Her eyes were sunk deep into lined and weather-beaten skin, and her body was thin and a little gnarled. When Ben kissed her, brushing her body with his lips, tasting her skin with his tongue, he did sometimes remember the days when that body had been smooth and young and firm. He hadn't loved her very much, not then. Her skin wasn't firm any more, and the muscles and sinews were stringy, lines and angles where there had been curves, but Ben sometimes thought he loved her more every day. He would work all through the day, hard and heavy work, in a bitter late spring rain, and finish in the evening cold and tired. Then Faith would smile at him, a warm and loving welcome, and every minute of that work was rewarded.

She was tired. She was rubbing her twisted shoulder, not really knowing she was doing it, not looking at it. Stiff, though. A bit sore. That

331

scrubbing had been hard on an old shoulder that hadn't been straight to begin with.

She was looking around the room. All this space. Cupboards to hang her dress in, and still room under the dress for shoes and things, and a cupboard over that one, how would she ever fill all these cupboards? So much space. You could walk around this big bed, right around it, except at the head where it was pushed against the wall. But you could pull that whole bed out away from the wall, and sweep behind it. Not fold it away during the day, leave it. Walk out of this room, and into another one. So much wasted space, it didn't seem right. It was extravagant, too much like luxury.

'Doesn't seem right,' she said.

It was a big cottage, nearly twice the size of the one she'd grown up in, the one where James had been born. There were only the three of them, with all this space.

'Could fit *Grey Lady*'s cabin into one corner of the kitchen.'

'You'll get used to it,' said Ben.

It took her months to do so, but James moved into his room without even remarking on it. He hardly spent any time indoors anyway: he was out in the yard at first light, checking the engines, wiping them dry, rubbing the brass and the copper, the non-ferrous metals.

It was William who came closest to sharing his love, big William, strong as a bull, looking a little like one too, with the slow way he'd turn his head to stare. James liked William, but Faith saw too much of his mother in him, and kept her distance.

332

They needed William. James might be a born engineer, but for the moment it was William who was the mechanic.

James seemed to ease himself into school, hardly noticing, hardly noticed, as though he had slid into the classroom through a side door when no one was looking, sat down at his desk and taken up the work. At reading and writing, he was already more fluent than any of the other children, and arithmetic was as natural as running and walking. He understood its logic.

Home in the evenings, and straight on to the yard, leaving his schoolbooks in his satchel on the table. He would help the men, if he could, with whatever they were doing, but his only real interest was in the engines, and in the way they were mounted. He watched his father shaping the oak keelsons, long and strong to spread the load of the engine as far as he could, and the cross members, and when he had fitted them James would look closely, see they were tight and firm, and he would smile. Yes. Yes, that was strong enough for an engine. That would do, that was just fine.

They all waited for James to come home before they mounted an engine. They'd have the slings ready, and they'd wait until they heard him running down the track. Then they'd smile at each other.

'Engineer's here now.'

James treated engines as though they could feel. He slid the massive straps into place, pulling them until they were exactly right, where the heavy weight would be balanced, lifting evenly, not dragging, not slipping, but just right, comfortable. Then a nod, and Jed would start pulling on the chain, and slowly the engine would lift off the ground, swinging just a little with young James's hand steadying it, watching, listening to the creak of the slings, the rattle of the chain. Slowly and smoothly it would lift, and the men would watch the boy, watch his face, his hands on the engine as they lowered it into place, never tugging, never jerking, but using the weight of the engine, a little turn, a little swing, then steady again, and down, slowly, slowly, and settling on the smooth, hard oak in exactly the right place. The chains rattled, and the slings slackened, and James unhitched them from the big hook, and the engine had come home.

After the first few times, William didn't even bother to check.

James could use spanners now. Nuts and bolts seemed easy to him. He never struggled with machinery. If a nut was too tight he wouldn't wrestle with it, never got exasperated, he'd pick up a longer spanner, hold it further away, more leverage, and the nut would move. A little oil, a smear of grease, set that piece carefully to one side, and he never lost them. Where Ben would mutter to himself, hunting around on the workbench, James would reach out for the piece he'd put in that place two days before, and it would be there. No one had moved it, it hadn't fallen behind the shelf when something else was put down beside it, it was always where he had left it.

Magic. Luck. Love.

School was easy, but not very interesting. James made a few friends, and now and then brought them home, but none shared his love of engines. They liked the boats, and in the summer they enjoyed swimming in the canal. Sometimes, for a while, they would help with small tasks on the yard.

Faith, watching them, listening to them, knew that none would remain her son's friends for long. Perhaps he had been on his own too much, and would never make lasting friendships.

But with her and with Ben, he was always affectionate. Whenever he passed her he would hug her, or kiss her, at first reaching up on tiptoe, lips pursed to reach her face, and then directly, and soon, so soon she could hardly believe it, stooping to drop his kiss on her head. Or he would hug her, a loving grasp that sometimes, as he grew stronger, hurt her, although she never protested. It didn't occur to the boy that his gesture might crush ribs and leave his mother a little bruised. She always laughed or smiled and patted his cheek. Her darling, perfect boy.

In his teens, James took to sport, to football and cricket. He played for his school in the first teams, and enjoyed it, but if his father needed his help with an engine at a weekend, James would drop out of the team without a second thought. The engines always came first.

He knew now that the engines weren't alive, as he had believed them to be when he was a child. He knew it intellectually. Emotionally, he was never quite so sure. He tried to explain it once, to his first girlfriend, a quiet, stolid child with the air of a small engine herself, predictable usually, but inclined to stubbornness.

'They run better for people who like them,' he said. 'Why would that be, then? We send a boat out and she's running well. If they like engines, that engine goes on running just fine. If they don't I'll bet you a sixpence they come back, two, three weeks later, engine isn't running right.'

Susie listened to him, her mouth pursed, frowning.

'What's the matter with the engine, then?' she asked, and James shrugged. That wasn't the point, but he might as well not have tried. She wouldn't understand anyway. Logically, you could say that people who liked the engines took the trouble to find out about them, learned how to take care of them. It was never a good enough explanation for James. Engines ran better for people who liked them.

James was an easy boy. Ben and Faith, listening to other parents talking of their difficulties with defiant or disobedient children, were sometimes amazed, first by the problems of which they were told, and then by their own good fortune. It seemed that all they had to do was explain to him, and he did as they wished. Or sometimes he would explain to them, why he couldn't, or wouldn't, or didn't want to, but there was always some way of finding an answer, some compromise. They never had to shout at him, let alone hit him, as most fathers seemed to do to their children.

There was only one issue on which he would not be moved. Every January he visited his

Jacardi grandfather's grave. He didn't know the exact date of the death, but he knew it had been in January. He told his mother he wanted to go back to Middlewich, and she said it wasn't possible. It was just too far. He didn't argue at that point, but later he said again that he had to go. After all, they visited Grandpa and Grandma Carter's grave quite often. Once a year for Grandpa Jacardi wasn't much. Again, Faith said it wasn't possible, and James fell silent. But a few days later he presented her and Ben with a page of carefully written arithmetical calculations. It was just so far to the churchyard where Grandpa and Grandma Carter were buried. They went about every two weeks, which was twenty-six times a year. Added together, those journeys were longer than the single one to Middlewich.

Faith was astounded, and Ben stared at his son, almost in disbelief.

'How long did this take you?' he asked. James said it had been a few hours. He'd had to find out distances, and hadn't known who to ask. So he'd gone to Mr Piers, the curate at the church who came to the school sometimes to teach Bible, and he'd helped. He had a map, and he and James had measured it all with a bit of string, which they'd laid against a ruler. It had been interesting.

'I'll take you, then,' said Ben. 'I believe you've earned it.'

Ben took James to Middlewich on the train, and they went to the grave. James had wanted flowers, but there were none to be had in January, so he took some holly instead, carrying it carefully, but still pricking his hands. Something had to be left on the grave, and holly was all he could find. He had still been quite small then.

Every year from that time on, in January, Ben and James went back to Middlewich. James no longer took holly, or tried to find flowers. He simply went into the churchyard and stood by the grave, gazing at the headstone, thinking of the man whose body lay there, and why it was there. He wondered what Captain Jacardi would have done had he known Gillian Nicholson carried his child. After the sacrifices he had made to protect his other son, what could he have done for the child not yet born?

Ben began to leave the engines to James and William. He and Jed were happier working on the hulls, skills they had known nearly all their lives. Ben knew the feel of the grain of the wood, how far he could bend it, the shapes it could take, and those it couldn't. To him, metal was cold and dead, while wood lived in his hands. He watched his son working, concentrated and relaxed, confident in his new skill, in his understanding of the machinery, and he felt pride and love for the boy, almost choking him. His perfect son, tall and strong and straight, breathing quietly, clever and eager.

He and Faith would marvel, thinking about him, catching each other's eyes and smiling, knowing they had been thinking the same thoughts.

James.

They were a close family. They all loved each other, and spent time together, happily. They tried to please each other, to look after each

338

other. Even from his first few days at school, James thought carefully of what news he could pass on to his mother, and what he should keep to himself. Getting a gold star for writing was something she would like to hear. Becky Evans asking why he lived with his grandmother he never mentioned at home. His mother had told him, when he was very small, that he had been born too late to have brothers and sisters, and now he mused over what she had said. Why had he not been born earlier, then? But he never asked her. One day, he assumed, he would know.

He never mentioned either that he dreamed of his grandfather Jacardi, dreams so vivid he felt he could describe the man in clear detail. Tall and dark, with a cleft chin, brown eyes, a way of standing with the back of his left wrist on his hip, the fist lightly clenched, whenever he was thinking. How could he have known that? And why did he find himself imitating it?

He told Mr Piers the story of Grandfather Jacardi, and the curate listened. He had heard of the battle of Isandhlwana, and he knew there had been no survivors. But the young son of an illegitimate man was surely allowed a few harmless fantasies about his father's family. Time enough to correct the fault, to name it as a lie, when the boy was older.

James left school, and Faith cried a little, because she had dreamed he might even go to university. A foolish dream, she'd always known it was next to impossible, but dreams were allowed to be foolish, and losing that one hurt.

'But his son might go to university,' said Ben,

stroking her hair, and she smiled at him, and brushed away the tears. It would be good to have him at home, anyway, not just evenings and holidays. Good to have him working there, and they needed a full-time engineer now. It wasn't only the Bolinder engine that was being fitted in the boats: there were Petters and Nationals, and one called Russell Newbury, and Ben didn't want to learn about them. They were all different.

James reacted to the news of every new engine as though he'd been given a Christmas present. He had to see them all, listen to them, drive the boats that used them. He wanted to touch them and smell them, and learn them. All the time, there was more to learn, and now it was James who had to teach William.

He was a good boatman. He could steer neatly and accurately, never scraping against the walls of the locks, judging the turns and the wind, and, when there was one, the current, without thinking of it. He quite liked boating, delivering the new boats to customers, often on his own, once he was strong enough to handle the locks.

Faith, watching him setting off, sometimes remembered Nellie and Joey Dobson taking the boat away, small children handling a horse and a full-sized working narrowboat. She wondered what had happened to them. Sam Dobson had been in prison for a long time. Had big Sarah recovered from pneumonia? They'd never come back to the boats, the Dobsons.

Now her own son was taking a boat away from the yard, on his own, standing at the tiller tall and confident, fifty miles ahead of him and then the train journey home.

'He'll be all right,' Ben had said, the first time they'd let him take a boat alone, but Ben had been quietly restless until James came back, then had greeted his son with a grin that didn't mask the look of relief.

Nearly a man now, James, taller than most, and with skills that left Ben marvelling. How had he learned this? So deft, those hands, blackened with oil, the third time this boat's been back and the boy close to losing patience.

'You wouldn't feed a horse his own shit, would you?' he'd asked the man, and Ben had gasped. 'Don't give this engine its dirty old oil, then. It can't run on dirty oil.'

The yard was doing well. The railways had taken most of the trade now, but there was still call for good boats, and Armstrong's yard made good boats. Jed had watched Ben painting over the name 'Cartwright' on the scarlet and gold board, no expression on his face, but when he'd seen Ben chalking in the old name, not his own, he'd smiled, and said he'd do that. He'd always been a better signwriter than Ben.

Faith kept the accounts and wrote the letters, but she said she was finding it difficult now. She thought she was making mistakes. She looked over the books every day, and was becoming more and more careful, looking for the mistakes she thought she was making.

'Getting old,' she said, and it was true. She moved more slowly, and said she felt pain in her twisted shoulder, sometimes in her wrists. Everything seemed to take a little longer. Ben said

341

they'd get a girl in to type the letters, why not?, and she laughed at him for his big ideas. A month later she asked him if he remembered what he'd said, about a girl to type the letters. And maybe someone to help in the house?

So Mrs Judson came once a week to do the heavy work, scrubbing the stone floors and polishing the wooden ones, and Miss Ford, a thin girl with greasy brown hair, came in the mornings to type letters, and left a week later, Faith having lost patience with her. She was followed by Miss Bachelor, Miss Nainby, Miss Fairchild and Miss Quinn.

'They're all useless,' she insisted, when Ben asked why she was never satisfied. 'They make mistakes.'

'They're human,' Ben argued. 'Give the next poor girl a chance, at least.'

The next poor girl was Mrs Davis, a widow with a young boy, and Ben refused to allow Faith to dismiss her. This one needed the job, he said.

'I don't believe she's a widow at all,' said Faith, and Ben said she was probably right, and that was all the more reason to let her keep her job. If ever a woman needed steady work it was Mrs Davis.

When Mrs Davis left to go back to her family in Wales, Faith was indignant. She had made allowances for the girl, and this was how she was repaid. Left with only a week's notice.

Jed asked if she would give his daughter a chance. Emily had been unhappy away from home so she'd come back, and she was looking for a job. She had a little experience, and she could type.

'Suppose she doesn't suit?' asked Faith doubtfully, and Jed said in that case Faith would have to sack her. She'd had plenty of experience of how to do that.

Faith was not sure whether to be offended or to laugh, but in the end she laughed, and said Emily could try, for a week or so at least.

Emily Cartwright was probably no better at the job than any of the other girls, but Faith's wrists were too stiff to allow her to write much any more, so she tried harder with Emily.

'At least she doesn't paint her nails and drip that nasty stuff all over the table,' she told Ben.

'That's good,' said Ben. He was tired and his back ached. Jed was getting slow at the work now, and Ben was having to do more of it than he liked. William had fixed the engine bearers in this last boat and he was not so keen on woodwork. He'd done it well, but he hadn't enjoyed it.

Ben was beginning to wonder how they would manage when he was too old to do the heavy work on the yard.

'I can't forget she's Violet's daughter,' Faith fretted. 'I can't quite bring myself to trust her, Ben. I know it's not fair, but I can't help it.'

Still, Faith had to rely on Emily. There was nobody else who could type the letters, now that Faith's wrists were too stiff for her to do it. Now and then she would insist that she could manage, and she would try, but after a while the stabbing, aching pains became too much.

'Emily will have to,' she admitted. 'But I still don't want her doing the books.'

Time was becoming a little confusing to Faith. Her clearest memories were of *Grey Lady*, when she and Ben were working the boat alone, with the piebald horse. What did we call him? Billy. Of course, it was Billy, how could I ever forget that? She would look out of the kitchen window, and find herself mildly surprised to see a boatyard and not water. More importantly, she would see a tall young man, where she had expected a child.

'My, how fast they grow,' she would say to herself, and try to push a growing fear to the back of her mind. She had expected to see a child. James was no longer a child, why was she looking for one?

'Drat these hands,' she'd mutter. 'Rheumatism, takes your mind off everything. Can't think for it.'

Jed told Ben he was finding the work too much now. He dreaded coming in to the yard, especially on cold days, or when there was heavy work to do. He said they needed a younger man, even if it was only part-time.

'When did I get old?' Ben asked Faith that night. 'When did that happen, then? Never saw that creeping up on me.'

Faith smiled at him, reached out to touch his cheek. Her dear man, who'd always been good to her. Yes, he was getting old now. She hadn't noticed, but he was. She'd been too busy feeling sorry for herself.

'It's this winter,' she told him. 'We always did feel old in the winter, didn't we? Always did, my darling. And I'm the one that needs a walking-stick, not you.'

She'd dreaded the winter, this year. The first frost at the beginning of November, and she'd felt frightened, almost panic-stricken. Oh, no, she'd thought. Oh, no, not again. Cold made her wrists ache so. When she tried to hang out the washing a bitter wind felt as if it was cutting her with knives. Winter meant pain now, not just a bit of extra work with the fires but pain, and fear, too. Fear of falling on that icy path. Never used to worry about falling. Just pick yourself up feeling a little foolish, dust off your skirt, and walk on. But falling hurt now. Falling meant bruises that took time to heal, falling meant a fair chance of a broken bone. Coal was heavy to carry. Oh, no. Not winter again.

'James, my dear, would you bring me in a scuttle of coal?'

That Mrs Judson, she was a good soul. A bit too fond of a cup of tea mid-morning, could go on for half an hour, sitting at the table, but a good soul for all that. Kept the floors nice. Might ask her if she could manage Thursdays as well as Tuesdays. She could do the stairs and the windows then. Leave a bit more time for the books. Take an age to check, they do. Writing's getting a bit spidery, sometimes not too sure if it's a five or a three. Does take a time now. Ben's behind on that butty for Jorrocks. Said it would be ready by Christmas, not going to be, not this time.

Oh, my Lord, my hands. Drat this rheumatism. Why does it have to plague me? What was the idea behind rheumatism, then, Lord? Not one of your better notions, if you'll forgive me saying so.

Need another man on the yard. Dear Ben. Not quite as strong and agile as you were ten years ago. Never be another craftsman like you, though. That's why the yard's doing well. Boats that'll take their owners through to Judgement Day, that's what you make, my dear. Where will we find a craftsman like you?

'David needs a job,' said Jed, and Ben leaned back against the boat, and thought, We need a worker and he needs a job.

'David's getting married. Getting married a bit quick, Ben. He needs a proper job, not just what he can pick up on the farms. Not with a baby on the way.'

Ben thought, This place will be full of Cartwrights again. What will Faith say to that? But Jed taught David, and Jed taught me. He's probably as good as we're going to get.

'Place will be full of Cartwrights again,' said Faith that night, and she was bad-tempered about it. 'I don't trust those Cartwrights. I don't mean Jed. He's all right. But Violet's children. I don't like this. Oh, Ben. Can't we get someone else?'

He left it for a day or two, then Faith said she supposed David was as good as most. Give the boy a job, then.

'Boy? Boy?' Ben laughed out loud at her. 'Some boy, that. He's coming up for thirty.'

'Old enough to know better than to get a silly girl in trouble, then,' said Faith, but she was shocked. Thirty? Young David?

'Dear Lord, I am old now, and I never thought of that. Never looked ahead to getting old. You'll forgive me kneeling on a cushion. Your rheumatism seems to have got into my knees now. That's a good walking-stick James made me.

'I do thank you for that boy. That young man. I do, I do thank you. But I need a bit more help now to be a support to my Ben. If you could see your way. But why I'm here now, feeling this floor even through the cushion, is what there was on the wireless about Germany rearming. Dear Lord, I do beg you, not that again.'

17

'It looks as if I'm going to be a soldier, too.'

A once-a-year conversation with his grand-father, six feet or so below, nothing but black bones, if Ben had been right, but James liked talking to Grandfather Jacardi. January again, and bitter frost had whitened the grass so it broke under his feet, crackling. He didn't mind the cold. He stood, hands in his pockets, looking down at the grave, and thinking his conversation with the dead man who never answered, except in his dreams.

'I don't know if I'll be as brave as you. I'll try, I suppose. Mother's fretting about it, Dad's worrying, I don't say much, but I want to go now. I want to be a soldier. I want to get at them. Someone's got to stop them, haven't they? I suppose that's us again. It's all machines now, and I like machines. They say there won't be all that many horses in the army soon. You rode a horse, didn't you? I dreamed of her, your bay mare. I can't ride a horse, but you couldn't drive a tractor, could you? Well, I can. It's easy. So I'll be able to drive a lorry, too, and they'll need that, in the army. I don't suppose I'll be an officer, nothing like that, but I'll be a soldier anyway. A useful one. I bet I can shoot, too. I bet I can learn that. A gun's a machine.

'Wish me luck, Grandfather Jacardi. I suppose

every soldier needs luck. So. Wish me luck, please. I don't know if I'll be able to come back here next year, or not in January. I don't know when.

'It does seem there's a lot I don't know, but I do know I want to be a soldier. I don't want to wait much longer. I think I'll look good in a uniform. Women look at me now, even in my working clothes. They'll look a bit longer when I'm in uniform. And I'll look right back, I will. I'll look right back at them, and I'll smile, and when I'm in uniform I'll know what to say to them. I'll say something to make them laugh. But I won't laugh. I'll just look at them, and I'll be smiling, just a little bit.

'That'll be good. Me in a uniform, and a pretty girl on my arm. The sort that makes the other men look, makes them wish they were me. I'll have two girls, maybe. I'll have a good girl who wears pretty dresses and speaks nicely and never looks at another man, and I'll have a bad girl. She'll let me do anything, and I'll get into fights over her, and the dresses she wears, well... That'll be good.

'When I'm away fighting, they'll write to me. Every week. And I'll have their photographs, I'll keep them, and I'll show the others. "That's my good girl," I'll say, "and that's my bad girl." And when we've been away for a while, the others'll ask to have a look at my photographs, so they can remind themselves this is what women look like. I'll keep the letters from my good girl secret, put them away safe, but I'll show them the letters from my bad girl. We'll all read them.'

349

Grandfather Jacardi understood about secrets. James had had some difficulties with secrets as a young boy, because there was no one with whom he could share them. On *Grey Lady*, they had been on the move, and he had never had an opportunity to make close friends. Other boat families with children came, and moored, and went on, but were never there for long. Never long enough and, in any case, there were always brothers or sisters. James never met a family with only one boy.

Ben was special to James, not only as a father but as a man without parents of his own. When James learned the truth, this did not make Ben less special to him: it simply transferred a measure of magic to the idea of Ben's own father. And Miss Nicholson, of whom no one spoke, the bad woman, was a mystery. Only Grandfather Jacardi really knew about Miss Nicholson, and it was another secret.

As a young boy James dreamed of his grandfather, a fighting soldier in scarlet uniform, a hero, a master of magical secrets, and James spoke to his grandfather, knowing that what he said would be kept secret. Grandfather Jacardi learned that James had stolen a penknife, and was afraid he might be flogged and sent to prison. Grandfather Jacardi was the first to hear that James didn't really believe in God, but prayers had to be said even so, or his mother would be unhappy. The grave in Middlewich became a focus for unspoken hopes, fantasies, fears and plans.

A child told his grandfather of the theft of a

penknife, a boy told him of the loss of faith. A young man spoke of a girl in a cinema, who took him into a field behind the houses, told him she would do it for five shillings. He had pushed her away, then followed her, and went back the next week with the money.

'What do you do, when you feel dirty right through?' he'd asked.

There'd been no answer from the black bones in the grave.

There were other girls, but never again for money, although most had cost him more, what with flowers, and chocolates, and visits to the pictures.

There were bad girls, and none he'd wanted to keep.

He'd told his mother he was out with friends. Yes, Dave and Pete and Laurence. Playing football. Going fishing.

He told his father nothing, and his father didn't ask.

He told Grandfather Jacardi everything, and everything grew clearer for the telling.

In the spring of 1939, James decided to enlist. He would not wait to be called up, and he most certainly would not avoid the call-up, as his mother said he could, on the grounds that building boats was an essential service.

Ben listened as James explained how he felt, or explained as much as he could. He had nothing to say: if James wanted to be a soldier, he would not try to stop him. In the last war he, too, had tried to enlist. In any case, Ben's worries were reserved for Faith. She dreaded another war, and dreaded it most because it might put James at risk. Now, instead of avoiding the danger, James was throwing himself at it. How would Faith manage this?

Faith did not seem surprised. She grew pale and her lips trembled when Ben told her, but it was as if she had been expecting it, like a death after a long illness. For over a year, since she had begun to take notice of what was happening in Germany, the sickness had been taking hold, and now James had responded to it by enlisting in the army.

At night Ben lay awake staring at the ceiling, trying to plan. With James going, he would have to employ someone, and he'd never find anyone as good as his son. He'd have to learn about engines himself. Get James to teach him as much as he could in the time that was left, however long that might be. Not that you could learn the sort of magic James had in his hands.

He couldn't be sure either that William and David would stay.

Faith dreamed restlessly of bright-eyed young men, eager for a fight, for a share of glory. Bright eyes growing haunted and exhausted, hopes lost somewhere in a wilderness of mud and barbed wire, where nothing would ever be green again, and no birds could sing.

'Gas,' she murmured sometimes, and Ben's arm would tighten around her, his lips move against her hair until she slept quietly again.

James dreamed of a dark-haired man in a scarlet

uniform cantering up a bleak and dusty hill on a bright bay mare.

'This way,' the man called back to him. 'Follow me. This way.'

James followed easily, running up the hill after the man, never taking his eyes off him. He might look back, and James must be there, ready, and running.

'Dear Lord, take care of my boy.'

'When do I get to be a soldier, then? What are they waiting for? I bet I'll look good in a uniform.'

A summer fête in the village, and the sky was clear and blue, and Faith had baked a couple of cakes. James went with her, carrying them in a basket with a clean cloth over them to keep off the dust. Faith couldn't walk fast any more, and she nearly always used the stick he'd made for her. She stooped now, bending her back as they went up the path, and she needed to stop to rest. A white-haired old lady with a hunched shoulder and a tall young man at her side carrying a basket, dew on the grass and the spiders' webs and wild flowers turning their faces to the lifting sun. A jewelled morning, a day that would shine and glitter, and Faith, stopping at the stile to catch her breath, looked up at her son and thought, This is how to remember him, on a perfect morning in early summer, before the world turns into mud and barbed wire.

That evening James came home with a lovely darkhaired girl on his arm, and told Ben and Faith that this was the one he would marry.

She had been telling fortunes to raise money for the school. He'd gone into the little striped tent, ducked under the flap, and looked up to see her smiling at him. That was all it had needed.

She hadn't looked at his palm. She'd held her hand against his, and told him what she knew: 'Seven times we've been married in previous lives. More to come, I shouldn't wonder.' And he'd nodded, accepting what she'd said, not asking questions.

He'd gone out of the little tent and sat on the grass and waited for her. That was what she'd expected, and that was what he had done, so when she had come out of the tent two hours later he'd been there waiting for her when she looked for him. He'd stood up, and she'd slipped her arm through his, and they'd walked back through the fields to his home, to where Ben and Faith waited.

Mary.

Faith looked into the girl's smiling blue eyes, and felt her heart lurch and lift.

'Mary?'

'Mary Savage,' the girl answered. 'I do hope you'll like me, Mrs Jacardi. We're going to be close for a long time.'

Faith laughed, and held out her arms.

'Oh, my dear. My dear Mary.'

How could they not love her, this beautiful girl who would marry their son? She was quick and clever, and she laughed easily, and she loved James, and had spirit enough to manage him without him minding, and grace enough to give in to him when it seemed that he might.

They would be married as soon as the banns had been read, because there was no reason to wait, and plenty not to.

The man on the bright bay mare wheeled his horse and came to a halt, and smiled back at James running behind him, and when James woke the next morning he knew he had time to marry his girl, although he had forgotten the dream.

Mary Savage was a teacher, although, in her own words, not a proper one. Only handcrafts and games, she said, nothing like classroom work. One Saturday morning she plaited a bracelet for Faith out of a few bits of copper wire and some strands of James's hair, and they watched her making it, interested and mildly amused. Then, when she'd finished it, she handed it to Faith. It was a lovely thing.

'You're a marvel, Mary,' said Ben, and Faith pushed it on to her wrist and said it felt like a lucky talisman. For a moment she remembered the bracelets she'd made from Blackie and Silver's hairs, bracelets that still lay in *Grey Lady*'s ticket drawer. A little smile, a moment of sadness, and Ben, watching her, knew what had crossed her mind and echoed her smile.

The talisman Mary made for James was plaited out of gold wire and her own hair. A love-knot, she said, and he laid it on the palm of his hand and looked at it, a delicate series of twists and curves, and he could find no join in it, no place where his eye stopped at an awkward angle.

'It's perfect,' he said, and it was true. It was the first time he'd ever seen perfection in something

355

made by human hands.

Mary looked into his face, and looked down at her love-knot, and asked him, 'When you go away, will you be true to me?'

James thought about it. He thought of his silly dream of having two girls, a good girl and a bad girl, when he'd imagined his good girl would have blonde hair and blue eyes and wear dresses with flowers in the pattern and neat, high collars, and his bad girl would be dark, and wear bright colours.

Mary was standing in front of him, waiting for his answer, dark-haired, her face brown from the sun, wearing a scarlet blouse.

He thought of being away from Mary, when he'd be with men, and when they could they'd go looking for girls, for bad girls. He'd imagined he'd go with them. If he was to be faithful to Mary, he'd have to stay behind. They might laugh at him. They'd tell him, 'She'll never know, will she? Where's the harm, then? Come on, don't be such a bloody sissy.'

'You're not the first woman in my life,' he said, and she replied that he was not the first man in hers.

It didn't matter. He looked at his beautiful love-knot, and he looked at his beautiful girl, and he smiled.

'Yes,' he said, 'I'll be true to you. You're not the first, but you're the last. Will that do, my love?'

She touched his cheek, stood up on tiptoe to kiss him, and he put the love-knot in his wallet, in the inside pocket of his jacket, and he laid the jacket down on the grass under the trees and turned to his waiting girl.

He was very careful with the scarlet blouse, because he knew she was the sort of woman who would always take care, so he undid every button, not pulling at them, but sliding them through the neat buttonholes, one at a time, only turned his face to kiss the palm of her hand as she held it against his cheek. He folded the blouse and laid it on the moss by a tree root, and gently and carefully he took Mary in his arms, down on to the soft, clean grass, and thought, I've never done this before. This is so different, it's like the first time.

She was hesitant, a little shy, but she loved him and she trusted him. She watched his face as he looked at her, as his hands stroked the long, lovely lines of her body, and when he smiled again, in delight at her beauty, she smiled back at him, and the hesitancy and the shyness had gone, and would never return.

For Mary, too, it was like the first time, because this man loved her, as he had in the lifetimes before. Seven lifetimes, she'd told him, in the little tent at the fair, but each time new again. He had taken joy in the beauty of her body, and she felt a sense of wonder in his, in the brown skin, in the curving muscles hard under her hands, in the small bones in his spine.

A man and a woman, more than themselves because they were together, lovers, and loving. Naked under the summer sun, close against each other, whispering the words of love, smiling and touching and moving. There was love, and there was friendship, there was laughter, and something in both of them reaching out for the other, straining towards each other, finally meeting in an explosion of release, triumph and joy.

It had seemed almost unreal to both of them. Mary opened her eyes to see James looking down into them, smiling, his hair damp against his forehead, and she reached up to brush it back, and he kissed her hand. Reality again, the sun shining down on them, the smell of the grass, wind in the trees above them bringing a small shiver from Mary, and James clasped her close to him, as if to shelter her from the cold drifting in the air. Voices in the distance, the sound of a laugh, and he turned his head, listening, calculating, coming this way? How far?

'Are you cold?' he asked. 'Is that grass damp?'

'No. Yes, no. Don't get up.'

'People are coming.'

'Oh.'

She sounded so disconsolate that he laughed. She wrinkled her nose at him, and smiled.

'May they fall into an elephant trap,' she said, and added, 'That's an ancient Staffordshire curse.'

A few minutes later Mary and James stood on the path looking down on to a patch of flattened grass, and green moss under a tree root. James thought he would never forget exactly how it looked, with shadows from the summer leaves dappling the sunlit grass.

'In our bedroom,' said Mary, 'I will make something moss green. Maybe a chair. What do you think? A chair to leave our clothes on at night? Moss green, like that?'

'Yes,' said James. 'I'd like that.'

The breeze moved the leaves again, rustling them over their heads, a cloud crossed the sun. Two people came out of the woods on the path and broke the spell.

They were married in the village church three weeks later. It was the first time Ben and Faith had met Mary's parents, and the last time Faith saw either of them. They came up from London just for the day, small, pleasant people, who seemed a little in awe of their daughter. Certainly they would never have questioned her choice of husband.

To James and Mary, the wedding didn't seem important. They exchanged vows in the church that they had already exchanged under the trees by the fields, and they claimed each other with gold rings when they had already pledged themselves with a love-knot. There was a man with a camera who fussed around everyone, made them all stand in a line, told them what to do, until they both grew bored and a little annoyed with him, and told him to go away. He gaped at them in disbelief.

'But I'm the *photographer!*'

They had already decided not to go away for a honeymoon. Somehow, the idea seemed a little vulgar. They went back to the cottage, where the only changes had been that James had thrown out his old bed and made a new one, and Mary had installed a chair by the fireplace, a comfortable little tub chair, moss green.

'We could go away,' said James, 'if you'd like to. It might be our only chance. There is going to be a war, Mary.'

I might be killed, he thought, but she knew it too, and there was no need to say it, not to Mary.

'I might be killed,' he said to Grandfather Jacardi, the next time he spoke to him. 'If that happens, it happens. But I couldn't bear to be a burden to my Mary. I don't want to come back a cripple.'

In his dreams the dark-haired man sat on his bright bay mare on the brow of the stony hill, and waited, his sword in his hand.

'Would you like to go away?' James insisted. 'We could take *Grey Lady*.'

She'd never been on a canal boat, except a couple of short trips down to the locks, when he'd been giving a boat a test run and had taken her along for the ride. She'd never slept on a boat, never tried to keep house on one. *Grey Lady*'s cabin was like a toy to Mary, everything so small it was as if it was made in miniature.

No, she didn't want to go away on *Grey Lady*. She wanted to stay in the house and help Faith, who was very tired, and who needed her lovely Mary. The house wasn't the way Faith wanted it now, it was dusty, not clean enough, and Faith fretted about it. Mary had buckets and dusters flying around, brooms whisking into corners, beeswax polish, and she sang as she worked, so it became a game, a dance, and Faith sang too, a high little soprano voice that wasn't quite steady. Faith washed china ornaments carefully and slowly at the kitchen sink, drying them and standing them on white paper, while Mary's scrubbing brush threw up a foam of suds, and an old carpet beater was found in the attic and brought back into service, clouds of dust thrashed out of the carpets.

'Whitewash,' Mary told James. 'And I saw a ladder at the back of the woodshed.'

'I'm no painter,' he protested.

'Not today, maybe,' she answered. 'Tomorrow you will be, or I'll know the reason why. And get those boots off before you come into this kitchen. You can leave your overalls out there, too.'

The kitchen floor shone, dark red quarry tiles rubbed over with Cardinal polish, the range freshly blacked, the big table scrubbed nearly white, and Faith sat in her chair looking around.

'Isn't she a love, your Mary?' she said, as James came in, and he looked across at Mary, standing in the door and smiling at him.

'A love?' he asked. 'A *love?* That one? She's a harridan. She's chased me up a ladder and kept me there all day, I was too scared to come down. I can't wear my boots in my own home. A *love?*'

The news from Europe was bad, and getting worse. War was coming, everyone knew it. The politicians denied it, and people smiled when they heard there would be peace in their time. They began to make sandbags.

A letter came for James telling him to report to a training camp. There was a travel warrant. He had ten days.

'They shouldn't make you go,' said Faith, and there were tears in her eyes. 'You've got a wife. They shouldn't make you go.'

'I volunteered,' he reminded her, and that night as he lay in the dark with Mary's head resting on his shoulder he asked her if she understood why he'd volunteered.

'I think so,' she said. She'd been quiet all day, since the postman had come.

'It's even more important, now I've got you,' he said. 'We've got to stop them. If we don't stop them they'll be over here in the end, ordering us all around. Telling *you* what to do. I couldn't have that, my darling. I couldn't stand for any damned German telling you what to do. That's the best reason of all, for fighting them.'

It wasn't exactly what he had meant to say, but he thought she understood.

He still wanted to be a soldier, but all his reasons had changed. He would carry a picture of his wife in his wallet, and he would carry the love-knot, but looking good in a uniform no longer mattered.

After a little while Mary fell asleep. Moonlight was flooding through the open window, turning white the moss-green chair on which their clothes lay, all colour gone. In the distance James heard an owl.

Mary should be safe here, with his parents. She'd told him that if there was a war she'd go back to work. Someone had to teach the children, Hitler or no Hitler, and she supposed, if she had to, she could teach them to read. There were four teachers in the village school, and three were young men. She thought they would enlist.

Mary worked in the house, and sang as she did so. She took as many of the burdens off Faith's shoulders as she could, but behind her smiling face she considered the future and tried to plan.

James would go away, and Faith would be desperate with anxiety. Already, there was something in Faith's eyes when she looked at her son that made Mary uneasy.

'It's only a training camp,' she said, and Faith smiled.

'He'll have a grand time,' Mary insisted. 'He'll get up to all sorts, playing cowboys and Indians all over Salisbury Plain. He'll love every minute of it.'

Neither of the women put their fears into words. To do so would give them strength and form. Instead, they agreed that James would have a grand time. It was good for a young man to be with others of his age, learning new skills, being out in the fresh air. He'd enjoy it, and when he came back on leave he'd be as brown as a berry, fit and strong, and full of stories about all the things they had done together.

When he left they didn't pretend to each other. Mary was crying as she waved goodbye, and Faith watched in silence, her eyes bright. There were no songs in the house for the rest of the day.

Ben, too, was silent. William and David worked quietly, leaving him alone, painting a new boat they had launched. His fears for the moment were almost entirely reserved for Faith. James would come to no harm in training camp, he thought. The lad was clever and strong, but Ben knew Faith saw these few weeks, and they were so few, to learn how to fight and survive, like some sort of preparation for sacrifice. Her boy was being groomed, trained, and decked out in his finery ready for his death.

Faith took longer over her prayers at night. She still knelt to say them, still closed her eyes and held her hands with the palms pressed together in front of her chest, and Ben, sitting quietly on the edge of the bed, waiting for her to finish so that he could help her to her feet, thought he could draw some kind of map of their life together from the way Faith prayed. Now, there was a kind of hopeless resignation. Tears would sometimes glimmer under her closed lids, sometimes run slowly down her lined cheeks. She believed James was as good as dead, and her prayers would not be answered.

James wrote to Mary as often as he could, and the letters were meant to be read aloud to Faith and Ben. A little note, which was just for her, would be slipped into the envelope, and these she tucked into a drawer in her dressing-table, and read at night, again and again. If she could not have his body in the bed with her, she could have the memory of it, and these notes were meant to remind her.

He telephoned her, too. Faith would not answer the telephone at all because it made her nervous, and Ben would shout down it, hardly able to believe that voices could travel down wires. He would say a few words to James, his mother was well and sent her love, the new boat was giving trouble, it shook too much when they started the engine, what could that be, then, son? Here's Mary, now. And then he'd leave the room and close the door behind him.

But Mary liked the little notes best, which she could read again and again as she lay in bed, and look across at the pillow that she had left, foolishly, dented by the weight of his head, at the single dark hair against the white linen.

He came home on weekend leave in uniform, and he did look good in it, as he had once hoped. He was thinner, the bones in his face clearer under skin darkened by weather. He told them he was sick of running around with a forty-pound pack on his back and a wooden gun in his hands, but he was learning lorry maintenance.

'Easy for you, that,' said Ben, and James smiled.

'It is easy,' he told Mary later, 'but there aren't enough lorries to learn on. I tell you, my love, it's damned stupid, this. Not enough guns to fire, not enough lorries, not enough anything. Well, I don't know.'

Guns weren't quite as easy as he'd imagined. He supposed he was a fair shot, as good as most, but nothing more than that. But he hadn't come home to talk about guns and lorries, he'd come home to see his lovely wife.

There was more to it than that, and she knew it. Had everything gone well, James would have talked about it, told her everything he'd been doing, but instead he wanted to know all the details of her life, everything she'd done since he'd left, until the Sunday afternoon when she'd said she wanted to go for a walk. Almost as soon as they were out of sight of the cottage she stopped him. She stood in front of him, her hands on his shoulders, and looked straight into his face.

'Now tell me,' she said. 'And tell me the truth.'

There was no evading Mary in that mood.

James didn't see how they were going to win a war against Germany. They didn't seem to have enough of anything. There wasn't enough live ammunition for them to learn how to shoot, even. Two old lorries, not even the sort they were likely to be using, were all they had to learn maintenance. Their best lessons had come from a garage in the town, which had telephoned them every time a likely vehicle was in for repairs.

James put his arms round Mary, and rested his chin on top of her head. She said nothing, stood quietly holding him, wondering.

'I've got a bayonet,' he said at last. 'No rifle to fix it to. I suppose I'd better learn how to throw it.'

It was not a good joke, but it was the best he could manage, so she laughed.

'Don't mention this to my mother,' he said, before they went home.

When he went away again Mary tried to sing as she cleaned the house, and learned how to cook, and sewed new curtains for the cottage, but every so often Faith would see her standing quietly, looking out of the window, a duster forgotten in her hand, and she would remember the look in the girl's eyes. Her prayers that night would be more desperate and desolate than ever.

War again, and then nothing happened. What sort of a war is this, where no one does anything? Where we wait night after night for the bombs that are never dropped, where everything is so busy, and nothing is ever done?

A funny sort of war, this. In America they called it a phoney war. Men were training all over the country, bits of lead pipe stuck into wood instead of guns, little folding boats meant for crossing rivers. When the men tried to climb into them, they sank. There were warning signs on some of the armoured vehicles, Training Purposes Only.

'Could punch a hole through that with my fist,' James wrote to Mary.

Get the men as fit and as well trained as they could, and there were boys coming out from the industrial areas and the mines, pale-faced and hollow-chested, coughing as they ran.

Mary went back to the school the day after she received a letter asking if she could spare the time to teach a few lessons a week. Handcrafts and games as before, and Mr Sinclair had been called up, or volunteered, the flustered headmistress couldn't remember which, and didn't see that it mattered either way. Mary, Mrs Jacardi, rather, could you manage to teach the fourth form geography if Miss Elliot takes on history?

'I don't know much about it,' said Mary doubtfully.

Mrs Webb waved her hands around in despair.

'Read it up the night before, dear. Keep a few notes. I believe it's known as bluffing.'

James came home twice in the autumn. He was a lance corporal, then he was a corporal, and he had at last been given what he called real work. It was a strange assortment of trucks and vans that came to the depot, and they all needed to be stripped down, rebuilt and made ready for action.

'Have they given you a rifle yet?' asked Mary.

He shook his head. He'd fired one a few times.

367

Someone had found some ammunition, not enough, but at least they had been given a few lessons. James had thought it would be easy, but a gun was a different kind of machine, with new rules he had to learn. He could pull them apart in seconds, clean them, and put them back together as fast as fingers could fly, and they worked well for him when he had done that, but firing them was a different matter. Range and wind speed, elevation, words he knew and more still that he learned, but these skills did not seem to have been born in him. Where he could listen to the sound of an engine, and turn a screw, a little pressure on a spanner, and the beat grew stronger, steadier, faster, slower, whatever he needed, and he never needed to think, firing a rifle had to be learned, and practised.

Calculate the distance, set the sights, aim, and at first the target never seemed to be there, not in the sights. Should be there, he'd pointed the bloody gun in the right direction, where was the damned target? Never there, only there some-times, getting a bit better. Right, there it is, now squeeze that trigger, don't pull it, don't jerk the thing.

'You wouldn't *believe* how the things can kick,' he said to Mary, but the bruises were yellowing by then, and all she could do was kiss them.

He was teaching other men now, routine maintenance on anything with wheels, it seemed to Mary when he told her about it. Wheels, or tracks, and he'd been in tanks as well, huge things, no steering-wheels, it's all done with the clutches and levers.

She listened, and tried to understand. The driver couldn't even see, could that be right?

There were rumours. Germany would try to invade France. Steel supplies from Sweden were going into Germany. Soon, he thought, he would be sent abroad. He didn't know when, didn't know where. But soon.

Even if he did know, he wouldn't have been allowed to tell her.

Would they send him out to fight without giving him his own rifle? He'd joked with her about learning to throw a bayonet, about being an amazing shot with a number-sixteen spanner, but Mary listened to rumours too, rumours of huge armies of modern tanks and other fighting machines that had rolled into Poland and crushed it in four days. Dive-bombers too, wicked things, faster than anything had ever flown before, hundreds of them.

James came home for Christmas, and told Mary they'd be leaving early in the new year. He probably wouldn't see her again before then. Yes, he had his own rifle at last, wished he'd been able to bring it home to show her, but that wasn't allowed.

'France?' she asked, and he hesitated, looking down into her face. He'd been ordered not to say, so she laid her fingers on his lips and said it didn't matter. He would have told her had she asked again, so she didn't. She couldn't think of anything to say to him about it. She talked instead about school, the children whose fathers had also gone to fight, alongside their teachers for all she could tell. She never knew from one day to the next what she'd be teaching, because the other men had left now. Mrs Webb was nearly tearing her hair out. There'd been a relief teacher from Birmingham for a few days, taking history, and she'd had something wrong with her teeth. It had become impossible, the poor woman trying to teach a class of eleven-year-old thugs about the civil wars, with Voundheads and Voyalists and Vestorvationists. 'Oh, and another disaster. We've run out of raffia.'

Little things to make him smile. She'd decorated a Christmas tree with candles she'd made herself, and fir cones painted gold and silver. It looked beautiful.

On the night before he left they lay naked in their bed, twined together, arms and legs wrapped around each other, and while James was calm, controlled, Mary was almost frantic. She didn't want to sleep at all. She wanted every minute, every second, wanted to remember. There was a little white scar on the edge of his jaw where he'd been hit by a cricket ball. Less than an inch long, quite faint, but she would remember that. Two fading bruises on his ribs, a game of football, he said. The way the outside corners of his eyes seemed to tilt upwards just a little. His crisp dark hair. The palms of his hands with the calluses from the tools he used, the faint traces of black oil still etched into the lines. The way he smiled, like his mother. Whenever she saw Faith smile she would remember.

I wish I could see into the future, she thought, and then, No. No, I don't wish that. God forbid.

The way he loved her. The many ways he loved

370

her, gentle, and fierce, and slow, and wild. The joy she took in the lovely strength of his body, the pride because he found hers beautiful.

Whatever happens, there had been this.

James, drowsing, and waking, and drowsing again, thought, We'll have to stop them. I'll die before I'll let the bastards near her. Fight them off with my teeth, if I have to. If I'm anywhere near, when they come.

Tanks with guns that wouldn't fire, with tracks that came loose on uneven ground. Damned engines that only started one in four times. Bakers' vans converted into ambulances, tear out the racking and bolt in supports for stretchers, clamps to hold boxes of bandages, whatever it was they needed. What sort of an army is this?

They'll be over here, if we don't stop them.

Morning, and Mary still wide awake, smudges of weariness under her blue eyes, but smiling at him. Suppose he had never met her? Imagine that. Going off to France to face the Germans and not knowing Mary was here. You'd be half beaten before you ever set foot on the ships.

She went to the station with him, kissed him goodbye, and tried to smile, but there were tears in her eyes. Beside her there were other women saying goodbye to their men. Most were trying to smile, but there were some who made no effort to disguise their misery, and their fear.

Dear Lord, she thought. Oh, dear Lord, bring him back to me. Bring him back safe.

Faith that night said her prayers, and they were brief. I will never see my boy again, she said. I should thank you for him, for the time I had him.

371

I should try to thank you. But only twenty-one years, and you're taking him back. I don't think I can help it if I hate you now.

18

Emily Cartwright left the boatyard to join the army as a nurse, and Mary said she would manage the accounts somehow, and she could make fenders, although the tough hemp rope was ruination on her hands. But a boat needed fenders, and could not be sent out without them, no matter how good the boatman. Something had to protect the hull. So Mary wrestled with the ropes, plaiting, knotting and tugging at them to make them hard and tight, and it was a job she began to hate and dread. By the end of the school day she wanted to rest, not work with ropes. She was teaching geography and remedial reading as well as handcrafts and games, and sometimes history and English, although she did draw the line at maths. 'No, Mrs Webb, I will not. They all know more than I do.'

Mrs Webb tried to plead with her.

'I will *not*. I'm already in a muddle with the history and geography. You throw geometry at me too, I'll have a nervous breakdown, that's a promise.'

The British Expeditionary Force was in France, and James was somewhere with them. Letters came, saying little because there was little he was allowed to say, except that he was safe and well. There were names of his friends, Jacko and Pitboy, brothers from the Coventry coalfields,

Fred, Yank and Zulu. He'd been nicknamed 'Mule', because a door had jammed and he'd kicked it open, breaking the lock. No one, except perhaps Fred, used the names their parents had given them.

'We had a mule,' Faith told Mary. 'He was called Silver. He was a good mule.'

Mary wrote to James every week.

I suppose Emily worked quite hard, but I don't think she achieved much. She was very slow. There isn't a lot of work at the moment, and that's just as well. There's only William and Ben. I don't know what we're going to do for the cloths for this new boat. I wish William would understand that the engine has to be put in straight. This one's rattling, too.

They listened to the wireless every evening, but nothing told them what they wanted to know. Every letter that came said only that James had been well when he had written it. Mary, struggling with the fenders, remembered the pictures she had seen of the tormented fall of Poland, and remembered James's voice as he told her about the bakers' vans they'd turned into ambulances, about engines that wouldn't start. The truck he'd been given was the worst in the unit, because he was the best mechanic.

She said the names of his friends as she worked, Jacko, Pitboy, Fred, Yank, Zulu. They needed each other, so she would say their names. And Mule. Her James, they called him Mule. He was a corporal, but it was still nicknames. Someone had told them, 'Take care of a mule and he'll pull you through hell.'

Were they still using mules, then? Real ones?

James wished they were. Some of these engines he was supposed to keep running with no spare parts and few tools were hardly worth the time he was spending on them. He supposed the other mechanics were doing their best, under the same difficulties. Everything had to be done at the double, too.

'What's the matter with it, Corporal?'

'Technically speaking, sir?'

'Well. If you must.'

'It's fucked, sir.'

'Ah. I see. Well, do your best, Corporal. As quickly as you can.'

His best on that occasion meant waiting until the officer was out of sight, calling Fred and Pitboy, and pushing the thing over the side of the road into the ravine. They were already miles behind the others, bloody thing overheating, breaking down every half-hour. God knows if they'd ever catch up now, but they'd certainly be quicker on foot.

He wrote to Mary that night: 'With luck it'll fall into enemy hands. It'll slow them down a treat. We're all well, seeing a lot of Europe. It looks much like England from inside the trucks.'

That was the last letter he sent, although he did try to write to Mary. He wrote late in the nights, when they finally stopped to rest on the retreat that was nothing more than a headlong flight back across Belgium and France.

Zulu was killed, and James never knew exactly what had happened, even though he'd been right alongside him at the time. There was a bang, and Zulu dropped to his knees, folded down on to the road, and James grabbed him and dragged him off to the side, yelling something about taking cover. Men were throwing themselves down the bank into the ditches, and James was half carrying Zulu and calling him a stupid bastard, never did look where he was going. Zulu thought he'd done something wrong. That's good, James thought. Keep saying you're sorry, and I'll keep shouting at you, that way you won't stop and think. Stupid bastard, I've told you, I've *told* you, until a look of surprise crossed Zulu's face, and then nothing.

They'd been taught how to check if a man was dead, but James didn't need to check. He saw Zulu die, and knew it for reality. A sort of blurring, and then that look of surprise, and whatever Zulu had been wasn't there any more.

'Shit,' said Pitboy. 'Oh, shit.'

Fred was crying.

What the hell had happened? What had killed Zulu?

'Come on,' he said. 'No point standing here.'

They carried the body for a mile, then climbed back on to the road. There was a truck stranded by the side, its tyres shredded, steam still curling up from under the bonnet. James and Pitboy put Zulu in the back of the truck, and James levered open the bonnet and looked down at the engine. There was a gaping hole in the side of the block, a buckled con rod protruding through it.

'Can you fix it?' asked Fred. He was still crying. Zulu had been kind to him, patient with him.

James gave Fred a cigarette, told the men to take a break. Five minutes.

In England Mary told the fifth form to name the countries that bordered France. Yes, Anthony, Germany, that's one. And Italy, yes. And Belgium.

She stopped, and looked out of the window, her eyes seeming to cloud over. The borders of Belgium and France, and there was a stinging in her eyes, as if there was smoke in them, as if someone had just lit a cigarette beside her.

And the countries that border the English Channel, please, Thomas. Holland, yes, and Belgium and France. Well done.

Holland and Belgium fought, and capitulated, stunned by the force and the terror and the speed of the German army. France tried to hold on, tried, tried, and failed.

I wish I could send this to you [James wrote]. Writing's better than nothing, even if I can't send it, or speak to you. Apart from poor old Zulu, we're all well. I've got his blood on my tunic. Maybe it's just as well I can't send this letter. I can't wash the tunic. It's still red. It should have gone brown by now, but it hasn't. It's dried red. We're heading for the Channel. I hope I'll see you soon. This wasn't the way it was meant to happen. God forgive us, we did not do very well here.

He thought about God sometimes. It didn't seem quite right, now things were bad, to turn to a God he'd decided didn't exist. There'd been a chaplain too, driven around in a car, and he'd been drunk, shouting that they should make way for him.

'Get those carts out of the way and let me through.'

God of the mud and the barbed wire and the drunken priests. God of the dead engines and the shredded tyres. God of dried blood that didn't turn brown.

He'd kicked another door down, a barn with hay in it, where they could rest for the night, and Pitboy had worked the bolt of his rifle, quite calmly, when the farmer had tried to order them off his land.

'Want to get that door open, Mule?' Pitboy had asked. 'I'll deal with the Frog.'

He dreamed of his grandfather that night. The bay mare was sweating and nervous, but the man sat calmly, looking at him.

'Are you there?' asked James.

'Yes.'

'I don't know what to do.'

The man turned the horse and rode back down the hill.

'Come on,' he said. 'Follow me. Now.'

James woke the men, told them to move out.

'Now,' he said. 'Follow me.'

The dive-bombers, the Stukas, that was what he hated most. They howled, demon things, screaming as they attacked. He'd never anticipated a machine like that, a thing that seemed to be alive, malevolent, terrifying.

'Move,' said James. 'Come on, move.'

They were cold and stiff and tired, grumbling at him, but the man had ridden back down the hill, and told James to follow.

'This way,' said James. 'Jacko, pick your fucking feet up and move when I tell you, or you'll get my bayonet up your arse. Fred, you too.'

Back the way they came, and he made them run. They were nearly a mile from the farm when the two Stukas came, and they heard the screaming of the engines. Smoke plumed into the air, black against the grey dawn, drifted, and the Stukas went away from them, flashing light along the road towards the sea.

'All right,' said James. 'Halt.'

'That's the farm,' said Pitboy. 'They hit the farm.'

'So what?' said James. 'Never did like that farm. Right, turn round and go back the way we came.'

Mary sat up in bed early that morning, her hands clasped over her ears. There'd been a dreadful sort of screaming noise, and she thought she could smell smoke.

There was a telephone call that day from Robert Marston, who'd bought a boat from them two years earlier. He wanted to speak to Ben. Did Ben think *Eliza Jane* could get across the Channel?

'Maybe,' said Ben, doubtfully. 'If it was dead calm.'

'Tell this stupid bastard that,' said Robert, and

Ben found himself talking to a stranger about canal boats and the lack of keels.

'I suppose I can't stop him,' said the stranger at last. 'Damned fool.'

'Going down to Southend,' said Ben, as he hung up. 'Lots of them. They're going over the Channel.'

'In narrowboats?' asked Faith, incredulous, and Ben shook his head. He didn't know. But he sat down beside Faith and put his arm around her shoulders. She'd been so quiet for the last few days. Nothing but bad news from Europe, what could they say to each other? Only Mary smiled and sang, and Faith, remembering the last war, knew vaguely what that cost her, and tried to smile back at her.

Mary was very tired, but she didn't recognise tiredness. She wondered what was wrong with her. She managed the teaching during the days, learning as fast as she could what she would have to put across in the lessons, trying to remember enough so she wouldn't have to look down at her notes too often. In the evenings she would mark the books, and type any letters for the business, but then she seemed to feel ill. She wanted to close her eyes. It took so much effort, knotting up the fenders. She would look at the neat coils of hemp rope, at her half-finished work, and think, I don't want to. I don't want to do it.

But it had to be done, because the man was collecting the boat at the weekend, and it couldn't go out without fenders, and there was no one else. So, with an old screwdriver, a hammer, something Ben called a fid, which he had made her out of teak, and that harsh, rough rope with the fibres that seemed to work their way into her skin, she would knot, and lever, and pull, and hammer, and at last they would be finished. A set of fenders for the new boat, ready for the weekend. Then there were only the accounts to check, because Faith fretted and worried about them, and couldn't seem to keep on top of them any more. It didn't take very long, but it had to be done.

Sleep, just a few hours, four or five maybe, and often she would dream of a soldier on a horse who was talking to someone she couldn't quite see.

'Our Father, who art in heaven, please keep my James safe. Amen.'

'God, please look after Mary, and keep Fred going in spite of his blisters. Stupid bugger got his feet wet again. Amen.'

'You were the one who wrecked the fucking truck.'

'Lay off, Jacko. Spent more time pushing it than riding in it.'

'Mule's supposed to be an engineer.'

They were bickering more and more now. He supposed he ought to do something about it, but he didn't know what. He was tired, and he was fed up with marching, with being ordered to march the men somewhere else, and then to march back again. He was fed up with the men, who could talk about nothing worth listening to. He was fed up with the sounds of the guns, and most of all he was fed up with the Stukas. Just where the hell was the RAF?

Did anyone know what was happening? It wouldn't be so bad if he could believe someone knew, someone had a plan, but he didn't believe it. The officers he saw looked not only tired but harassed.

There were dead animals by the side of the road, horses usually. When the Stukas came the people ran off the road, into the ditches, some sort of cover, but the horses were harnessed to the carts. There were dead people, too, but usually someone had thrown something over them to cover them.

Not the woman. He wouldn't forget the woman. She hadn't reached the side of the road, and she'd been hit. There was a lot of blood, not much you could make out, except her face, one shoulder and one arm, which was crooked across her chest, damped against it. It was holding a baby's head.

They'd all seen it, but they'd gone past, not saying anything, perhaps pretending they hadn't noticed, but suddenly there'd been nothing to say. They weren't even grumbling. Silence, just the dragging thud of their boots on the road. That was what he remembered.

He knew it couldn't have been silent. There were refugees around, and there were guns in the distance, there was never silence. There was a staff car a minute or two afterwards.

'Where are you heading, Corporal?'

'You tell me, sir.'

'I see. Well, carry on.'

Mary supposed she would just have to carry on, no matter what happened. At least those fenders were done. She did wish Faith would try to rest in the afternoons. Dear Faith, so brave, trying to keep the house clean, to cook a meal in the evenings, but Faith was beginning to forget what she was doing. Mary would come home to find a pot of potatoes half peeled, a tin of polish and a duster lying forgotten on a chair.

If I make a start on another set of fenders, she thought, it won't be such a rush. I won't have to spend hours on them every evening. Maybe I'll start them tomorrow. I'll leave it for this evening.

'I can't go on,' said Fred again. 'You'll have to leave me.'

'It's only blisters, you whining bastard.'

There was no skin at all on Fred's heels, just raw flesh, bleeding.

James cut the backs out of Fred's boots and told him to shut up and march.

That night Yank lost his rifle. He didn't know what had happened to it. Another mystery, and one for which James would be held responsible. Yank said he knew he'd had it when they started.

'Started what?' demanded James, but Yank didn't know. He was sullen about it. He must have put it down somewhere and forgotten to pick it up. He didn't want the fucking rifle anyway, he was sick of it. Mule could go fuck himself.

James made them do the next two miles at the double, and after that they kept their complaints a little quieter.

They were shouldering their way through

383

crowds of refugees now, men and women who had no idea of where they were going, only that what lay ahead could not be as bad, as murderous, as terrifying, as what they had left behind.

Fred found a dog, an old hound of some sort with a weeping sore on its flank. It stank, and it whimpered all night, keeping most of them awake. The next morning James shot it, and Fred cried for the rest of the day.

There was black smoke in the sky ahead of them.

'Dunkirk,' they were told. 'Head for the smoke. Get on to the beaches, you'll be evacuated.'

'Fred?' said James. 'Fred? Come on, pick your feet up. We're going home.'

'What's all that smoke, then, Mule?'

'Looks like burning oil. Come on, let's go and find out.'

It wasn't rumours any more. The British Expeditionary Force and the French army were to be evacuated from France, and they were now in headlong flight to the coast. Behind them in the east, and to the north and the south, inexorably, rolled a huge machine, belching smoke and death. Above them, fast and ugly, the aeroplanes that not only spat bullets and dropped bombs but spread fear with the noise they made.

'Did you ever see anything as ugly as that?' Pitboy demanded of James, as they climbed to their feet again. 'Those wheels look as if they're coming down to grab you.'

Pitboy had a way of saying things, putting into words what they all felt. He of them all was the one James thought he would like to have as a

384

friend, after all this was over. The Stukas did look like ugly birds of prey.

He hated them.

Pitboy gave him a note that night and said it was his girl's telephone number. Mule could call her if Pitboy couldn't, but God help Mule if he did more than call. James put the note in his pocket, wrote Mary's number on a scrap of paper, and gave it to Pitboy.

They reached the beaches that afternoon. There was smoke from the oil storage tanks drifting around in the air. Far out, ships waited.

'How do we get to them, then?' asked Jacko.

They were too tired to care. They sat on the sand, looking out at the ships. There seemed to be thousands of men, all sitting, looking at the ships, all tired. Miles away, those ships, with a sea between them.

'It's shallow,' someone said. 'You can wade out.'

Fred pulled off what was left of his boots, and James tried not to look. He had a feeling Fred's feet were down to the bone in places.

The filthy, oily smoke rolled out across the sea, blotting out the ships. Overhead there were the Stukas, and James didn't care. There were only German aeroplanes in the whole sky. He looked at them indifferently. He'd been so frightened of those things, and only a bit more frightened of letting on to the others just how scared he'd felt. If he did that, they'd panic. It was bad enough as it was, him pretending it was all just part of the scheme, flat on his face with his arms wrapped around his ears, nearly crying, nearly wetting himself. But when they'd gone and he'd looked up, he thought his face had been calm. Look around, everyone all right, and make sure, when he spoke again, that his voice was steady. That was very, very important.

When he'd heard those machine-guns, when they strafed the road, every time it happened he thought they were going to get him in the backs of his legs. Every time they went over he was waiting for that, for the feeling of something smashing into the backs of his legs.

Still, they'd been lucky. They'd only lost Zulu. Left him in the back of that abandoned truck. What else could they do? And Yank's rifle. Fred's feet. Not one of them had been in a battle at all. All they'd done was drive across Belgium, then drive half-way back, and march the rest, that damned truck crumpled at the bottom of the ravine, wherever it had been. James didn't know. Follow everyone else by then, try to find somewhere to sleep at night, he'd done his best, but it hadn't been good enough. He'd lost a man. Zulu.

Daylight, bright morning. He must have been asleep. It was a beautiful day. There was the stink of burning oil in the air, but those clouds of smoke were being blown out to sea. He couldn't see the ships.

Two Stukas came at them out of the sun, quite low, strafing the beach, and someone yelled at them. There was the sharp crack! crack! crack! of rifle fire. You'd have to be dead lucky. Weren't there any guns at all?

Just as well it was sandy. James looked along the beach at where the Stukas had been, looked at little holes dug in the sand by the machine-gun bullets. There were some bigger holes further along, bomb craters, he supposed. Quite small. The sand must have absorbed the force of the explosions.

How do we get out to those ships?

There were men forming into lines down on the beach, officers walking up and down talking to them. Some of the lines were moving into the water. But it had seemed like miles, miles out into the sea. He couldn't see the ships at all now, because of the smoke. Sometimes it drifted away, blown by the wind, only a little wind, enough to make it drift, and then he'd see the ships again, waiting. There was the sound of gunfire too, not far away. The Germans must be quite close. They wouldn't have very much time to get out to those ships.

Salt water and sand, and Fred's feet. Fred couldn't do it. The others would be all right, but not Fred.

'Who can swim?' he asked. Yank, Jacko and Pitboy raised their hands. Fred didn't even seem to have heard him. He'd have to carry Fred. He wouldn't be able to do that swimming, but it was so shallow out there he thought he could get him most of the way. Then, they'd have to see. See what they could do for him. But it would be torture, sand and salt water on Fred's feet.

There were men wading out into the water, lines of them, moving quite slowly. They were a long way out before the water came up further than their thighs.

'Look,' said Jacko. 'Look.'

387

Boats. He couldn't see what sort of boats they were, but there were three of them, pulling out of the smoke towards the beaches. They were still a long way off.

Further out, still several miles from the beaches, the *Eliza Jane* struggled towards Dunkirk. The engine was overheating, but Bob Marston could do nothing about it. There was only him, and he couldn't leave the tiller. He'd never been so frightened. There were tears running down his cheeks, and he no longer cared if anyone saw them. He wished he'd never come, wished he'd never heard of the call for the little ships. They'd told him not to, and they'd been right. The sea was flat calm, but so often the *Eliza Jane* had nearly been swamped by the bow waves of bigger boats going past him. He was driving her as fast as he dared, but every time there was one of those waves he had to slow down, hope she would ride over it, not dive. She'd done that once, and he'd thought she wouldn't come up again. Water right over the bows, washing over the top of the cloths, and she'd been so sluggish he'd thought she was going down. It had stopped her dead, and then the bows had come up again, slowly, reluctantly, but they had come up. She was much lower now, must be nearly a foot of sea water in her, so she was rolling. That was the big danger, a bow wave coming in from the side. Too fast, and she'd dive; too slow, and she'd roll over, and he didn't know enough about boats to be sure he was judging it right. Never thought he'd be out on the sea in a narrowboat. Only bought

388

her to carry coal, just a few loads up and down the canals.

Don't go, they'd said, you'll never make it, but he'd always been a stubborn man. Mines and sand bars, but he'd been able to laugh at that.

'The *Eliza Jane* only draws a couple of feet when she's empty,' he'd said. 'I can ride over them. And I'm going anyway, you can't stop me.'

'If your boat goes down someone will have to stop and pick you out of the water, that's a place a soldier could have had,' but he'd had an answer for that, too, although he didn't give it. Hadn't told them he couldn't swim. If the *Eliza Jane* went down, he'd go down with her, and he must have been mad to think he could get a narrowboat across the Channel.

But they had given him diesel and oil, and they'd wished him luck. Go down the coast to Dover, they'd said, then cut across almost due east, but look out for the Goodwin Sands if it's low tide. He'd done that, and he'd enjoyed it. It was only when he headed out into the Channel, leaving the white cliffs behind him, that there'd been other boats. Only then had he begun to realise what he had taken on, what could happen. She hadn't been built for this.

The bigger ships had had to take a different route because of the Goodwin Sands, but now here was a ship coming towards him, only about a mile away, a destroyer. Fast, you wouldn't believe how fast they could move. Bob stared at her, felt the tears hot in his eyes again. A bow wave like that, it was going to sink him. White

389

water right over her bows, they called it a bone in her teeth. Going to pass him only a few hundred yards away, and that bone, that would be it.

Bob watched the destroyer, listened to his engine, tried to think. Turn her so she goes into it as straight as possible. Straight, but slow, so she won't dive, but enough way on her to steer, keep her going, so she'll ride over it. Maybe.

Oh, God, here it comes. Oh, God.

Straight at it, and *Eliza Jane* lifted, slowly, lifted but rolled, and Bob could hear the water in the hold, it would take her over, she'd never come back from this angle. She'd never come back, with all that water in her.

Come on. Come on, sweetheart, please.

It was right under her, he'd been going too slowly, she was going over.

Propeller out of the water now, suddenly a sound like roaring, and the bows going down, water over them again, but she was coming back, coming back up. Oh, God, please. Come on. Come up again. Come on, sweetheart.

We're all right. She's even lower now, but we got through, just. Rolling and lifting again, because of the waves behind that first big one, coming up, and lying steady on the water, low in the water. Please, no more of that, please.

Black smoke ahead, that must be the oil-storage tanks, they've hit the tanks, all that smoke. We might make it. We might. If there aren't any more like that. If she isn't taking in any water. If the engine doesn't seize up. It's hot, God, it's so hot, that engine. Not much further, though. We might.

We're going to be one of the last. Doesn't matter. I'll beach her. I'm not taking her back, I can't. I can't. They can use her, find someone who can handle her. Leave her there if they have to. I can't take her back.

Wish I hadn't come. Wish I'd stayed in Oxford.

Heat haze over the engine room, that's not just the sun. Look at that, she's going to seize up, I know she is.

Not much further. Might do it.

Sailing boat going past. Hardly any wind, but she's going well. Lovely little boat. No, not so little, bigger than us. And that's a Thames cruiser. All brass and mahogany, and the fishing boats over there. All racing over, who's going to win, then? Like a regatta, this. Who's going to get there first, the Thames cruiser or that little Bermuda rigged sloop? Fishing boats, they're a different class, that's not fair.

That paint's going to start blistering any moment now. How much hotter can an engine run before it stops? Then we're finished.

There's another bloody destroyer, like the one that nearly sank us. Not so fast now. Stopped. Too shallow, can't get any closer. Bloody stay there, then. Bastard.

We've made it. We're there. Can see the beaches, all those men, lines of them coming out into the water. Find someone else who can take her, I can't. Must be someone. Just get her to the beach, and then that's it. I can't do any more.

Men walking out into the sea, so call out: 'Anyone know how to handle one of these?'

That tall young corporal with blood on his

391

tunic, carrying another man on his back, he looks familiar, somehow. He's smiling.

'I can handle that one, anyway. I built her.'

19

The army was coming home. The time for secrecy was over, the secret that everyone knew was well and truly out, and the newspapers and the radio broadcasts were full of the story. The boys were coming home, and the little ships were bringing them. Defeated heroes, bedraggled knights in crumpled khaki. They came home, leaving France to Germany, exhausted and beaten.

It didn't matter. They'd come back alive, or most of them, those who made it at all. They were apprehensive. What sort of a welcome could they expect from those who had waved them off with such high hopes? They'd gone to France to beat the Germans, as they'd done before, and many had never even fired a gun, some had never seen a German tank, not even a German soldier. They'd driven across France and Belgium to defend a line they'd been told was impregnable, and the Germans hadn't come that way. They'd gone to the south, and before anyone could understand what was happening it had turned into a race back to the coast. Get back before we're cut off, before we're surrounded. Drive, and march, and run. March and run alongside the refugees. Race the exhausted women and the old men for the ditches beside the road when the divebombers attack. Tin helmets beside coloured cotton headscarves and old black Homburg hats, khaki tunics in the dust beside flowered print dresses. Get up again, maybe help the girl to her feet, and march on, leaving her behind.

Not the way a hero was supposed to behave. What sort of welcome, then?

There were heroes among them, and there were even more stiffening under the sun in the dusty fields of France and Belgium. And there were others. A man who'd shielded a child with his own body when the Stuka attacked the village stood in the train to London beside one who had two silver candlesticks in his knapsack, candlesticks stolen from a church in the same village. How could you tell? That artilleryman with the dramatic bandage on his hand and arm had cut it breaking open the window of a shop. The one just behind him, the small, ugly one, shivering, hadn't told anyone about the wound in his back, because they'd all seemed too busy.

For James, there was a sense of enormous relief. From the moment he had pushed Fred into *Eliza Jane* and scrambled aboard himself, he had known what to do, for the first time for weeks, it seemed. A blast of heat had hit him as he scrambled down into the engine room, and he had known the Bolinder was in danger of seizing up at any moment. He had clawed sand and weed out of the mud box, felt the filter clearing under his fingers, felt the water begin to move again, and felt, deep within himself, within what must have been his imagination, a huge gasp of relief from the exhausted engine.

Eliza Jane had been rocking at first, but then she had steadied, and he had known she was

394

beached, quite hard, on the sand as men climbed aboard. Pitboy was standing on the locker in the bows, shouting, telling the men to climb in on both sides, and Jacko and Yank were stripping off the cloths, rolling them back so the other men could climb aboard. Nearly all of them came in from the side nearest the beach, despite Pitboy's orders. It didn't matter by then, because she was aground. James called out to them to bail out the water. There was nearly two feet of it, it was a wonder she hadn't foundered.

How many men could she take? He'd never had to calculate that. He stuck his head out of the side door, squinted along the gunwales. Allow six inches of freeboard, should be enough, nothing would be moving too fast here. No, that was all right. They'd be packed like sardines, and still leave enough.

Bob Marston was sitting on the steps, his hands dangling between his knees. He'd told James he couldn't do any more.

'You'll have to take over,' he'd said. 'I can't.'

James had glanced up from his efforts with the mud box, nodded, gone back to his work. Marston was looking ill. Exhaustion?

'I can't do any more,' Marston kept saying.

James realised the man was close to tears.

'You did well to get her across,' he said, and at that Marston buried his face in his hands and cried.

It hadn't been easy, getting her off the beach. There was sand swirling under the propeller, the engine thudding like a racing heart, but the boat was on the sand, weighed down with men, he didn't know how many, couldn't begin to count.

He shouted out to them, 'Rock her! Rock her!' Heard voices answering, the sounds of men scrambling to their feet, and a few moments later she began to sway, slowly, swinging from side to side.

'Go on!' he shouted. 'Go on!'

There'd be more sand in the mud box now. He'd have to keep clearing that, but she was coming off, she was backing off the beach, and the men were cheering. He smiled, feeling the propeller bite into the water, hearing the splashing die away as she found enough depth, and he swung the tiller slowly to bring her nose round, still backing away from the beach, and she was moving cleanly and sweetly through the water, low and deep, but steady, working away from the lines of men who moved out from the beaches, turning again into the deeper water, and heading into the smoke that hung around the waiting ships.

That had been yesterday.

He'd held *Eliza Jane* steady against the hull of the destroyer, watched his men, his friends, climbing up the scrambling ropes to where ready hands helped them aboard, watched the other men, watched Bob Marston, who hadn't looked back. Pitboy had been grinning down at him, waving.

'Telephone Mary!' James had shouted.

Pitboy had called back, 'You've still got my girl's number. You call her now you're dead, Mule!'

'You do more than telephone my wife, you'll

pray for death!'

Then he was on his own, on a canal boat he'd built, on the other side of the Channel. Funny old life, he'd thought. Not one of those buggers even thought to give me a shove away. Oh, well.

There'd been a young guardsman on the next trip. When James had called out to ask if anyone knew anything about boats Nicholas Maitland had looked around to see if anyone else was volunteering, and had then raised his hand.

'A bit,' he said.

Racing yachts had been Nick's passion, and engines had no place on them. Racing yachts and thoroughbred horses and English springer spaniels, but Nick Maitland had water sense and could steer a boat, leaving James to tend the engine whenever it needed him.

Nick had sought and gained permission to stay with James, and they'd lost count of the number of times they'd beached her, helped men aboard, rocked her free, backed away, and crossed the sand bars out to the ships. The destroyer had gone, and there'd been some sort of tramp steamer, a filthy thing with rust and coal dust streaking her hull, and now there was a mine layer, half full, already beginning to make smoke and turn away to the north with three lifeboats still clinging to her sides, and men climbing.

The divebombers were still there, but James tried to ignore them. They didn't frighten him any more. He watched some of the other boats, jinking in the water, weaving, trying to escape, and he knew that, if he had had that option, he would have been frightened. *Eliza Jane* couldn't do that. She wasn't quick and agile.

She'd been hit three times now, shells thudding into the wooden hull, and she'd shuddered, as if in pain. James had flinched, then patted her, as if she was a horse who'd been hurt, and needed comfort, reassurance. The last time she'd been hit there'd been screaming from the men she was carrying, stifled quite quickly, but when they reached the mine layer a lot of men were pulled aboard with ropes, and he thought some of them were dead.

Nick went to see if the boat was taking in water. He came back looking a little pale.

'The holes are above the water line at the moment, but we're empty. We'll be bailing, I think. Mule, she needs cleaning out in there before the next trip.'

He'd done it, too. A bucket, rags, no comments, no questions, no complaints. He was pale, and he'd been sick, and his hands weren't very steady, but the boat was clean, and ready for another trip, and he'd been right: they'd been bailing all the way, with water splashing through the shell holes with every wave they met.

There were lines of lorries stretching out into the water now, men climbing over their roofs, boats using them as jetties. James and Nick ignored them, driving *Eliza Jane* on to the beach, gently backing her away as the men climbed aboard, and now they could judge well how close they could bring her, how hard they could run her aground, how many men she could take. They hardly needed to rock her to bring her off the sand; they'd backed her away as she settled lower into the water. They were quicker now, except when the men were panicking. Nick tried to make them board from both sides, had even threatened some of them with his revolver, but they didn't seem to hear him. When that happened, James drove the boat hard on to the sand to stop her capsizing, but then it was difficult to bring her off. He'd back her away down the channel she'd dug for herself, he'd shout at the men to rock her. Were they too exhausted to hear him? Too exhausted, too frightened, too demoralised, and he couldn't blame them. He was frightened enough himself, now that it wasn't only the dive-bombers. He could hear the guns.

The wind was beginning to rise, to veer to the east, and there was surf.

But then it was over, and they were told, 'Get back across the Channel. Dover, or wherever you like. Don't stop to offload this lot, take them with you, that's an order, Corporal.'

Don't argue when you've been given an order, even if the half-colonel who barked it at you is a half-wit. *Eliza Jane* had been holed, and with all these men in her the water would be pouring in, and not only when they met the waves. If they ran into anything more than dead calm water she'd go down, and they'd all be left clinging to a rolling wooden hull, and hoping for a sea boat.

Nick and James had exchanged glances, and Nick had shrugged. He'd gone into the hold and relayed the order to the men. Nearly two hundred of them, James thought. He and Nick had worked it out on one of their early trips. If she can carry twenty-two tons, how many men can we take? It had been nearly three hundred, but they agreed there wasn't room. In the end they'd given up. Pack them in until there isn't any more room, then back away.

Sitting on the gunwales, clinging to the stands, crouched in the hold, how many lives had that fool officer risked, with his order to take them across the Channel?

By now, Mary would know what he was doing. Pitboy would have called her.

Pitboy's last thought as the water rushed through the gaping hole in the side of the torpedoed destroyer had been, Mule will tell Janet.

James didn't think he could get *Eliza Jane* back. He didn't see how they could avoid being swamped. The men would bail, and that would keep the water down, but they could do nothing if a big wave hit her. It would wash over the gunwales, she would dive or roll, and that would be the end.

At least the engine was running well.

The wind was blowing surf against the hull, white foam frothing, some of it scudding into the hold. Nick and a few Royal Engineers raised the side cloths. Water was still coming through the holes, and now the men had to stand to throw it overboard. The extra movement made the boat rock, but there were enough men to bail, and quite soon Nick had them doing it to some sort of routine, which kept her level.

Something to be said for the Guards, thought James.

They were alone now. In the distance, when he looked around, he could see the ships, smudges of smoke on horizons, and far behind them the black clouds that drifted around Dunkirk. But the other boats had left them behind, the cruisers, the yachts, the river tugs. *Eliza Jane* was struggling to make headway in the sea, calm though it was.

A few hundred yards to the north a thin shape was standing high out of the water, black against the sky. Someone shouted, 'Submarine!' But Nick laughed and made a reply James couldn't hear. He looked again, narrowing his eyes.

It was a wreck. A mast and rigging. The Goodwin Sands. They must be over halfway across. How much further, then?

They'd been one of the last to leave. He hadn't noticed at the time. He hadn't even noticed what sort of a ship it was they were ferrying the men out to, beyond the sandbanks. Some sort of coastal steamer, not as big as a destroyer. She'd gone, he thought. When they came out, when that Lieutenant-Colonel had barked out his ridiculous orders, he didn't think they'd passed her. She'd already gone. There were ships burning in the water, wrecks, broken and blackened, and he'd hardly noticed. None that could have taken these men. Just a few boats, cruisers he thought, and a narrowboat, and still men on the beaches. The sounds of surf, of flames from a ship, and of guns.

They'd been ploughing their way through bits of wreckage, abandoned boats, broken wood, he'd heard them scraping against the hull, looked down. There were some bodies, too. Nothing he could do for them.

In one or two places Nick had called back to him, warning him, rope floating in the surf, and he'd dropped into neutral and let *Eliza Jane* drift over and past it. Rope wrapped around the propeller could stop the engine, and then he'd have no control: she could turn broadside on to the wind and the surf.

She was a good boat. He remembered Faith writing down the order for her when Bob Marston had telephoned one evening to ask if Armstrong's would build him a boat. Just a working boat, carry a few loads of coal here and there. Spent a bit of time on the canals as a lad, always thought he'd like to come back to it.

Gone back on that destroyer, had Bob Marston. He'd be wondering what was happening to *Eliza Jane*, if he'd ever see her again. Some of the little ships hadn't made it back. They were easier targets than the warships: they didn't have guns.

Nick called out sharply, and James jumped, looked at him, looked where he was pointing.

There were men in the water, swimming. One was waving. He couldn't hear them, but he knew they'd be shouting. How many? Fifty? More?

'Can't take them,' he called back. 'She'll sink.'

Can't leave them, either. Can't leave men drowning.

Ropes, then, but long ones: they could hold on, *Eliza Jane* could pull them, not too close or they'd be sucked into the propeller and cut to pieces. Nick might not know that.

'Take her,' he called.

Check the engine while he could. He had enough diesel, but the oil was low. Daren't run out of oil. Pour that dirty black stuff through again?

He told Nick they'd have to tow the men behind them, make sure they didn't try to board her, and keep them away from the propeller.

Not much further. The white cliffs were clear now, they seemed to glitter. Come on, they said. This is home, and safety. Not much further. Then you can sleep.

Tow them on long ropes, he'd said, but the men in the water were exhausted. He brought *Eliza Jane* round, turning her bows into the swell, into the scudding surf, and he didn't know what to do now. Those men would drown. They couldn't hold ropes. They couldn't even hold the gunwales. He watched helplessly as the men in *Eliza Jane* pulled the side cloths down, dragged the men into the hold. Watched the water creeping up the hull, watched it lapping over, watched the men's faces as realisation dawned. Heard them shouting to those still swimming towards them, 'Keep off! Keep away!'

The shell holes were well below the waterline now, and the sea was pouring through. He could hear it, a surging, splashing noise behind the shouts, behind the noise of someone screaming.

Not much further, said the white cliffs, as he looked across at them. Nearly home.

20

When Mary saw the telegram boy cycling up the track she thought only of the farm up the hill, of Tommy Stapleton. Poor Derek and Freda, she'd thought. Young Tommy, how dreadful, those poor people.

Faith, standing in the garden, thought, This is it. They've killed my boy.

Ben laid down his tools and waited. Ride on past, he thought. Ride on up the hill.

That evening when Mary stood in the garden where Faith had been earlier, she tried quite hard to believe that James was dead. Why do I still feel alive? she asked herself. If James is dead, why am I standing here and looking at the flowers?

James is dead, and I am here, and this isn't right. This can't be.

Earlier she'd sat on the edge of Faith's bed, holding Faith's hand. Faith had watched Ben's face as he read the telegram, and then she'd pulled herself to her feet, and said she thought she'd like to lie down. Mary helped her up the stairs, thinking, James is twenty-one, and I don't know how old Faith is, but now she has grown as old as anything I know.

Neither of them had cried. Mary had helped Faith undress, helped her into bed, and sat beside her, holding her hand, until Faith fell asleep. Then she had drawn the curtains so the evening sun wouldn't fall on the old woman's face and wake her, and she'd gone downstairs, walked quietly past the living room where Ben sat on the sofa, his face buried in his hands, and out into the garden.

James is dead, she told herself, but the words had no meaning, no reality. James is dead, she insisted, and a blackbird sang in a tree on the other side of the canal. The blackbird was probably warning others away from his territory. His song meant something, and Mary thought she knew what he was saying in his song, but the words 'James is dead' were incomprehensible.

'*Il est mort*,' she said aloud. '*Er ist tot.*'

French, German or English, it made no difference. The words were nothing.

If I am alive, he cannot be dead. I cannot be here, listening to a blackbird, looking at the flowers, feeling the sun warm on my skin if James is dead.

'There'll be a letter tomorrow,' said Ben, behind her. 'Or the next day. They'll write, won't they? Tell us what happened.'

'I expect so.'

His eyes were red, and his breathing quiet. Pain in his chest? she wondered. He only ever breathed quietly when he was in pain.

'Are you all right?' she asked.

'No,' he said simply. 'But I will be. I don't know about Faith.'

Old beyond imagining, Mary thought, but Faith's son is only twenty-one. Faith looks like dust, as if she will crumble in the wind.

Ben was grieving for James, but he was heartsick for his wife. My little love, he thought. My little Faith. Darling Faith.

Somebody had told Ben that men see their whole lives in the instant before they die, but now it was Faith's life that passed through his mind, from the time he had first seen her, and not noticed, so now he wasn't sure. He thought it had been in town, when he was still at school. The Carter family had been there, in the high street. Faith would probably have been with them. So he told himself he remembered. Yes, she'd been there. In a grey dress, beside her mother. Yes.

Then he'd taken her out for a walk and asked her to marry him. He'd needed a wife to help him work the boat, and Faith Carter was a worker. Also, a little deformed, so she might be glad of a man, and a home of her own, and would take him, despite the noise he made, despite his breathing.

Darling Faith. Working *Grey Lady,* crying for a baby, and the little one who'd died. Peggy, bonny Peggy Trafford. He hadn't thought of Peggy Trafford for months.

He remembered the fight with Paddy, when he'd been hurt and had needed his wife, really needed her. Loved her by then, didn't know it, not for sure.

He turned his head to look up at her window, a blaze of gold where the sun shone on to it, bright, making him narrow his eyes. She was asleep behind that golden fire.

Faith slept quietly, dreamless.

Mary was listening to the song of the blackbird.

Ben watched his wife's window, and remembered her poling *Grey Lady* through a tunnel while he rode the piebald horse over the hill. Knowing then how much he loved her only when he thought he might have lost her.

Knowing now how much he loved her, now that he knew she was dying.

'Don't leave me,' he whispered to her late that night, as she slept on and he stood beside the bed, looking down at her. 'Stay with me.'

The next morning, Mary was up early, out in the yard, in the garden, back into the house, unable to be still. She repeated the words, 'James is dead', over and over again, but they floated away from her, leaving no imprint.

Mrs Webb came to the cottage carrying flowers. She stood on the doorstep, said she could only stay a moment because of school, but the Stapletons had telephoned, they'd seen the telegram boy.

'Oh, my dear,' she said, and she burst into tears, so it was Mary who had to comfort her, to hug her, bring her in and sit her at the kitchen table and put the kettle on.

'What happened?'

The postman had been, with a brief letter. Mary told her: 'It seems they were on a destroyer on the way back. It was torpedoed. Three of them are still missing. James is one of them.'

'So there's still a chance, then?'

'Not after four days, I don't think,' said Mary.

'I must go now,' said Mrs Webb. 'I'll cancel your classes, they'll just have to...'

And she burst into tears again, and was still crying when Mary saw her off at the door.

I'm the one who should be crying, thought Mary. James is dead, I should be heartbroken. Why am I so calm?

Because I don't believe it. I do not believe he is dead.

There were dead men all around him. When they died, or when they became too weak to hold on any more, they floated away. James had tied some of them to the hull, loops of rope around their wrists, and he'd killed two of them like that, because *Eliza Jane* had rolled and dragged them under. After that, he would do nothing to try to help. He and Nick told them to hold on, because the boat wouldn't sink. Just hold on. Wait for rescue.

He laid his face against the elm planks, looked down the length of the boat at the iron studs standing out from the wood. My father did that, he thought. Hammered those spikes through, and split them, fitted the roves. My father's hands held that iron.

Some of the men were lying on the boat, but most were too exhausted to pull themselves out of the water. Heavy boots, waterlogged greatcoats had sucked many of them down, and he'd watched, helplessly.

'Hold on,' he said, but the boy beside him was beyond hearing, and the thin white hands uncurled, loosed their grip, and the boy floated away.

Mary felt as if she was floating, as if she was still and quiet in the centre of the events that surrounded her, and rolled by, and left her untouched. She supposed that they saw her as they usually would, with them, and speaking and moving, but that was not her. That was her shell. She was alone, apart from them, waiting for timelessness to pass.

The part of her that they saw was with Faith, holding her hand, speaking to her, then to the doctor, who said something about medicine to calm Faith, but Faith was calm. Faith lay, placid and quiet, waiting.

Ben thought of his tall, perfect boy, drowning inside a sinking destroyer, and tried to force away the dreadful pictures that broke into his mind. In their place he put his wife, and begged her not to leave him. What will life be for me without you? I know you want to go now, but please think of me too. I love you. Don't you love me enough to stay with me? Please don't go, my darling. Please don't go.

Faith opened her eyes and looked at him, and her bones were sharp under her wrinkled skin, small features. Little sharp-faced wife, he thought, with a crooked shoulder. Thin little thing, poled a full-sized laden narrowboat through that tunnel for me. Carried me down into the cabin, near enough. Who would have thought you could do that?

Oh, my Ben. My dear. I do so love you.

Two days after the telegram came Faith died, and James raised his head from the wooden planks because something had woken him. Something had happened. There was a choking feeling in his throat, burning in his eyes that was more than the salt, and a sound he couldn't place, something more than the lapping of the water.

Stones rolling. Stones. He could hear them. He could feel them, under his feet. Shingle, under his feet.

'We're ashore,' he said, but his voice was cracked, and they didn't hear him. He tried again, and still they didn't hear, so he hammered on the wood, banging his hand down hard, and they raised their heads.

'Look!' he said.

This time they heard him.

One by one they let go of the boat. They dropped into the sea and began to wade to the shore. They were very quiet. They didn't look at each other, didn't speak, just waded off towards the shore, clambered up the rolling shingle.

There weren't many of them left.

James would not count them. He sat on the shingle with his arms wrapped around his knees and tried hard not to think of the men in the water. He should have left them. Brought the others back to shore, then turned round and gone back to the Goodwin Sands to look for them. How many men had drowned because he hadn't left them? And the ones he'd tried to help by tying them to the boat.

'We're home,' someone said, beside him.

Nick. What could he say to the young guardsman? Nothing.

'Why didn't you go into the navy?' asked Nick.

Because of my grandfather, he thought. Because I dream of a soldier in a scarlet uniform on a bright bay mare, and he talks to me. I can't explain all this to you, Nick. You did well. Please leave me alone now.

'I didn't think we'd get more than a mile out,' said Nick, sitting down on the stones beside him. 'That idiot half-colonel, if I can find out who he is I'll get him court-martialled, I swear I will.'

'He didn't know,' said James.

'Then he shouldn't have given the order. When you don't know you ask questions, you don't give orders.'

'I'm tired,' said James. 'You did well, Nick. Please leave me alone now.'

Nick sat quietly for a little while, then began to throw stones into the sea.

'There are more than a hundred men here who would be dead if it wasn't for you,' he said. 'I'm one of them. No, I will not leave you alone.'

A hundred? thought James. There were many more than that when we left Dunkirk. Or wherever it was. We'd moved about a bit by then. La Panne? No, it was Bray, that last one. I think it was Bray.

Nick was still talking. He meant to be kind, but James knew he had made a terrible mistake.

'If I hadn't tried to pick up those men...' he said, but he couldn't go on. If he hadn't, if he'd left them to drown, brought the others back... If.

'It doesn't make any difference,' said Nick. 'You can only do what seems best. That's war. It's always nightmares, no matter what you do.'

411

There were no nightmares for Ben and Mary, because there was no sleep. A nurse had called, and had washed Faith, dressed her in her prettiest nightdress, and folded her hands. Mary picked flowers from the garden, made a small posy, and tucked it into those quietly folded hands, then kissed Faith's forehead. Ben sat in a chair beside the bed, looked at his wife's face, and thought, Couldn't you have stayed? My darling, I wish you could have stayed.

He missed her.

Her hand was still warm when he touched it. Her eyes were closed, and her mouth too, although it had dropped open a moment after she'd died, and her eyes, they'd been open as well. He supposed the nurse had done something.

When Kathy had died it had been Mrs Webster who had looked after her. Josiah had asked her to help. She'd picked rosemary for Kathy, and put it in her hands. Mary had picked little white roses for Faith.

Ben looked into his wife's face, and tried to think of all the time they had spent together. He tried to remember, as he felt he should, but could only hear words in his own voice, Darling Faith. My darling little wife.

James is dead, Mary thought mechanically, and now Faith has died, too.

Faith's death was real and true, and she understood it. Poor Faith. She was so sad about Faith, so concerned for dear Ben. What could she do to help Ben? They had been so close.

The doctor had offered her medicine as well,

412

when he had called to see Faith. For the shock, he'd said. And Ben, he'd need something, wouldn't he? His son, and his wife. Poor Mr Jacardi. He'd need something. And the doctor would call the next day, if he possibly could. In the meantime, his deepest sympathy. To them both.

Neighbours had come, with flowers, with food. So kind, at a time when they hadn't much for themselves. Derek and Freda Stapleton had brought a roast chicken. That was a real luxury. Faith would have enjoyed that, if James had been here to eat it with them. Now, Ben and Mary, and neither of them were very hungry, but it had been so kind, and the pork pie from the Cattermoles, a flan from Mrs Dixon. Bunches of wild flowers from the schoolchildren, already wilting in their vases.

The vicar came twice on the day after Faith died, and offered to pray with them. Ben wanted to talk to him, so Mary left them alone. There were letters to write, and the account books to check. People offered to help. I'll do that for you, they said, but what would there be for Mary, if they took it all away? What was Mary to do?

Cry, they thought. Cry for her husband.

When will I believe he is dead? she asked herself. When?

When will I understand that he is dead? was what she was asking herself as she watched him walk along the track towards the cottage, and there was no sense of surprise. They said he was dead, and I didn't believe it, and now he has come home. How has this happened?

413

Faith had believed he'd been killed, and she had died. Ben believed he was dead, and what sort of a shock will this be now?

Now he's here, and holding out his arms to me, and I'm running to him, and all these questions. Why? What happened? Why did they say you were dead?

James looked into her face and saw tears, and shock, and joy and bewilderment, and he asked, Didn't Pitboy telephone you? I asked him to. I had to stay behind.

Pitboy?

Yes. God, what's his real name? Edward. Ted? Ted Pearson? Didn't he telephone? Oh, darling. Darling Mary.

James. Pitboy, Ted. James, the destroyer. Darling, we thought you were dead too.

Ben was at the door, holding on to the frame, looking across the garden at the track where Mary stood in the arms of a tall man who looked so like James. Who looked so like him.

James. My son. They said you were dead, drowned in the destroyer.

So much death, thought James. The men in the water. The bodies, the two I tied to the boat who went under her when she rolled. The ones I should have left, and now Pitboy and Jacko? Yank and Fred? Oh, no.

'I stayed behind,' he said. 'There was a narrow-boat, I was working her. *Eliza Jane*, remember? Bob Marston took her across. Oh, God. Bob was on the destroyer, too.'

Which of them would tell him about his mother?

414

He was holding Mary so close, clinging to her, and he was crying for his friends. The names he'd written in his letters, now he was saying them, and they were dead, and something about the others who'd drowned. Who would tell him about his mother?

Ben, standing at his side, saying his name over and over again, Ben dressed in black, while Mary smiled through tears, and she'd been standing in the sun in a black dress. She'd been mourning, his lovely Mary.

'I didn't believe it,' she said, and through his confusion came another. She hadn't believed he was dead, yet she'd been wearing a black dress. Why, then, if she didn't believe in his death, was she in mourning?

But so much death was more than he could bear, and this question was put aside as he raised his hands to his face, and began to cry. His friends, all gone, all drowned in that destroyer. The men in the Channel, the bodies that had floated past *Eliza Jane* as she set out from Bray. All dead. And then the ones on the Goodwin Sands that he'd tried to save, and the many, many more who had died because of that. So many deaths. Even old Bob Marston, who hadn't looked back as he'd climbed over the railings into the doomed warship.

They led him into the cottage, and he looked around at the familiar places, all the things he had known since his childhood, and something wasn't there.

Ben, old and grave, with the tears drying on his cheeks, Mary in black, even though she had not believed him dead. Neither of them had to tell him about his mother, nor tell him why. Faith had never believed he would survive the war. She had hoped, and she had longed for his return, but she had never believed she would see him again.

There was nothing to say. Mary held his hand, but he reached out for Ben, hugged him close, felt him shaking with grief, with relief, with sorrow and joy, and still he could think of nothing to say.

So there was silence. A very long time passed as they stood together, close, giving what they could of comfort to each other, sharing their loss, holding each other, and it was enough. What could there be in the way of words?

Love, and silence.

James could never remember breaking that circle, although Mary thought often of the three of them making their way upstairs, Ben following, then hesitating and turning back, and Mary had gone down again to collect him. Much as she loved James, much as she longed to be alone with him, she would not leave Ben at such a time.

James fell asleep almost immediately. Mary sat on the edge of the bed and looked down at him, and Ben moved between the two rooms, between his dead wife and his living son until he, too, slept, in the moss-green chair by the window, the evening breeze stirring his thin white hair, his breathing once again loud, roaring, slow.

It was Jed who helped Ben most over the next few days, through the funeral and the pain as the numbness wore off, as Ben began to realise, to believe, and at last to understand, that he would never see Faith again, that she was truly dead. Jed stayed with him in the yard, helped him with little bits of work, sat with him in silence, listened to him and answered him. Jed took him to the churchyard where the flowers were wilting, held him when he cried, watched him as he remembered.

James thought, Jed must be older than my mother. He doesn't look it, but he must be. She'd always seemed old, but she wasn't, not really. How did she die like that? Just because she thought I had?

Mary knew, but could not explain, that Faith had had a strong spirit, a very strong will, and that although most of her love had been for Ben, the spirit and the will had been for James. Without James, there was nowhere she could turn except to death.

Mary washed James's clothes, washed salt water away, but a dark red stain would not come out, no matter what she did.

'Zulu,' he said, when she showed him, and asked. 'Still red.'

Why? she wondered. Cold water, salt, everything. But there it was, dark red on the khaki, it would not move, as fast as dye. And why red? Why had it not turned brown? The blood of a dead man, still red.

She laid it aside, almost reverently. The army would have to buy him a new one. She would do no more to it.

'Why did you call him Zulu?' she asked, and he gave her the simple, obvious answer. He was

417

black. He wasn't a Zulu, he was West Indian. He'd been all right. A bit slow. Not as slow as Fred, but still. He'd been kind to Fred. Fred was just about borderline. Wouldn't have got into the army if there hadn't been a war. Yank was half American, had a bit of an accent. Funny thing was, Yank was as near as could be a Communist. Used to spit on the ground when an officer went past. Not when they could see him, mind. Oh, no. Not much of a hero, not Yank. He lost his rifle. He could be an idle bugger, too.

Jacko, he was Pitboy's younger brother. Jacko, he wouldn't do anything much unless Pitboy said... Unless Pitboy...

He couldn't speak of Pitboy. He would try, because he wanted to share Pitboy with Mary, but he couldn't talk of him yet. Later, maybe.

Mary had found a torn-open cigarette box in a pocket, with something on it, too faint to read. Pencil marks had washed out of cheap cardboard where blood would not come away from khaki serge.

His girlfriend's telephone number. I promised. How can I do that now?

'I'll have to go to Coventry and find the family,' he said. 'I promised him.'

Ben was helpless in his despair, clinging to some vague idea that James could stay at home now, in hiding if necessary.

'They'll know you're alive if you go,' he said.

Mary explained later that they already knew. He'd been given a travel warrant to come home. But Ben didn't want facts and arguments. He wanted James at home. He wanted evenings with

418

James and Mary, not counting the days they had left.

'I have to go back,' said James. 'They haven't been beaten yet.'

All the old arguments remained the same, although looking back on them James saw them as faintly ridiculous. Unanswerable, but still faintly ridiculous. Far from having fought to keep Mary safe, he hadn't fought at all, and he'd simply been one of tens of thousands flooding back across Europe.

Mary asked him to calculate how many men he had ferried out to the ships in *Eliza Jane* before he'd been sent across the Channel. How many men did she hold? He wasn't sure. If they were wounded and lying down, they needed more room. Standing? Well, she was nearly seven foot wide, and the hold was how long? She hadn't been quite standard, Bob Marston had wanted a bigger cabin, but maybe fifty foot?

'Oh, I don't know,' he said, but Mary insisted.

'Think,' she demanded.

'Well, say seventy or eighty each time. But that last time, she'd been packed, Mary, well over a hundred.'

'Thousands, then,' she said. 'You saved thousands.'

She wanted to comfort him, so he tried to be comforted. He tried to accept what she said, that nothing had been his fault, and he had done his best. He hadn't meant to kill them. Mary loved him, and held him, and listened to him on the few occasions when he wanted to talk about it, but he felt he was alone in this. He took more

419

comfort from Nick Maitland's words: 'It's always nightmares, no matter what you do.' They told him that he was not the only one to have made the wrong decision.

He was given extra leave because Faith had died, and he spent his time helping Ben and Jed with another boat. It was good to install an engine in a canal boat, a machine that wasn't going to war. Good to work with his old tools, to listen to the water and the birdsong.

It couldn't last. The day came when he had to leave, and Ben cried while Mary stood dry-eyed, watching the train pulling out of the station. He was going to a depot in Hampshire, to train mechanics and to work on the new tanks. He could come home from there. He'd be given leave, now and then. Weekend passes. They'd see him soon.

Mary kept repeating this to Ben, but he was helpless with misery. He'd once thought, when Faith was so ill, that if she died his only friend would be a horse. Now, he had this lovely young girl, and he had a son, but Faith had gone, and taken with her the sunshine, the songs of the birds, and his love of life. All he had left was fear for his son, and affection, admiration for Mary.

Lovely girl. So glad James found her.

James went back to the army, and worked as he was told, dismantling vehicles and reassembling them until he was familiar with every part of them, then teaching others to do the same. Sometimes he found mechanisms that didn't work as well as he thought they might, and then he'd puzzle over them, make drawings, find a better way. His drawings and his notes went back to the factory, and sooner or later he'd work on a new machine, and find his own designs no longer on paper but in steel.

When that happened, he'd smile.

He went to Coventry on one of his weekend passes, and found Pitboy and Jacko's family, and then a redhaired girl who lived two streets away. He told her Pitboy had asked him to call, but the telephone number had been washed out of the piece of cardboard, and he gave her the little scrap of cigarette box that Pitboy had handed him. Then he held her while she cried.

That seemed to complete his farewells to his friends.

By then he was a sergeant. He was well liked, quite sociable, but he made no close friends. He dreamed too often of the ones he had lost.

He dreamed of Jacko and Pitboy, but never of his grandfather. He remembered the dreams of the soldier on the horse, and he thought about them, and about the reasons why they had stopped. He decided it was because he had failed. Even though he'd been officially exonerated of blame for those deaths, he could not bring himself to accept that they had not been his fault.

Nick Maitland had been at the inquiry, and had said that the order to go back with the men still on the boat had put Corporal Jacardi in an impossible position. They hadn't been able to find the Lieutenant-Colonel who had given it. Some of the survivors gave evidence. There were questions about whether they should have attempted to rescue the men off the Goodwin

421

Sands, but no one seemed to have an opinion either way. No one except James, and they didn't ask him.

He and Nick met afterwards in the sergeants' mess, but James couldn't think of much to say to him. They compared canal boats with racing yachts, made a few jokes about them, then said goodbye without suggesting they should meet again.

The men James trained went to war. He stayed behind. He felt detached from them, as though he was watching himself from a long distance, seeing himself talk, demonstrate, then work alongside the other men, oil streaking his arms, words drifting from his mouth. He heard himself laugh, saw himself smile, but never felt that he was laughing or smiling. It was another man who did that. The real James Jacardi only watched.

Only with Mary did he feel as though he came together. When she was with him he could feel the laughter, and the smiles were for her. In the boatyard, where they kept the engines in their crates until he could fit them, he not only worked, oil streaking his arms, he felt the tools in his hands, he heard the song of the engines, he smelt the oil. He would hear footsteps on gravel and turn his head, smiling, as Mary approached. Here, he was alive. Here, with her and Ben, and with the two London evacuee children who were staying at the cottage, Carol and Simon Edmunds.

Ben, too, found time unreal. His anxiety for James had lost its edge, and the war seemed a distant thing, happening to other people. He worked slowly alongside Jed, glad there wasn't so much demand for boats now. Mary taught at the school, not for the money but because the children needed teachers. James sent money home. Boats were sold. Money didn't seem to be a problem. And rations, they must be a nuisance, he supposed, everybody said so, but they seemed to manage. Stapleton's Farm, he and Jed went up there sometimes to help out a bit, harvest time, or haymaking, and there was often a slab of butter, a piece of ham. It was only when he went into the towns and saw the bomb damage that it really came home to him. It was war.

He liked the children. Carol was a bright girl, and she adored the boats. Six years old, and where most children asked, 'Why?' Carol always wanted to know 'How?' She played house in the boatman's cabins, hiding toys in the cupboards, pretending to cook on the ranges. How do you light the fire? How do you make that? How do you learn to be a teacher?

Simon, two years younger, was shy and homesick. He cried for his mother almost constantly throughout the first week. While Carol was climbing up the ladders and looking at the boats, Simon was hiding in the kitchen cupboard, sobbing. Mary put his bed in her room, and offered to do the same for Carol, but Carol was happy from the first day. Only when she woke in the night did she say she wanted her mother. At any other time she was too busy to think of her.

Sharp tools had to be put out of reach now, and an eye always kept open for small children who could open cupboard doors, climb on to unstable timber piles, fall into the canal. Mary watched anxiously at first, but it was Ben who looked after them best. James had been on the boatyard from the time he was a baby, and Ben knew where the dangers lay, what would attract a child. He carried Simon around on his shoulders, telling him to look for things that had been lost.

'Where's my hammer, young Simon? Can you see it from up there? And where's Jed's coat? Can you find that for him? Jed might catch cold.'

The resignation that had settled like a shroud around Ben since Faith had died lifted a little. Mary watched him with little Simon, and thought, He's not so old. His hair's white, but he's not so very old after all.

James moved around the country, teaching young soldiers how to care for the massive machines that were fighting the war in so many distant places. The sense of unreality began to fade a little, and one night he dreamed of his grandfather, this time riding towards him, but a long way away.

The day after the dream he went out on to the rifle range, and this time he concentrated on what he was doing. It was time to be a soldier again, and to take this seriously. Range, elevation, wind speed. Think. Calculate, work on it until it's quick, and go on working until thought is no longer necessary. Again, and again, and the bullseye is quite good, but that little white egg right in the middle of it would be better. Wind speed, look at the flag, look at the grass, look at the leaves over there, near the target. Look further away, the wind's coming from over there, so look. Look there. And quicker, work that bolt. Quick fingers, quick wrists. Think and aim, and squeeze the trigger.

'Not bad,' said the instructor, and as James walked away he looked at him, thoughtful and a little surprised.

That was the morning Mary woke early feeling sick, and accepted what she had suspected for some time, that she was pregnant.

'We'd better not tell James,' she said to Ben. 'There's nothing he can do. He'll only worry.'

If James worried he might not concentrate on what he was doing, and then he would be in danger.

Ben looked in the kitchen and made sure there was tea in the cupboard, and dry biscuits in the tin. He would have to get some beef, too. He must keep her strong. Tea and biscuits, and beef, and perhaps apples, if he could find some. They'd be dry and wrinkled at this time, but they might still be sweet.

He went to the graveyard, sat on the bench, and thought, It goes on, my love. James and Mary now, a baby coming. I'll take care of Mary. Her man should be with her now. You'll understand how she feels.

A Christmas baby, and perhaps it would all be over by then. Perhaps the baby would be born in a world at peace.

The army was going back to Europe. Everything was to be thrown into this push, everything, every machine, every man, everything.

I don't want to kill anyone this time, James thought. I don't want to choose between bad and worse. The night before they left he woke early in the morning with tears on his cheeks, and felt sick, and he knew.

She's pregnant, he thought.

Mary was awake, too, a hundred and fifty miles away. James lay on his back, his hands clasped behind his head, staring up into the darkness, thinking of her. Mary sat in the moss-green chair by the window, looking out over the garden.

I love you.

I love you, too.

Take care.

There was no reply to that. Take care? Take cover, if there is any. Be alert. Listen and watch, and be quick, be very quick.

He'd been out on the landing craft, testing the trucks and the tanks. It had been building up for weeks, months probably. He'd been given tape and a substance like putty, and told to waterproof a lorry, drive it through a tank four feet deep and see what happened. He'd done it, and asked no questions, but it hadn't been difficult to guess, and the exercises on the boats had made it certain. Somewhere in France, the rumours said, and he only hoped it wouldn't be on the borders of Belgium.

He'd become a very good shot. A rifle needed different skills, but in the end it was, as he had first thought, just another machine. It would do the same thing time and time again, and if anything changed, it wasn't the gun. Range, and beyond a certain range, wind speed, and he no longer had to calculate, any more than he had to think when he heard an engine missing, or something grinding in a back axle, or felt a shudder in a steering mechanism.

They'd been training for weeks, hard physical work, running over difficult terrain with heavy packs on their backs, and he was probably stronger than he had ever been before. There'd been rumours, and one that he had believed was that troops who had been at Dunkirk and had not been abroad since would lead the invasion force. It seemed only fair.

Now they were in a camp surrounded by barbed wire, with sentries patrolling, and no contact with the outside world. No letters, no telephone calls, no civilians allowed within shouting distance of the perimeter fence, so it wouldn't be very long. Days, maybe. They were strong and fit, they'd been trained as well as they could be, and all it needed was one bullet, or a landmine, and it would be for nothing. Just another number.

Once again, if he prayed at all, it was that he wouldn't come home a cripple.

That night his grandfather rode through his dreams at a flat-out gallop, low over the bright bay mare's withers, her black mane streaming into his face as he crouched in the saddle, a pistol in his hand, urging the horse on. There were other men there, but James couldn't see them. He watched the horse, watched sand scudding from under her flying hoofs, heard the sounds of revolver shots. Today, then, he thought. Action today.

He wrote to Mary, a letter he could leave behind that someone would post for him. He thought of her as he wrote, pictured her in the scarlet blouse standing in the garden. Pictured her in their bedroom, smiling at him, taking it off, laying it on the moss-green chair. Dark hair, brown skin, blue eyes, so beautiful, so vivid, so loving. Mary, laughing up at him, her hair swirled on the white pillow. Her hands on his body, her eyes growing drowsy, her voice slow, nothing mattered more than Mary, nothing more than turning the languorous movements of her beautiful body into wildness, the drowsy eyes wide and gleaming, the desire and demand answered, and answered again, until the moment when she would seem to leap into tumultuous oblivion, long, long moments, timeless and ecstatic, ended with a slow, deep sighing, and sometimes quiet tears, and the gentle smile as he kissed them away.

Would he ever see her again?

Mary, wiping sweat from her face and smiling as bravely as she could at Ben, who had made her yet another cup of tea, wondered, Will I ever see him again? Dear God, will I see my James again?

It must be today, thought Ben. Today they'll go. What will I do if...?

Faith had always found a cup of tea and a dry biscuit helped, when she was pregnant and sick with it. So, now James isn't here to make her the tea and find the biscuits she'll have to make do with me. And I can take care of the children, until she's feeling better.

There was another teacher now, and Mary had given up the school. She hadn't wanted to let them down, but there were too many times when she felt too ill, and Carol and Simon needed her at home, needed more of her time when they came home in the afternoons. But, most of all, she felt too sick.

James, in the landing craft, didn't know whether he was seasick, or affected by the stench of vomit from all those others who were. He wouldn't have believed a boat could move so violently. He didn't feel particularly frightened, but he did hope he wouldn't let anyone down.

There was more noise than he had anticipated, although it didn't worry him. They'd grown accustomed to noise during their training, but the guns from the big ships were almost deafening, and when he looked up he saw spirals of black smoke, quickly swirled away by the wind. Rain was coming down, sporadic but sharp. He felt cold. Bullets hit the sides of the boat, slamming into it and making it rock, and he heard someone near him crying. His stomach heaved, and he thought that no matter what awaited them on the beach he would face it. Anything to get off this boat.

He knew the men around him, but none were his friends, and that was good. He thought he could rely on them, hoped they could rely on him, would do his best for them, but nothing more. No more grief.

Sand was grinding under the boat, and it lurched, and the engine roared. They were driving in as hard as they could, as close to the waterline as possible. They couldn't know what lay under the ramps, better to be close. If there were shell holes they could drown. Swimming, carrying so much weight, would be impossible.

The ramp dropped, and they were on their feet, running almost as soon as they could see, down the ribbed steel, and into the water, then wading. There was machine-gun fire, but it was away to the right, and he saw men fall. More noise, more guns, explosions all round him, but he was still running. Someone near him fell, he thought he heard a scream. Another man down, and it was hard, running on the sand carrying so much weight, but there was smoke blowing across in front of him now: somebody had thrown a smoke grenade.

The noise seemed to come and go, at one moment loud and close, the next muffled, then again loud, and the ground was shaking under his feet. Flail tanks were coming up the beach, and in front of him were the dunes. He threw himself to the ground, heard a machine-gun, a thudding noise, and he thought of the horse galloping in his dream, sand flying under her hoofs.

There were two more men beside him, one whimpering, 'Sarge, I've been hit, I'm hurt.'

James looked at him, at his shocked white face, and blood on his chest.

'Someone will come,' he said. 'Wait here. You'll be safe enough here.'

Time to move on. There were more men now, so he spoke to them, voice calm and steady, and

430

he checked, quickly. Two missing, and where was Captain Rowley? Well, they'd waited long enough. He wasn't coming.

Someone counting, was it him? Then they were up and running, heads down, running through the sand and across a road, more and more men around them as they moved away from the beach. There was still gunfire, still explosions, still, more relentless than anything else, the bombardment from the ships out in the Channel.

A wall. They reached it and crouched behind it. They were through the worst. They'd come off the beach and over the dunes.

'Everyone all right?' he asked. 'Everyone here?'

On again, towards the village. He could see the church spire. That was the objective, the village, reach it, take it, regroup. The machine-gun from the pillbox behind them was silent now. There'd been Royal Marines landing there, they would have done that. But there was still plenty of gunfire ahead.

'Everyone all right?' he asked again, and saw them nod. Tense, pale faces, but they were ready. They could go on.

They were firing as they went, not aiming, and he shouted at them: they were wasting ammunition. The shots became more sporadic for a little while, but then there was the crack of bullets around them, and they threw themselves down.

'Where is it?' someone shouted from behind him. 'Where's that coming from?'

Cautiously, they moved on again, but this time, when they started shooting, he didn't try to stop them. He was doing the same, shooting from the hip, running towards the hill that stood between them and the village. He saw some German soldiers coming out of a bunker, their hands raised, saw them fall, heard the shots. More came out, shouting, hands high in the air, and they, too, went down. He didn't think it was any of his men who had shot them, but he wasn't aiming, and didn't think they were either.

It didn't take very long to reach the village, but from the moment they'd left the wounded boy by the dunes time hadn't meant anything. It was only distance, that road, that field, this hill, the orchards and the wall beyond them, the houses where there were some people, frightened faces and a crying child, some sort of stone shed with the door smashed open into which they ran, and the noise of tanks coming up the road, and some German soldiers in the square, their hands on their heads, sappers pointing rifles at them, and a look of relief on their faces.

'We're there,' he said. 'We've done it. Well done.'

Time to draw breath, to find Major Roberts and tell him they were there, except three of them. To learn that Captain Rowley had been killed before he reached the shore, and two of the trucks were overheating, 'Amazing what a bullet will do to a radiator, isn't it, Sergeant? Get on with it, will you?'

21

Letters came from James quite regularly. He was well, he said, and they'd come through the landings better than he had expected. Once again he was up to his armpits in oily engines as more and more vehicles were brought to Normandy, while officers raced around with maps and clipboards dealing with bigger pictures.

I don't know exactly where we are, but at least I know what I'm doing. It's spanners and screwdrivers again. I think of you all the time, my love. Soon, we should be getting letters from home again, but there's been another mess, so they've gone missing. The news in those letters hasn't reached me, at least not officially. Take care yourselves, my darling.

In England the summer brought the doodlebugs, which were hated and feared, and one landed in a field behind Stapleton's Farm, killing two horses. Once the carcasses had been removed Mary took Carol and Simon up the hill to look at the crater.

'They're getting these in London, aren't they?' asked Simon, after they'd looked at the hole in the ground in silence for a minute or two.

'Everywhere,' said Mary.

'But they're aiming them at London?' he

insisted, and all she could do was squeeze his hand and smile at him.

Mrs Edmunds was in London, driving an ambulance. Mr Edmunds was a stoker in the merchant navy, on an oil tanker. Every night the children said their prayers, and 'Please keep Daddy safe' had been the most important one. Now their mother was in danger too.

She came when she could, weekend visits when things were quiet, bringing presents, not only for Carol and Simon but for Ben and Mary too. When the ships came back there was always something. She telephoned, talked to the children, asked for news of James. The two families became quite close.

Mary had extra rations because of her pregnancy, and Freda Stapleton always set aside an extra half-pint of milk for her. They weren't short of food, but when Pamela Edmunds came down from London with a lemon that Tony had brought back from America everyone wanted to see it. A little yellow thing with a sharp, fresh smell and a wrinkly skin, something most of the children had never seen before, except in pictures. Mary cut it in half, and each child pressed a finger against the fruit then licked the finger. Sharp and sour, and they pulled faces, but they all wanted another taste.

Then a letter came from James saying they were on the move again, east and north, probably towards Belgium, and Mary began to worry. He had told her he hated the idea of going back to Dunkirk, but after that first one, which said they were somewhere in Normandy, the letters didn't

434

mention the areas at all. He said the vehicles were going well, which was his job, so that was good, and then he mentioned, almost casually, that he had shot a sniper.

'We came into the village in the evening, and I heard a knocking in the back axle, so we stopped to check it. There was a sniper. I shot him.'

She read that paragraph again and again.

They'd reached the village late in the evening, pulled the lorries up into the shelter of a wall by the church. James wanted to deal with whatever it was that was causing the knocking, and Major Roberts had agreed.

'No point in risking a bloody truck, is there? Sort it, Sergeant.'

Then the sniping had started, too bloody accurate for comfort one of the subalterns said, trying to sound unconcerned.

'Where is it, then? Where the fuck is he?'

He'd been ready with his rifle, looking at the woods. That was where it was coming from, not the houses by the road, the woods. The wind stirred the tops of the trees, enough to make a difference? A little, perhaps, the wind moving the branches, and below them, another movement. But the wind was high in the trees.

'Right,' he'd said, and the rifle was at his shoulder, and that place where the movement had been that wasn't the wind, it was in his sights. 'All right.'

They'd watched him, and they'd waited, and he'd squeezed the trigger. Nothing, nothing, but then a scream, a high, wailing sound, the most

435

pitiful sound he had ever heard, and he'd brought the rifle down and was staring across at the trees and the men started yelling and shouting, banging him on the back, and he thought there was another shot, a quieter sound, but he couldn't be sure. Once all the shouting had stopped, and Major Roberts had said, 'What about that bloody axle, then, Sergeant?', there was no more screaming. Nothing, from the trees.

He was under the lorry working on the axle, and the men were laughing on the other side of the square. They'd cheered him, slapped him on the back, cracked jokes about the shot. It had been a good shot, an almost impossibly good shot from that distance and at that angle, with nothing more to aim at than a little movement in the trees, and he should have felt elated and proud, but all he could think of was that he was tired, and he had had enough. It didn't matter that he'd spent the last four years in England training mechanics, he was tired of being part of the army, always doing as he was ordered, never free of the mastery of other men.

Now he had shot a man. Killed him. It was enough. He had had enough.

He laid the spanner down in the dust, and he lay on his back under the lorry, his hands clasped behind his head, looking up at the steel axle, at the chassis members, at the springs, and he saw none of them. Tiny flecks of rust drifted down on to his face.

His wife was pregnant. His father was old, and alone, and doing work too hard and heavy for an old man. He should be with them, working for

436

them. He didn't want to be here, in a foreign land.

He turned his head and looked across the square to where the men stood in groups, talking together, relaxing. Didn't they ever feel this, too? This weariness?

He saw himself rolling out from underneath the truck, climbing to his feet, and walking away, walking northwest, towards home, just walking until he reached them, his pregnant wife and his old father. Not running, not frightened, simply going home, where he should be.

He'd be shot, if he did that. Shot as a deserter. Mary and Ben would never know why he had deserted, what he had done.

He looked up again at the axle, at the heavy brass nut that was finally coming free, where the crossed threads showed bright where they had frayed, where the oil had seeped out.

He didn't care. Someone had done a bad job on that axle. Hadn't bothered to set the nut in place properly, had forced it rather than take the trouble to get it right. And James didn't care. He was looking up at a piece of machinery that had been abused, and for the first time it didn't matter.

The sniper didn't matter either. He'd been trying to kill them, and this was a war. Somewhere, behind all this, there must be a point to it, but James couldn't see it. All he could think, as he lay in the dust gazing up at steel and brass and iron was, My wife's pregnant, and my father's old, and I'm hundreds of miles away in a foreign land doing what strangers order me to do.

There was another burst of laughter from the men, and James thought just once more of rolling out from under the truck and walking away, and then he sighed, reached for the spanner, and thought, I'll have to replace this nut, it's ruined. And I hope there's the right sort of oil somewhere around here, because this thing won't go much further if there isn't.

'I shot him.'

When Mary wrote back to James, she didn't mention the sniper. She didn't know what to say.

Antwerp was the objective, and they reached it early in September. They were tired, because they had been fighting nearly every mile of the way at the beginning, and it had often been confusing. There had been times when communications had been so bad they hadn't known where they were, they hadn't been sure whether the gunfire had been from German positions or their own artillery, hadn't been able to make out whether the vehicles moving on the roads were the enemy retreating or the British advancing. More than once they had been attacked by their own aircraft. Then they seemed to have broken through the main defences, and they reached Antwerp in a final, furious drive, and captured the port intact.

It really did seem, now, that the war was coming to an end, not immediately but soon. Surely, soon.

Mary took on some part-time work at the school, once the bouts of nausea subsided. Ben and Jed went on at the boatyard, and William came back to help them, blind in one eye as the result of a training accident.

'Place is full of Cartwrights again,' Ben murmured, over Faith's grave. 'They're all right. It was only Violet, really, my love. Just a bit too big for Jed, I reckon.'

Violet had grown huge. Ben was shocked when he saw her. He could hardly believe that this was the woman who'd been so kind to Josiah when the old man went senile. He'd never seen a woman that big.

She could hardly walk. She looked diseased, unclean, raised red blotches on her arms and legs, her face bloated, eyes sunk in creases of fat. The thought rose in Ben's mind that Violet looked like the victim of a curse, and as soon as he thought it he remembered Mrs Webster, and then Faith when he had told her Josiah had left them the boatyard, her sudden fury.

Stupid idea, he told himself, and brushed it aside. Must be dropsy or something. Poor Violet.

She died that autumn, and this time it was Ben who held his old friend as he cried, and listened to him as he remembered, and tried hard to understand how Jed could still have loved that monstrous creature. Ben could hardly think of her without shuddering.

He went to see the vicar, and asked if Violet could be buried somewhere not too close to Faith. He found it difficult to explain his feelings, but they were too strong to be ignored. So much hatred, all wrong, in consecrated ground. All wrong. But the vicar could not, or would not, understand. Hatred, like other sins, would be washed away.

The whole funeral service was held at the graveside, the great coffin already in the ground. Jed had told Ben they'd needed a big cart to take it to the grave, and sheerlegs and pulleys on the ropes to lower it. Not very dignified, for a funeral service, so that was how it was to be, the coffin in the ground ready for burial, flowers on it and laid ready on the heap of earth.

The four Cartwright brothers and Emily were there, all in black, all solemn, but there didn't seem to be much grief, except from Jed. Emily wiped her eyes with her handkerchief, but Ben could see no sign of tears, yet he thought Violet had been a good mother. She'd been a kind woman, when he'd first known her. Couldn't they remember that, even now?

Barely ten paces separated the two graves.

Mary hadn't come to the funeral. She'd made an excuse that the Cartwrights accepted unquestioningly, that such events upset her and she was afraid it might harm her baby. Ben knew it was a lie. Mary's loyalty lay with Faith, and Faith had not been a forgiving woman, not to Violet. Mary went to the Cartwrights' house in the town that afternoon and prepared a meal for the mourners, what she could manage on the rations. Two of the neighbours brought a little food, and she'd put together a salad from their own garden, but there wasn't much. What there was in the way of gifts and kind words were for Jed. Violet had not inspired friendship.

She told James about it in her next letter, a factual account, nothing of her feelings. His

440

letters had become the same, a mechanical recitation of what he had been doing, this Bren-gun carrier, that truck, an ambulance, spare parts not getting through very quickly, breaking up three bad vehicles to make two good ones. Nothing more of how he felt, not even whether he was tired. That he still loved her, that he missed her, he would write that, and those words sang to her from the page, but that was all. What he had been doing, his part in this war, was stark and bare.

That was how he felt, and he was struggling hard to do his work effectively. He was having to think now, to go through routines, searching for problems that previously would have been immediately clear to him, but that was when it had all mattered, when it had seemed important. When the steering dragging to one side had to be corrected quickly so they could go on, when the Bren-gun carrier was wanted urgently, when the machine of which he was a small part had to be kept running smoothly.

'How much longer is that going to take, Sergeant?'

'Doing my best, sir.'

He *was* doing his best, but Sergeant Jacardi's best had always been something magical, and now he was no more than very good.

No, the war would not be over soon. Not this year, anyway. Supplies were the problem, spare parts, petrol, all to be brought over sea and land, damaged roads, mined ports, and Antwerp was clear and free, but the approach to it was not.

Tyres, brake shoes, grease, tools, welding rods, I should be at home.

'Are you going to be much longer with that, Sergeant?'

'Fuck off, sir.'

'What? What was that?'

'Not much longer, sir.'

Not much longer until the baby was due, and Mary knew James would not be home for Christmas. Had someone made the wrong decision somewhere? It had all seemed so close, back in the summer, once they were in France, moving towards Belgium and the Netherlands. Doing their best.

Cold rain and strong winds, November, but at last the approaches to Antwerp were clear, and surely it couldn't be much longer. Christmas was coming, and Mary sat at home, by the fire, growing dreamy as the baby's time drew near, listening to the two children, wondering how much longer they would be in the cottage, when they could go home. Dear God, please keep Daddy safe, and thank you for letting the soldiers stop the doodlebugs. Please God make the war end soon.

Violet's grave settled, grass began to grow over the mound, and there was a headstone, 'To the Memory of Violet Cartwright, Beloved Wife and Mother', a piece of sandstone, quite plain and simple. A week after it had been put up there was a heavy rainstorm, the ground became sodden and marshy, and the headstone slipped and cracked.

Subsidence, said the stonemasons. The ground's too wet. Leave it until the spring. It was bad luck, we'll do the next one at a special price.

The borders of Germany were drenched in rain, and the mud, the forests and the flooded rivers seemed to have trapped the armies. How much longer?

The Germans attacked, tanks and guns driving into the Ardennes, bombers flying into Belgium. For a brief time it seemed that the desperate tactics might be effective, that Germany might reach out into the Low Countries and retake Brussels, even Antwerp, but the young Americans held their ground until all elements of surprise had been lost, and the armies closed in again.

Christmas Day, and the baby was born, a quick, simple birth. Mary hardly felt tired after it. A little girl, with puzzled blue eyes and a mop of dark hair, and the children were enchanted.

'Are you going to call her Jesus?' asked Carol, and Mary smiled.

'We'll just call her 'Baby' until her father comes home.'

Ben found the cradle he had made for James, in the cabin of *Grey Lady*. He stepped down into it and stopped, looking around at damp, at mildew, at paint peeling from the swollen wood, at rotting curtains and blankets.

'Oh, no,' he said. 'Oh, no. I'm sorry.'

He took the cradle back to the workshop, sanded it and painted it, pink for the little girl he somehow hoped Mary would name Faith. Funny little thing, looking so surprised all the time. But a perfect baby. Perfect. Breathing quietly, and lying straight, tiny hands clenched around his finger. Perfect.

Rip out the old curtains and the blankets, make a bonfire and light the range. Smoke billowed into the cabin, dusty and yellow. She was so cold, poor old boat. Sorry. I'm sorry.

They were pushing towards the Rhine, and the tracks were narrow, only one road and it was often blocked. James supposed he knew where he was, but he hardly ever thought about it. He was always on the way to another crisis, something broken down, blocking an essential route, get there fast. A tank, the track torn off, behind it supply trucks with the drivers out in the woods looking for a way through, but there was nothing.

'Couldn't have happened in a worse place,' said the Captain. 'Do you need anything you haven't got?'

'No, sir.'

Space. Give me a little space. Quicker to repair this than move her, can't do that anyway, not without the track, she'd go straight down three feet into the mud.

'Call me if you need anything.'

'Sir.'

That's what an officer's for. This one knows it. Some way of jacking up the wheel, get it a little way out of the mud, it's a routine, they know how to do that. Officers are there to get us what we need so we can do what we're there for. What a tangle, words and steel, but I know what to do. It's all coming together. Move it on until we can get it off to one side, see why it came loose.

They'd done well, the men. All right, stand aside. That captain, can tell him, two minutes and you can, and a tremendous crashing noise, so loud it almost seemed like silence, throwing him against the side of the great monster, and it was lifting, and coming down again, and there was darkness.

'Sergeant?'

Torch in his eyes, bloody fool, want to draw the artillery, do you?

'Get up, Sergeant.'

'I can't, sir. There's a tank on my leg.'

Darkness again, and swearing, and someone had switched off the torch. All those trucks behind them, and no way through, a drop on one side down into a river, well, a stream, and two feet of pure mud on the other. Drive on, then.

'Amputate? Amputate his leg? Sorry, but we can't wait any longer.'

'Drive it,' he said.

'Ah, Sergeant. You're awake, are you?'

'Drive it,' he said again. 'I'd nearly fixed it.'

Get it a hundred yards further on, clear the track, then he could do it properly, one more tank back in action. Not difficult, not really, not once it was out of the mud. Off his leg.

Roaring and rumbling, shouldn't be that loud, and shaking, and then there was darkness again, and a sort of stillness.

'You'll be all right now. There's an ambulance somewhere. Thank you, Sergeant.'

'Sir.'

Sitting by the side of the road in the rain, his leg straight and stiff in front of him, splinted. He couldn't feel it, not really, sort of throbbing, warm. If the blades from the tank track had dug into his leg, he would probably lose it. But perhaps they hadn't.

'You all right? All right, mate?'

'Yes, thank you.'

The trucks moved on. Kind of him, to ask. Funny voice, like from a long way away. Someone must have given him morphine. That captain, the one who knew why he was there. Spanners and split pins and morphine. Why had that track come off in the first place? Something wrong there.

Might go home now. See Mary, and the Christmas baby. Call her Carol? After the little girl, and because of Christmas? Would Mary like that name?

'You the sergeant who got caught under the tank?'

'Yes.'

'Can you walk?'

He hadn't thought about that. Hadn't tried. Perhaps he could, if he tried.

'Bogged down, back there. Fifty yards? Can you make it? If I help you?'

Darkness again, as if he was rolling in it, a centre of silence, and then a moment when he was being carried over someone's shoulder, the boy who'd asked if he could walk, staggering in the mud. More darkness.

'Am I going to lose that leg?'

'I don't know.'

There didn't seem to be much blood but there was a bandage, very clean and white. There was another man in the ambulance, unconscious

446

probably. Very quiet. There was blood on his chest, which was rising and falling slowly, so he was breathing, he was alive. That was good.

'May I have some more morphine, please?'

If I ask very politely, they may give me some. I do hope so, because this is becoming more than I can stand. I think I'm going to scream.

'Nearly there now.'

Mary, darling Mary. I do wish you were here. I wish.

'Morphine?'

'Not much longer.'

Back into the darkness then. Was it him making that noise? Into the silence, where the pain was further away. He knew the pain, but it was a long way away, here in the darkness and the silence. There were voices, and the sound of an engine. Running too fast, that engine. Needs tuning. Lights through the darkness, he was being carried, on a stretcher this time. Into a lorry. Two lorries, backed up to each other, close together. Voices, a face over his, saying his name, saying, 'I'm a doctor.'

'Morphine? Please?'

'Yes. Yes, of course.'

This time he felt the needle, and he heard the voices. Shell landed by the tank, rocked it, he was blown under it. Leg crushed.

Crushed?

Warmth and dreaminess, and the doctor, cutting his boot, cutting the leg of his trousers, 'May I see, please?' But there were no words.

'Going to knock you out, old chap. Don't worry.'

447

Crushed? By the tank they'd said they'd amputate, but that was so they could move it. They hadn't known he'd nearly fixed it. But he'd told them, and they'd driven it. Hope there's someone who can sort out that track, once they get it off the road. It's not difficult, you just have to know what you're doing. You must have the right tools, and you can't do it alone, but it's not difficult.

'No, no, old chap, not difficult at all. Now, I want you to start counting down from ten. All right? Ten, nine, that's right.'

'Eight, seven, six. Five.'

Into the warm darkness, and Mary was there, smiling at him, eyes half closed, she was almost asleep, lying beside him.

She slept late that morning, and the baby slept too, quietly, in the painted wooden cradle by the bed. When she opened her eyes it was warm, but there was a thick frost pattern on the window, and the fire was out. She'd dreamed of lights in the darkness and someone counting. Broad daylight, why had she slept for so long?

James woke to broad daylight in the back of the lorry where the bright lights hung and the generator hummed and there was a man looking down at him. His leg. He wanted to look, but he couldn't move. Was that the doctor? He hadn't seen him in daylight.

'Leg? My leg?'

'Not as bad as we'd thought. You've still got it.'

Later that morning they moved him, strapped

to a stretcher, into another ambulance. Going to Brussels, to a real hospital. Yes, beds with clean sheets, you lucky beggar. Might even be nurses, real female ones.

There were four other men in the ambulance, two with chest wounds and the other badly burned. James lay silently, staring up at the roof and listening to the laboured breathing of the other men. There was a medical orderly sitting on a box, his back to the cab, watching them. He, too, had little to say. The burned man was unconscious, and kept that way with morphine. Every now and then the orderly asked them if they wanted some.

There didn't seem to be anything to say. James began to feel depressed. The other men's wounds were so much worse than his. He felt he should be explaining. I didn't ask to be sent back.

'You'll be going home,' said the orderly. 'You'll all be home soon.'

It was a long, slow journey. For much of the way they could hear gunfire. Several times they had to stop, pulled in to the side of the road to allow other vehicles to pass. James listened to the rolling, rumbling of the tanks, and wondered if anyone had repaired the one that had fallen on him. The track shouldn't have broken. There had been a break, it hadn't worn evenly. One of the wheels was out of line, that must be it. They ought to be told.

He felt sick and feverish. How could he tell them? He didn't even know where he had been. Out of hundreds of tanks, how could he tell them which one had the wheel out of line? The track might break again. They ought to know.

The orderly was wiping his face and telling him not to worry, not much further now.

'Sorry,' he said.

Brussels, and they were in a courtyard, men coming out to carry the stretchers. There were nurses with long white headdresses, smiling at them, walking beside them into the big building. He heard his name, Jacardi, and someone questioning it, but they were speaking in French. He only understood Jacardi, so he raised his head, and called out:

'I'm Jacardi.'

'It is only paper,' said one of the nurses. 'There is here a man with the same name.'

Tired. Been lying down for hours, but still tired. Another man with his name?

He slept, woke, dozed, moved as they asked him, was taken to a big, white room and his leg X-rayed. Slept again.

'Broken in two places,' they said, when he woke.

'Everything else, only little.'

A doctor came, and told James he wanted the torn skin and muscle to heal properly, and he could not put a plaster cast on the leg.

'You were very lucky,' he said.

Days of boredom, of lying still, of intolerable itching in healing skin, of a weary, dragging pain in the bone, and the doctors warned him to keep his leg as still as possible.

'You are Jacardi?' a small old man asked him, and he said that was his name.

'We have here another man with that name. He

is badly hurt. It is not a common name, I believe. A relative of yours, perhaps?'

They asked him if he would be willing to see the other man, to talk to him. He had been blinded. He was a fighter pilot, and he had been shot down. The Spitfire had burned. He was badly hurt and, of course, depressed. Perhaps Mr Jacardi could help? A member of the family?

'I don't know anyone else with my name,' he said. 'He's a stranger.'

The doctors said he could have his plaster cast, the danger of infection had decreased enough.

'It is good that you are so healthy,' said one of the nurses. 'You have a good body, I think.'

She looked him directly in the face, smiling, a question in the smile, and James looked back. Nice little thing. Pretty.

No.

He told her about Mary.

Last time he'd seen Mary she'd been slim and quick and graceful. Since then she'd been pregnant, and had had a baby. Would she still be slim and lovely? Or would she become slower, the way some women did, her waist thickening, her energy drained by the child?

Pretty nurse, smiling at him, telling him it is bad for a man not to make love to a woman. It is bad for the health, not to have sex. Here in the hospital we try to make you better. This is my job.

'If you do not use this,' she said, squeezing cold water from the sponge held high over his body directly on to his penis, 'you may go home and it no good. Not working.'

'I'll risk it,' he said, through clenched teeth.

'I think perhaps you are not normal. I shall tell Dr Anton. He, too, is not normal. He will be very pleased.'

James wrote to Mary that night: 'I love you and I miss you. I am beginning to need you desperately.'

The old man came back and asked him again to see the other man named Jacardi. Squadron Leader Jacardi.

'Does he want to see me?' James asked, and the old man hesitated, then shook his head.

'No. He wants to see nobody. He will tell you to go away.'

More days of boredom, of wondering when they would let him go.

They cut away the plaster cast, and James looked at a pallid, thin leg with a startling growth of long black hairs, and dark scabs falling away from a network of scars.

'That's disgusting,' he said. 'That's really revolting. Can I scratch it?'

'Don't move,' said the doctor, smiling at him.

'Are you so afraid of facing an angry man?' the old doctor demanded when he came back again. 'I think you are our only chance, now. Please.'

They gave him a crutch, and a nurse took him to a small room and opened the door for him.

'May I come in?' he asked.

The man lying on the bed with his face turned away sighed.

'Which are you? A bloody psychiatrist or a bloody surgeon?'

'I'm a bloody sergeant with a broken leg and

452

the same name as you.'

'Oh, really? Well, I'm not in the mood for a family party, so be a good chap and piss off, would you?'

But James was ready for this. After all, the old man had warned him.

'I'm not here for your benefit, sir. I'm here for my own.'

There was no response at all from the man lying on the bed. His face was still turned away, and he remained silent.

'I would very much like to know about Captain Samuel Jacardi,' said James, and waited, leaning against the doorframe. He wasn't sure what he would do if the man refused to speak, and it seemed, for a long time, as if that was what he would do.

'The gallant captain?' The voice, when it eventually came, was light and ironic. 'Got himself killed by a pack of niggers in South Africa.'

Nothing more. He might have been asleep.

'Did he ride a bay mare?' asked James.

The man stirred, almost turned his head, then seemed to remember.

'He did, as it happens. He called her Vienna. That was where he bought her. He thought a lot of that mare. The regiment shipped her home. My grandfather learned to ride on her. Why do you ask?'

Dreams, thought James. They were right, then. Well, it's not such an unusual colour.

'Where did the name come from?' he asked.

The man shifted impatiently. 'Why did you ask

453

about the horse?'

'For God's sake, sir, what does it matter?'

'Because I'm interested, that's why it bloody matters. Now, answer my bloody question, why did you ask about the horse?'

Well, let him make what he likes of it, then.

'I dream about the Captain sometimes. He's always riding a bay mare.'

He couldn't tell what the man on the bed made of his answer, and again there was a long silence, broken at last by a sigh.

'I've got Vienna's great-granddaughter. She's bay, too. A bit shaky on her legs now, the old mare, but she was good in her time. We're still breeding from that line. Most of them are bays. Bright bay with black points, head carriage a little too high if you're being fussy, but we're getting it down, slowly. There are photographs of Vienna on the tack-room walls. Yes, a bright bay mare, very fast, and very brave, and the Captain had a high opinion of her. That was why the regiment shipped her home. For his son.'

He turned his head, suddenly, without any warning, almost as if he was trying to shock this man who had spoken of the horse, and James didn't know whether, had he not been blind, the maimed man might have seen a reaction.

It was not recognisable as a face. It was not even the colour of skin.

'I was planning to ride Copenhagen in the Grand National, after this lot was over. If they haven't bombed Aintree out of existence. But I hadn't calculated on this. Stupid of me. Well, there you are. That's your question answered. Yes,

454

he did ride a bay mare, and I'd planned to ride one of her descendants in the greatest race in the world, and he's bright bay, too.'

He turned away again, the parody of a face hidden once more.

'And the name?' asked James.

The man sighed. When he spoke again his voice, which had become animated as he talked of the horses, was once more bored and weary.

'It's an abbreviation of Jack Hardy. He was thrown out of his family for whoring and drunkenness. He started up a gang down in Gloucester. The Bishop of Gloucester put a curse on him.'

'Why?'

'Because he was a murdering bastard. They called him a devil. Devil Jack Hardy. So if you and I come from the same family, that's your ancestor, Sergeant. Now, do what I asked you in the first place, would you? Be a good chap and piss off.'

'I'll be back,' said James, and heard the heavy irony in the reply: 'I'll look forward to that.'

22

They sent him home a few days later, back through Antwerp, but this time there were no guns, and the ship moved quietly out of the port, down the approaches and into the Channel, into wind and rain, towards England.

James stood on the deck and watched the shores of Europe turn into a horizon, a dark, blurred line against the sky, and disappear.

He would tell his father what he had learned in the hospital.

There would be no more information from that source. Squadron Leader Jacardi had died. No one would tell James how or why, but the old doctor had said he should not feel badly about it.

He'd killed himself, then, James decided, but how he had managed to do it he could not imagine.

The old man had given him an address in London, and said Squadron Leader Jacardi's parents lived there, in case James felt like calling on them. James had taken the piece of paper, slipped it into the back of his wallet, and thought he would probably never look at it again, but would remember it was there. He had a child now, and she might want to know about her family one day.

There was another horizon now, and he leaned on the railings and looked towards England, with the wind and rain blowing into his face, and thought, Home.

Ben sat in the churchyard on the bench that stood only a few yards from Faith's grave, and thought, He's coming home, my love. He'll be limping, but that won't matter. That'll heal. I'll tell Mary about willow bark, shall I? Just from one side of a healthy branch, not too much from the same tree. I won't forget that. It will be good to have him home again. William never did have his touch with engines. Born engineer, our boy.

He looked further away across the graveyard, to where the grass grew over Violet, and he thought, Let her be, my love. Let her be now.

There was no answer in his mind, and he thought, sadly, That new stone, that'll break too. Will she ever forgive?

A cold shiver, the wind lifting the long grass at the edge of the path, and Ben looked down at it. Rain coming from the south. It'll be raining when he comes back, but that won't matter. He never minded the rain.

He's coming home, he thought again, and said it aloud, 'He's coming home, my love. Our James. He's coming home.'

The ship drew slowly in alongside the grey stone walls, and James thought, Home. This is home, this grey place in the rain.

His leg began to hurt, quite fiercely, and he thought, That was stupid of me. They told me to rest it. Too late now.

'Are you all right?' someone asked.

457

He nodded. 'Yes. Thank you.'

'Will you need some help on the gangway?'

They'd helped him on, in Antwerp, but he hadn't thought it had been necessary, just part of the routine. Wounded man, going home, help him on to the ship. Now, as he shifted his weight, he winced and drew in his breath.

'Oh, damn. I think I may.'

All the way across the Channel he'd been on deck, looking towards England, when he should have been resting his leg, and he'd forgotten all about it. He hadn't noticed the pain.

Mary wondered whether he would be in pain when he reached home. It would have been a tedious journey, with little chance to rest, except on the ship, and she doubted if he'd have taken the chance when he had it. He wouldn't have been tired, then. A broken leg, that can start to ache quite fiercely after a while. What should she do for him?

For the last two days she'd hardly known what to do with herself. The cottage shone and sparkled with cleaning, she'd swept the garden path and weeded the borders, mowed the lawn and hoed the vegetable patch. She could not bear to be still. She hadn't slept, and couldn't rest.

He's coming home. He's coming home.

Baby Carol slept peacefully in the painted cradle, dark curls vivid against the white pillow, her fists curled beside her head.

Mary looked at herself in the mirror, touched her hair, moved away, then went back and looked again, critically.

She did seem tired. Her eyes were smudged and a little heavy. But she was slim again. She hadn't changed much over the last year.

I don't know what time I'll be arriving, so don't try to meet me. I'll walk the last bit. I need the exercise. I'm coming home, my darling.

He'd be limping quite badly. He'd told her there were scars on his leg, where the track on the tank had cut in, where they'd operated to set the bone. She'd read that part of his letter, read anxiety into it. Would she mind? Would the scars worry her?

I'm looking tired, she thought. Will he still think I'm beautiful?

He'd wanted so much to be with her when the baby was born. He'd worried about Ben trying to do work that was too heavy for him. Ever since the letter that said he'd shot the sniper she'd read weariness into his words, worry about her and Ben and the baby, and a sense of dull futility about his own work that she'd never thought to know in her James. Then there'd been the letter from the War Office that said he'd been wounded, and he was in hospital, his leg broken, the muscles torn and crushed. She'd written every day, but not all the letters had reached him. The war wasn't over.

It wouldn't be over until he was home. They were still fighting the Germans. Ships were still going down.

She went into the garden again and looked up the lane. That's the way he'll come. From the bend around the hawthorn tree where you can first see the lane it takes five minutes. It might take him a little more, because he'll be limping.

Ben came the other way from the town, along the towpath. The ship wouldn't even have docked yet, for all he could guess, but he wanted to be there to see his boy come home. Not to interfere, and James and Mary would need time together, but somebody would have to look after the baby. She'd be bound to wake.

In his hand, rolled up to keep them cold and moist, were strips of willow bark. He would put them in a bowl of water when he got back to the cottage, the way Faith had done when his leg was hurt, to keep them supple and cool. Mary could use them when the boy came home. He could show her how, if she didn't know.

Maybe there's a little bit of magic in a willow tree. You never could tell with Mrs Webster.

There were boats moored against the bank, moving a little in the wind, the squeak of a fender against a hull. Old *Grey Lady*, there she lay, as good a boat as he'd ever built, *Grey Lady*. Empty now, so her front end was high in the water, the weight of the engine settling her low at the back. Black tar gleamed on her planks in the rain.

He'd cleaned her and painted her again. When he'd been in to get the cradle for Baby Carol, when he'd seen her all damp and the paint peeling, he'd almost felt his little wife at his shoulder, felt her dismay.

Oh, that's bad. Oh, Ben, that won't do.

So he'd lit the range to dry the cabin. Sanded down all the wood that had swollen and peeled, and then he'd painted her, painted over those panels where he and Faith had worked with their brushes so many years before. Took a while, but it didn't matter. Have to keep the old boat right, can't leave her to rot. Might be the best boat I ever built, *Grey Lady*, and you never know, the boy might need her one day. So paint that again, where it peeled, where the damp marked it, but paint it the way it was. Faith painted that castle, yellow castle over the blue water. See the marks on the wood, those lines? She made those. So paint it the same, yellow castle by the blue water, and remember how she did it, the way she looked, the little frown.

He hadn't hurried the work. He'd sat for long minutes at a time, the paint drying on his brush, remembering Faith crouched over her work, the quick, careful brushstrokes, the way she'd sat back and looked, head on one side. Often as not reached for the rag and wiped it off. Not perfect, and that won't do.

My darling, I'll never make this as good as you did. But I'll keep to your colours, and I'll do my best.

Leave the engine. Leave that for the boy. He'll want to do all that. It won't be long after he comes home that we hear the song of the engine again, that was what he used to call it when he was little. The song of the engine. Used to hum along to that, he did.

Well, Faith, my darling, he's coming home now. We thought he'd died, and that was the end for you, and I do miss you, my little wife. I do wish you could have stayed. But *Grey Lady*'s dry and clean again, and the paint's bright, and our Mary washed the crochet lace and polished the brass.

I remembered the willow. I do forget things now, sometimes, but not important things, and I brought the willow for him.

'Who are you talking to?' asked Mary as she came into the kitchen.

He didn't hesitate, when he answered:

'Faith.'

Buried her with three bracelets on her wrist, he thought, as he ran the water into a bowl over his strips of willow bark. Blackie and Silver, and the copper wire with James's hair plaited into it. Her prettiest nightgown and her memories, and all his love.

He's coming home, my darling. He's coming home.

The publishers hope that this book has given you enjoyable reading. Large Print Books are especially designed to be as easy to see and hold as possible. If you wish a complete list of our books please ask at your local library or write directly to:

Magna Large Print Books
Magna House, Long Preston,
Skipton, North Yorkshire.
BD23 4ND

This Large Print Book for the partially sighted, who cannot read normal print, is published under the auspices of

THE ULVERSCROFT FOUNDATION